SECRET

AGENDA:

ONE MAN'S FIGHT AGAINST HIGH-TECH TERRORISTS & THEIR BIOLOGICAL/ NUCLEAR WEAPONS OF DEATH

BY HOWARD H. SCHACK

New York

DISCLAIMER

The author has used composite names, places, events and dates to protect his sources. Any resemblance to actual persons, living or dead, is purely coincidental.

An SPI Book

Copyright © 1998 by Howard H. Schack

For any additional information, contact:
SPI Books
136 West 22nd St.
New York, NY 10011
Tel: (212) 633-2023
Fax: (212) 633-2123

Library of Congress Cataloging-in-Publication Data available

Schack, Howard H.
SECRET AGENDA: One Man's Fight Against High-Tech
Terrorists & Their Biological/Nuclear Weapons of Death
1. Title

ISBN: 1-56171-956-0

Peace need not be impractical and war need not be inevitable. Contacts among nations need not be transformed into an exchange of threats.

—John F. Kennedy
June 10, 1963

ACKNOWLEDGMENTS

I am deeply grateful for the interviews granted by many intelligence professionals and advisors at the Institute for Intelligence and Special Operations. Because they were involved in clandestine ventures, they requested anonymity.

For her understanding, unquestioned loyalty, and support during my frequent absences over the decades, I gratefully recognize my wife Ruth, and thank her for her creative ideas and invaluable contributions to the preparation of this manuscript. I owe more to her than I can possibly record. I also thank our family for their inspiration: Michael, Toby, Barton, Paul, Anne, David, and Karen, and our loving grandchildren, Rebecca, Zoe, Arielle, Ilana, Elizabeth, Rachel, Joseph, and the extended Schack family in the United States and Israel.

For their friendship and painstaking insights into the dangerous world we live in I thank Congressman Benjamin A. Gilman, Chairman of the Congressional Foreign Affairs Committee, In addition, I thank Mr. Jerry Lipson, Marice Wohlgelernter (Professor of English at Baruch College, New York), and the library staff at Finkelstein Memorial Library.

My appreciation to Michal, Avner, Moshi, Colonel Yossi, and Colonel Langatz, who helped me explore alternatives to terrorist tactics with an expert's perspective. And I am grateful to a devoted group of retired Mossad colleagues for their encouragement.

I acknowledge the guidance of my publisher, Ian Shapolsky, and Isaac Mozeson, Editorial Director of SPI Books. A special acknowledgment to Christopher Thornton, Professor of Literature at Massachusetts Institute of Technology.

Most important, thanks go to my many lifelong friends who will travel through these pages with me to determine how the problem of world terrorism might be solved. I hope you enjoy the adventure.

CONTENTS

INTRODUCTION
BY CONGRESSMAN BENJAMIN A. GILMAN

For most Americans, terrorism has meant airliners blasted apart in mid-flight, killing all on board, or car bomb explosions devastating buildings and wreaking havoc on innocent victims.

While such incidents were perceived to occur far from the United States, in February of 1993 the bombing of the New York World Trade Center brought the plague of terrorism home to all Americans.

Such terrorist attacks are often followed by statements from one "revolutionary" group or another, claiming responsibility in the name of a higher justice or moral cause.

Regardless of the motivation, terrorism has been seen as the perpetuation of random acts of massive violence designed to instill fear in a civilian population, thereby forcing its government to capitulate to the demands of the perpetrators or their sponsors.

This book is about a different type of terrorist. As it was once said, "It is but a step from a mariner to a pirate." *Secret Agenda* makes clear that it can be but one step from an espionage agent to a terrorist.

This book lays out a frighteningly plausible scenario that shows how "terrorism" need not be confined to small bands of desperadoes wearing ski masks and brandishing Kalashnikovs, or anonymous agents placing time bombs in cars and planes.

For Americans who believe that the end of the cold war also ended the possibility of war between Russia, the principal successor state to the Soviet Union, and the United States, this book will not help them sleep better at night. *Secret Agenda* is a reminder that all Americans must be informed of and continuously vigilant to the constant threat of terrorism against the United States around the globe, as well as here at home, from sources that may be totally unexpected.

The book makes clear that most terrorists are seeking economic gain, political power, or revenge for a personal grievance, and are prepared to strike without mercy or conscience at whatever targets are available, wherever they can be found. And it makes evident that, under the right circumstances, not only can well-armed terrorists overthrow a government, but they can actually act in its stead before seizing the reins of power.

Anyone who has read *A Spy in Canaan*, Howard Schack's account of his activities for more than a decade as an under-cover agent, will find this sequel equally absorbing.

Drawing on his personal experience, in *Secret Agenda* he has written a powerful description of how a massive con-spiracy of highlyconnected rogue die-hard Communists could use terrorism to bring on a major conflict between Russia and the West, returning Russia to the deep freeze of Communist despotism.

BENJAMIN A. GILMAN,
Chairman, International
Relations Committee of
the U.S. Congress,
Washington, D.C.

AUTHOR'S NOTE

The fifteen years that I was privileged to serve with Israel's equivalent of the CIA, known as the Mossad or the Institute for Intelligence and Special Operations, helped me focus on areas of genuine potential conflict, especially involving those nations which have cloaked themselves in an erratic cultural and political fog.

Experience as an intelligence operative helped me portray a consistently credible true-to-life espionage storyline in this novel *Secret Agenda*, while also affording me the opportunity to reconstruct clear and penetrating scenarios from real-life situations.

Arguments, disagreements and opinions among politicians cannot dispute the fact that in Russia the inflation rate has risen 2,000 percent over the past three years; or that 45 percent of the population has dropped below the poverty line. All of this and more has taken place in Russia since the end of Communism.

Conditions in Russia today make our own Great Depression seem like paradise. Crooks and murderers have made the streets of Moscow more dangerous than any city in North America. Spontaneous and organized crime have surged. Russian Mafia thugs now control the distribution of food and other commodities. Private business people are paying a corrupt police force for little or no protection. The health and education systems have deteriorated. It is an evolving story of the so-called good guys against the bad guys—endemic to the Russian business and political establishments.

In Russia the only people who are truly making money since the beginning of their so-called democracy are brash entrepreneurs, criminals and the good-old-comrade network of bureaucrats. This is accomplished through private companies set up to trade in physical commodities, land and foreign currencies.

Russia today has become a Mafia power, involving illegal exports of military equipment, technology, oil and other natural resources, and then shifting billions of dollars in profits to "safe" Western banks. The profiteers pay off police and government officials so that they can operate outside the law. They are overwhelmingly responsible for the steep rise in crime while at the same time running protection rackets, accepting and offering bribes, imposing political monopolies and provoking artificial shortages.

While doing business in Russia after retirement from the Institute, I was able to witness an ambiguous statehood emerging after the cold war, and the first phase of a new era in strategic and economic relationships between the great powers. Cynics will be startled as they learn that Russia's nuclear force is well maintained—its missile-firing submarines are still on active military patrol—and that even with Russian citizens having to sell household goods to buy food, the military is developing three superior new missiles: one silo-based, a new submarine-launched missile and a newly improved mobile missile to replace its single SS-25 warhead.

Furthermore, readers will here learn of the U.S. defense department's spectacular and unacknowledged secret plan to purchase 400 MIG fighter jets from the Confederation of Independent States (C.I.S) for the purpose of bringing them to the United States to be retrofit and then released to the American military as drone aircraft.

As a more-truth-than-fiction composite of many actual events that I experienced in my life as an undercover operative, *Secret Agenda* reveals the activities of a group of former intelligence agents from various backgrounds, men who deal with a dangerously unstable moving target—today's Russia.

This group's major discovery is the clandestine construction of a vast underground command post, deep in the Ural Mountains, being built by Russian engineers. Equipped with the latest computers and communication technology, its antennas will be capable of communicating with Russian land-based mobile missiles and missile-carrying submarines around the world.

Additional revelations include how a group of intelligence operatives become involved in a joint crusade to minimize the likelihood of a future crisis that could re-create the

Soviet Union, revive Communism and heat up the paranoia of the cold war.

During their grand-master intelligence chess game, the former agents of *Secret Agenda,* with all their inherent strengths and weaknesses, attempt to stem a dangerous new violent plot of combined alliances. This coalition to counter democratic reforms consists of the Russian underworld, a number of former secret KGB operatives and a die-hard group of Communists who are planning a breathtaking coup.

This carefully researched combination of historically accurate events from firsthand knowledge of numerous intelligence operations is intended to make readers more conscious and questioning of today's dangerous international developments. Nothing is as it seems, and Russia's penchant for cloak-and-dagger intrigue did not end with the cold war!

PREFACE

During the current changing political, religious and nationalistic beliefs among nations there are individuals who, as undercover intelligence agents serving their country, in some way have violated the standards of responsibility set by their secret community. And while endeavoring to protect national security, it is often difficult for their superiors to control or monitor every act of the crucial, sometimes difficult-to-predict human components who make up every intelligence agency.

A more dangerous scenario occurs when a group of these agents, at the pinnacle of their careers, retire—joining what has become an exclusive club of "formers." After coming in contact with their erstwhile enemies, some eventually realize that they had served on different sides of the trenches for too long. In retirement these unique individuals, many of whom were accustomed to working alone in the shadows of secrecy, display an unusual flair for joint ventures in free enterprise, public relations and diplomacy.

Shadowy underlings of intelligence organizations, including the CIA, KGB, Interpol, and the Mossad, eventually must retire from the inner hell of their agency's clandestine operations, giving them their first opportunity in many years to peek around the corner of the *real* outside world to discover fabulous new opportunities for financially rewarding missions.

At one period in our recent history, as long as there were mechanisms for mutually assured destruction between the Union of Soviet Socialist Republics and the United States, everyone was relatively safe. During the cold war, it was clearly defined to the intelligence community who the enemy was and what it was up to at any given moment. But with the formation of the unstable C.I.S., a group of Russian individuals comprised of frustrated politicians, power-hungry ex-soldiers and out-of-work or soon-to-be-relived KGB agents have embarked on a plan to regain power and reinstate Communism. These malcontents have formed a loose association of fellow die-hard pro-Communists, seeking their former glory in a plan of attack that had never been previously imagined—a plan that must be kept secret until the attack is launched against the free world.

On the other side, an unlikely group of former intelligence colleagues, representing the spectrum of views from the intelligence community, with extensive operational experience have come to a consensus that something has to be done—outside the jurisdiction of their former agencies—to thwart the efforts of the dangerous renegade group. By joining East and West in an exclusive society of "formers," they immerse themselves in the new world order of biohazard chemical warfare, creating a quasi-new intelligence force of "terrorist hunters without portfolio." They demonstrate an outstanding ability to organize, screen and evaluate facts that their former intelligence agencies could not mobilize in time to protect international security. The "formers" realize that international coexistence depends on their establishing an effective and smoothly functioning security and intelligence operation to thwart the serious new enemy.

Secret Agenda deals with the constant threat of terrorism that now faces the Free World. Terrorists today have a host of new weapons that amplify their danger to democratic societies. These frightening possibilities involve nuclear proliferation, chemical warfare and biological warfare attacks.

SECRET AGENDA

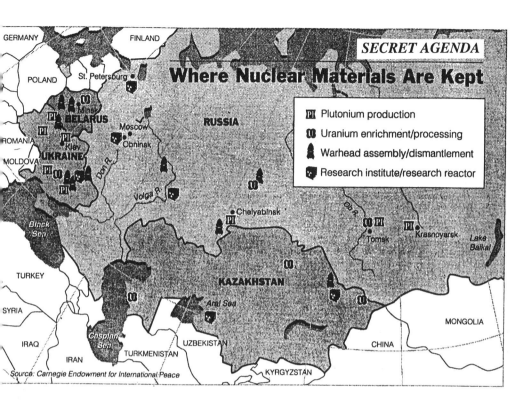

Where Nuclear Materials and Weapons are kept in Russia. *Carnegie Endowment for Intenational Peace.*

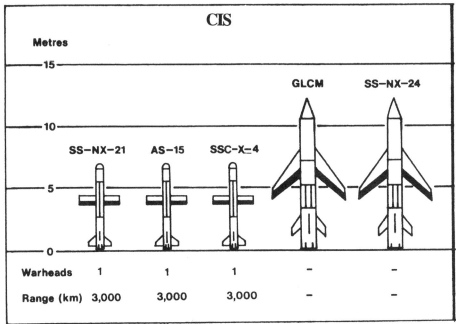

CIS   **Long Range Cruse Missiles**

The CIS is beneficiary of an expensive and technological array of Intercontinental Ballistic Missiles developed during the reign of the USSR. The cruse missiles are capable of accurately delivering a nuclear or chemical device to a predetermined target. The GLCM and NX-24 series missiles have a classified range. *Soviet Military Power.*

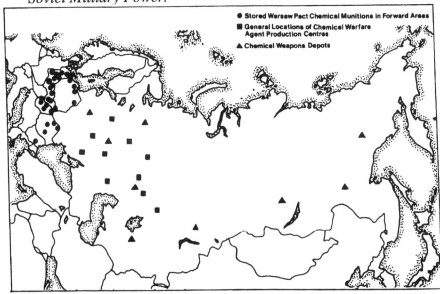

Main CIS chemical weapons depots, storage areas and production facilities for chemical related weapons. *Soviet Military Power.*

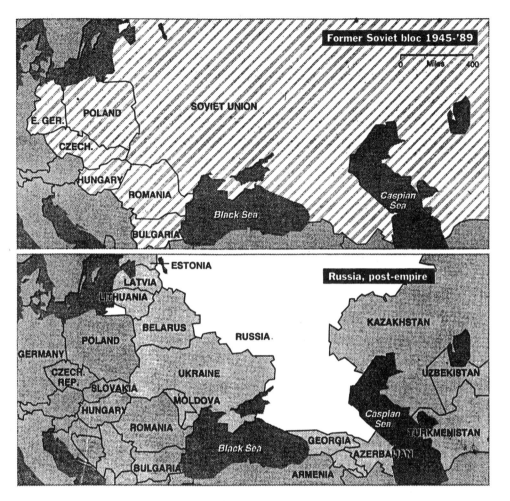

Top: Map of the Soviet Union booc, pre-empire.

Bottom: Map of Russia (CIS) post-empire 1989
to present. *Carnegie Endowment for
International Peace.*

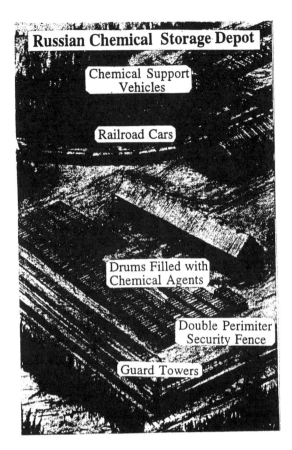

Artist's rendering of a typical Russian Chemical storage depot.
Soviet Military Power

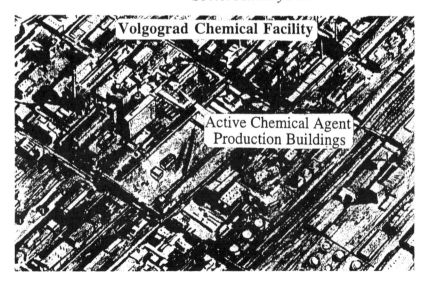

Artist's rendering of the Volgograd Chemical Facility, derived from satalite image. *Soviet Military Power*

Chapter One

PARIS, FRANCE

1975

She asked him, "Got your passport, dear?"

Hershel Shemtov could have responded, "Which one?" It crossed his mind, but that would have only prompted unnecessary questions.

"Have you got it or not?"

"It never leaves my person, dear," he replied.

"Take care, have a safe trip, and call me every day."

"Don't I always?" He fought hard not to say anything. How could he possibly tell her that he, a former Mossad field operative, was now on a special mission, working under the anonymity of his business?

He paused a second to look in the hallway mirror as he walked by. The stubble on his face had not taken long to grow into a well-trimmed beard.

"I don't know if I like it," his wife reluctantly declared.

Anyone else's spouse would have objected or suspected some sort of mid-life crisis. But not Ruth, who was accustomed to Hershel's doing the unexpected without prior warning. He had done so fifteen years earlier when, one day, he decided to follow up on his new hobby and learn how to fly.

As he boarded an Air France flight to Paris he thought back to the flying lessons he took from an old friend and ex–World War II fighter pilot, who now operated a crop dusting business. The pilot had been chief cook and bottle washer to his business—booking orders, servicing and fueling the plane, and then piloting the ugly but highly maneuverable beast. The lessons turned out to be cheap. At first his pilot friend

1

would not take any money, so Hershel negotiated until it was agreed to let him pay for the fuel.

Hershel learned by the seat of his pants as he went along on crop dusting jobs, climbing, diving steeply to just a few feet above the telephone pole wires, pulling back on the stick to level off at several feet above a farmer's field and instinctively activating a control which released the dust of a foul-smelling chemical that covered the crop. With a gut-wrenching feeling Hershel would pull back on the stick and climb again almost vertically, to avoid hitting the trees. After a number of lessons he still could not properly fly the plane level, but his climbs and dives seemed professionally executed.

His flying experiences were positive, for he learned about cloud formations, studied radio communications, frequencies, radar vectors, VOR approaches, expanded on his map reading expertise, and memorized the "survival guide." All of this would come to good use in later years. From his past flying activities, Hershel could almost anticipate the slow and deliberate moves of the big jet's pilot on his present commercial flight.

In the Mossad, Hershel had also become familiar with the art of walking the narrow line to get in and out of countries—something that came easy for intelligence agents and determined terrorists. It was easier than the average American could imagine: Both practitioners were balancing artists, trained to travel via the "green borders," otherwise known as unofficial points of entry. Hershel would always have some sort of cover in reserve. His amazing work with the Institute for Intelligence and Special Operations (another name for the Mossad) was a well-kept secret. Once you met Hershel, nimble and in the prime of life, you would never confuse him with anybody else. He had the sixth sense of the professional intelligence operative, intuitively feeling the presence of enemies when they were close by, but not knowing why.

Hershel heard the news as he arrived at De Gaule Airport outside Paris for a meeting with business associates. Just as he had surmised, the Arab League met as scheduled, and with open arms the United Nations invited PLO Chairman Arafat to address the General Assembly. Nevertheless, at the moment, Hershel would have to concentrate on a dinner meeting arranged by his associates.

Once on the Parisian Left Bank, his taxi came to a halt at the intersection of the Quai de la Tournelle and Rue Maître-Albert, near the wooden bookstalls that ran along a wall of the Seine, and just south of the massive Cathedral of Notre-Dame.

The driver, gratefully acknowledging Hershel's generous tip, pointed down the narrow alley, indicating where his passenger was heading. "The restaurant Atelier Maître-Albert, monsieur," he said. "On the right, you will see the small sign."

The maître d' hastened Hershel across the darkened room to Mr. Pierre Robert's table. Three men already at the table had risen to their feet to introduce themselves, buttoning and unbuttoning their blazers. *"Meestaire Hershel, bonjour,"* he was graciously greeted.

After ordering a bottle of vintage wine, his hosts began with projects they were reviewing for bid in Iraq. It was a rather long and dreary discussion, describing various building materials and highlighting difficulties their firms had encountered while working in Saddam Hussein's hostile environment. Their competition was primarily Japanese and Korean.

It would not have been hard for anyone to have fallen asleep if they were not as interested and involved in this area as Hershel was. But all the strategic material he was given as to where the Iraqis were deploying construction of their bomb-proof bunkers sank into his memory bank. His stock smile was still in place as he insisted to the group that he receive the exact coordinates of these bunkers—so he could compute his costs of transporting equipment and building materials, he informed them. A perfect explanation.

Within days of this meeting, he was told, he would leave France with those exact locations, along with complete plans for the proposed structures. Saddam's projects in Iraq would require installation of special blast-proof doors. Saddam must be preparing for something serious—but what, he wondered? Was it only to protect himself against his enemy, Iran? Hershel casually inquired of Pierre Roberts, his dinner companion. No one in the restaurant had a clue. And no one cared. They were only out after the almighty franc. The meeting ended with an orgy of handshakes.

Before leaving for this trip Hershel was shown pictures of the Mossad contact he was to meet in Paris. He would make contact at a prearranged public rendezvous in the way expected of him. He would be able to confirm his recognition by the fact that both agents would be carrying red pens in the top outside pocket of their jackets. The Mossad agent would reach for his pen first, remove it, and then put it back. Hershel would follow his actions to acknowledge recognition of his contact.

It did not take long for Hershel to accompany his contact to a place a bit more private—the back seat of a Renault—where at the right moment, Hershel would turn over the information he had gathered. The Renault was driven by a man in a black hat who immediately turned the vehicle into a narrow street and slowed down. Hershel could see that they were being followed by two other men driving a green Estafette. It was standard operating procedure for Israeli agents to follow one another as backup.

The Mossad agent spoke with his lips so close together that at first Hershel did not realize it was he who was speaking. "You have a manuscript for me to read?" he asked. "Only non-fiction sells to-day." Those words were code, confirming that the man was prepared to accept any information Hershel had available.

"Non-fiction indeed," he acknowledged. "I hope you enjoy the author's work." Hershel knew he would, that the architectural drawings would be photographed in detail, the specifications copied, and the originals returned to him later the following evening.

When he spoke again, the man's voice was reassuring. "I will consider the author's writing and advise in due time if his work is something that fits into our publication schedule."

"Done," said Hershel.

Hershel's expression must have appeared rather severe. The Mossad agent reached out and squeezed his shoulder to break the tension.

The agent reached into his briefcase and pulled out a spiral-bound book. He handed it to Hershel saying, "It would not do any harm for you to read this report on the political situation in the so-called confrontation states. It was published here in France by the leading newspapers. I know what you are doing is preventive intelligence. You can't afford to be depressed, even though I know you must be, going into the areas you travel. Who knows, in your travels you may come up with a piece of information that will put an end to all this insanity. Or if not the end of it, perhaps the beginning to the end. *Know thou thine enemy,* is an expression I like to remember."

The agent did not sound like a typical Israeli. It appeared to Hershel that from this guy's accent he'd most likely been educated in Great Britain.

Whoever wrote the report—and Hershel had his suspicions as to who was the responsible party—it certainly could have added some excitement to those typical travel guides one gets in bookstores. It began with a concise and practical overview that started with Arab countries farthest removed from Israel—Algeria, Libya, Morocco, Sudan, and Tunisia—concluding with neighbors surrounding Israel: Egypt, Jordan, Lebanon, Saudi Arabia and Syria. There appeared an analysis of each country, a description of its geography and a review of its history.

The conclusion presented in the report's analysis was that all the Middle Eastern countries and kingdoms had ongoing rivalries dating back to ancient times. But they were all drawn together by a common cause: destruction of the State of Israel.

The report quoted communiqués that had been issued following Arab conferences in which heads of various states—themselves involved in regional military confrontations—expressed their unified support for continuous confrontation against Israel. It continued to assert their joint opposition and resentment against the chief supporter of Israel, the United States. The policy had been coordinated into a unified movement after the Yom Kippur War, when oil-producing nations imposed their oil embargo. The report insisted that Israel would never leave itself vulnerable and totally dependent on the support of the United States.

This left Hershel somewhat depressed. But it also renewed his determination to do all in his power to provide Israel with anything which might be useful in a future challenge that could come from a confrontation state.

Sometime later he understood from his handler that the Mossad contact whom he briefly met with in France was one of the participants in Israel's hijacking of missile boats from the French seaport of Cherbourg, in 1969. The boats were intended for the Egyptian navy. Hershel, not one for adulation, nevertheless wished he had known this fact before he had met with the man. The Mossad agent probably would not have wanted to talk about past missions; however, Hershel would not have missed the opportunity of at least trying to ask him the many questions he had about these past exploits.

Before leaving on this trip to Europe and the Middle East, Hershel thought continually about his wife's last-minute advice, instructing him to take care of himself. For there was much to be concerned with on this mission, even here in beautiful Paris. Car bombs were going off outside prominent buildings in the heart of Paris during working hours, and it became extremely unhealthy for any pedestrian, let alone someone in his line of business. All Hershel could do to reduce risk was to restrict his movements within the city as much as possible.

Hershel was now living in a time where many radical groups believed that only violence could change the world the way they wanted it to be. The terrorist acts, these days, were attributed to a long list of fanatics including Ilich Ramírez Sánchez, better known as Carlos, or "Carlos the Jackal"; Commando Mohammed Bouda; Wadi Haddad; Michel Moukharbel; and such groups as the PFLP (Popular Front for the Liberation of Palestine), Black September, and Al Saiqa. In addition, Basques, Corsicans, Irish, Bretons, the Baader-Meinhof, the Second of June movement, and the Japanese Red Army were creating havoc in various other parts of the world. No country, it appeared, was safe from terrorism.

The Israelis had quietly hunted Bouda, and finally caught up with him in Paris a few months before Hershel's visit.

Bouda had spent a night with one of his mistresses at an apartment in the Rue Boinod in the 18th Arrondissement. He left soon after dawn, driving to another of his safe houses, located in the Rue des Fosses-Saint Bernard. Precisely at 11:00 A.M., Mohammed Bouda of the Haddad terrorist group emerged, unlocked his car and got in. As he leaned forward to place the key into the ignition the land mine under his seat exploded. Carlos ended up replacing the assassinated Bouda, and it was back to business as usual for Haddad.

After Bouda's death, the terrorists decided that their Palestine issue would now no longer know frontiers. The former understanding that there were "no-go areas," such as Europe, was expunged from their vocabulary. Recent Paris bombing targets had included the newspapers *L'Aurore* and *Minute,* the magazine *L'Arche,* and the television and radio station ORTF. Even the THKO (Turkish People's Liberation Army) decided to get into the act by planning to assassinate the United States Secretary of State, Henry Kissinger. They wanted to wipe out the domination of the United States in the Middle East.

Few men, either real or imagined, have provoked such fear as did Carlos. No man had read his obituary more frequently. Thousands of "Carlos" posters were distributed everywhere. Underneath his photo was a cryptic two-word biography: "Extremely Dangerous." He'd been wanted by Israel ever since he led the Arab group Black September in an attack on the Israeli Olympic team in Munich in 1972. Reports of positive sightings came from everywhere, equaled only by reports of his demise. Carlos was a man with unlimited terrorist money and resources at his disposal. He had safe houses, women, bombs and guns in dozens of cities throughout the world. In a single day he was reported to have been seen in Cuba, London, Chile, Libya, Lebanon, Israel and Colombia at exactly the same moment.

Counterterrorist experts whom Hershel later spoke with were asking with increasing urgency, "Is 'Carlos the Jackal' a Moscow-trained terrorist who has gone out of control?"

The Mossad wanted to know whom Carlos was working for when the Uruguayan military attaché fell dying in an underground Paris garage with six bullets in him. To the best of Hershel's knowledge, the question was never answered.

After that incident, Carlos moved on to a bigger project and was rewarded with a payment of twenty million dollars by Libyan ruler Muammar Qaddafi, as a result of his holding the OPEC oil ministers hostage at their Vienna headquarters. For years now, Carlos seemed to be everywhere simultaneously. Legend had it that he'd carry a gun in one hand, a grenade in the other and a rocket launcher strapped to his back.

His Haddad PFLP group took credit for the hijacked Lufthansa Jumbo jet that was diverted to Aden. Ransomed among the 170 passengers was Joseph Kennedy, son of Robert F. Kennedy. The ransom demanded, and quickly paid by his family for his return, was five million dollars. As a result, finances for the Haddad group were no longer a problem.

On a rampage throughout Europe, Paris-based Haddad and his following were murdering people on a wholesale scale. They blew up oil tanks in Holland, a factory in Germany that was working with Israeli companies and oil pipelines in Hamburg.

Palestinian gunmen and bomb makers seemed to have taken the initiative. Two PFLP terrorists threw hand grenades and opened fire with automatic weapons at an El Al airplane at Athens airport, killing one Israeli passenger and wounding two stewardesses. An identical attack by PFLP gunmen took place at Zurich airport, killing an El Al pilot and wounding five passengers. No target, if connected to Israel, was off limits.

The world continued reeling from still other terrorist attacks: A Black September unit hijacked a Sabina Boeing 707 and forced it to land at Lod Airport in Israel, where the group demanded the release of 371

Arab prisoners. An Israeli rescue team attacked the plane, killing two of the hijackers and a female passenger.

Three months later, Haddad, using the services of his non-Arab fellow terrorists, demonstrated to the world from Lod Airport how to create terror on an Air France flight from Rome. Three Japanese pulled out submachine guns and hand grenades and began firing into the civilian crowds until twenty-seven were killed and sixty-nine injured.

Terrorist carnage continued. In a single day early in the '70s a TWA Boeing 707 carrying 155 passengers and crew from Frankfort to New York was hijacked over Belgium and forced to fly to the Middle East, where it landed at a desert airstrip in Jordan. A Swissair DC-8 airliner flying from Zurich to New York with 155 aboard was hijacked two hours later over France. It, too, landed at the same airstrip. At almost the same time, hijackers attempted to seize an El Al Boeing 707 flying from Tel Aviv via Amsterdam. When three of the passengers who claimed to be Senegalese insisted that their first-class seats be near the pilot's cabin, it aroused suspicion. Their tickets were returned and they were told to fly another airline. Undeterred, the hijackers who had been turned away proceeded to Pan Am, where they seized a 747 jumbo jet flying from Amsterdam to New York. With fuel almost exhausted, the plane finally landed at Beirut, where it was blown up just as the last of the passengers jumped clear.

The PFLP accepted full responsibility for all of the hijackings. It was war without frontiers. How could anyone be careful? Hershel questioned. Those who were killed or injured did not have a say in the matter and, unlike him, were civilians minding their own business.

Aboard his plane while on the final leg of his journey to the Middle East, Hershel thought about all that the terrorists had recently done. He had waited a number of months to walk the hot sands. It was difficult to understand how and why so much terrorism had been suddenly unleashed. Hershel turned his attention to the immediate task at hand: Iraq and Saddam Hussein.

Chapter Two

BAGHDAD, IRAQ

1975

There are several expressions in Arabic which every expatriate who comes to the Middle East eventually finds he cannot be without. One is "Alhamdullah", "Praise be to God." When an Arab asked Hershel "How are you?" He would reply "Alhamdullah."

His other favorite word was *"Insh'allah."* It means "As God wills." He found it to answer almost every question that one could ask him about the future. Will the sun shine today? Will the plane be on time? Will our order be signed? Will the check be in the mail? His answer when in an Arab country would always be the same.

"Why don't you become a Muslim?" the taxi driver asked of him when he discovered that Hershel could say a few key words in Arabic. Little did he know those words were all too few. The driver could not understand how anyone capable of reading or understanding the language in which the truth of his God was enshrined could not accept that truth and embrace it completely. Blowing his car horn constantly as he spoke, the driver instinctively swerved around several pedestrians crossing the busy street without bothering to slow down.

"Insh'allah," Hershel said under his breath.

Not far from Baghdad the driver stopped the car among the lighted hibiscus at the hotel where Hershel was staying. Sight of the hotel brought back to him his conversations with his Mossad handler before he left for the Middle East. Hershel had waited a long time to be able to participate, to see, to question, to listen, and to personally begin what he had volunteered to do for the Israeli intelligence service. Part of his motivation was out of patriotism for the State of Israel and what it stood for. He believed that the Jewish people deserved a homeland, especially after the horrors of the Holocaust and the equal horrors of an indifferent world that had refused to assist them until more then six million had been exterminated. Hershel saw the signs of another Holocaust emerging from the Arab world and he was determined to do whatever he could to help stop it. He also wanted to understand how and why such unremitting evil had been unleashed among Arab people over the centuries. He was transfixed by what he had been told about master terrorists like Saddam Hussein, Wadi Haddad and the infamous Carlos the Jackal.

Hershel had been shown dossiers on the "Carlos Terror Network" that had been carefully monitored by the Mossad and the myth of Carlos being in a number of different places at the same time had doubled and redoubled since the Rue Toullier murders in Paris. He was advised that airports around the world were on full alert against Carlos' impending attacks, oil rigs were under armed guard and heads of state were being given maximum protection. A variety of reports alleged that Carlos even had atomic weaponry at his disposal, as well as hydrogen bombs and chemical weapons.

The international media had a field day. To them Carlos was an extraordinary phenomenon. Account after account stated that he was about to blow up embassies, kidnap and kill top politicians and heads of state, and that Algeria and Libya had given him additional millions. He was alleged to be ruling Libya and controlling Qaddafi. Still, no one looked in the direction of Saddam Hussein or the possibility that he was the one backing Wadi Haddad and the incredible operations of Carlos.

It required greater effort for Hershel to maintain his composure each time he encountered another hidden agenda planned by Hussein. With Hussein there was always a secret agenda.

In 1975, the latest terrorist plan that Hussein and his advisors had outlined to his henchman Wadi Haddad was, in its concept, quite chilling. When Haddad was told by the Iraqi leader of the details of the desired operation, it gave him particular delight and he readily agreed with Saddam's wishes. Haddad was promised and eventually provided with every available logistical support necessary by Saddam, along with weapons, money and, most important, information. It was specified that the composition of the group was unimportant as long as it was led by Carlos.

A Carlos-led commando team was to attack OPEC headquarters in Vienna, during a meeting of the oil ministers. All the ministers were to be seized and held captive. Carlos was to demand that a plane be put at his disposal by the government. Fear and terror would have to be an essential ingredient if the operation was to be successful.

Carlos was instructed to tell the Austrian government that all the ministers would be released when the plane landed in the Middle East and after each minister had made a public statement rejecting any negotiations with Israel on the Palestinian question. Actually, strong political pressure was the best excuse for Carlos to get the plane sooner rather then later. Once out of Austrian airspace the plane would head for Aden. Upon arrival in Aden, all the ministers were to be freed, except two: Sheik Ahmed Yamani of Saudi Arabia and Jamshid Amouzegar of Iran, who were both to be executed.

Saddam Hussein knew his man Wadi Haddad well. He knew that Haddad would find his plan irresistible.

Israelis were grateful that Saddam was not preparing for war against them, but instead against neighboring Iran. That unfortunate move would keep Iraq occupied for some time to come.

Saddam made Haddad understand that his war with Iran would be a war to avenge a personal and national humiliation. At its heart were two main elements: oil and the Kurdish people.

The Kurds have spent most of the twentieth century fighting for their own homeland. The Kurdish region stretches across four countries in the shape of a crescent, including parts of Iran, Syria, Iraq, and Turkey. This territory they claim as their homeland contains some of the world's richest mineral deposits and the richest oil fields in the world.

In 1974, full-scale war started out again between Iraq and the Kurds. With a fresh supply of Soviet weaponry, Saddam Hussein resolved to crush the Kurds once and for all. He committed his entire fighting force—120,000 men, 750 tanks, the air force and 20,000 police—to the fighting.

The Kurds, descendants of an ancient warlike people, fought with a spirit that was superior in every respect. The Iraqis took no prisoners. The Kurds fled into the northern mountains of Iraq and into Iran.

What Hershel saw by now was political turmoil in the area he traveled, and he filed a detailed intelligence report of what he observed through his handler. The Shah of Iran continued to give ever-increasing support to the Kurds, which infuriated Saddam Hussein. The Kurdish cause had also been supported by the United States and Israel since the early 1970s, Nixon secretly allocating to the Kurds sixteen million dollars, bypassing his State Department. The Kurds were hard pressed by early 1975, but continued to tie down the Iraqi war juggernaut with casualties numbering in the thousands and a mounting daily cost of two and a half million dollars. They continued to press the Shah for more aid and to escalate an already active Iranian participation against Iraq. The aim of the Kurds was to achieve an honorable and advantageous settlement with Saddam Hussein.

The Shah recognized the Kurds' plight, and pulled an old and bitter dispute out of his hat. A major area of contention was the Shatt al-Arab waterway, an outlet to the Arabian Gulf that is extremely vital to both Iran and Iraq. Iran had no legal access to the deep parts of the waterway under a treaty of 1937, and its attempts to negotiate rights since that time had gone downhill. Then came the OPEC conference of oil ministers in Algiers in March of 1975.

At the close of the OPEC summit, the Shah of Iran and Saddam Hussein shook hands, embraced and kissed. Everyone attending rose and applauded. A public gesture of friendship of this nature was no exception to the rule in the Middle East. Instead of applauding, everyone should have hidden under the nearest table for protection. Because of Saddam's embarrassment, he finalized the seeds of war with Iraq that day.

Iraq and Iran's mutual hatred amplified during a 1963 OPEC meeting when the Iraqi oil minister accused Sheik Yamani of representing a country that was little else than an agent of American oil companies. The Saudis boycotted further meetings until the Iraqis apologized and their statement was expunged from the meeting's minutes. Now, in 1975, Saddam had been obligated to lose face in front of the entire OPEC membership and in humiliation he had to even publicly kiss his enemy, the Shah. It was expected of him and he was humiliated before the entire group of snickering ministers and their support staffs. A Carlos-led plan of attack at the very next OPEC meeting would be the inevitable payback in Saddam's vengeful mind.

Meanwhile, the Kurds, not able to receive sufficient military or financial support, soon ceased to be a problem to Saddam Hussein. But the seeds of hatred, anger and humiliation had burned deeply between all parties. The decision by Saddam Hussein to wage war against Iran and to tear up the Algiers accord was made even before it was signed— as was Saddam's decision to fly to Paris in September 1975 to negotiate with French Prime Minister Jacques Chirac to purchase a nuclear reactor. When those who found out about the transaction announced their concern that the reactor was powerful enough to shortly make nuclear-grade plutonium for a bomb the size of the one dropped on Nagasaki, the French attempted to assure everyone that Iraq only intended for the reactor to generate electricity.

While he was in Paris, Saddam heard about the extraordinary ter-rorist exploits of the by-then-famous Carlos, and he began to form an incredible plan. Paying for his ambitious five-year development plan, in addition to paying for his war, would require approximately fifty billion dollars every year. His present oil revenues were eight billion. There was no alternative other then to force up the world market price of oil. The obstacle to his plan was moderate Sheik Yamani and the Saudi Arabian government he represented, which had dominated OPEC meetings for years, preventing the price of oil from going through the roof.

Just three weeks before the Algiers OPEC meeting, King Faisal had been assassinated, and the Saudis were still in disarray. But oil minister Yamani continued to resist a major price hike. The sheik had in effect signed his own death warrant as far as Saddam was concerned. Hussein no longer had any doubts about unleashing Wadi Haddad and his under-ling Carlos. He knew that the only way he could get his price increase would be to permanently remove Yamani as well as Jamshid Amouzegar, the oil minister of Iran, who would most likely fill the void and keep the prices stable if Yamani were the only one killed. They both had to go.

To ensure that the finger of blame would not be pointed at him, Saddam's plan took on the perfect Arabesque touch. The hijacked plane with the hostage ministers aboard should stop at a number of Arab coun-tries, where at each stop the oil minister of that country would to be forced to make a public speech denouncing the Israeli-Egyptian treaty prior to their release as hostages. The exact same scenario by the Iraqi oil minister would be played out at Baghdad International Airport, to prove to the world that Saddam Hussein was not involved with the outra-geous Vienna scheme.

Haddad was up to Saddam's challenge of keeping him out of the picture, so he selected an unlikely mixed team: two Germans, three Pal-estinians and Carlos. Khalid, one of the Palestinians, was appointed by Haddad as Carlos' number two, as was Samir, one of three experienced terrorists-survivors of the Munich Olympic Games massacre.

Haddad learned a lot from the Munich siege. The reason that opera-tion had failed to achieve its goal was that the first of the Arab commandos to die was their leader. Because all the details of the plan, as well as which country the Israeli athletes were to be taken to, were only known to the deceased leader, the operation was doomed to fail. If Carlos were to be killed during the proposed Vienna mission of terror and fear, the "military operation" would still continue to its conclusion.

By the end of 1975, the commandos began to gather at the Vienna Hilton, along with their backup team of six Germans, dabblers from various revolutionary cells. They obtained full intelligence details of the meeting, complete with two machine guns, six automatic pistols, eight hand grenades and enough explosives to blow up a score of OPEC buildings. The weapons came directly from Baghdad by way of an Iraqi diplomatic pouch, and on the very same plane as the Iraqi oil minister.

On Sunday December 21, the terrorist group walked past a lone security guard and into the OPEC building, overburdened with duffel bags heavily laden with munitions. In less than five minutes the terrorists seized absolute control of a group that included eleven oil ministers. Those eleven represented the richest assets and the largest revenues in the history of the world, some $100 billion each year.

Only one solitary policeman in a white trench coat and brown beret guarded the entrance and all of the talent assembled in that room. As the group approached, the guard saluted and permitted them to pass without asking them for identification or requesting to inspect their heavy bags. Some of the people in the reception area laughed at the ragtag group as Carlos and the balance of the commandos walked up the wide flight of stairs leading directly to the main OPEC conference hall.

A security guard inside the building and two assistants to the ministers had died during the initial phase of the attack when they resisted the takeover of the building. Further bursts from machine guns were now fired into the ceiling as Carlos shouted to the ministers and everyone else in the room, "Get down. Lie on the floor, facedown."

A switchboard operator was brave enough to dial Vienna police headquarters from beneath her desk, seconds before the switchboard was shot out.

Most were convinced that they would be slaughtered. Sheik Zaki Yamani lay on the conference room floor reciting verses from the Koran, certain that he would die as he learned that Ilich Ramírez Sánchez, alias Carlos, led the terrorists. The seventy hostages knew well his version of democracy: All decisions would be made democratically by Carlos; any who disagreed would be shot.

Carlos got down to the business of negotiating his way out of Vienna. He handed his handwritten list of demands to an assistant of OPEC's secretary-general:

> We are holding hostage the delegations to the OPEC Conference. We demand the lecture of our communiqué on the Austrian Radio & Television Network every two hours, starting two hours from now. A large bus with windows covered by curtains must be prepared to carry us to the Airport of Vienna tomorrow at 7:00; there a full-tanked DC-9 with a crew of three must be ready to take us and our hostages to our destination.
>
> Any delay, provocation or unauthorized approach under any guise will endanger the life of our hostages.

The message was signed: "The Arm of the Arab Revolution," a name created by Haddad exclusively for this operation.

The communiqué was just one of Saddam's tricks, a device with one purpose only: to convince everyone that they were simply a group of Palestinian fanatics seeking attention to their cause.

Allegations would eventually be made by Egypt that Colonel Qaddafi, their advisory, was the one who masterminded the attack. The Mossad knew that this was not so.

The communiqué continued, laying out the demands in the form of a manifesto, and was read over Vienna radio. It stated the familiar ground of the hard-line Arab states that rejected all treaties or negotiations with Israel. The Egyptian army was called heroic, and they were requested to lead a war of liberation with the armies of the northeastern front.

Shortly before 7:00 a.m., Carlos, sitting next to an Austrian pilot, took off from runway 12 at Vienna Airport with his hostages, and phase one of Wadi Haddad's plan as ordered by Saddam Hussein came to a satisfactory conclusion. Carlos had no intention of releasing all of his hostages at the first touchdown. Saddam's plan called for the murder of Sheik Yamani of Saudi Arabia and Jamshid Amouzegar of Iran at Carlos' secret destination in Aden.

Most of the Arab nations saw the whole affair as a frontal attack on OPEC and realized that loss of life on a ministerial level would result in a most serious disruption of the organization and create a critical diplomatic situation within the Arab world.

The plane first landed at Algiers, but Carlos was not given a long-range Boeing 707 as demanded, which could fly nonstop to Saddam Hussein's headquarters in Baghdad. Refueled, the jet instead had to take off for Tripoli, Libya, where air traffic controllers refused to give the plane permission to land. They could not chance a landing until the Libyan oil minister, Ezzedin Ali Mabruck, was forcibly taken into the pilots' cabin and advised Libyan air traffic control by radio that all aboard would be shot if permission to land were not immediately granted.

Wadi Haddad and Carlos had made a serious miscalculation in assuming that Libya would give them a plane with a longer range. Even though Qaddafi supported revolutionary movements, he would not come to the support of this particular operation, probably because he realized that the world would then make him the prime suspect in masterminding it. Libya had recently been very firmly on the side of OPEC moderate nations like Saudi Arabia, and would not assist in murdering its leading moderate, Sheik Yamani. In fact, another unanticipated problem was that Qaddafi was especially furious for two additional reasons: first, because one of his own delegation had just been killed by Carlos in this terror operation, and second, now the finger of guilt had been pointed at his nation because the plane was landing at Tripoli. Unfortunately, Carlos had antagonized the wrong person with that series of missteps.

One has to have had business dealings in the Middle East to fully appreciate the mentality of Arab negotiators. With years of experience negotiating contracts, Hershel understood that even after contracts were signed following lengthy negotiations with Arab clients, it meant nothing to them. It was simply an excuse for them to take a breather and then to open negotiations anew.

Qaddafi would surely come up with his own plan to point the finger of guilt for this operation away from his shores. The Libyans demanded that the Carlos-led Haddad group release all the hostages and then immediately leave his country. However, loss of face is always of prime importance in the Arab world: Exploring a variety of solutions for almost two hours, the negotiators moved among the hostages on the plane, and to keep up the hostages' morale they reassured Yamani and Amouzegar that they would not be killed.

The Libyan negotiators were comparable in deceit to those Arabs with whom Hershel had usually bargained. "Well, yes, we can let you have a bigger plane, a Boeing 737," they told Carlos, "but I'm afraid it's at the Tobruk airport and we understand that you wish to fly on to Baghdad. We're afraid that the 737 is of no use to you, it does not have the range. You need a Boeing 707. We do not have one of those available at the moment. Our people are trying to charter one for you from another airline. By the way, Carlos, we've just heard from Baghdad. They've refused permission for you to land."

One has to have experienced this kind of obfuscation-jerk-your-chain negotiating technique firsthand to appreciate how good Arab leaders and businessmen are at it. Hershel remembered how he had chuckled at the idea that any airline on this wide earth would willingly charter a multi-million-dollar piece of prime equipment and crew to a Carlos-led terrorist group. Carlos always bragged that he knew all the tricks in the book, but the Libyans were cut from the same cloth and he was certainly up against his equal in these negotiations.

By now, Carlos and his terrorists were keeping themselves going on amphetamines after two sleepless days. Perhaps that is why he could not see that the Libyans were not being truthful to him. As the Libyan delegation left the plane, they promised that another would be made available "as soon as possible."

Carlos brooded; he decided to refuel and leave immediately. Before departing he released another group of hostages, but he still held another ten. He was coming down to the wire, complaining that everyone was conspiring against him, even the Baader-Meinhof group, whom he called incompetents. He was paranoid. He said that he resented that the West German government paid the Baader-Meinhof group two and a half million Deutsche marks a year to ensure that there were no attacks on German airports or Lufthansa planes. He could not understand Qaddafi's attitude. "After all," Carlos stated, "Qaddafi financed the attack at the Munich Olympic Games."

As they flew toward the city of Tunis, Carlos became more and more agitated. He ordered the pilot to land, with or without permission. The pilot protested, stating that the runways would certainly be blocked with vehicles or the plane would be attacked by missiles.

"Don't worry about missiles, Captain, I should know what armaments Arab countries have. And I know for a fact that they don't have any missiles."

The pilot was advised to fly low over the airport and had no choice other than to comply. But someone in air traffic control had another idea. At a precise moment, all the lights were shut off and the airport was plunged into darkness.

Carlos ordered the pilot to fly on to Algiers. After landing there, racked with fatigue, Carlos demanded a larger plane, but was given the exact same excuses he had heard in Libya.

Then the heat was turned on. Algerian president Boumédienne offered Carlos sanctuary in his country and a large amount of money in exchange for his not killing the hostages. "After all. Carlos," he said, "if you carry out Haddad's orders who is going to protect you once the Saudis and Iranians come after you? Saddam Hussein? Never! His advisors and military have been infiltrated by Iran for years. And don't forget that just a few months ago he kissed the Shah and signed a peace treaty. If the Saudis put pressure on Wadi Haddad, he will give you up for a few rivals. Yes, my alternative is the best. Everyone has a price, what is yours? One million, two million, five?"

Carlos was no longer demanding large planes. He became obsessed with the idea of making money from this operation. This became his new primary motivation. He enjoyed the game of haggling as much as terrorism, and he did both well. The final figure rose to ten million dollars for each life, guaranteed as demanded by Carlos from the State National Bank of Algeria.

Money was the oil that kept Carlos rolling. Carlos had made a deal, he sold out, but he had to sell it to his colleagues aboard the plane, who were still holding the hostages. This could yet be another story. Yamani and Amouzegar still did not know if they would live or die, since the other terrorists became incensed at the suggestion that the operation be aborted in return for a ransom. Unable to control their anger, the terrorists screamed, cursed and threatened the Jackal. Carlos turned on his sales charm, used his leadership mentality, telling his associates that the Algerians had listened to their discussions. They were not going to be permitted to take off for Aden and were all going to be killed there, at the airport, if Yamani and Amouzegar were harmed.

From the reaction of the terrorists, Yamani was convinced that he would die aboard the plane. From the moment he was taken hostage, Yamani was not allowed off the plane. Khalid, one of the more violent, began to harangue Yamani, vowing that the sheik's time on this earth was limited and that he would die sooner than he could imagine. The next instant, Khalid was surrounded by Algerian security, preventing him from carrying out his death sentence.

Fighting terrorism from the safety of editorial rooms, hostile press appeared everywhere. Media began to thrash around for the real mastermind and reason behind the Vienna attack. Hershel recalled that he had had to laugh aloud again when he saw that Arab papers agreed with Saudi press releases, pointing the finger of guilt at Israel. He though it interesting that they came up with the incredible thought that it was in Israel's interest to disrupt the precious Arab commodity of oil. Iranian papers blamed the CIA and their British counterpart for being behind the attack. Even the KGB were being blamed. The Egyptian newspapers accused Muammar Qaddafi for planning and financing the attack. Still no one pointed the finger of guilt toward President Saddam Hussein of Iraq.

Incapable of staying in one place for any length of time because of his restlessness, Carlos left Algeria for Aden, returning to a very turbulent reunion with Wadi Haddad at his headquarters. Haddad, beside himself with rage because Carlos failed to kill Yamani and Amouzegar, accused him of being a revolutionary with his mouth, never with his heart. When Carlos argued that he had little choice because he could not get a long-distance plane from Libya or Algeria to fly to Baghdad, Haddad's response was: "Better to die with honor than to live with dishonor."

The story Hershel later heard about the ransom was ironic. The Saudis had promptly paid their ten million dollars, but the Shah of Iran reneged. Anxious to ensure that OPEC would not be threatened by Haddad or Carlos, the Saudis made up the balance that was due and paid a second ten million dollars. It was paid to Carlos' designated Algerian account, where "handling charges" of five million dollars were levied—highly profitable Arab banking blackmail among Arabs.

The Mossad had known that Carlos always functioned with a secret agenda, and they suspected he was involved with Saudi contacts, well before the group assembled in Vienna.

"Perhaps two and two do not always make four," Hershel recalled that his handler had often said. As far as he could see, the millions paid to Haddad and Carlos the Jackal by four major airlines, including Lufthansa, to avoid terror in their installations, and with the full knowledge of their governments, had only succeeded in creating more terror. And to what end?

It was during this period, that Hershel agonized over reports that Saddam Hussein had plans to become a nuclear power and that he had huge stores of chemical weaponry. Saddam had been picked up on Israeli eavesdropping tapes as having firm plans to use chemical weapons against his enemies. "Sounds like a bad dream, and the dream's not over," Hershel had commented to his handler when he filed his report.

"For bloody hell sure!" was the reply he'd received. "There's just you and the jungle out there. No policemen on the street corner to protect you. No justice handed down by chaps in white wigs acquainted with Western law. *Nothing*. I know you're rubbing shoulders with the Arabs. I don't think I have to remind you to always watch your back, don't trust the best of them, even if you think they are your closest friends."

Chapter Three

ABKHAZIA, GEORGIA & FAIRFAX, VIRGINIA

OCTOBER 10, 1995

"How do you feel we should please the Chechen rebels?" Morat inquired, holding his head in both hands as if he had a migraine headache. "Run it by me," he asked his partner.

"What would you do?"

The answer was a simple shrug of the shoulders.

Morat Progalin spoke to his associate with a tone of impatience, but indulged him for the moment. "You know the Ruskies write their own rules, hold their own kangaroo courts and put innocent people in prison. Just imagine what the new regime would do to your indecent hide if you are caught." Progalin was getting even more aggressive.

"That answer should be really obvious," Progalin added. "What most likely will happen is that some big bloke in Moscow will up and tell some big cheeseburger in Washington that they are having trouble with the warthogs, and that they do not want anyone to arm the Chechi-Chechens," he said authoritatively, purposely mangling the word. "They will make their statement in the form of a demand and threaten to take their argument before the UN Okay?"

"So far," replied Morat's partner.

"Alright. Then Washington will acknowledge that the message was received and understood. They will state that they never intended to arm the Chechi-Chechens and agree not to do so in the future. By this time I expect to have been on the horn with brother Fritz, requesting that the old sport do us a favor. I will explain that the new administration in Moscow has the Chechi-Chechens embargoed, that they need a few new toys and there's a few bucks in it for him. Of course he will immediately assure me that he doesn't give a rat's ass about any Russian embargo and that he will get our requirements from the extra toys earmarked for Saddam."

He added to his premise with a lyrical tremor in his voice, "Fritz will get on the hotline to his trusted gun-runner of the month: 'Great News, Abdul. Got a green light for the Chechi-Chechen deal. You'll have to get the goods in via the back door, and our buddy Morat will make sure it is wide open.' Then I will expect the P.S.," Progalin said, looking into his partner's eyes.

"What P.S.?" his associate questioned, rubbing his nose with the back of his hand. "There's more? You must be joking."

"The postscript," Progalin said. "The sugar in the coffee. My offer of a few bucks will be settled at the rate of ten percent of our action for Fritz's introduction and services. It's a piece of cake."

"I'll grant you this," his partner said approvingly. "You summed it up perfectly."

Progalin continued, "And incidentally, before Fritz concludes with us, he is going to add that he doesn't want to get caught with his hand in the till, so payment is to go to the account name of Guns and Bullets, in care of the orphans fund, at the Bank of Crook and Crook in Switzerland."

Hypnotized by his buddy's smoothness and humor, Morat's partner in crime flashed a luminous smile. "You're a laugh a minute. Yes, I like it," he said cheerfully. "I'm all for it."

His partner snapped back, "Never mind the compliments. Let's hear it for the Beluga caviar!"

Though clearly on the wrong side of the law, Morat Progalin had never thrust a knife or fired a gun in anger or fear. Always capable of finding someone to carry out a "contract" on his behalf, he never had to get his hands dirty. The only punches he had ever thrown were in bars, and those were only in self-defense, as the alcohol made men braver than they should have been. His standard for choosing targets: He took from those who could well afford to loose it. And so as not to discriminate, he also took equally from the poor.

"Better to live like a rooster for one day than to live as a chicken all your life," a reporter for the Itak-Tass news agency quoted the Chechen officer commanding the brigade that was charged with the hopeless job of assaulting the attacking Russian helicopters. "Boris Yeltsin and his democratic society are like camels trying to put their nose into our tent," he said.

The officer was a compact man with an apologetic grin. Nimble and in his prime, he was the kind of man who would not think twice about eating his lunch while sitting under a dead, hanged prisoner.

The place where the interview took place was called the "ridge." The ridge overlooked an old military highway that was a road traveled by armies moving from Russia to Chechnya. Steep mountains rose in all directions behind low hills and the road disappeared behind a distant plateau.

When the Chechen commander was asked by the reporter whether the Russian military was picking its targets carefully or bombing indiscriminately, he replied, "The Russian empire was never capable of using a scalpel. It always barged into other people's houses with a bear's claw. Yeltsin insists that we are all one nation and that we must all cling together while Russia's problems are being solved. But of course we disagree, we are not all one nation: The boundaries we are obligated to live by were established by force and not by consent. I am Chechen because I say I am. This is our native land we stand on, and we are prepared to establish that fact by force and not by your consent."

The Chechen conflict was the beginning of something that would not soon end. Many people in strange-sounding places were moving off in directions and on missions for any cause that they mistakenly thought they understood.

History will be served by what I read in today's paper, Hershel realized, as the early-morning New York to Washington shuttle approached the D.C. airport from over the Potomac River. For Hershel, there were times when the future of the world was almost too fearful for contemplation, and certainly events were constantly unfolding beyond the expected.

He tightly folded the *Wall Street Journal* and carefully fit the sections he had not yet read into his scuffed brown briefcase, which lay open at his feet. His puffy hands finally found the car rental reservation slip for his short drive to Fairfax, Virginia, in his inside suit pocket.

A few minutes later, taking a moment to adjust to his surroundings, Hershel gripped the steering wheel loosely as the car drifted slowly ahead. A few pieces of gravel from the parking lot flew out from under the tire treads and then silence—except for the steady hum of the engine.

At Hershel's age most men had settled down into second careers as grandfathers, part-time guardians of their children's children, as abused and weary joints eased down into well-worn recliners and arteries began closing up from the internal clutter of a busy, unhealthy lifetime. His mouth curled in displeasure at this thought.

As a former intelligence officer he was accustomed to operating covertly under deep cover, Hershel was never known to be a loose cannon. A longtime agent for Israel's equivalent to the CIA, to defend himself he had been well trained in the use and concealment of deadly assault weapons. Hershel never spoke in specifics over the telephone, and made it a practice to shred all notes and memos, while concealing his every move to the point that he almost didn't exist. Without question, ten years earlier he was in such good shape he could have easily qualified for service as an Israeli commando.

When he retired from the Mossad, Hershel had not become one of those foolhardy or bloodthirsty, devious son-of-a-bitch military weirdos. He was just the opposite, a regular, stable guy who performed his tasks flawlessly and truly loved his work, regardless of the task.

Hershel's expertise lay in the fact that at this point in his life he was a top intelligence analyst, with a sterling record and an incredible, creative, deductive mind. Never considering himself a spy, he concluded that now he was simply a gatherer of loose intelligence—a packrat of valuable information. Even after being retired for some time, he never wearied of looking through the knotholes and cracks in the military intelligence woodwork—it had become his hobby. From early in his life, the more complex a situation, the more he enjoyed it. Boredom was Hershel's greatest enemy.

For a man just beginning to feel his years, he always brimmed with enthusiasm while working on his latest interesting projects. His challenging job allowed him to constantly sharpen his voracious inner mechanisms for analysis, not only for the sake of his survival and well-being, but for his own enjoyment. His work and family were his reason for living.

It had been less than a week since he'd been a guest at Automatic Technologies Inc. in Fairfax. His assignment there was to learn all he could from a seminar offered in the recent technology of "soft-kill solutions." "Soft-kill" was a new category within the intelligence community for nonlethal disabling technologies.

Surprisingly, the first workshop took place at a local fast-food restaurant on the outskirts of Fairfax, Hershel and the other attendees viewing the serving area through the one-way mirror of the manager's office. As he and the others watched, two suspicious-looking men walked in, one brandishing an automatic handgun. Their green facial camouflage makeup made them look especially threatening. Each wore a black scarf covered over with a green, floppy fatigue hat. Unlike U.S. military outfits, their military fatigue uniforms were rip-stop khaki, and hanging from their web belts were several hand grenades, frags, smokes and extra ammo.

One of them ordered the cashiers to "empty the registers and be quick about it!" The second intruder reacted like an Irish setter on point, waving a gun toward the dining area and shouting, "Everyone facedown on the floor!"

Hershel studied the play with the slack-jawed intensity of a floor broker eyeing the Big Board at the New York Stock Exchange. It was hard for him to believe the scene was not for real.

The rules are sure changing, he told himself. This is no routine holdup, it's developed into a terrorist-hostage situation.

Someone tripped the silent alarm to a police station, and within seconds police cars with red lights flashing screeched into the parking lot.

The two criminals continued to hold those inside at gunpoint.

After a few moments, a hostage-barricade situation ensued, with more police vehicles arriving, along with a police hostage negotiating team.

After opening a telephone line to the restaurant, an acting police negotiator succeeded in making phone contact and initiating a dialogue with the gunmen. But they remained belligerent, making demands for $10 million and safe passage to Panama, while continuing to escalate their latest threats to kill one hostage each hour.

As darkness began to fall, the two gunmen turned off the lights. Then two rather strange-looking vans arrived in the brightly lit parking lot. These were not the usual Swat trucks Hershel was expecting to see. They had dozens of car headlights mounted honeycomb-like along their sides.

Policemen lifted and carefully positioned huge speakers adjacent to the vans, carefully aiming them at the restaurant.

Hershel was impressed with the equipment, but felt that this entire scene was so unusual compared to what he was used to seeing in hostage situations; he compared it to a circus high-wire act. Regardless, for once he was happy to step back, relax and take the passive role of spectator.

A low, gradual rumbling could be felt in the restaurant, even in the isolated area where Hershel and companions were observing. First the windows, then everything inside began to vibrate as if an earthquake were in progress. The situation became annoying, then uncomfortable and finally nauseating. The smell of cold greasy food added to the problem. Minutes passed; the rumbling continued and became more intense as the gunmen and a number of the hostages vomited. Even Hershel began to feel somewhat queasy.

Suddenly, a brilliant strobe light whitened the entire scene, as the rumbling came to an abrupt halt. A stern voice shouted over a hand-held loudspeaker, "Police! Freeze!"

The hostages squinted to see silhouettes of heavily armed men hustling around throughout the restaurant.

All at once a very bright, pulsating, multi-colored beam of light splashed onto a gunman's face.

"Police!" barked a Swat team member. "It's over! Drop your guns! Put your hands on your head."

When the lights came on, the hostages were in the middle of a protective circle, surrounded by members of the Swat team, who were all wearing strange-looking goggles and ear protection. A number of the officers shouldered bizarre weapons that looked exactly like science fiction ray guns.

One gunman was covering his eyes, screaming that he couldn't see. His partner in crime was on the floor, throwing up.

Actors dressed as Swat-team officers, also feeling the same nauseating discomfort, escorted the disoriented hostages from the restaurant.

After they saw how well the game played, Hershel and the others attending the seminar did not take the time to cheer. Instead, they were amazed at the breathtaking action and immediately questioned the leaders of the workshop about the unusual ordeal they had just witnessed. Why did that blinding strobe light cause everyone to become so disoriented? What was that resonating sound and the rumbling that gave everyone such a queasy stomach? What was the intensely bright pulsating light that illuminated the gunman's face for a split second, and what exactly did it do to his eyesight?

The seminar leader casually responded, "NLT—nonlethal disabling technology."

He waited for a few moments to see if everyone grasped the new technology.

"What you were looking at are counter-terrorist weapons of the future, which could defeat an opponent and save lives at the same time. In this post-Cold War era you have seen just a few of our future weapons of choice."

The seminar leader went on to discuss a recent partnership between the U.S. Department of Justice and the Defense Department, focusing on seven main technological areas that were being developed for mutual benefit, including concealed-weapons detection, improved body armor, limited-effects technology and locating sniper fire.

"The National Institute of Justice recently instituted a program," he said, "to improve concealed weapons detection. The program selected four methods to develop: an X-ray sensor; a combination of passive millimeter wave and infrared cameras; an integration of ultrasound and radar; and a low-frequency magnetic technology. The devices are intended to be affordable—safe and as inconspicuous as possible. They will be able to detect weapons made of steel as well as those with little or no metal content, well over thirty feet away. I am sorry that we are not so far advanced as to be able to give you a demonstration of the different technologies today."

By learning this information Hershel felt reassured and anxious, in equal parts. He listened intently as the speaker continued.

"Different alternatives are also being sought to serve as limited-effects technology from crowd-control duties during peacekeeping operations to stop fleeing suspects. The program is testing a ballistic, electronic-stun projectile that sticks to clothing. The device emits a strong electric shock designed to halt individuals. The projectile is gas launched, wireless and has its own power supply. There are also plans for an 'eyesafe' laser device to disorient an individual. Consideration must be given in the research and development of the devices so as not to unintentionally harm bystanders or damaging property.

"The most extensive area of cooperation between law enforcement and the military has been in the field of body armor development. As you know, current body armor worn by the police and military is heavy, restricts movement and offers little if any protection against Teflon and rifle bullets. The vest being developed contains titanium and ceramic inserts and is designed to be worn as a concealable undergarment. The armor weighs no more then eight pounds, and provides optimum protection with the inserts positioned over the heart and spine.

"A design requirement for the new concealable body armor was to stop a bullet from the Russian AK-47 assault rifle at a range of 328 yards. During the initial test the inserts stopped the bullet at a range of less than 200 yards. There is also an outer-garment body armor being developed that will protect against a 30-06 armor-piercing bullet. This new garment weighs 40 percent less than the current type worn. Both the Secret Service and the military have ordered these from the prototypes.

"Both military and law enforcement are equipped with nothing more than their sense of sight and hearing to detect sniper fire. In urban environments, tall buildings or congested neighborhoods create echoes and offer cover for muzzle flashes and other visible clues as to the location of a sniper.

"Scientists are presently experimenting with laser sensors that use integrated acoustic-infrared beams. The system locates a sniper by tracking the heat generated by the friction of the bullet traveling through the air. This information reveals the bullet's three-dimensional trajectory, and the snipers' position.

"In addition, the Defense Advanced Research Projects Agency is working on a program to improve technologies that identify and monitor movement by individuals and vehicles: electronic miniaturization and packaging, navigation tools such as the global positioning system, and reduced power consumption. There are two main projects that the agency is developing: Soldier 911 and tagging. The former can emit a distress call when an individual is in danger. At the press of a panic button, a signal is sent that provides a receiving station with the soldier's location, complete with geographical coordinates. Presently the Soldier 911 is about the size of a brick and can be hand-held. But in the future it will be considerably downsized. With these improved technologies, emergency medical care will be provided with more expediency, and movement of contraband tracked more accurately."

Impatient with all of the generalities he was being fed, Hershel was suddenly pleased that he'd agreed to come to the seminar instead of deciding that a technology update would be uninteresting. By agreeing with the concept that everyone should learn how the "big boys" play he was only being realistic. However, Hershel was also convinced that in today's dangerous world, we should no longer deal with threats to national security through local police agencies.

Working internationally on a consulting basis for a defense contractor, Hershel had one more assignment to take care of today. He had to travel a few miles away from where he was in Fairfax in order to analyze and interpret information of interest to his client that would be released shortly in a press conference.

Chapter Four

WASHINGTON, D.C.

OCTOBER 10

Hershel shook his head, throwing back his hair in anticipation of mounting the steps to the large government building, amply supported by tall Grecian columns at the entrance. A security ID tag with his latest picture was clipped to his gray suit jacket. It flapped against the collar as he vigorously bounded up the long flight of wide stone stairs.

The warm early-autumn afternoon, with the fresh smell of the Chesapeake Bay in the air, seemed too nice for him to be inside this dingy building, he thought.

As he walked across the white marble floor of the lobby, quickly passing through the security checkpoint, Hershel headed to the large auditorium where the Defense Secretary, Lester Vaspin, would shortly be speaking.

Bored-looking cameramen, journalists, news reporters, commentators and dignitaries were everywhere, impatiently awaiting the already late arrival of the speaker.

Compared with some of the other guests and reporters attending the press conference, Hershel's intelligence background gave him the unique, decisive edge of being able to interpret more of what was about to be revealed than the others in the room.

No longer involved in covert Mossad campaigns to protect his biblical homeland, Hershel was now responsible only to himself and his private clients. He had undertaken the press-conference assignment today as a consultant to ADA Aerospace and his friend, Jack O'Neal. They wanted him to learn everything possible about the recently created U.S. Ballistic Missile Defense Organization. They specifically were interested in its likely future purchasing activities.

As marketing director for ADA Aerospace, Jack greatly feared that as a result of these changes his company might lose ground to foreign and domestic competition, which led him to aggressively revamp his company's technological capabilities and marketing efforts.

Even though there was some opportunity for diversification into commercial markets, O'Neal had decided to gamble, continuing with defense production as his company's primary source of profitability. In fact, ADA Aerospace had recently won a 105-million-dollar contract for an unmanned guidance system to be constructed in Fort Polk, Louisiana.

With Jack two steps behind him, Hershel found two seats near the rear of the auditorium and made himself comfortable. Jack's nervousness over his company's future truly showed. He approached his aisle seat so cautiously it looked as though he might catch some highly contagious venereal disease by sitting on it.

The door at the back of the podium opened and a gray-haired man walked to the speaker's table with ramrod military posture and announced: "Ladies and gentlemen, as usual, Secretary of Defense Vaspin will take a few questions at the end of his statement."

Hershel certainly expected that Les Vaspin would have more than a few perfunctory words to say in this well-publicized major announcement.

"That's a laugh," Jack said to Hershel in a hushed tone. "You can always ask Les any question you like. If he knows the answer, he'll answer you. And if he doesn't know the answer, he'll also answer you!"

Chapter Five

ST. PETERSBURG, COMMONWEALTH OF INDEPENDENT STATES

OCTOBER 10, 1995

It had been five years since Yoel Melman retired from the Mossad to begin his private life as a businessman, and it had not been an easy time.

Trying to conduct barter deals in the new Russia as an Israeli entrepreneur was even harder than Yoel had imagined. This was due to the simple fact that Russia was in a period of profound change and upheaval that included being in the primitive stage of an economy struggling to accumulate and attract new sources of capital. Yoel did not care to conduct business according to the new Russian Mafia standards, if he could avoid it.

A well-educated man, handsome, with a full head of gray hair and a perfect command of Russian, Hebrew, English and Arabic, he had also taught himself to speak German and French with some proficiency.

In Russia, the obstacles he encountered could not have been predicted without actually traveling in the country and trying to do business as an outsider. Resisting as long as possible, out of desperation he was eventually forced to play the game and bribe Russian bankers in order to have them properly expedite his clients' letters of credit. He was never quite sure if those bankers were not in fact connected in some way to the Mafia. He always assumed the worst.

Orders and contracts emanating from Russia without guarantees from prime Western banks usually did him little good, for they were often simply ignored by skeptical Western traders and sellers, who were well aware that Russian banks were unable to back up the letters of credit they issued with transferable, hard currency. His Western clients usually lost interest in the risky Russian deals he would set up, generally failing to make delivery to Russia and instead selling their goods to other countries that were safer to do business with.

Zipping along in his secondhand Russian-made Zhiguli, Yoel drove from business to business in St. Petersburg, forming friendships with an outer circle of former government officials—only to learn that they, too, were surrounded by unbelievable layers of new, inner-circle government officials, bogged down in their own red tape.

He befriended one such outer-circle former high-ranking Communist official, a middle-aged Russian named Emil Matonsky, who, Yoel later learned, regularly enjoyed the bar scene and the few late-night places of St. Petersburg.

Emil soon became Yoel's escort and his prime contact with the outer circle. Yoel did not have a bottomless wallet, but he always managed to pick up the tab when they went out and that went a long way in befriending Matonsky. Yoel never knew when he would have to call in his "chits" with him, but it was well worth the investment in all the dinners and drinks to know they were there.

One evening, entering a small eatery that Emil had chosen, Yoel's eyes focused on the glass at the center of each table, which held elongated bread sticks. To him they resembled soldiers standing at attention. Then a lonely paragraph from his ancient family Passover ceremony suddenly came to mind, allowing him a momentary escape from the present:

"This is the bread of affliction which our forefathers ate in the land of Egypt. Let all who are hungry enter and eat thereof."

Yoel smiled to himself. Some of my Jewish background showing through again, he thought silently, but immediately dismissed this line of thinking and focused on the matters at hand: how to do some serious business using all the contacts he had amassed in a lifetime of intelligence work.

Emil was no sooner seated than he ordered a vodka, straight up. And then two more, downing them "neat." Yoel was astonished. He knew that Emil liked vodka, as did his many other Russian acquaintances, but not to this extent.

It was obvious that something was bothering Emil tonight. He was acting as if he were trying to drown his convictions with liquor. But this was the wrong time and place for Emil to drink—if Yoel hoped to get any useful information out of him.

Yoel held the side of his glass to his cheek to cool his flushed face, and suggested they order some food. His plea was ignored.

The drunker Emil got, the more his tongue loosened in offering his opinion of the "new Russia."

"By now you should be able to see," he slurred, "that this new entrepreneurial activity in Russia has divided…all new and potentially successful business activities into…categories, from which I can see that many different factions are…beginning to take shape."

So this is what has been bothering Emil, Yoel reasoned. He refuses to accept and welcome the development of the new democratic Russian society. It somewhat surprised Yoel that Emil wanted to re-open the book on Communism.

"Sounds like bullshit," Yoel said, trying to find out why Emil had begun babbling on this strange tack.

"Juss hol' it, you'll see what I…tell you is true," Emil said as he slurred his words while signaling the waiter for a refill. He paused for several moments, closing his eyes to reorganize his thoughts before taking a few more mouthfuls of the potent Russian vodka before him.

Then his head began to bob from side to side drunkenly, as he continued to slur his words. "The new…legit Ruskie businessmen are trying to be and act like the…Americans. They are not only engaged in tough business competition, which they are not used to, they have *us*…to conten' with, and we die-hards are planning to hinder them at every opportunity. We…are going to resort to whatever means available to us, to restore our good ol' way of life." His look became even more serious and self-righteous.

"You can…call us the Mafioso or the bourgeoisie if you want, but lishen carefully." He said this softly, holding up a wavering first finger. "We ex-officials have a…strategy—an' we're gonna have our day with our good frien' Mr. Yelsin, an' get our good ol' ways back…at the same time. It's just a matter of time before he gets wha's…comin' to him an' we get wha's rightfully ours!"

"I…I'm not so sure about that, Emil. You mentioned strategy. What strategy are you exactly talking about and what do you mean when you say you and your friends are getting what is rightfully yours?" Yoel questioned him in a surprised tone.

A man with a mustache and a short beard sitting at an adjoining table, obviously overhearing at least part of the conversation, stood up, put on his muffler, hat and heavy coat, and walked out.

"Maybe we should have something to eat before you have another drink," Yoel gently suggested, but Emil appeared to be in a fog and Yoel's words of advice fell on deaf ears.

Discontent shows up at the most unlikely time and place, Yoel thought. His former Israeli intelligence training instinctively pushed him to investigate these strange comments further. He planned to question Emil further, to understand his attitude and the meaning behind this brief mention of the Mafia and die-hards in the same breath. Was there a connection? Yoel's probing would have to be hurried, as his Russian associate was getting drunker by the minute.

Reaching for Emil's pack of Marlboros from the middle of the table, Yoel extracted one, almost shoving it in Emil's mouth. Maybe this will keep him awake for a while, Yoel thought as he picked up a book of matches to light up.

As soon as he took the first puff, Emil's head jerked up with another burst of brilliance. "We're givin' it away—we Ruskies are even givin' our birthright away...in sellin' our space propulsion technology. Even those big RD-170 booster engines that waz used to place our space vehicles in orbit...waz sold for a few rotten rubles to those even more backward than we are...Chinese. There's no point...in my carin' about the new Russia, this environment is jus' too hostile for us."

"You are so funny when you drink! You shouldn't drink this much," Yoel replied, loud enough for the benefit of anyone who may have been listening.

"Very few of us in Russia are...Moslems," Emil grunted, and then laughed. "It's not agin my religion to drink!"

"Some things are best not said," Yoel quietly whispered to his associate, trying to calm him down in case they were being overheard. Cautiously and discreetly he continued questioning his drunken friend. "So tell me, Emil, who are your die-hard friends, eh?"

Emil just laughed.

"Come on now, Emil, you don't know what you are talking about. You must be drunk."

"I...don't, eh? Is that what you think? We have plans...We'll get it back...can't keep givin' it away...long live the die-hards..." he exclaimed as his head slumped. "But shh...top secret!"

Yoel was fully aware that Emil was only the "joker" in this Russian house of cards. But his gut feeling told him that he was on the fringe of learning something important. He figured that if all his investment in entertaining this guy led nowhere and gained him no new business, maybe he could at least get him to spill some juicy information that would be valuable in a non-business sense to others with whom Yoel was connected.

However, before Yoel could come to any conclusions, he had to find out exactly what was going on in Emil's head. Was this just a lot of angry bluster from an ex-Commie who was bitter over not making a big financial score, like many of his buddies did, or does Emil have some valuable information that might be worthwhile to Yoel's old intelligence friends? This was the question.

"Who are these die-hard friends," Yoel repeated while they huddled at the table.

To Yoel's disappointment, for the moment the question could not be answered directly, because in a final gesture of defiance Emil's head kept leaning forward until it finally hit the table in a drunken stupor. It was obvious that the Russian's system had little tolerance for this type of drinking.

As he looked into his half-filled glass of beer, the more Yoel thought about it, the more he concluded to himself that he had stumbled onto something important. He felt he was at the very tip of an iceberg. Perhaps I should leave it alone and mind my own business, he told himself. If I learn anything of a political nature I'm just going to tell someone else, and that will obviously irritate an already bad situation here in Russia.

Yoel's inquisitive nature could not let this story die from lack of further information that evening. But for the moment he had no choice other than to discontinue his unproductive chat with Emil and wait for yet another evening of drinking, when his guest might be more cooperative.

Yoel was aware of the intrigue, swindles and bribes. These were hardly phenomenal in Russia. They had been going on for decades, even in the old Russia. While the old Communist system had its own pattern of crime, peculiar to its economy, with shortages of material and food at any given moment, Emil's not-yet-clear version of today's discontent had certainly begun to sound bolder and more sinister than Yoel had previously heard.

He was familiar enough with history to know that Russia was authoritarian at heart and expansionist by habit. If it could only rid itself of Communist baggage like Emil and his out-of-work Communist buddies, with the country's highly educated population and vast resources it could gradually rise again to superpower status. But that might not be Russia's manifest destiny, Yoel thought. He recalled that Emil did speak, openly, of some "hard-liners" and their jealousies toward these old Communist bureaucrats, who now promoted themselves to corrupt millionaire businessmen. Suddenly Russia was sitting pretty in a most comfortable position between state socialism and the new market economy.

Early in his lucid drunkenness, before he had begun slurring his words and passed out, Emil had started to babble in a definite direction, blurting out with great conviction: "The people and most of our corrupt former government officials are...now out for themselves and all they can get. Anything goes in this new democratic, capitalistic Russia....People like you aren't even aware that there is a total breakdown. A breakdown...in the trust and discipline that was famous for bonding our society together for so many years. Today...there is just a feeling of what we call *noglost,* or brazen insolence...everywhere you look. Corruption is rampant. There is more crime, prostitution, alcohol and even drug abuse than...ever before.

"Look out there." Emil gestured, pointing to the window at an imaginary speeding car. "Drivers don't even bother to...obey traffic rules. Better yet, look at me," he demanded. "Am I not the perfect...example of this new democratic society drowning in its own elixir? I feel that I am a perfect representation of those people...who have come to realize that they are like a pendulum...only swinging in one direction."

Yoel wondered what the hell that meant. But he knew that once a bottle was opened, the primary objective was to empty it. The elixir was cherished. Many times he had heard the saying "Vodka left in the bottom of a glass is bitterness thrown in the face of a friend." Indeed, one very important thing that Yoel learned to appreciate in Russia was that vodka was akin to patriotism.

Emil had then continued his rambling rhetoric. "Don't think that all of us former government officials have...sold ourselves and our access—to the highest bidders. There are still many of us who have maintained our honor and our loyalty...to Mother Russia—something you capitalists would not understand. You cannot begin to contemplate what motivates *us,* the few remaining...true patriots of the U.S.S.R. You may think we're all slaves to the lure of your mighty dollar, but I promise you that this is not the case…and there are still thousands of good Russian officers—men of high honor—who will be heard and will influence the final outcome of this disaster…that has afflicted our great country.

"Mark our words, you capitalists have not defeated the great men who…built this country and who still have a profound influence over what direction it will finally take!"

With that last burst of brilliance, Emil grabbed the glass and polished off what was left of his drink, obviously very pleased with the convoluted lecture he had just given as his head sank lower towards the table.

Yoel's Mossad friends did not hang out with him anymore. Nevertheless, Yoel had not given up on the old habits learned in his intelligence days of saving every bit of information he considered even slightly important. To him bits of information were like fighter planes sitting in warehouses, always there in case they were needed in an emergency. His observations of what he had just heard and seen were no different, and the political ramifications of his findings could one day indeed prove to be extremely useful.

He also still had the sixth sense of the professional intelligence agent, knowing an enemy is close by but not knowing exactly who or where.

When he was an intelligence agent for Israel, Yoel did not have to observe an immediate and spectacular military action against an enemy to know that he had succeeded in obtaining important information for his government. Results were usually more indirect: a subtle shift in government policy, the sharing of secrets between military agencies, a hint that came in the form of a whisper from his immediate superior. In such ephemeral matters Yoel could only judge his success and the impact of his discoveries by continuing to read the newspapers. At this time of his life, knowing that something positive did happen because of his work was often his only reward.

While a member of the Mossad, Yoel had also been able to maintain total solitude. His greatest attribute *had* been *that he was* a one-man spy network. In his circles he was known as a lone wolf. But this could eventually prove to be a security disadvantage if the circumstances were anything but ideal. Professionalism *had been* one of the prime secrets to his success.

In today's Russia, Yoel could understand, there was a lot of social sympathy for heavy drinkers, who realized, as others did in the bar, that the pain and tragedies of life were more easily resolved through alcoholic oblivion. Vodka had long been a natural part of life to Emil, who saw drinking to excess everywhere he went.

Yoel paid the tab and the bartender helped him with Emil, half dragging him into Yoel's Zhiguli, to be quickly driven to his home a short distance away. Yoel had been on the road ten minutes, driving at a leisurely pace to the rectangular sign that the bartender told him would point to the street on which Emil lived.

Guiding his car slowly through a left turn, he was captivated by the quaint churches and quiet atmosphere of the neighborhood's unhurried, residential peacefulness. Steering with one hand, he reached over to push Emil's head back as it fell forward.

He lightened the weight of his foot on the gas pedal and permitted the car to coast to a stop when he located the number on the door to Emil's building. Emil's apartment was on the second floor of a building on Najorkya Street. Yoel glimpsed the identical apartment buildings on both sides of the street and the crumbling asphalt pavement on uneven sidewalks. The street was lined with large oak trees whose leaves would fall like a snowstorm at the slightest breeze. Other leaves that had fallen previously lay in drifts on the asphalt as a remnant of summer's end.

Yoel helped Emil get out of the car and turned to close the Zhiguli's door. As he turned back, Emil stood facing him, feet apart and nostrils flaring with each breath. His head was thrust forward and his hands hung limp by his sides—a pose Yoel imagined would be perfect for an anti-drinking poster. He took Emil's arm.

Emil tried to halt him, but Yoel had a firm grip on his arm. "Keep walking," Yoel said in a firm, low voice.

Once inside the Russian's apartment, Yoel decided it would be a perfect opportunity for some private investigating. He was intrigued, and decided he would never have a better opportunity than this moment to look around Emil's apartment for anything of interest.

Emil, meanwhile, fell onto his bed comatose. But when Yoel tried to help him off with his trousers, Emil temporarily became lucid and began to shout, "Whasa matter, I hav' za right ta drink!" Yoel left him to his oblivion.

Emil's proved to be a small, sparsely furnished two-room apartment. One room included a bed, dresser and closet. There was a small bathroom and an alcove with a refrigerator, table, sink and stove. The unusual number of large plaster patches on the walls surprised Yoel. Could there be some secret documents hidden there, he wondered? There was little in the room that gave a clue to the occupant's personality.

Yoel examined the grim room. Beginning cautiously at first, he looked behind every picture, door, window frame and under the tables for any sign of a frequency-designed listening device, which would be voice-activated, transmitted and recorded at another location. Even though he didn't find anything suspicious, he still surmised that Emil was most likely a trusted member or a group leader of a renegade band of Communist die-hards.

Continuing to snoop around the apartment, Yoel noticed a closed door on the opposite side of the room. Walking in its direction, he drew his revolver, pushed on the door and peeked into the darkness as the door slowly gave way. Reaching in, he pulled on a light string attached to the single bulb hanging from the ceiling, and then stepped into what appeared to be a small laboratory of some kind. It was full of scientific equipment: a microscope, several sterilizers, culture dishes, beakers and numerous small thermos-like silver containers.

Yoel took one of the containers from the shelf and then paused. He thought carefully, weighing the practicality of opening it. This home-made lab didn't seem like a crack or drug factory, he thought, as he carefully replaced the container in the same place from which he had taken it. Something told him it was better not to touch anything—there was something strange about this place. Emil or one of his close former Communist official friends could be among those insane terrorists looking to cash in on the former Soviet Union's nuclear-grade raw materials. These canisters might even contain a dangerous biological sample or even an explosive.

Toward the end of his career in the Mossad, Yoel had become a counter-terrorist expert, trained primarily in Middle Eastern affairs. During his last two years of service he was promoted to coordinator and re-stationed at the Mossad home base. One of his duties was to keep tabs on several Arab high-rollers, attempting to figure out what they were up to when they were not involved in their usual terrorist operations. So this kind of search was nothing new to him. If he'd still been on active duty, he could have written the report on the results of this search before it was over.

Yoel continued his search and opened a dresser drawer, rummaging through it while carrying on an inaudible angry dialogue with himself: But why here, in Russia? Why is so much bad shit in the world still coming from this miserable, run-down, joke of a one-time super-power? Yoel felt like shouting out that this entire state of affairs in today's world was preposterous. But his intuition told him to continue looking for some definite telltale sign of involvement with die-hards. He found only rumpled clothing in the drawers.

However, it was not difficult for Yoel to spot the small cardboard box jammed behind the sofa. He dumped its contents on the kitchen table and made himself comfortable in an old wooden chair. Slowly picking through the rumpled papers ,one at a time, he noticed a crude map of Russia. He traced what appeared to be roads and reviewed the numerous coordinates circled in pencil. At the bottom of the page was a memo in the margin referring to "book."

He spread out the remaining papers on the table, looking for what could be the book referred to on the piece of paper. There was a thin, worn, pamphlet with a militant-sounding title, "Return to Communism," by General Yevgeny Lukyanov. In flipping through the pages he realized it was mostly a detailed description of the hard-liners' recent attempted coup against Mikhail Gorbachev. It described how Gorbachev had completely lost control of Russia's nuclear arsenal, as well as other never-before-revealed tidbits of recent Soviet history. The author, General Lukyanov, took credit as the one responsible for planning and executing the cutting of the communication lines to Gorbachev's villa.

In reading on, Yoel came upon a startling section where the author bragged about how the plotters managed to totally isolate not only the president, but also Gorbachev's special security team assigned to guard the "nuclear suitcase."

According to the pamphlet, the situation was so dangerous and out of control that it had every military man in Moscow wondering what was going to happen next. What was even more surprising to Yoel was the fact that the hard-liners in the Soviet military apparently had the means to trigger a first strike against Europe or even the United States, without their president's approval.

Yoel was fascinated by Lukyanov's authentic behind-the-scenes version of events. He described how, at 4:32 P.M. on August 18, the lieutenant on duty in the guest house where the nuclear codes were kept under tight guard, some 100 yards from Gorbachev's dacha, saw his emergency light flash on. This indicated that his direct communication lines had been somehow broken and he was to go on "full alert status" because something was very wrong.

The pamphlet stated that when the lieutenant was finally able to contact the emergency communications center at Mukhalatke, he was told that indeed an accident had occurred and that he should not worry— the matter was under control.

Immediately thereafter, the lieutenant was contacted by General Varennikov, a hard-liner and co-conspirator who had planned for the lines to be shut down for a number of days. Varennikov told him that the situation was normal and he should not worry about the communication lines that were down.

The lieutenant was not a fool and didn't accept Varennikov's explanation that everything was normal. Instead, he followed his training instructions for these sorts of nuclear emergencies. He was supposed to contact Military Headquarters in Moscow if the emergency light ever flashed on, but apparently General Varennikov's people would not relay his urgent messages beyond their command. He was never able to reach Moscow, and Varennikov's staff soon stopped taking his calls altogether. The next morning the new military shift arrived from a nearby army installation, but was turned away by a KGB general who was in charge of securing the Gorbachev villa.

It was only the following morning, after the coup was announced on television and radio, that Lieutenant Viktor Boldyrev, the man in charge of the nuclear watch station, understood why he had lost communication with the guards at 4:32 P.M. on August 18.

General Lukyanov realized that the coup had failed on the morning of August 19, when communications with the nuclear watch station at Gorbachev's villa were reestablished on orders that came via the KGB's "special telephone lines."

Some of the plotters were caught, arrested and eventually released. But from the information provided in General Lukyanov's writings, it seemed to Yoel that the hard-liners' conspiracy to seize power would not end easily. These powerful generals had too much at stake to lose this power grab. They were not about to give up everything without some kind of major battle to try to take it back. This was obvious, predictable human behavior. Only the place and time when the plotters would carry out their future actions was still in question.

Raising his eyes from "Return to Communism," Yoel let his thoughts wander. I simply can't believe I'm reading this, he said to himself. What determination they have! But more important is how much power these guys once all had! There were no checks or balances on their power, as in democracies. These generals were stronger than the country's politicians. And those who didn't profiteer during the past few years of the dismantling of the Soviet military were certainly not happy campers.

After reading a few more pages of the pamphlet, it became obvious to Yoel that another planned coup was looming in the background, waiting for the right opportunity.

Suddenly, like the bursting of machine-gun fire, Emil's snoring shattered the stillness of the room. Startled, Yoel steadied himself, and then placed the papers and pamphlet back in the box, putting it behind the couch where he found it. He then walked to the bed to examine the drunken heap. Emil's head was slumped to the side, his eyes shut tight in happy oblivion, his nose snoring as he inhaled, his mouth wheezing as he exhaled.

Yoel wrote a short note to Emil and placed it on the kitchen table, set the alarm next to the bed for 6:00 A.M. and laughed aloud. "Won't he be surprised when it goes off so early. It serves him right for getting so wasted that I had to carry his sorry drunken ass back home!"

Finally, looking down at Emil, he said, "How's the world feeling, old boy? You should heed the Russian proverb 'Morning is wiser.' Surely there must be some truth in it for you."

Before leaving the apartment, his last act was to empty the contents of the trash can onto some old newspapers, which he placed on the kitchen floor. From a tightly squeezed ball of torn paper, he put back together a few pieces of handwritten notes that matched the writing he had noticed in the margin of the map. Yoel placed these scraps of paper in his coat pocket and put the balance of the garbage back in the pail.

It was the end of an amazing, confusing and startling day, filled with discoveries. Yoel put on his muffler and heavy coat, secured the buttons and prepared to leave the apartment.

Yoel, he thought to himself, you are inviting serious trouble if you keep thinking about and looking for the dangerous ex-Communist die-hards everywhere you go. Who would ever believe there was any sort of threat at all from this group of presently powerless angry Commies? But they are here, waiting in the tall grass, preparing their next moves to regain their lost power!

Yoel had no idea what their next step would be, but the history of the Mossad was not one of failure or charity; its strength was in study-ing the facts and understanding the truth. Having been one of their top agents, Yoel had spent enough time in Russia, bumping into various ex-government and ex-military types, to know that the level of discon-tent was so high here that if he was in their shoes, he too would be looking to do whatever was necessary to get back what was taken from him. It was human nature, and the ex-Commies were not great humans to begin with, particularly if one remembered their dark history of corruption, gulags, murder of millions of their own party members— and worse. The Soviet die-hards were one of history's great cesspools. In reviewing their abominable track record of plunder and greed, how could anyone who understood their past not fear their attempted revival?

Turning toward Emil before opening the door, Yoel said softly, "I know there are several ways to tell when a man is lying: One is when he says he can drink vodka all night and not get drunk. The other is when he says that he understands what is going on inside Russia. I'll wager a worthless ruble that more attention comes out of the bits of information collected here tonight than anyone would ever expect.

"Well, Emil, you're living proof that former Communists are great company," he said to the man as he turned out the light and pulled the door closed behind him.

Yoel should not have dismissed his sixth sense when he thought he saw the shadow of a man in the corner of the dark hallway as he quickly walked toward the stairs.

Chapter Six

CAPITOL HILL, WASHINGTON, D.C.

OCTOBER 11

It was a typical Friday for Hershel. He had taxied downtown early to join Jack O'Neal before their planned attendance at a congressional hearing. He liked to put the week to bed with a big event before leaving for the country. Jack was younger than Hershel by some ten years, and even though his eyes gave the appearance of being tired, he did not lack in aggressiveness or ambition. Known for his short fuse, Jack was too shrewd an operator to ever let his temper get the better of him when the stakes were high.

"Jack, you look like you need some fresh Washington air to cool you down; let's take a stroll before we go in to the congressional meeting," Hershel suggested.

It was a sunny autumn afternoon; the leaves on the trees shone gold and red. Tourists in groups gathered on the pavements, and Hershel bestowed a paternal smile on them as they passed.

After their brief walk, the men entered the Capitol. Defense Secretary Les Vaspin approached the speaker's lectern and announced: "I am pleased to announce the formation of the new United States Ballistic Missile Defense Organization," he asserted in a mike with the volume set too high. "This signals the end of the Star Wars era. This new defense organization will be totally prepared to respond to those missile threats that can be anticipated in this post-Cold War period. He paused to take a sip of water from a glass left for him on a shelf under the podium.

"The decade-long Star Wars debate," the Secretary continued, "centered largely on the best means for us to avoid nuclear war. In past Senate battles, the argument was over whether we should build a massive defense against a missile attack from the Soviet Union or press for arms reduction backed by a tradition of deterrence.

"Like many other of our Washington battles, it wasn't decided on its merits. Our battle went on for so long that circumstances simply changed the terms of the debate. The fate of the Star Wars plan was finally sealed by the collapse of the Soviet Union," said Vaspin.

Hershel knew that before Vaspin's statement was made, bidding *adieu* to the Strategic Defense Initiative Organization, the most pressing priority was the much-needed development of a theater-defense capability for the United States, with short-term costs amounting to about $1.8 billion. This would be followed by a plan for an antiballistic missile national defense system located at a single site in the United States' heartland. Even Saddam Hussein knew that the initial site would be located at Grand Forks, North Dakota.

Vaspin disclosed that the target acquisition sensor and tracking for the national shield would be code-named Brilliant Eyes, and could be in place by the year 2000 if properly funded. Vaspin added that command and control for the national defense system would be centered at Cheyenne Mountain Air Force Base, in Colorado.

Hershel understood that the name and policy shift had not drastically curtailed congressional funding for the current ballistic missile destroyer program for the upcoming fiscal year. While Les Vaspin stated that an expenditure of $3.8 billion was planned, he cautioned that funding would be reordered to reflect the dramatic shift in system priorities. He also warned that short-term focus was making it difficult to preserve critical technologies in a number of other projects. When SDI was launched by then-president Ronald Reagan in March 1983, Reagan had stated, "…the Star-Wars system would render nuclear weapons impotent and obsolete."

"Twelve years later," Vaspin now said, "we find we have a real need for ballistic missile defense, but not the massive program of space-based weapons that Ronald Reagan envisioned. Saddam Hussein and his SCUD missiles showed us that we need ballistic missile defenses for our forces in the field."

As Vaspin spoke, Hershel listened in silence as he used his small memo pad to note all details precisely. He was relaxed and enjoying what he was doing, but did not want to forget any of the important points.

"Unfortunately," Vaspin continued, "that threat is here and now. In the future, we may face any number of hostile or irrational states which have both nuclear warheads and ballistic missile technology that could reach the United States."

And then came the key to the points that Hershel was waiting for the Secretary of Defense to make: "Ballistic missile defense will be geared to focus on follow-on technologies that offer promise in both tactical and strategic defense. These changes represent a shift away from a present crash program for deployment of space-based weapons designed to meet a threat which today has receded almost to the vanishing point: the all-out surprise attack which was always a threat from the former Soviet Union.

"This new plan will better reflect the shift from research to development and acquisition of systems. It will allow us to manage our work on ballistic missile defense in a way appropriate to its place in the overall defense program."

Always suspicious, Hershel now had all the confirmation he needed to conclude that the nation's ballistic missile defense strategy was being guided by a new set of primary considerations. The first new scenario was the prospect of more regional conflicts in the 1990s.

Another was the realization by Hershel of the still significant threat from unfriendly groups within the former Soviet Union, like the Nationalist Party leader, Vladimir Zhirinovsky, the big winner in Russia's recent parliamentary elections. Zhirinovsky insisted that he was not a reactionary or a fascist, but charges kept coming because of his emotional, often inflammatory oratories targeting the West, the independent-minded Baltic Republics, Yeltsin reformers, and Russia's dark-skinned minorities from the Caucasus Mountains, among others.

Other strange comments attributed to Zhirinovsky included his accusation that the Jews started two World Wars, his threat to drop 100 nuclear bombs on any country making territorial claims on Russia, his demand for the return of Alaska from the United States, along with the return of Poland, Finland and other parts of past Czarist empires.

Hershel had read that Zhirinovsky first burst on the Russian national scene in June of 1991, when he ran for president and finished behind Yeltsin, with six million votes. In the subsequent two years he helped organize demonstrations against Yeltsin's administration. In 1992, he made a speech to the extreme right that won him notoriety. In it he said, "Japan, China and the West should understand that they can torture Russia for a long time, but when Russia rises, there will be nothing left of Japan or Europe."

Even though Hershel totally disagreed with Zhirinovsky and compared his campaign style to that of Hitler, he knew too well that many hard-line Russian citizens found his sense of humor and flair for the dramatic to be appropriate and even charming.

Hershel also worried about many other power-hungry people in the C.I.S. who were just like Zhirinovsky, although they were discreet enough to keep their outrageous beliefs to themselves. Hershel's experience made him alert to the fact that at any moment the political instability throughout Russia could be explosive.

Most U.S. politicians to whom Hershel spoke about the lack of stability in Russia were aware of this pressing problem, but felt that their duty was twofold. Their first priority was to protect the economic security of the United States, while maintaining the imperative to develop a shield against weapons of mass destruction, which became a secondary problem as Communism ended.

Hershel recalled that the Gulf War clearly disclosed to the world that deterrence, and threats from superpowers, don't always work.

A perfect example of this was Iraqi dictator Saddam Hussein, who used the SCUD missile in his desperation to provoke a retaliation from Israel, despite the placement of Patriot missile batteries in key locations within Israel. At the time the world believed the Patriot missiles were reasonably effective against SCUD attacks, yet Saddam was undeterred, and still tried to inspire an Israeli counter-attack in a wild attempt to drag other Arab nations into his war.

Today, Vaspin had concentrated his talk on the enhanced technology of current U.S. defenses. He indicated that while the Patriot performed far better than anyone could have expected, the United States needed to update its defenses, especially against weapons of mass destruction. "Sensors with greater acuity are also needed to identify and target mobile missile defenses," he said.

Hershel knew, from speaking to contractors manufacturing the Patriot, that it had a long way to go before being perfected. At this point in its development it was nothing but a joke.

During the question-and-answer period, one aspiring news-media participant cautioned Vaspin and the Defense Department to pay more attention to the peril of cruise-type missiles, which, he said, were relatively simple for Third World nations to produce. The reporter added that cruise missiles could easily be modified to deliver nuclear, biological and chemical weapons against the United States or its allies.

From speaking with several members of the Defense Initiative Organization, Hershel knew that they were in favor of moving abruptly away from an orbiting grid of space-based weapons and sensors to defeat a massive launch of enemy nuclear missiles. Instead, they had adopted a plan that called for a smaller system of killer interceptors planted on terra firma.

"Buy, buy, buy, and screw the cost" was no longer the order of the day in the U.S. defense establishment. Some big things were about to take place in a down market, and the smart defense contractors in that rather large fraternity of elite weapons developers were going to rebound from that fantastic seesaw of economic balances that the department had been putting them through for years.

Hershel was about ready to suggest to Jack O'Neal and APA Aerospace the feasibility of proceeding at once with their new defense research plan, which had been shrouded in mystery for the past year. In preliminary discussions, the plan already impressed Les Vaspin and the bigwig generals at the Pentagon.

Jack's face was alive with anticipation as he turned toward Hershel. "We have to go with the tide and God," Hershel said, smiling.

What Hershel alluded to was the approval of his plan by APA, for an initial purchase of 40 MIG-21 and MIG 29 fighter planes from the C.I.S. These would be sent to the APA Aerospace plant in the United States to be retrofit for reconnaissance, target and high-altitude unmanned drones for use by the U.S. military. They would cost a mere fraction of the expense of the former U.S. ICBM program. Some of the planes would be outfitted as remote-control units and loaded with explosives to bring down enemy ICBMs. The proposed cost of each MIG would be $14 to $17 million, plus parts, compared to the previous expensive, unworkable program.

The plan to purchase the surplus MIGs was absolutely brilliant, Jack believed, since it would also keep the Russian fighters out of the military arsenals of unstable Third World nations.

Hershel's next assignment would be to go to the C.I.S. to locate the MIGs and commence preliminary negotiations with those in charge for the purchase of what was formerly hostile equipment. And he knew full well that any kind of negotiating in Russia today was no easy task.

Chapter Seven

ST. PETERSBURG & MOSCOW, C.I.S.

OCTOBER 12, 13 & 14

For Yoel Melman, guessing Russia's future was among his most frustrating pursuits, so on a Sunday, whenever he had a few moments of spare time, he tried to enjoy Russia's history. He delighted most in recalling his parents' stories about Russia and learning about their roots, as well as the Jewish history of St. Petersburg, while slowly conducting his own walking tour of the city.

When he was a youngster, many times his mother repeated the story of her grandfather, who was among the first Jewish leaders of St. Petersburg during the 1850s. One day, as Yoel waited at a bus stop, he approached a coin machine that changed Russian kopek coins. Handling the coins reminded him that Baron Horace Guenzburg and his family's Guenzburg Bank pioneered the development of credit financing to help build Russian railroad systems and the mining industry, not far from where he was now standing. For years the family and their descendants had headed up the Jewish community. Yoel was surprised to see that the home on Profoyusov Boulevard, where his mother was born and lived as a child, was still standing and occupied.

It was not until Lenin's time that hundreds of square, monotonous apartment buildings were constructed. These were so ugly that he knew they had to have been designed by someone without compassion. Anyone with compassion could not have permitted such terrible buildings to house fellow humans.

Originally built on swamps, St. Petersburg was a city of canals and bridges along the Neva River, with endless embankments along which

Yoel enjoyed walking, especially during the "white nights" of late summer, when there are almost twenty-four hours of daylight. It was the busiest seaport in Russia, ships waiting their turn for up to a month in the outer port before offloading. Founded by Peter the Great in 1703, St. Petersburg was the second largest city in Russia and had been for a long time its capital.

Among the earliest settlers of St. Petersburg were Spanish Marranos and Apostates. Over the years, Jews became somewhat influential, and a Portuguese Jew even became the first Police Minister of the city. Other Jews followed to escape the persecution in their homelands. They were allowed to serve in the Russian military and live in relative peace in their own ghettos in the city. Yoel knew, however, that the small Jewish community of yesteryear had suffered greatly from the anti-Semitism of the eighteenth century, which continued to sweep through Russia today.

Russia's partitions of Latvia had brought masses of Jews under Russian control, and a good deal of them, such as Yoel's ancestors, found their way to St. Petersburg. By 1863, not only had the city become the center of the Russian-Jewish press, the government had encouraged the establishment of the Society for the Promotion of Culture Among the Jews of Russia, uniting the Jewish intelligentsia throughout the Russian Empire.

Yoel learned from his mother that not only was St. Petersburg the home of the Winter and Summer Palaces, the Hermitage, Vasilyevsky Island and the Peter and Paul Fortress, it was also the home of the oldest Torah scroll in the world. Stolen from Crimean Jews, the Torah dated back to 912 A.D. THAT in itself was enough challenge for Yoel. He set out to find where it was kept—which proved to be more difficult than he anticipated.

Stopping by Marx Street, he found a telephone on the wall of a building. He cursed at the phone as it ate the first two of his two-kopek coins, but accepted the third. He dialed his friend Emil to see how he was doing and to inquire about the exact location of the scroll. Emil agreed to try to find out where in St. Petersburg the scroll was on display. However, when Yoel called Emil back later to get the information, the man's voice was muffled, as if he were speaking through a cloth. Yoel could not be sure why Emil sounded so strange, but became suspicious and put the phone back slowly on its cradle.

One had to assume that all phones in Russia were still tapped, as in the bad old days, but he dismissed the thought for the moment as he walked south quickly onto Trotsky Street, following Emil's directions. His excitement rose with every step as he realized he would become one of the privileged few to see the Torah scroll in recent years. He found it precisely where Emil told him it would be, located deep in one of the storage rooms of the State Public Library and covered in dust. But it could not be unwrapped for fear the ancient scroll would be damaged. It was enough for Yoel to gaze at it from a distance.

Yoel's parents had explained to him that the good fortune of the Jews in St. Petersburg—and throughout Russia, for that matter—rose and fell on a constant basis, according to the ever-changing moods of the ruling czars. Some Jews left during Czarina Elizabeth's reign, though her successor, Catherine the Great, attracted Jews. Under Nicholas I, in the nineteenth century, the situation for Jews deteriorated, but improved under Alexander II, only to decline yet again under Nicholas II.

Yoel was told by his family that except for periods when it was totally forbidden, Jewish residence in St. Petersburg was highly restricted, though it gradually was permitted to grow. The first lease for a Jewish cemetery wasn't granted until 1802. And his parents described how when Nicholas I came to power, in 1825, there were only 200 Jews living in the city. In those days other Russian citizens knew little of Jewish life, and widespread libels and slanders were often perpetrated against them.

Yoel was taught that over the years the murderous attacks known as pogroms finally spurred Jews to form self-defense units along with the creation of an All-Russian Zionist Congress; but this was short-lived. Jewish communal life continued to disappear, and by 1929 the last of the Jewish schools were closed down, along with the historical and cultural societies.

From some of the families he visited on the left bank of the Big Neva River, Yoel learned that there were approximately 140,000 Jews now living in St. Petersburg. That made him feel that if he had to, he could probably survive living here, just as his parents had, years ago.

Monday morning brought Yoel back to the reality of the day, and the beginning of his new work week. It was 5:00 A.M. when his small travel alarm clock rang, and still dark outside as he raised the window shade.

Yoel's plan was to board the early plane to Moscow. He washed, shaved, dressed, then went to the closet to take the long knit sweater that his wife had given him at his last birthday from the top shelf. He quickly slipped it over his head and smoothed his ruffled hair with his fingers. "Come on, hurry up, you decrepit old bastard," he said to himself as he looked in the mirror to see if he had put his hat on straight.

The drive to the airport did not take long, and once aboard the flight Yoel could not keep his mind from drifting to Saturday's tangled web of events, which had involved Emil—and possibly others. Was there really a conspiracy or possibly a coup attempt in the works, planned and promoted by the angry good-old-boys network of the former Soviet military? The more he thought about it, the more the conspiracy theory seemed to be a plausible scenario. It seemed clear to Yoel that the hardliners might attempt to engineer opportunities for themselves at the expense of the C.I.S.

Just to see if this scenario could be further supported, Yoel planned to continue collecting information and evidence on the activities of these die-hard ex-Communists. He started writing down his thoughts and bits and pieces of information he had so far gathered regarding them. He planned to present this to a small group of visiting former Mossad agents with whom he had previously worked and who were coming to Moscow.

The "formers" were already scheduled to meet with him for their planned reunion early next week.

He smiled in anticipation of this fabulous opportunity, as he imagined the formers sitting seriously in chairs around a table filled with food, discussing old times and new, including this spectacular scenario on the possibility of a military putsch by the die-hards. He knew they would enjoy the challenge; they would spend many pleasant hours, perhaps days, helping him put together the numerous exciting pieces of the puzzle that did not yet fit.

Yoel knew that his close friend and former colleague Avrum Hamo would, as always, be impatient while he laid out the Generalities of his premise. Avrum always sought specific, snap answers to specific questions. Yoel opened his briefcase and took out a blank pad of paper. He could not wait to begin his usual practice of listing the many relevant questions that revolve around intelligence-related mysteries like the one he was trying to solve. In anticipation of the grilling he would be put through by Avrum, he began a comprehensive list:

One: Is Gorbachev as isolated at his dacha as the reports say he is?

Two: With access to the mountains of tapes, notes and other information found on the defense minister's desk, why has the KGB still not presented a clear case of conspiracy against the accused?

Three: Why did the hard-line coup leaders, having isolated President Gorbachev at his seaside dacha in the Crimea, not move at the same time to isolate the outspoken and troublesome Boris Yeltsin at his country villa outside of Moscow?

Four: Why did the KGB not cut off communications once it became clear that Yeltsin would mount resistance from the Russian Parliament building?

Five: Why have only some of the coup's hard-line followers been arrested by the KGB and not other guilty individuals?

Six: Were there plans, which would obviously gather large crowds, to storm the Parliament building on that rainy night of August 20, 1991? If so, why were they not carried out?

After examining the questions, he smiled. He mused about the contradictions: the mass confusion on August 20, on the part of those carrying out the coup (if there was one) and the lack of detail and urgency on the part of the hard-liners who had obviously planned the whole thing.

But wait a minute, Yoel thought, after he considered another possible scenario. Could the planning have really been as bad as it now seemed, or had it been purposely intended to be a failure to begin with, in order to get rid of some of the coup's participants? Could the true masterminds have set this all up to flush out a faction of hard-liners that they wanted to lose as sacrificial lambs, anyway? And are we still in the middle of a well-timed military putsch, he asked himself, that will eventually take place once everyone in Russia is relaxed and confident that the first attempt failed? In addition, there was the possibility of a scenario in which a second group might attempt an independent coup sometime soon.

Yoel was so engrossed with this possible new scenario that he absentmindedly placed his notes inside his briefcase, which he left on the floor in front of his seat. He stood up, excused himself to the passenger in the aisle seat next to him and walked to the lavatory at the rear of the plane.

In a few minutes he slowly wound his way back among several passengers who were standing. Casually stretching himself as he walked, his eyes discreetly went from face to face. Yoel suddenly recognized a man, seated several rows behind him, as the one who had gotten up and walked out of the restaurant the previous Saturday evening when Emil was drunkenly shouting his mouth off about "the men of honor." I hope my face doesn't show any anxiety, Yoel thought.

The stranger looked up at Yoel, and Yoel returned his stare, studying the man narrowly and feeling uneasy under his hostile, penetrating gaze. In the back of his mind an alarm went off. There was something unusual about his demeanor and Yoel just couldn't put his finger on it. Is this just a coincidence, a case of mistaken identity, or am I being set up, Yoel wondered? As farfetched as it seems, it is conceivable that this character is following me!

Yoel again excused himself to gain access to his window seat, and for the moment he put the thought in the back of his mind.

When seated, Yoel suddenly realized that something was wrong. His briefcase was turned a different way than when he'd left, and one of the snaps was undone. I always lock both snaps, he thought, so this could not just be my imagination or a simple coincidence! More likely, someone is a bit too inquisitive about what I am working on.

Yoel knew that the KGB still covered the country like a blanket. He felt rising indignation. Perhaps it is the passenger seated next to me, he considered. He seems to be engrossed in his book, but is he? He is taking a bit too long reading a single page. Could he be KGB? The KGB has long since stopped its old cloak-and-dagger routine. But if he *is* KGB, wouldn't he have detained me by now?

This was indeed unnerving. Yoel decided to consider his old Mossad instruction manual, the chapter on survival.

Meanwhile, he did not loose his sense of humor, but did start feeling uncomfortable. He believed it was unlikely that the KGB intended to pick him up or harm him, because they could have him arrested anytime they wanted. More likely, they were just following him in an effort to gather information. He assumed they would keep him under surveillance until he led them to something they wanted.

For the moment Yoel knew he had few options while he was on the plane, so, pretending he had not noticed anything wrong, he continued what he was doing before: thinking about the information he planned to share with the formers.

"While it may be difficult," his memo continued, "to accurately reconstruct the events of the coup and to conclude who the ring leaders really were, there is no doubt in my mind that the true die-hard leaders are still running loose, eventually expecting to triumph!"

Yoel continued to list his thoughts in the memo. Why were the real leaders of the plot not willing to publicly assume responsibility? Even though the first plot failed, the publicity might have been good for them.

Was this merely a test for a larger and more successful coup to come? Why was the prosecutor's case against the few conspirators caught in the coup attempt pursuing political goals and not legal ones?

He concluded that perhaps the military was waiting for clearly defined leadership to come forth, while the KGB was waiting for any of the other government units to move first.

Yoel, a decent, hard-working man trying to achieve decent things— for which he had no immediate backup protection because he was not even working for the Israeli government on this *pro bono* assignment— carefully folded his few handwritten pages and put them into a pre-addressed, pre-stamped envelope, without a return address. As he turned his head toward the window he sealed it by wetting the glue flap with his tongue. The envelope was directed to Nikolai Mikoyan, a former with a temporary "dead drop" address in Moscow.

Yoel had decided it would be best to forward his thoughts to one of his friends, on the remote chance he was stopped, detained or questioned by the KGB. His plan was to perform a sleight of hand: When exiting the plane, he would drop the letter on the steward's counter as he had done countless times on previous flights. Yoel was sure that, once found, the steward would most likely mail the letter, relieving him of the one thing that might give the KGB something they could be interested in.

The air inside the plane seemed to become as oppressive as the man he was sitting next to, who quite likely was the person who rifled his bag. Then, instantly he was snapped back to reality by a sudden turbulence. The seat belt light came on, followed by an announcement from the steward. An experienced flyer, Yoel automatically kept his seat belt on while in his seat. Unavoidable potholes, he thought, but the turbulence seemed to intensify.

Waiting so that he would be one of the last passengers to disembark, Yoel's plan to discreetly drop the envelope worked just fine. Now it was a question of whether it would ever get to Nikolai. In Russia, someone might even steal the envelope just to recycle the unused stamp. But probably not a flight attendant. And he didn't believe anyone that desperate would be flying aboard a plane.

Yoel had made every effort to reason out his dilemma. The entire ordeal had become a strain, the added uncertainty while on the four-hour plane trip making him yearn to get to his final destination without any incidents; so, once in the terminal, Yoel collected his bag, walked out the front entrance and down the lengthy broad sidewalk that led to the taxi stands and car garage.

Again, by sheer instinct without bothering to turn his head, he became aware that someone was slightly behind and to the side of him, walking a little too close to Yoel for comfort. Why was this person so close? There was plenty of room on the walk. It was not all that crowded.

But his mind was too weak from lack of sleep to think of possible answers or solutions to this latest dilemma. Nevertheless, his Mossad intelligence training had taught him that indecision could be one's worst enemy. An inner warning alarm sounded for him to take decisive action as his pulse rate escalated.

Yoel did not turn his head until he felt unexpected pressure under his ribs. The force of the gun was pushing him to walk in a direction he did not intend to go. He knew instantly that his transient moments of peace and comfort would soon be forgotten. His fears had not been misdirected.

"Shall we explore the inside of my car?" the man with the beard said in Russian as he pointed his free hand in the direction of a black car parallel-parked at the curb.

"Did you expect me to refuse your invitation?" Yoel shot back with as much attitude as he could muster.

He looked down at his watch before speaking again. "Why shouldn't I join you? I'm in no rush to go anywhere," Yoel said with a forced laugh. Not only was his anxiety about to get the better of him, so was his curiosity.

As he climbed into the back seat, Yoel tried to suppress his fear, even hide it from himself, as the mystery driver pulled out into the traffic. At a time like this, he felt the worst thing he could do was lose his ever-present sense of humor.

The stranger was a man of heavy build, medium height and a gray face, accented by a prominent brown beard. "It's strange how events bring people from different lands together," the man now added, making the entire incident even more mysterious for Yoel.

"Look, I don't know who or what you think I am, but you must admit that you could be making a mistake. And I'm willing to give you every benefit of the doubt," Yoel bluffed, thinking all the while that the best defense in this situation was a good offense. "If you're kidnapping me for money, you're wasting your time. My family is as poor as I am. If you'll just open the door and let me get out, I will forget all about this incident."

"*Da,* we can probably work something out," the man with the beard said, grabbing Yoel's arm tightly. "We will let you go. But not this moment. We will talk first. Tell me what agency you are working with, what are you carrying in your briefcase and what are you looking for here?"

Yoel was suddenly relieved to be able to confirm that the stranger did not have the letter he'd left on the flight attendant's counter for mailing, otherwise there would have been no need to ask these questions. It took him a second to realize he had to come up with some plan of action, in case things took a turn for the worse.

"That's ridiculous! I'm not part of any agency and no one sent me here! You are looking at a legitimate businessman trying to conduct legitimate trade with your country!" Yoel blurted out very convincingly in his excitement.

It was easy to sound convincing, because this was, for the most part, the truth. His past was another story.

"I work for and by myself," he continued, "and I spend my spare time learning about and enjoying the culture of lands other than my own. You are not going to get any loans or cash advances from me. Long gone are the days of finding businessmen's briefcases packed with thousand-dollar bills. Yes, I work alone. Okay? And that is the only truthful answer I am able to give you."

Instantly, he recognized that he had made a gross error—a silly one, yet a significant one. Emphasizing that he was working "alone," without help, was a slip. He realized that he would have been better off not saying anything on this subject.

He hoped that perhaps this scorpion did not pick up or understand his last sleight of tongue. By God, Yoel asked himself, have I forgotten everything? Have I finally risen to my own level of incompetence? I have to think fast and maybe divert this man's ugly thoughts.

He tossed a question over his shoulder as if it were a hand grenade, and waited for the explosion: "What kind of credentials do you have?" Yoel asked aggressively of the stone faced man as he looked directly into his glassy eyes.

Countless times he had trained other people to defend against just the sort of predicament that he was in now. He knew that he would have to take action, and soon, but how? When was the right opportunity for him to pull out his single-shot cigarette pistol and use the one bullet?

Yoel did not like to think about being kidnapped, the likelihood of a ransom demand, of torture, or the possibility of being killed—especially by some unknown, die-hard, radical group in a faraway land. The recognition of the seriousness of his situation suddenly sank through Yoel like a stone in water.

Well, here I am, Yoel reasoned in silence. Maybe if I humble myself, and in a matter of speaking bare my soul, admit my mistakes, that will give me some sort of a chance with my captor? "To err is human, to forgive is divine," Yoel quoted, trying to soften up his Russian adversary.

"Drop it," the Russian shot back.

"At least consider what I said," Yoel appealed.

"I'll sleep on it," the man said as he signaled his driver to pull the car next to the trolley station, at an intersecting street.

Yoel tried to recover lost ground with yet another gambit. "A bad compromise is better than a good battle. Let's go back a minute, just reach in my briefcase and pull the green folder out of the side pocket."

Holding a gun against Yoel's temple with one hand, the man carefully reached into the leather briefcase with the other, cautiously looking for a concealed explosive dye or gas that could incapacitate everyone in the car if activated.

Satisfied that the briefcase was harmless, the man found the green folder and removed some papers.

Yoel said, "See? Those are the food orders I am working on for commodities…sugar, coffee and wheat for the people of your nation! How much of a threat can one businessman like me be to your country?" Yoel coughed in nervousness. Bringing his hand up to his throat, he wiped the sweat from his brow.

"I can accept that," the man said slowly, but he pressed on. "I have another problem you can possibly help me with. What do you know about a General Lukyanov and his memo book?"

Yoel leaned back in the car seat, his eyebrows raised, his fear obvious. Good God, he thought, immediately realizing that he had given himself away by not reacting casually and with a poker face. Where did all my Mossad training go? My reflexes are not working properly today, I must be getting older, or I must be really tired.

"I don't know a General Lukyanov. Does he want to buy sugar?" Yoel replied nervously. "And I do not have the slightest idea what 'memo book' you are referring to. Is it the title of some novel *The Memo Book*?

Who is the author?" He asked his captor these questions in a voice that seemed to float off into the distance.

The man studied Yoel with his cold eyes, stroking his beard with his free hand, thinking.

Yoel was still contemplating that the best way for him to play out this scenario was to be unpredictable, to act on impulse and try to get the man to answer a few questions. In the process, Yoel adopted a brazen, arrogant style that contrasted sharply with the tweedy professorial facade he usually imitated. He blurted out, "Do you work with the KGB?" This surprised the bearded man.

"I don't have to tell you anything," the man replied arrogantly. "But no harm. I did work with them, but that was long ago. I am now a member of the new personal militia of the Russian Parliamentary Security Service." And with a flash of wrath and indignation in his voice he allowed himself to state that he was deeply disappointed in the new C.I.S. "There are those of us who don't want the C.I.S. to last."

The man then started spitting out meaningless words.

"There is no need to dramatize our country's problems. Please get out of the car very slowly and walk just in front of me to the trolley station. We are going to take a short trip. Remember, my gun will be in my coat pocket and my finger will be on the trigger. I will not hesitate for a moment to shoot you if you try to escape, but I want to show you something important."

The man was experienced, all business. Yoel was sure that this guy had done things like this before.

"All right so far?"

"Keep it moving," Mr. ex-KGB said.

There was a long silence. "I am ready to meet my maker," Yoel said. "Whether my maker is ready for the ordeal of meeting me is another matter." His new attempt at humor did not receive a response.

Yoel hadn't had a cigarette in almost twenty years, but now he desperately craved a smoke. Still, he knew that a sudden move on his part could lead to disaster. His immediate objective was to wait for the right moment—hopefully a moment of confusion, perhaps when the man with the gun would be inattentive or indecisive. At that instant, he would swing to the left while grabbing for the man's arm holding the gun. He would then use his past training to silently disable the Russian with a blow to the throat or the groin, whichever was more convenient.

He felt that he would be able to disappear among the many people waiting at the trolley stop before his captor would know what hit him and regain his composure. Maybe there was one more rabbit in the hat after all.

"Walk slowly," said his mystery captor. "You will board at the front of the trolley when it stops."

"Disrespectful," Yoel said out loud, trying to distract the man.

"Just do it, and now!" the man insisted.

If this guy has a car and driver at his disposal why the hell are we taking a trolley? Yoel asked himself. As the trolley rapidly approached, Yoel flew forward. It was sudden, unexpected. Too sudden.

Yoel was used to seeing violent death in Israel at the hands of the Palestinians, and in an instant he realized that he had been shoved from behind, that death was now coming for him.

"Shema Yisroel!" he cried out as he fought desperately to regain his balance.

He spun his body, using his outstretched arms to try and roll off the tracks and out of the way of the trolley that was now almost on top of him. Like a haunted man, he felt as if he were dreaming. Everything was in a fog, as if it were happening to someone else.

He heard a burst of laughter and then the drum of voices filtered down to him, together with the loud clang from the trolley bell, which sounded like a jet plane droning directly over his head.

It was too late. He heard the screech of brakes, the momentary pain was excruciating. At that split second he knew he was dying. Everything became blurred, a white flashing light. It was an inauspicious end for a man whose promising new career and future with his young family was just developing.

"I don't have time to be bothered by small dragons," the man with the beard was heard to say as he turned and walked away, totally disinterested, into the gathering crowd. He continued mumbling under his breath, "Kill the messenger and destroy the message." His job had been accomplished with the accustomed precision.

Even with the sudden confusion, a balalaika player continued to play on the opposite street corner as a crowd began to gather around the body.

Chapter Eight

FRANKFURT AM MAIN, GERMANY

OCTOBER 14

Opening the newspaper wide to screen off the troublesome children in the opposite aisle of the plane, Hershel buried himself in the headlines. Automatically he glanced up as the stewardess, empty serving tray in hand, suddenly opened the door to exit the cockpit.

Within, a profusion of red and green warning lights, control dials, pressure gages and gridded flashing computer screens were visible in front of the navigator. The pilot and copilot were listening to voices coming from their head sets.

Looking out the small window of the commercial 747 transatlantic airliner, Hershel saw the maintenance hangars and support buildings near the runway rush past. As the plane quickly touched down, he felt his body press against his seat belt as the pilot thrust the large engines into reverse to help brake the aircraft.

Clearing her throat before announcing that flight 806 had just landed at Frankfurt airport, the stewardess added, "Please remember to remove your belongings as you leave," while static crackled over the loudspeaker.

Feeling for his passport in his inner jacket pocket for the tenth time, Hershel relished the thought of meeting his former Mossad handler and longtime buddy in Helsinki in two days. They planned to continue on to Moscow together early the next week for a reunion with the liaison and collection group of intelligence agents with whom they had worked. Until now, he had not been fully reconciled with his feelings about his former colleagues. But for days now, in the conscious and subconscious parts of his brain, he had been looking forward to this moment, savoring it, and now the time was almost here. He was filled with an excitement that he tried his best to suppress. Then, he realized how tired he was from the long trip, and recalled how in the past he had been able to cope for years at a time with travel complexities on an almost daily basis.

There had been much more challenging flights than this—secret intelligence missions, where the unmarked black plane he was aboard cut its engines so the Israeli military pilot trained in short field landings could guide the aircraft over a strip of hard beach, a cutout area in a wooded forest, or make an odd intrusion on a concrete-like desert floor somewhere in the Middle East. Hershel remembered how the high-soaring plane would avoid all commercial routes and military installations, landing so rapidly from an altitude so high that the probability of detection by the enemy was slim. If there was a sudden blip on a ground-defense radar screen, it would appear and disappear so quickly that the controller would generally not bother to investigate.

Hershel now realized that this current means of travel was more to his liking. At least it left his stomach intact. But seven hours of flying in tourist class had given him pains in his lower back. He rose, stretched and gently eased himself back into his seat.

Staring blankly out the window as he waited for the plane to taxi slowly up to the waiting ramp, Hershel's mood changed as he came to the realization that there was so much history he had been involved with that could not be comfortably revisited. Just thinking about some of his past missions brought on anxiety and bad memories. Now, as Hershel momentarily struggled to close the stubborn zipper of his briefcase, he recalled how he had countered the numerous hours of travel boredom in years past by writing his intelligence memos and formulating reports for his handler.

With his retirement, for his own enjoyment Hershel had begun to do more and more casual traveling, revisiting all those places he liked but had never had the time to explore in the light of day while on a mission—all those good places, with great-smelling food, that were not located behind the borders of unfriendly Islamic countries.

When he was not traveling, he enjoyed reading, sketching, oil painting or writing in his diary about his many experiences while a member of the Mossad. He developed contacts around the globe: from Swiss

bankers in Geneva, to the Minister of Finance in Panama and other help-
ers or collaborators—anonymous and otherwise—from Singapore to
Saudi Arabia. And there was even a lawyer in Miami who, when speaking
from his desk, affected to Hershel the gruff murmur of a godfather-like
character.

But if there was anything Hershel longed for this late afternoon, it
was having a gourmet dinner in a quiet German restaurant, accompanied by a great stein of beer.

Going through customs, Hershel appreciated the fact that this was the
first time in fifteen years that he was not using a forged passport.

"How long do you expect to stay in Germany?" the customs inspector asked.

"Just for a day," was his reply, in German.

"Are you here for business?"

"No, for pleasure. This is a stopover. I am on the way to Finland.
Here are my tickets."

The customs inspector acknowledged Hershel's explanation with a
nod as he hand-stamped the passport.

"Guten tag."

"Danke," Hershel replied.

Walking through the terminal building, he took particular notice of
the large number of security police, some with attack dogs on short
leashes. All were provided with obvious sidearms as well as automatic
Uzi machine guns slung over their shoulders or tucked under their arms,
and all had a finger on the trigger. They flanked both sides of the baggage conveyor belt, obviously on the lookout for suspected terrorists. A
few of the security police walked among the passengers like a flock of
strutting peacocks, a visible threat to any who were attempting to smuggle
narcotics or explosives.

These uniformed guards with guns are not all that comforting, Hershel
thought. But neither are the lunatic terrorists who are out there somewhere at this very moment, seeking a target....

He held his breath. She smiled like an actress in a television commercial. The beautiful ticket agent with long-flowing blond hair at the
Finnair counter reconfirmed Hershel's Sunday-morning flight to Helsinki.
Hershel imagined that if he were only younger and not married, he would
convincingly request her company for dinner that evening.

Claiming his bag, he exited the main entrance and took the next available Mercedes cab, giving the driver the name of his hotel as he closed the passenger door. With Hershel's lone carry-on bag safely in the trunk, the driver floored the gas pedal, never slowing down at the end of the ramp leading to the *Autobahn*. Once on the open highway, the driver seemed to be trying to show his passenger and the other drivers how the Daytona 500 should really be run.

The car's interior was spotless. A miniature palm tree hung from the rearview mirror. Hershel grimly thought that with this sort of driving, they might both wind up in the land of palms.

Placing his head against the rear-seat headrest, Hershel barely had time to notice the silver BMW with the rear passenger window open as it sped up in the passing lane, pulling parallel with his taxi. For an instant, as light swept through the darkness of the passing car, he thought he saw the outline of a man with a gold tooth, and the reflection of a gun muzzle pointed in his direction.

Instinctively, Hershel reacted by sliding lower in his seat. Then there came the flash of a gun and the swish of the bullet going upward as it tore a small hole in the far corner of the car roof. A small piece of broken glass from the dome light landed in his lap as the shock and suddenness of the incident quickly sank in.

The BMW immediately veered into another lane and sped off.

What in the...? Who? Why? Was this just a random drive-by attempted shooting?...A gold tooth? Who in the hell wears a front gold tooth in this day and age? Many questions would have to be answered. The answers would be essential to his continued security, although they would have to be postponed until the taxi got to the hotel.

The driver had never heard the report of the gun or the breaking of the glass of the dome light over the noise of the traffic and his blaring radio. Hershel saw no point in bringing the damage to his attention.

Sliding to the opposite side of the seat, Hershel did not know who, other than he, could have been the target of this attack. He wasn't planning to take any chances. Too many terrorist organizations were using terror incidents or assassinations to send messages. He did not intend to be the messenger. He was shaken from what had just happened, but could still think clearly. He decided it would be safer to assume that this was no misunderstanding or accidental drive-by shooting. Most likely, he had been marked and followed.

Reacting automatically from his many years of training, Hershel reached down for his holstered gun for comfort, only to realize that it was not there.

"Damn it," he mumbled in a low breath, as he remembered that he was no longer officially part of the Mossad and was not armed. When he was on active duty, he was able to conceal a weapon in an aluminum-plated secret compartment of his luggage while traveling. When X-rayed at airport security, the compartment would simply show up as a Polaroid camera case. But independent businessmen, like himself, without government affiliations, had to look out for themselves. Now he had only his wits as his defense.

"Welcome to Frankfurt am Main," said the large letters of a sign across the highway.

The burst of gunfire had brought Hershel back in touch with the reality of the day: Some welcome indeed! He was glad the driver hadn't heard the short blast of the gun or the impact of the bullet—the man could have lost control of the car, Hershel thought. Furthermore, he wouldn't have appreciated being detained by the authorities for the inevitable questioning that would have followed.

Still, what was the significance of the driver of the attack car speeding up and disappearing in the darkness before he could see if he hit anyone? Maybe he was the kind of guy who blew up buildings before breakfast just for the fun of it.

Hershel continued to seek an explanation. He believed in having everything under control. Leaving nothing to chance. No matter how he thought it through, it was obvious that this was not just a random shooting committed by someone who could kill without compunction, indulging in some insane form of barbaric highway terrorism.

He did not imagine that drive-by shootings occurred frequently in Europe, and theorized that likely it was a greeting from an old enemy who only recognized him by chance. This, if true, made him uneasy. But the feeling lasted only an instant, and belonged somewhere in his past life. He had been out of the intelligence game for long enough that any past enemies would have found him and taken their revenge by now.

One thing was certain, however: From this point on, he would have to watch his step or he could find his body floating down some dimly lit German canal.

All Hershel wanted now was to enjoy the good things that retirement had to offer; and that included his safety. He felt he had earned that with his rites of passage as an intelligence agent. He knew he had been marked by his enemies fifteen years before. But now? He was beginning to feel as if someone still had his name on an Arab "Wanted" poster.

In Frankfurt the streets were crowded. The shops were doing a brisk early-evening business as the taxi wound its way through the inner city and pulled up in front of the Plaza Hotel.

The driver still had not discovered the broken glass. Hershel promptly paid the fare and awarded the driver a handsome tip.

"Good driving," Hershel said in German, remembering his German from way back in Spring Valley Senior High School. He then stepped out of the cab, looked around briefly and quickly proceeded into the spacious hotel lobby.

Signing the register, he quickly checked in and settled the method of payment for the hotel, which would be by credit card. After dealing with that paperwork, the desk clerk efficiently requested the bellhop to show Hershel to his fourth-floor room.

As he entered the elevator, he went to the very back corner of the car so that the bellhop would be in front of him and he could watch the man's every move. He could not trust anyone at this point.

Since the shot fired at him in the taxi was not successful, he knew that he might have been followed to the hotel. By now the shooter might even have the number of his room, although it was unlikely he would make any rash moves before Hershel went to bed. And that is just fine, Hershel thought. This will give me time to collect my thoughts.

And these were that he not stay in the hotel room that night. Hershel had come to grips with his immediate problem. He knew he must survive.

What would I do if I were the shooter? he tried to imagine as he took a deep breath. Let's see, I would place myself in the lobby or at a vantage point somewhere in front of the hotel. I would try to figure out precisely when the person I was stalking would be alone in his room. Therefore, if I stay in the room, he and his friends will certainly come for me during the night.

Hershel shrugged his heavy shoulders as he realized that he would be damned if he stayed in this hotel—but that he'd be in an equally precarious situation if he went downstairs.

His reactions became instinctive at this point. He removed his pin-striped suit and put on casual clothing from his carry-on bag, selecting the common favorite of Europeans: a well-worn pair of Levi 501s and a pair of sneakers. He also put on a dark-colored heavy turtleneck sweater, a crushed Irish hat with a brim that would help cover his face when turned down, a long muffler, and his carry-on bag—which he easily converted into a backpack.

If the weather forecast proved correct, he would also be needing his overcoat the next day. Rolling it as tightly as possible, he tied it up with a cord he cut from the window blind and attached it in a neat roll at the very bottom of his backpack. He laughed as he imagined how his back-pack would resemble those carried by the hippies of the '60s.

Looking in the mirror at the final results, he realized that on the street he would not even recognize himself. He looked nothing like the Hershel who walked into the hotel a few minutes ago.

With his ear to the door, he listened as a number of people walked down the long corridor in the direction of the elevator. Waiting a few minutes after the voices faded, he slowly opened the door and cautiously walked into the corridor, gazing carefully in both directions. Given these circumstances, the less dependent he was on anything he did not have complete control over, the better off he would be. Getting stuck in an elevator for any period of time was not part of his battle plan. He chose the stairs instead.

Consciously putting one foot in front of the other, he wound his way down the stairwell, stopping and listening for other footsteps at each landing. At the first basement level, he opened the door and casually walked through the busy kitchen area, eyes straight ahead, looking like he had a reason to be there. He looked just like one of the maintenance employees going off duty.

His timing proved to be perfect; other employees were also leaving and some were coming in to their shift. He waited for his turn at the time clock, picked out a card that belonged to an unknown employee and punched out, leaving through the rear employee entrance.

Knowing that entering the unfamiliar street alone would be like walk-ing into a minefield without proper training, he watched for an opportu-nity and soon spotted a waitress who was about to leave alone. He saw her name on her ID tag before she put her coat on.

"Hello, Olga," he said.

Almost before he could finish, she blurted out, "Who are you?"

"My name is Hans. Today is my first day working here as a waiter. It is also my birthday and I have no one to celebrate with me."

He then added that he did not often have reason to celebrate and asked if she would join him for a drink in the bar across from the hotel. He continued to explain that because it was his birthday, he was a little lonely. It appeared to him that this waitress without a wedding ring might possibly be just as lonely as he pretended to be.

Olga noticed that he had an unfamiliar accent, but she dismissed the observation as unimportant. Maybe he was convincing, looked safe, or was just convenient. Anyway, the bar was right across the street and it was crowded, so she probably felt safe going there with this total stranger.

As he and she passed the alley at the front of the hotel, Hershel's face suddenly turned rigid, his eyes zeroing in on the middle-aged man standing partially hidden by a column of the building across the street.

Even though Hershel had not seen or recognized his attacker when in the taxi, intuition told him that this had to be the man. The attacker obviously worked for some "company," but which company was the question.

This would be a good test of his disguise, and Hershel almost enjoyed the moment. He hoped the attacker would never expect his target to come right at him from behind. After all, who would be so foolish as to purposely brush shoulders with his would-be assassin? With the girl on his arm, he walked right next to where the man was waiting, almost brushing up against him, as he escorted the girl toward the bar.

Although Hershel felt confident about not being recognized, his up-close observation of the man would have to be fast. He smiled as he passed his enemy.

"Now I am sure," he commented to himself as he walked past the attacker. Ugh! He could have used a bath and some deodorant, and that strange smell...was it hashish? Looks as if he hasn't slept for days. Those are indeed the hands, face and nose of an Arab. And, damn it, a gold tooth right in front of the man's mouth. A sign of wealth in some countries.

Now it began to come together for Hershel. The man had all the features of an Arab, in all likelihood a Palestinian from one of the radical terror groups. Hershel was sincerely tempted to allow this fellow his martyrdom by deep-sixing him on the spot. All this terrorist needed to do was give him a look or move in his direction and it would be the unfortunate terrorist's last move.

The attacker proved to be alone, which meant that he did not have time to call for backup or didn't think he needed any. Or it was even possible that he might not have reliable backup in this city. If this assumption were true, and the situation got much stickier, Hershel would have no problem using his camping knife, which was sharpened, when unfolded, to a stiletto point. But he wanted to avoid an incident.

For the moment he saw no urgency in resolving the problem of his stalker in a violent manner. He believed that his situation would be better if he left this bad guy alone, and that it would be best if he could simply disappear in the secure departure area of the airline terminal until his flight left the next day. He was reminded how appropriate the old Russian proverb was: "A hundred friends are not too many; one enemy is."

Once a shining knight in the world of secret intelligence, Hershel refused to run, for while he was inconvenienced, he was not afraid. Threats like this were once routine. An occupational hazard, characteristic of his former life. All he needed was to properly arm himself if things turned ugly.

Inside the bar, he bought the girl a drink and ordered one for himself. He regarded her for a moment, then with a smile and considerable charm said: "To the good old days!"

"To the good old days past!" she added hoarsely.

He touched his glass to hers so hard that some of her vodka spilled.

She laughed. They drank in silence for a moment and then she thanked him for the drink and walked over to another couple she recognized in the cafe.

"You're welcome," he said before she left. The artificial lights of the cafe glowed in the semi-darkness as she walked away. Then she turned to look back at him. He waved, and so did she.

Well, nothing is forever, Hershel reflected. He was relieved that the small talk was over and she was gone.

Finding an empty table near the front window, Hershel ordered another drink so as to blend into the bar's scene. When it came, he looked into the glass on the table in front of him, as if looking into a crystal ball trying to see what the future held in store for him.

He angled his chair to a good vantage point for sidewalk surveillance and by sitting in a slightly awkward position could look over the half-window curtain and observe the scene in front of the hotel.

Suddenly he realized that the name of the bar he was in was *As-Sa'iqa*. In Arabic that meant lightning bolt. He remembered a Palestinian terrorist group by the same name. Was it just a coincidence that a place of business had the same name as an Arab terrorist group? He had no idea that this terror organization was even still in business.

All of this day's events were beyond Hershel's wildest expectation. He would never have predicted that someone would take a shot at him. He knew that contrary to what most laymen believe, when the cause was mutual intelligence, strategists from opposing services often made contact in strange ways to confer. "We are just practical men doing business in a deadly profession," he had been heard to say to others on occasion. But Hershel had the feeling that the guy outside the window was no strategist—and that his specialty was the killing fields of the world.

Now that Hershel had had time to collect his thoughts, he believed that the shot could have been just bad aim, or even a warning statement: Yes, I recognize you, I know who you are, and I am going to stay on your trail until I find out why you are here and what you are up to, and all the while I will always have the option of killing you.

God, how I hate to leave this one behind, Hershel thought. Unfinished business, so to speak. I'd damn well like to retaliate against the man who fired at me. But I trust my instinct: The man probably did not want me to consider operating in his territory.

Hershel chuckled at his own dark humor as he recalled street signs in New York City stating: "Don't even think of parking here!" Maybe the local chamber of commerce should have posted signs saying: "Former intelligence agents—don't even think of visiting Frankfurt am Main!"

Hershel's feelings about his future and his wondrous expectations for retirement had been shattered like a hundred broken mirrors. Perhaps, he speculated, he could discreetly get word out to the Intelligence Community that he no longer had anything to do with its world, that he was just an independent businessman trying to earn a living. Then, on reflection, he realized this message would take ages to become accepted. People in the know would assume the worst about someone—as they had been trained to do through their years in the intelligence field.

Hershel decided that the best approach was not to open that can of worms. An old Arab friend once told him of a Bedouin saying: "Never let a camel's nose into your tent, or the next thing you know, you get the whole camel." Relating that saying to his present circumstances, he decided that he would never give this guy the opportunity to get into his tent. It was time for him to put some distance between himself and his attacker—A.S.A.P. "Silly fool, you should have killed me while you could have," he muttered, as if speaking to his attacker.

He jumped at the first opportunity to leave the pub—a silhouetted figure tagging along with a group of boisterous half-drunk patrons. He soon disappeared into the darkness. "Child's play," Hershel mumbled to himself.

In a situation such as this, he was trained to escape and never look back, but he could not resist the temptation. After a few steps he turned around, confirming that he was not being followed and had made a clean getaway.

Chapter Nine

HELSINKI, FINLAND

OCTOBER 15

The elegant-looking man was in his late fifties, slightly on the heavy side but still looking dapper in his wool two-piece pinstriped gray suit. His long black topcoat was unbuttoned, a gray muffler flowing in the slight breeze as he stood beside the modest entrance to a small hotel and rathskeller, waiting uneasily with his back against the turn-of-the-century building. Standing in downtown Helsinki reminded him of the hazards he had gone through over the years while on special assignment with the special "AL" unit of the Mossad.

Avrum Hamo was holding the international edition of the *Herald Tribune* partially folded in front of him, giving everyone the impression that he was absorbed in reading. In fact, he was peering over the top of the paper, keeping alert for his immediate target, Hershel Shemtov.

A car rapidly pulled up to the curb and a man wearing a black fur hat climbed out after paying the driver. He slammed the door just as the car pulled away and walked directly toward Avrum.

At first glance, Hershel noticed that Avrum appeared worried. It looked as if Avrum had not eaten or slept during the past week. His eyes were hollowed and red-rimmed, but whatever the problem was for the moment, it didn't seem to bother him. He quickly folded the newspaper and broke into a smile.

"*Shalom*, Avrum, it's good to see you again," Hershel said warmly as he extended his right hand. The other arm went around Avrum's shoulder as he gave him two pats on his back in the usual gesture of greeting.

"I have something for you. I think you call them nails." He pulled a carton of Avrum's favorite cigarettes out from his coat pocket.

"*Shalom*, Hershel," Avrum replied, as he inspected the labeling on the carton. "Still trying to get rid of me? Only joking. You're always true to form. You never seem to forget me. Thank you. And you look well, Hershel. You haven't aged a bit since I last saw you."

"Lay it on thick. I love it, Avrum!"

"How's the world treating you, old boy?"

"It's hard to keep the score."

Hershel was of medium height. Regardless of the fact that he was pushing fifty-four, he had the body of a gymnast and the muscles of a weightlifter. His stomach was flat, his head full of hair, and he looked good wearing his old jeans and sweater. When Hershel was with the Institute for Intelligence and Special Operations, he'd been a "barracuda," with a natural ability and instinct, especially when it came to analyzing a tight situation.

Finished with their genial greeting, the two strolled down the stairs and through the narrow entry of the rathskeller without saying another word, making themselves comfortable at a round table strategically placed in the corner of the nearly empty room.

"My poor aching feet," Avrum complained. "I think they've had it for today."

The smell of fresh baked bread filled the restaurant. Avrum sized up the other people in the room and gestured with an affirmative nod to Hershel that all was clear.

Hershel smiled. He appreciated the fact that some people could never change their old set habits. After taking a few moments to consider the menu, Hershel gestured for the waitress to place an order for drinks.

The waitress hurried to the bar after taking their order. Hershel wanted a few moments to unwind, so he pushed his chair away from the table, leaned back with his legs crossed, inspected the shine on his shoes, brushed the lint from his sweater off his jeans and decided to wait for Avrum to speak first.

"How are your wife and children?" Avrum inquired.

"Couldn't be better. I now have seven grandchildren, and hopefully more will be on the way. There is just one variation on the theme," Hershel added. "So far my four boys took all this while to find the right combination, and between them all they've finally produced a boy! But to tell you the truth, I have no complaints. Girls are in fact my favorite people! Have a look for yourself."

Hershel smiled proudly, pulling out several pictures from his jacket pocket. Avrum peeled them back, one picture at a time, toying with one group picture of Hershel's grandchildren.

Hershel broke the silence, identifying them. "The oldest is Rebecca, on the left. Sorry, but I didn't have a wide-lens camera to get all her boyfriends in the same picture. Next to her is Zena, with the great-looking hat. This is Alice, with all her curls, and Irene, with the big smile. Unfortunately, her great sense of humor does not show up on film. Ellen Anne is the one dancing in the middle. Rifka Julia is laughing at her mother and father. She thinks they are pretty funny. Just look at those knowing eyes! And the youngest is Jonathan—named for my father. A great honor indeed!"

"Congratulations! Each one is a beauty. Thank goodness they resemble their parents and don't look anything like you," Avrum laughed, as he carefully handed the pictures back to Hershel.

"How is *gesheft* (business)," Avrum inquired. "I'll bet you don't have any pictures of that."

"Don't bet on it!"

The waitress brought the stein of beer and two glasses, and placed them on the table.

"Cheers," said Avrum.

"Mmm, delicious," murmured Hershel, sipping the beer, "*L'chaium* (your health)!

"No, fortunately for you there are no pictures of the business. But I really can't complain at all. Business has been rather good. The scale of international economics in the import-export business seems to go hand in hand with my former intelligence training. In fact, I just concluded the purchase and resale of a warehouse full of Russian titanium at a price surprisingly below market. It was fascinating, since the titanium was once owned by some former Politbureau members of the Communist Party."

"Since the C.I.S. came into being," said Hershel, "the cost of their free-enterprise overhead—including warehouse rental and insurance in Latvia where the titanium was stored—has become too costly for them. But that's not the best part." Hershel had a look of contentment on his face. "I was able to get this super-good buy because, with the breakup of the C.I.S., Russian interests have to liquidate their holdings and get out of Latvia."

He paused, took a sip of beer, and dabbed the corners of his mouth with a napkin while he continued his story.

"Because of this urgency, I was able to take advantage of this opportunity and I quickly re-sold the titanium to another import broker in Bahrain, who sold the goods to yet another Arab buyer in the Middle East. Just the usual good business of buying low and selling high," Hershel interjected while smiling.

Avrum listened with great interest and was a little jealous of Hershel's success. This was the kind of deal he too would have loved to discover. Then Hershel changed the subject. "To tell you the truth, Avrum, getting back into the active international life feels just great. I always needed something stimulating to keep me going. My wife tells me that I'm just not cut out for retirement. Well, not right now, anyway."

Avrum smiled in grim agreement as he reached over to fill their glasses for a second round.

Avrum, a professional with family responsibilities, had a large mortgage on a new condo-apartment in Tel Aviv and children whose company he greatly enjoyed. Now an independent consultant for a public organization, he objected to wandering around exotic countries working and living under difficult and sometimes dangerous physical conditions. However, because he had the ambition and vitality that drives younger men to greatness, he put up with the unpleasantness and focused on what he enjoyed about his new line of work since retiring from the Mossad.

While traveling through the former Soviet Union, in addition to his business activities Avrum enjoyed meeting and socializing with new people of different backgrounds. He particularly liked encountering East Europeans who had ethnic Jewish roots similar to his own and who could trace their ancestry from nation to nation. He would spend hours with these new fast friends, comparing notes on what twists of fate caused their parents and grandparents to settle in various towns and cities throughout Eastern Europe.

But for the grace of God, Avrum and his own family might have ended up as captive citizens in the former Communist nations. Luckily, his grandparents were wise enough to see the handwriting on the wall with the rise of the Nazi Party in pre-World War II Germany, and they left for Palestine, in the 1930s. The Jewish people he came in contact with, although very poor by Western standards, were quite warm and would regularly invite Avrum to stay with them. They would constantly question him on every conceivable aspect of life in Israel and the United States and the differences between these countries and their own.

The upcoming gathering of the "formers" would be the fourth such meeting of Avrum's group since the discovery of the Jonathan Pollard spying affair in Washington. While none of the intelligence groups Avrum or Hershel had been formerly involved with had any knowledge of the event, while members of the Mossad they carried the embarrassing heartache of the incident.

Their intelligence group had comprised a small number of former American and Israeli members of the Institute for Intelligence and Special Operations. Every several years or so, this former team of unconventional fighters, anti-terrorist guerrillas and elite paratroop commandos, who had worked closely together as a unit at one time or another, held their reunion in a different country. It helped them view their homeland, the land of Israel, from a different perspective, while recounting their past escapades. Their favorite topic of discussion was the daring raid on the nuclear reactor in Osrack, Iraq.

They also enjoyed discussing future hypothetical plans for taking out their favorite terrorist target, Sabri el Banna—alias Abu Nidal—the Arab "father of struggle."

Two musicians in local folk costumes strummed their small balalaika guitars as they accompanied others in popular folk songs. A young waitress rested her tray next to a table on a serving stand and carefully began setting out appetizers.

After a few seconds of silence, Hershel asked, "What have you been up to over the past two years?"

"Well, God must have chosen me...to contribute what I can to humanity." Avrum explained. He laid his cigarette carefully in the ashtray, not looking at Hershel. Slowly he settled back in his chair, seemingly relaxed for the first time. He went on to describe what he meant by this cryptic statement.

"The fact is, I am on a new mission, totally unrelated to our former intelligence organization. As part of the human race, my belief, as always, is that former intelligence people should do all they can to change the world for the better."

Hershel uncrossed his legs and leaned forward. "Uh-huh. Now, that's a very lovely thought."

Being realistic, Avrum took a bleak view of what the new Russian society ultimately held in store for minority populations, particularly those of Jewish ethnic backgrounds.

"I am now a man of peace and honor. Peace for all men and honor for Israel and the Israeli people. The small Jewish agency I am now associated with here helps me to explain to young Russian Jews the meaning, strength, beauty and understanding of their long-suppressed heritage. I have been helping to give them an extraordinary opportunity for an organized and structured future if they should decide to emigrate to Israel."

"Admirable," Hershel interjected.

"Here in the C.I.S. they come to my organization as a quiet and confused people, similar to the Woodstock generation before they woke up. They object, in the meekest way, to the frightened life-styles and traditions that their parents were forced to live under in order to survive the anti-Semitic former Soviet Union. And now that there are several independent new states and a multitude of new problems and economic disruptions, they feel the rise of a new tide of anti-Semitism sweeping their region.

"As convenient scapegoats for all of the ills of the new post-Soviet societies, they see the writing on the wall, just as the lucky ones to leave Germany realized what was brewing in the 1930s. But this new generation, as meek as they were when I first encountered them, have fire in their bellies and have the means and the will to confront this new Jew-hatred in ways their parents could never have dreamt of. They can easily get the hell out of here and start new lives where they are welcome with open arms, in a country they can proudly call their own: the State of Israel.

"Their music is now louder, their hair is longer and their skirts are shorter. At present, to me they appear disinterested in everything close to them in the sick post-Soviet society. And they realize that they will no longer be arrested for thumbing their nose at authority or conventional values, so they feel they can finally do almost anything they want. This is a luxury their parents never had or even thought possible."

Hershel listened attentively, enjoying a feeling of exhilaration. He had been waiting a long time to hear exactly what Avrum was up to. He was impressed.

The waitress collected the empty beer stein and returned with a full one, while Avrum continued speaking.

"I help them, as Jews, to make *aliyah* (to become new citizens of Israel). In getting them to recognize their potential, they achieve, in most cases, a deep-felt commitment to their new homeland and eventually may experience the spiritual dimension of the modern Jewish life-style."

Hershel saw the glow in Avrum's face and realized that he had graduated to a new cause, beyond his past life of petty bickering with his former intelligence handlers, political in-fighting and putting his own gratification first, rather than caring about the well-being of others.

"Talk about operational bonuses!" Hershel said encouragingly. "It must be quite satisfying to be involved in this sort of good work, especially compared to our past resumés, which focused us on deception, stealth and subterfuge!"

"In the C.I.S.," Avrum continued, running a finger around the rim of his glass, "those young people I speak of are vulnerable to attack from all sides. They are hated for being Jewish and are not really strong enough, yet as an ethnic group to defend themselves against possible attacks from the growing right-wing, angry, Russian Jew-haters. In Israel they would be given the opportunity to find their true values, be independent, cohesive and could turn out to be instrumental in our nation's future. I suppose if you tried to analyze what I am doing, you could probably say that I am trying to do my part to improve mankind—one person at a time."

"It appears to me," Hershel interrupted, "that you are focused on something more than simple emotions, and certainly there are many of us at fault for not putting more effort into this important cause you have embraced. Perhaps my point would be best put if I would quote the words of Shakespeare: 'The fault, dear Brutus, is not in our stars, but in ourselves.'"

Hershel's attempt at humor failed to arouse emotion in Avrum. He continued to tap the table and gaze straight ahead. Hershel did not have to be a member of the Sayaret Matkal (General Staff) to perceive that something deeper than just helping the cause of Russian Jewry was on Avrum's mind. He realized that Avrum had suddenly stopped listening to him and respected his friend's few moments of silence. Hershel's instincts proved correct, for Avrum continued hesitantly, seemingly looking for the right words to say.

"I am hearing about disturbing activities that seem to be arising from various sources throughout Russia, and I would like to run some of this information past you, just to get your opinion," Avrum said, with glint of mischief in his eye. "I want to see if you are as sharp as you used to be when you wrote your intelligence reports."

In their service with the Mossad, Avrum had been one of Hershel's "handlers," and Hershel never asked for or expected openness from any of these. He fully realized that while serving in his official capacity, Avrum's actions were on behalf of his nation and he openly acknowledged the fact that nations have no friends, they only have interests.

It was after their long stint together with the Mossad that Hershel and Avrum found common interests. As far as Hershel was concerned, he felt that he worked within the most important department of the Institute for Intelligence and Special Operations—the liaison and information collection areas. In Hershel's intelligence days, he had developed and operated his own network of agents and informants who obtained and analyzed information from behind enemy lines. He then was able to send his analyses to headquarters in Israel by way of a series of dead drops and his one-time liaison, Avrum. Along the way, Hershel always felt an obligation in each of his cases to protect his sources, so he respected whatever Avrum was contemplating regarding his mysterious comments about disturbing activities in Russia.

Avrum now asked out loud, "I wonder why it is taking the world governments so long to come to the realization that the collapse of the U.S.S.R. has now created vast possibilities for the spread of nuclear and biological technology to Third World countries—not to mention the outright sale of Russian nuclear weapons themselves and weapons-grade nuclear explosives."

Hershel replied, "Well, I expect it may be unreasonable to hope that the post-World War Two 'empire of enemies' would quietly collapse and all of the former generals and intelligence people would go their many ways into happy retirement. This is just not going to happen. I think, Avrum, that you have to bring yourself to understand that the old world, as we both knew it, is dying. A new world is beginning, and the only way its security can be maintained is, unfortunately, by the old, traditional military methods. We can not afford to be naive, Avrum." He added, "This is today's real world, and those generals and intelligence operatives are certainly still out there trying to carve out various roles for themselves."

Avrum managed not to flinch at Hershel's statement. He took a deep breath and nodded in agreement as Hershel continued. "Unfortunately, the world drastically changed with the end of Communism. The UN and NATO lost even more influence. We all know that the United Nations was created and still functions in accordance with the world as it was, back in 1946. Today, NATO is an almost empty shell, and no longer an effective defensive alliance. What do you think, Avrum?"

"I think that I am technically fit for intelligence, but I lack the political sophistication needed to be a politician. And hell, politics aren't supposed to have much place in the intelligence directorate." Avrum smiled to punctuate the irony of his statement.

"What I *think* is influenced by what I *know*. And what I know is a function of my inner drive and my curiosity and need to know more about the survival issues of the twenty-first century. What I already know would frighten anyone—even you! Let me make you aware, if you don't already know, of some of the wild things that have been going on in this part of the world lately. For instance, on December 20, 1992, a detachment of heavily armed Russian Special Forces, on a tip, raced onto the main runway of Moscow airport and surrounded a Tupolev-42 airplane preparing for takeoff. Inside the plane were thirty-six nuclear weapon engineers from the former Soviet nuclear facilities at Arzamas-16 and Penza-19. The commandos stormed the plane, arrested the scientists and seized the plane's secret flight plan. The plane was bound for Pyongyang. Although *this* group was captured, a nuclear exodus of other Russian experts is currently underway. Amazing, isn't it?

"And according to my friends at German intelligence, two hundred and fifty former Russian nuclear weapons and missile experts are right now at work in Iran. Others are arriving in Iraq, Libya and Algeria. I have also been advised that Russian experts are helping to dramatically upgrade the nuclear capabilities of China. China, in turn, is accelerating nuclear exports to still other countries.

"If you are uncomfortable with that," Avrum added, "consider the fact that twenty thousand Russian strategic nuclear warheads are still poised to be fired at pre-arranged Western targets at a moment's notice, with no possibility of recall. Much of the Russian missile force is on a hair-trigger 'launch on warning' alert status, controlled not by President Yeltsin, but an automatic 'dead hand' doomsday system of unreliable, obsolete and deteriorating Soviet computers. It is only a matter of time before there is a failure of some sort, and you can imagine what that would mean for the West. It will take some fast talking to talk these facts away, no matter what nonsense is being fed to the Western media about disarmament and the repositioning of strategic nuclear warheads away from their former targets."

"And what about the political dimension of Vladimir Zhirinovsky," Hershel inquired. "What the hell is going on with that brash neo-Nazi?"

Avrum shot back, "Didn't you hear about the new book he just published, titled *The Final Thrust South*? In it he proposes a war to extend Russia's borders to the Indian Ocean and the Mediterranean. He reasons no country or alliance would be able to stand in his way while Russia still possesses nine-thousand strategic nuclear warheads capable of reaching any region in the world. The possibility of Zhirinovsky becoming a constitutionally elected president of Russia are not entirely remote. He is far from being a clown or a lone phenomenon any more then Hitler was. He has had considerable popular support and a strong growing political base in the Russian parliament, which not long ago voted overwhelmingly to grant amnesty to Yeltsin's enemies.

"Zhirinovsky has the means to use superior nuclear or biological weaponry to terrorize, which is the essence of international blackmail. The Russian government is suffering from a serious case of schizophrenia. While it demands foreign aid and IMF credits, the Russian military continues to upgrade its strategic missile forces to make it more reliable and to improve its accuracy."

"What I'm hearing, Avrum," said Hershel, "is that there is ample physical evidence to have an open-and-shut case against the present Russian leadership, and that the world could very easily end up in flames after the collapse of the U.S.S.R., and there are no firemen around to put it out. If you have come up with your frightening information as a retired intelligence agent with limited, old sources and almost no resources to gather fresh, new information, we can only speculate how much information on this subject our friends in the CIA and other agencies have."

"Exactly!" Avrum exclaimed.

Until this moment, Hershel felt far enough away from the problems of the world so as not to be all that uncomfortable.

"You have to remember," said Hershel, "that in the early 1980s, only one country had been publicly accused of having a biological weapons arsenal, and that was the Soviet Union. Although most countries denounced biological warfare as repulsive as early as 1925, Iraq's use of chemical weapons against Iran during their war in the 1980s and against Saddam's own Kurdish population clearly demonstrated that such weapons could have a devastating impact.

"Because the world let Iraq get away with the terrible use of chemical weapons, the example became obvious to small and middle-rate powers that anyone could get away with developing a chemical or biological arsenal with impunity and that these weapons could potentially make a difference on the battlefield.

"Incidentally, do you recall the documented history of the Japanese invasion force that occupied much of China from 1931 to 1945?"

"Can't say I do," replied Avrum. "Give me the details."

"A lone Japanese plane flew out of the Western sky in August 1942, and circled low over the rice paddies that surround a huddle of ornate, upturned roofs in Zhenjiang Province, spraying a kind of smoke from its tail.

"The first signs of the coming epidemic emerged two weeks later, when rats of the village started dying en masse. Then came the fever— an outbreak of bubonic plague, transmitted by fleas that had carried the same Black Death through Europe in the Middle Ages—struck. It raged for two months killing hundreds of residents before Japanese troops moved in and started burning down plague-ridden houses. The screams of the Chinese civilians shattered the nights. Many of the delirious victims ran or crawled down narrow alleys to gulp putrid water from open sewers in vain attempts to quelch the septic fire that was consuming them from within. The living died most excruciating deaths. They buried the dead knowing full well that the next day they too would be buried.

"As a matter of fact, China is pushing Japan at this very time to dispose of the almost two million chemical bombs—most of them loaded with mustard gas and many of them corroded and leaking—left by the Japanese Army in Manchuria."

"I agree, Hershel," said Avrum, "that little has been said in the West about the atrocities committed in China by the Japanese or the Iraqi attacks against Iran and the Kurdish people. And don't forget the Sarin nerve gas attack on the Tokyo Subway.

"At the end of the 1991 Persian Gulf War, United Nations inspectors discovered that Saddam Hussein had secretly loaded SCUD missile warheads with deadly anthrax bacteria that could have terrorized any battlefield or city into which they were fired. General Schwarzkopf was fearful that a last-ditch use of chemical weapons by Saddam could have reversed the Allied momentum with a devastating blow. I am concerned about the potential of Communist die-hards in this area."

Avrum tilted back in his chair once more, and seemed to be concentrating on one of the light fixtures hanging from the ceiling. His features were those of a man who had been blessed with a revelation, or one who had just discovered a time bomb ticking under his chair.

"It's awfully funny!" Avrum said as he abruptly came to life and leaned forward in his chair. "Here we are, only casual acquaintances since our last meeting, talking about world problems. It's good that we are not just discussing casual subjects—such as the weather—when we have hard cold interests to face."

Looking thoughtful, he paused for only a moment. "I dare say," he muttered almost under his breath, "that it may be of interest if I told you a remarkable story related to me by our mutual friend, Nikolai Mikoyan. I must tell you that he had heard it from various sources over the past several months. At first it sounded rather farfetched, but the same story was repeated by too many people in separate cities within the C.I.S. to be a coincidence. And Hershel, as you can appreciate from your long experience, in our former business there were no farfetched intelligence stories regarding our children's well-being that should not have been followed up."

Hershel looked at him, understanding. The coming bombshell certainly sounded as if it would be important.

"But not here and now," Avrum went on. "I am sure you remember the old sayings: 'Walls have ears, loose lips sink ships,' and all the other has-been expressions of that sort."

Hershel had put his faith in Avrum before, and he would probably do so again. He knew that Avrum had always been completely truthful with him, that he loved intrigue, even thrived on it. There was nothing more satisfying to him than uncovering a conspiracy around every corner and behind every door. He could see where Avrum would fit right into any sort of sophisticated intelligence operations, even in this day and age when he was supposedly in his retirement. Avrum had not finished.

"There are many former intelligence and military veterans who are totally committed to their country while in official service, but ignore their old loyalties and interests and would not lift a finger or take any risks, once retired," Avrum said, as his face reddened with emotion. "However, that's not Yoel Melman's story. I know that you were involved with Yoel as your one-time handler and that after your retirement he became a good friend to you and your family. He was also my superior before I retired."

"You sound as if he were not going to meet us in Moscow tomorrow," Hershel exclaimed.

"We lost him, Hershel. We lost another former. It was just hours ago when I checked in with Nikolai. He gave me the bad news. Police authorities in Moscow told Nikolai that Yoel fell or jumped in front of a moving trolley car. There were no witnesses to be found, and I believe he very likely was pushed."

He spoke about Yoel as if he'd just found a hair on his tongue.

"I can't believe it! Poor Yoel—just think of the tragedy for his unfortunate family!" Hershel offered. "But you sound so doubtful about the accident part of the official explanation. Could it possibly have been an accident? Maybe he slipped on some wet pavement?"

A scornful laugh rose to the surface from Avrum's stomach. "Never. He was too careful. Anyway, Nikolai checked the weather bureau and it was dry for several days before and during the time of the accident. The streets were not washed for weeks. And he certainly didn't commit suicide—he enjoyed life and his family too much."

Avrum paused for a moment to collect himself before continuing. "But I think I have a lead on what Yoel was working on and maybe he got too close to the heart of the problem. I feel he may have gotten carried away with one of his private investigations and had a momentary lapse regarding just how dangerous his investigation was. I think he was operating alone and without any backup. Maybe he even got so caught up in what he was doing that he forgot he was no longer working for the Institute. I don't know. We may never know what he was thinking," he said as he spread his hands in an all-encompassing gesture.

Avrum filled his glass and drank some more. For the moment, Hershel did not push him for any additional information. He simply pondered the situation.

"If we are lucky enough to get out of here and to the station on time, we will be able to catch the morning train to Moscow. Nikolai has made arrangements to pick us up when we arrive. It's a good thing that he has some *blat* (influence). With a few extra rubles he is an expert at cutting through red tape."

No one had to issue a formal typed-out, signed directive for Hershel to understand what was coming down the pike. Avrum took a deep breath and continued: "As you well know, the intelligence business is a lot different today than when we were all involved. A few years makes a big difference. That's why I am asking you to plan to stay on for an extra week or so. Our reunion may develop into a search-and-destroy mission, and I want you aboard if at all possible."

"Sounds reasonable. Let us see what has to be done."

"We 'formers' will not only have to be the spymasters, but also the analysts—and that's where I need your expertise, Hershel, to sift through and make sense of the material that we will collect. We will review the objectives and target our mission in the next few days, when all of the group arrives in Moscow."

Hershel looked at Avrum, who was waiting, and what he saw worried him. "Uh, there are many dangers and difficulties in Russia, I know," said Hershel. "And what Yoel may have been involved in—what do you expect that we can do about it?"

"I hope you will refresh your memory and appreciate my viewpoint. I try never to leave any unfinished or unresolved business behind. Hershel, you are a man of good faith, I am sure you will help us if you can. Not only for me but for Yoel's memory, his honor and dignity. And by the way, what happened to Yoel can easily happen to any of us. We are here in the equivalent of the Wild West. No one gives a damn about what really happened to our friend Yoel but us! No justice will ever be served and probably no official investigation will ever occur. If we don't at least try to do something, who will?" And with that heartfelt lecture, he was silent.

Hershel wondered if Avrum could be alluding to bringing him back into the fold on a full-time basis after the reunion—back to his old love, and new hobby, of gathering and analyzing intelligence data. If so, Avrum would be disappointed. That proposal would meet a premature death, for Hershel had no illusions about returning to the Mossad and becoming officially active again. He had been there, done that and bought the T-shirt.

Avrum abruptly pushed his chair away from the table. He slid from the chair to stand up, catching Hershel somewhat off-guard.

"We meet at 0700, and we can discuss further details at that time. Have a good evening. *Shalom*." Avrum extended his hand to Hershel.

"Did anyone ever tell you that you would make a great bomber pilot?"
Avrum shrugged his shoulders. "Why is that?"

"If you were a bomber pilot," Hershel said with a twinkle in his eye, "your ending to this conversation would be the equivalent of a direct hit on target. *Shalom*. Sleep well—I know I won't."

Hershel smiled. He was instinctively aware of the inner strength of this man who had practically ordered him to work on this new, troubling assignment.

Chapter Ten

MOSCOW, C.I.S

OCTOBER 16

By 5:00 A.M., Hershel was awake, lying in bed, thinking of the various escapades over the years that he had planned and worked on with Avrum.

In particular, one that came to mind had been painstakingly arranged by him for the Sayaret Matkal, Israel's elite hostage rescue and retaliation commando force. One of the truly remarkable qualities of the Sayaret Matkal, Hershel discovered while working with them, was how they prepared for an operation. No matter how small or large their intended target, they had Hershel study it exhaustively. He had to personally instruct each soldier, in detail, about the responsibility of his assigned task, taking into consideration every possible contingency for failure. If there were a million things that could go wrong with a mission, he would have to be prepared for a million and one.

When Hershel was introduced to the unit, he found that unlike the rest of the Israel Defense Force it had no written manuals or regulations restricting what the men were permitted to do during covert operations, which only made his planning for this assignment easier.

"What we need you for, Hershel," Avrum had said to him when he was recruited so many years ago, "pure and simple, is your mental strength, not your bulging biceps. I just hope you're up to it."

Both an enigma and a source of pride for Israelis, operations of the Sayaret Matkal were state secrets of the highest order. Hershel had learned this the hard way when accompanying them on a search-and-destroy mission in Beirut. The code name for the mission was Operation Spring of Youth. It was a dramatic reprisal for the massacre of Israeli athletes at the 1972 Munich Olympics and gave the terrorists a clear message.

On the eve of this special operation, a storm lasted all through the night, dropping several inches of rain. In addition, lightning had touched down with a ferocity not often seen in Lebanon. It was like an artillery barrage, sudden bursts of light followed by a tremendous rumble. After an hour of that, it was just a wet and miserable morning.

During this bad weather Avrum and Hershel sat quietly in the front seat of their Opel sedan on the Rue Verdun in the upper-class section of West Beirut. The driver and the three young men in the rear were clutching their loaded but slightly inaccurate Mac-10 machine guns. These were the preferred weapon for this mission because they were not traceable.

They were anxiously awaiting their fellow commandos and the Mossad agents in the two cars following them to signal that the patrolling Lebanese armored car had passed down the block and was out of sight. Some of the Israelis were carrying sleek Kalishnikov assault rifles and AK-47s, stolen from a Syrian storage facility.

Convincingly made-up as disheveled European male hippies accompanied by funky, provocatively dressed women, the men bolted from their cars at the appropriate signal from Avrum, to assume assigned positions around the block.

"Look to the right front," Hershel whispered urgently.

"Roger that," Avrum spoke into his radio over an encrypted radio channel. Despite the secure radios, chatter was kept to a minimum.

"Stay cool everyone, we got some of them unfriendly terrorist folks some one hundred meters in front of us in a car. Over."

"Got 'em," a voice crackled back. "We have target."

"Read you, five by five. Move out! Go! Go! Go!"

"Roger, copy that. Going in NOW! OUT!"

Parked in the street at 23 Rue Verdun were two black Mercedes with 17 PLO bodyguards, talking, listening to the radio and smoking.

The overconfident Palestinians took no notice of the hippies and their women, or "flower children," casually walking down the street toward their cars—until the first PLO member slumped over from a bullet through his temple.

In a matter of seconds most of the terrorists were shot dead or had been mortally wounded, but not before a stray bullet cut through the dashboard of one of the Israelis' cars, short-circuiting the wiring and unfortunately setting off their car horn.

With the horn sounding and the Israelis' hearts pumping, the commandos bounded up the steps of a luxury apartment building to the sixth floor. Avrum hand-signaled the team leader to blow the door off the apartment, which, he knew from intelligence reports, belonged to Abu Yusef—the leader of the Black September movement, who had planned the massacre of the Israeli athletes at the 1972 Olympics.

One 30-round burst from the Ingram Mac-10 instantly killed Abu Yusef as he tried to reach for his gun, the very same one that had been presented to him as a gift by Yasir Arafat.

Before the last shot was fired, Avrum was already busy cramming every last scrap of paper into bags, including maps and other documents, that he found throughout the apartment, before exiting, leaving Yusef's wife and child unharmed there.

Synchronized to the second by Hershel, he quickly led two other Sayaret teams into an adjacent apartment building in time to see the instant elimination of Kamal Adwan, a Black September terrorist who was guilty of leading operations in Europe and Israel. Also killed was Kamal Nassar, a Black September spokesman and operations officer.

As the Israelis, led by Avrum and Hershel, simultaneously exited the apartment buildings, they found their lookouts on the street engaged in a furious close-quarter gun battle with several dozen Lebanese police. Now joined together, all the Israelis retreated in a gradual firefight, regrouping at their cars before the Mossad drivers reversed their vehicles into the intersection of Ibn Walid Street. They performed some daredevil high-speed car stunts as they raced toward the Mediterranean shore, blowing up the few automobiles full of terrorists and police that were following them.

Abandoning the cars and unused satchel charges of explosives on the beach, the Israelis loaded their bags, laden with documents, onto rubber dinghies and headed out to sea for a rendezvous with an Israeli boat.

Hershel never tired of reliving that stunning operation, but he pulled his thoughts back from the past and into the present. At the appointed time of 0700, Avrum joined him in the lobby of his hotel.

"Good morning! I was just thinking of you, and the good old days. Remember Operation Spring of Youth?" Hershel asked nostalgically.

"Wow, that goes back. I remember it well. Then we were considered the elite of the intelligence community. We were respected as war heroes by some, while others looked down on us as spies. Don't forget that after that operation there were some, in other countries—countries considered friendly—who had the nerve to called *us*, and not the murdering terrorists, the scoundrels.

"I can't wait to go into Moscow," Avrum continued. "Just wait until you get a whiff of this new Russian dreamland, Hershel, ever since Gorbachev lifted its barbed wire and Yeltsin set the country's economic course.…Anyway, you will be able to visit a new stock exchange and a parliament—in or out of action—and as you would imagine, they are usually out of action," he added jokingly.

"You'll also be able to enjoy some of the fruits of the West: kiwis, bananas, Mars Bars, Cokes and Big Macs, while driving around in a Cadillac, smoking Marlboros—but only if you have the bucks! That is the real problem. Most Russians can't afford such goodies, and they resent it. The abundance of new wealth only makes the ordinary Russians on the street realize their poverty. Now, knowing the history of the Russians, you know what that kind of unrest can lead to."

Hershel nodded. "It sounds like you're planning to have an interesting time."

"It doesn't look all that promising from where I'm sitting," Avrum replied.

When Avrum spoke of going "into" Moscow, Hershel found it most unusual. Hershel often heard other seasoned travelers speak of going "to" and "from" Russia, while others referred to it as going "in" and "out."

The train they were traveling on was quite clean and there was no graffiti. As they left the last border outpost, a lone Finnish guard in a gray uniform watched almost with disinterest as the train passed through the forest of seemingly endless dark green pine and birch trees before entering Russian territory.

The large number of trees reminded Hershel of a time in his youth when his grandfather taught him to listen to the symphony of the forest as they walked among the fallen leaves and branches. It was not until Hershel was an adult that he realized what his grandfather was trying to teach him.

Years after his grandfather's wise advise, he came to appreciate how every movement in a symphony is created for the delight and pleasure of the listener. For Hershel great symphonies revealed birth, life, struggle, intensity and climax—all of which were balanced by interludes of quiet insight, revealed only to delight those who cared to listen, as he now did whenever he was in the forest.

"The trees and woods, Hershel, are at times a peaceful interlude not understood by all, but available to those who are trained to listen to the gentle murmur of the forest," his grandfather used to say.

Hershel did not it know at the time, but his grandfather was helping him to develop the power to think, the power of self-realization, the power of awareness. This evoked in Hershel a complex spiritual and intellectual growth that he never would have experienced without these influences.

Immediately beyond the border there was a much different kind of forest, a forest of barbed wire that remained from the Soviet regime. Beyond that there were now-unmanned watchtowers on stilts at the tops of most hills, and the visible cut through the forest for the tracks on which their train now ran.

Avrum sat in a window seat while Hershel sat closest to the aisle. With the compartment door left open, their space offered a friendly invitation, and a strange man in a baggy, old-fashioned jacket and soiled trousers approached, saying in Russian, "Beautiful day, eh?" as he leaned against the side of Hershel's seat.

"Da," Hershel replied, as he turned his head away, not wishing to get involved in a long-drawn-out game of verbal chess with this stranger.

Hershel casually noted the man's features and appearance as he pulled a book of anecdotal history of Scotland Yard out of his bag. Because of his gangling height, the man's pants were pulled up over a slight potbelly, leaving them short at the ankles. He had rather long arms and big reddish hands, a full shock of black hair, peaked bushy eyebrows, blue eyes, a flat nose and cleft chin, all drawn on a long face. He walked with a jerky gate.

Hershel felt grateful that he had not lost his ability to I.D. and analyze someone on the spur of the moment. The man returned Hershel's gaze, summed him up, lost interest and walked away.

Since the incident in Frankfurt, Hershel wanted to keep strangers trying to be friendly at arm's length. It would only take an instant for a stranger to pull out a needle-sharp stiletto and silently put it through his heart or into his skull behind an ear.

Hershel noticed that his observations had become more sophisticated over the years. He had learned to depend on a good deal of intuition in order to stay alive. His subliminal warning system was now geared to observe every face that came near him; he looked deeply into any stranger's eyes. He searched for any pronounced features, or perhaps the extension of veins in their necks, anything that might be an indication of stress. Even an excess amount of involuntary swallowing, frown lines in the forehead, a sudden raising of the eyelids, or holding the breath might indicate an agitated state of mind in a suspicious-looking individual.

Avrum, too, appeared uncomfortable, as if his legs were getting stiff from sitting still. He put both hands on his seat and pushed himself to a standing position. Hershel looked up as Avrum negotiated getting through the compartment door.

Returning Hershel's gaze Avrum said, "Just taking my constitutional," as he pulled the door closed.

And then, casually, it happened. Standing in the shadows between the rail cars with an automatic pistol pointed at Avrum's head was the man who had annoyed Hershel just a few minutes earlier.

Why the gun, Avrum wondered? Why the gun?

No formality, no commotion, no screams—scarcely a sound beyond the iron wheels rolling across the tracks—and then came the strange man's demand for Avrum to stand still and hand over his money.

The Israeli's thoughts developed slowly, the same way a large orchestra starts a rehearsal with determined players leading the way. The man had a gun and Avrum understood the rules. He could make no objections, offer no resistance or unpleasantness at all, for his own good and safety, while the nervous thief held up a small cloth bag intended to receive the valuables.

But Avrum didn't always play by the rules, particularly when he sensed things were even worse than they seemed. Like a splash of red fury, Avrum felt an internal alarm go off, a call to battle stronger than any he could remember since the day Israel was attacked on Yom Kippur in 1973. He felt a call so loud that he wasn't thinking anymore, he was only reacting. He had not even reckoned with the consequences.

"If it's money you want, you can have it," Avrum heard himself say while his eyes remained fixed on the man. "Here it is," he exclaimed, feigning anger and insult as he yanked the wallet from his hip pocket, tossing it angrily at the man's feet.

The blood was pulsing in Avrum's hands, each fingertip throbbing. As the man's eyes groped for the wallet on the floor he instinctively passed the gun from his right to left hand so he could more easily pick it up. Avrum didn't need a second invitation. The man heard Avrum move. His horse voice panted, "What the hell!...Good God!"

Avrum instantly slammed the stranger's face with the sole of his shoe while lunging for and smacking the side of the gun with his fist, sending it chattering to the floor. With his right hand he seized the arm that had held the gun and gave it a ferocious, bone-breaking twist. The stunned man gave a prolonged scream.

Hauling the stranger and his damaged arm to the exit doorway of their car with a chokehold, Avrum grabbed the handle, threw his body weight up against the door, guessing it would open, and proceeded to shove the man through the opening between the cars and off the train. Avrum couldn't believe that no one heard this struggle, but as he scurried back to his compartment no one seemed to have heard a thing over the loud noises of the train.

He picked up the gun from the floor, putting it in his jacket pocket as he opened up the compartment door.

The entire incident had not taken more than five minutes.

"How was your walk? Was it long enough to get your heart rate up?" Hershel asked, as the door closed to the compartment.

Not wishing to alarm Hershel, Avrum answered with a voice filled with vagueness. "You should try it sometime. Nothing more stimulating."

By now it was quite dark, and an occasional light from a distant farmhouse could be seen dancing through the trees.

The train got up to full speed, with a steady click-click of the wheels at the rail joints, as it rumbled toward its destination. Then, after a few miles, it came to an abrupt stop. Everywhere in the cars there was the aroma of tobacco, combined with the odd smell of old wet wool.

Avrum and Hershel looked up as several young Russian border guards in green uniforms, high black boots and hip pistols went about the boring business of gathering up passports, half-heartedly looking for secret storage places in luggage, checking compartments and washrooms, while others checked on the roof and under the train. For Russian citizens who were traveling or working abroad there was no longer the extensive customs check and search there had been under Communism.

"Just a short time ago, all traveling Soviet citizens had to undergo intensive investigations where *everything* was checked—back to their grandfather," Avrum said, leaning toward Hershel.

Hershel enjoyed watching as passengers popped their heads around corners or out the windows to watch the proceedings, while others laughed, mimicking the guards. He overheard several other passengers speak openly about how this sort of disorderly conduct would never have happened prior to the dramatic change from Communism.

Avrum again leaned toward Hershel, explaining that this was the first time travel controls had been relaxed and freedom of travel made available to the average citizens in the C.I.S. Such freedom had not existed since 1785, when Catherine the Great had given the right to travel abroad only to the privileged nobility and gentry.

Except for the excitement of going through customs and viewing the countryside, Hershel found the balance of the trip uneventful. He looked around trying to spot the man he had picked up the bad vibes from, wondering where he had gone.

The train slowed to a walking pace through the outskirts of Moscow. Space between the buildings of the sprawling city became less and less. Then he could see workers trudging to the Metro, now only a kilometer or two away.

The conductor came up the aisle. He had the air of an owner in control. "Don't forget to take your belongings," he shouted out.

Avrum jotted down the address and phone number of Nikolai on a small piece of paper and handed it to Hershel, in case they became separated in the railroad terminal. Hershel surveyed the note, and before putting the slip of paper in his wallet confirmed with a nod that he understood.

At the station a few old Russians in heavy coats and scarves were hawking sweet buns, homemade pickles, hot boiled potatoes and newspapers. Police checked for hostile signs and suspicious people.

"I wonder if it ever gets warm enough for those old Russians to bother taking off their heavy coats in the summer," Hershel joked. "The cool evenings of Moscow this time of the year will empty your mind of all your troubles. It will give you clear vision and new thoughts."

Hershel had learned long ago to expect the unexpected from Avrum. But now Avrum's eyes appeared distracted, his behavior more contrived, and small talk came hard to him. He wondered what was wrong and why Avrum was now acting so seriously. What had come over him?

Then, suddenly, Nikolai Mikoyan, a former Mossad agent and a close friend of both Avrum and Hershel, acknowledged them from a distance with a wave of his arm.

After a warm greeting that included kisses on both cheeks and big bear hugs from Nikolai, the trio hurried out of the building and into a black, chauffeur-driven Chaika, the Russian-made car that Nikolai had hired. It had plenty of room inside but was rather bulky, high-bodied and resembled a pregnant 1950 Packard. Other black automobiles waited outside the station, some Volgas and Zilis, and one that resembled an older Lincoln Continental.

Driving through downtown Moscow, their chauffeur raced down the center of the street, the so-called Chaika lane, a special lane reserved for VIP automobiles of cabinet ministers, field marshals, foreign dignitaries, and in this instance, Avrum, Hershel and Nikolai.

While policemen frantically motioned other traffic out of their way, Nikolai said in Hebrew, "This driver has some chutzpah."

"For sure. Especially since the Russian police are not exactly required to read you your rights when they arrest you," Hershel added with a smirk.

Avrum asked the driver to take a short scenic detour so they could view the Lubyanka, the dreaded Cum Prison, KGB headquarters, Pushkin Square and 2 Granovsky Street, where Nicolai Lenin spoke to the commanders of the Red Army before they headed into battle with the White Russians during the Russian Civil War.

The three could not help staring at the stark, empty windows of the large Gum Department Store as they drove by.

"I wonder if Gum will eventually be a division of Macy's," Hershel suggested, unsuccessfully trying to improvise a joke. "You have to laugh once in a while, Avrum," he said, "or you'll go stark raving mad. Raving as in lunatic," Hershel persisted.

"Raving as in drunk," Avrum responded.

Now, with his reading glasses tilted on his prominent nose, the cigarette clenched between his teeth, his bony fingers slowly massaging his jaw, Avrum's entire appearance underwent a metamorphosis in Hershel's eyes. Gone was the fervent look of the Old Testament prophet. In its place was a man of intelligence-gathering—the nuclear age's Sherlock Holmes, sitting hunched in his chair.

It appeared to Hershel that Avrum was holding something back. He was close-lipped, almost afraid to talk shop and make small talk about their past together in the Mossad.

Hershel's feeling had been building ever since he had told Avrum of his close call in Frankfurt. Then, for a moment, a strange thought flashed through Hershel's mind. Was Avrum still operating deep undercover for the Institute and not disclosing it? No, he quickly convinced himself, Avrum would not do that. He knew him too well. He was a friend and they trusted one another. Hershel could see no reason why Avrum would not be straight with him about something so important. He was not the type to play a game of cat and mouse with former colleagues.

Hershel decided he'd had enough of this tour around Moscow. He concluded it was more important that Avrum snap out of his dark mood, and he had an idea.

"'Say first, of God above or man below, what can we reason but from what we know?'" Hershel's quote from Milton did the trick. Avrum raised his head, chuckled and came back to earth.

"Sorry, but I have been considering a lot of things. I've been having a lot of second thoughts and, frankly, I feel very reluctant in asking you to help me when I am not sure myself what the hell is going on."

Hershel peered at Avrum, waiting, but Avrum paused in thought for another moment, a complacent smile on his face.

Then Avrum leaned forward and said something in Russian to the driver. The car suddenly slowed and came to a rather abrupt stop at the curb. For some unknown reason the driver appeared annoyed as he squirmed around in his seat. He kept looking at his dashboard clock, but from the time it indicated, it probably had not worked for years.

Could we be making him late for his evening vodka? Hershel wondered.

"Touchy, touchy," Avrum remarked to Nikolai in Hebrew. "There has to be a reason for his fussiness. Let's go for a walk, I need a little air."

There is an intelligence agency tradition of taking the standard security precaution of "going for a walk in the park," while sensitive subjects are discussed. Nikolai always believed in copying a good thing. In the park you two should be out of earshot of taps or bugs.

Hershel knew exactly what Nikolai was referring to. He was aware that the many trees would distort almost all sounds of conversation, which would ordinarily be picked up by a listening device planted in the car, or by visual beams from electronic surveillance devices in nearby buildings. There would be a small delay while they walked silently out of listening range.

Nikolai remained in the car with the driver as Avrum and Hershel pulled up their coat collars. They began their walk in silence down a deserted street, past communal apartments with lines of hand-washed laundry hanging behind some of the windows that were not covered with lace curtains. The dark street was lit only by small street lights and the glow of a bright moon.

Avrum stumbled momentarily on an uneven piece of slate sidewalk, and Hershel quickly put out his arm to assist his friend, keeping him from falling.

"Steady, old boy," Hershel laughed.

"Thanks," Avrum offered, regaining his composure.

Avrum was looking around carefully. On the opposite side of the street stood the Victorian homes of former intellectuals and nobility, with peeling stucco and faded wood trim. Nothing appeared unusual and there were no other cars in sight as they entered a small park.

"I'm sorry to drag you around the cold streets, but I know that you want to learn more about Yoel," Avrum said as he walked—his head turning from side to side, his hand under his left armpit, wrapped around the cold handle of a PPG pistol which he always carried, ready to react to any irregularity that would endanger them. For anyone with ready cash, obtaining a weapon such as his PPG in Russia was not a problem.

He first noted to Hershel that the devastating information that he was about to disclose was obtained in the strictest of confidentiality; then, Avrum began to talk slowly and deliberately as he told his friend what few sketchy facts he knew.

"Before he died, Yoel found out that former officers of the KGB are involved with other Russian and German criminal groups in exporting highly enriched plutonium-239. I assume that the plutonium obviously came from one of the many Russian deactivated submarines, or from a nuclear power plant. We are also going to have to consider the missing weaponry, chemicals, cesium 137, osmium 187 and uranium. These are all weapons-grade materials."

He paused for a momentary thought. "Some can be used as fusion materials while others may be used as gas vapor, pulse lasers or neutron weapons."

Hershel shook his head from side to side. "This sounds great. It seems that everyone who is anyone in Russia is now freelancing in the black market. Just wait until some terrorist group gets its hands on these goodies."

"Exactly!" Avrum shot back. "I have reason to believe there are any number of groups opting to do just that."

He then added that he had no idea down which road this entire situation might lead them. "I am sure you read the book written by Aleksei Tolstoy, in which he describes details of a secret Russian 'death ray' device. Today the most powerful laser that the United States has exists in Livermore Laboratories in California. This monster occupies an enormous building needed to achieve its power concentration. The device tests, at best, once a month—which results, as some Americans joke, in the dimming of light throughout California—so tremendous is the electric power demand that it creates.

"This is not the case with the very powerful Russian laser, which uses nuclear pumping, a device created by Tolstoy's fantasy. The device, located in Obninsk, is now capable of producing as much energy as can be produced by all the nuclear plants of the world in the short time of between 40 to 100 microseconds. The nuclear pumping laser has been officially named Okuyan, which stands in Russian for Optical Quantum Amplifier with Nuclear Pumping."

"I always claimed that Russian research was more advanced than they were ever given credit for," Hershel interjected.

"True, but a good deal of that was due to the stealing of industrial secrets from the Western superpowers by the KGB. Now, what is important is that in this Russian device there is direct conversion of nuclear energy into laser radiation. For Okuyan, fission energy is directly transformed into light and, therefore, it is possible for the Russians to produce a powerful laser beam by this compact device. I have recently been informed that the next step in Russian laser weaponry is already in development."

Hershel shrugged. "This takes a while to penetrate the analytical part of my brain," he said as he followed the painful drift of Avrum's dissertation. Merely the thought of all this power out of control in some corruptible Russian military officer's hands was depressing.

"The brotherhood of arms manufacturing is a powerful influence in Russia," Avrum added. "The unseen problem at this time centers around the momentary shortage of funding, and for the past several months the working personnel at the laboratories have not been paid. That could mean even more danger, for the technology will be available to anyone who has the rubles to pay. We are playing here on dangerous turf."

Hershel considered this dilemma for a moment. "What can we possibly do to alleviate this dangerous problem?" He was at his inquisitive best. "And do you think this has anything to do with Yoel's death?"

"Unfortunately, I don't have the answer either," Avrum continued. "But it's you who will have to do the quick study and give us some actionable options on how to proceed. These urgent problems are why I, a former intelligence operative without an organization behind him, have to call on dependable formers like you and the others we will soon be meeting with," he said sternly, pointing a finger at Hershel's chest.

Hershel stopped in his tracks.

"Yes, you especially, and a few others," said Avrum, "are the only people I can assemble on the spur of the moment. I need a lot of help to hunt up the missing pieces of this story. Intriguing, isn't it? It may also prove to be the perfect opportunity for me to call in some favors."

"Favors? Missing pieces? Avrum, we used to call this sort of impossible challenge 'reading tea leaves.'"

"What do you mean reading tea leaves. We're not a bunch of Gypsies. We know that we only go on hard, solid, verifiable information— so don't jump to conclusions just yet. And furthermore, we have the combined resources of the elite former members of the world's most respected intelligence service. If every one of these talented agents focuses on our goals, we will have a fighting chance to achieve them."

"Do you really think all of them will agree to cooperate?" Hershel interrupted.

"I'd bet my life on it," Avrum shot back. "Not only will they jump at the opportunity. Knowing them, they would *want* us to take advantage of their knowledge, experience and technical spying skills and inventiveness. Without a doubt, Hershel, they will agree to continue Yoel's investigation."

"You haven't told me exactly where Yoel fit into all of this."

"That's what we must now discover."

"We're probably looking trouble right in the face, Avrum…. But then, in this career, have we ever faced anything other than trouble?"

"I'm afraid you're right."

"Do me a favor Avrum: Just keep in the back of your mind that, given our circumstances in a place like this, useful information has a price.

Russian mentality in these sorts of intelligence matters is to dole out minimal amounts of information. There is not going to be much cooperation, even from our former sources and contacts, as they know we are 'out of the game' and will have little or nothing to give them back in the future.

"What we will be looking for is not going to be easy to find. It would be nearly impossible to proceed on this mission, even with the full backing of our government and our former agency. We don't even have access to the sorts of weapons, communications gear, gadgets, undercover identities, not to mention the big bucks we will end up spending to try to make this all work!"

"Hershel, I know that we are on an impossible mission. But remember what we were all taught in our beginning training classes: 'In the Mossad, the impossible takes a little longer to accomplish.' I also know that if we were still in the Mossad instead of the Israeli Intelligence Veterans Association, we would certainly have the contacts and resources to do the proper job. By now, I would be working on the real meaning of the information gathered about Yoel's murder. And even if those tips were unconfirmed, Mossad headquarters would have officially classified them top secret."

"Of course you're right, Avrum. But headquarters is no longer at our beck and call and we don't even know where the enemy may be. The smoking gun could be behind any lamppost!"

"Ah, but we do have a lead as to where we should begin looking.... We know that when he was in the Mossad, Yoel worked mostly against Arab fundamentalist groups. Because of this history, we should focus our initial efforts in that direction. I believe it is possible that a member of a radical group may have suddenly recognized Yoel from the past and conspired to do him in. But I feel that it would be rather remote for an Arab fundamentalist to be working alone, here in Russia. So there might be a well-organized group and they could be based anywhere—even in Chechnya."

"That's certainly a plausible theory," Hershel agreed.

"My intuition tells me there had to be more than one person involved in following Yoel and pushing him in front of the trolley," Avrum reflected morbidly. "Yoel had to know that he was about to die. We can only hope that the end was fast. Unfortunately, we know that he did have those few moments to realize what was about to happen. His end was certainly not without pain. Yoel, I fear, suffered unfairly."

"Goddamnit, Avrum," Hershel said, taking his hands out of his pockets and gesturing, "how do you expect me to react? That I wouldn't help you find Yoel's killer? I am realistic enough to know that we are inviting serious trouble for ourselves. And the Good Lord only knows what you really have in mind for me. From past experience, I probably should expect something most unusual, but I'm convinced that we can turn this damned liability into an asset."

When he spoke, Hershel had the ability to project strength and confidence to anyone close to him, but right now he was also trying to convince himself. Taking advantage of the opportunity to speak his mind, Hershel explained to Avrum that he could not and would not deal directly with the Mossad again. He explained that he did not have the patience to sit still for the bureaucratic shuffling and political indecision that were part of any intelligence agency's makeup.

Avrum looked him in the eye and said coolly, "There's no way that I would even try to officially involve our former bosses in the Mossad in this affair. And believe me, there's no way they'd ever agree to use this group of retired agents for anything as serious as the operation we are about to embark on, Hershel. They would not want us, and wouldn't ever *consider* us—because we have all been on our own for too long. We could not be expected to reliably follow their orders or procedures. So, don't worry yourself over something that's not going to happen."

Both Avrum and Hershel knew that in a short time their own sources of intelligence could be developed and they'd be every bit as reliable as those used by the Institute for Intelligence and Special Operations.

The next point that came to mind, one that was appreciated by both men, was that they were thankful they only had each other and their small group to account to, and not a long chain of command. Avrum and Hershel also agreed that at this moment they had not the least clue as to where the mission would lead, and no accurate plan as to how they would go about accomplishing their goal of learning more about Yoel's killer.

"Come on now, Hershel, cheer up! I know that we are probably both certifiably mad for agreeing to proceed on this matter, and all of this is deeply disturbing. But let's reason this out. First, we can be assured that Yoel did not bring us disinformation. Second, we can keep digging into what Yoel said in his letter, what he heard with his own ears or had seen with his own eyes. Once we make the right contacts, we may possibly have to change our safe house again. And remember that there will be little or no contact with the outside. Like old times, you will have to prepare excuses for your family. They may not see or hear from you for a while. And don't forget our *age*. We're not as young as we used to be."

"Uh-oh, I hear age talking," Hershel interrupted. "I think it was you who once told me that age was only a state of mind."

"God, that's magnificent! I must have been much younger when I was so philosophical, poetic and brilliant," Avrum replied, chuckling. "Before you make your final decision that you will join us, Hershel, just remember that time is not in our favor."

"Isn't digging for information what we've been trained for? And just forget your damned reference to our age! I don't want to hear it. You know damn well I'm with you," Hershel said convincingly. "If you feel we're too old, then we should all go back to our hometowns, stand in line at local restaurants, wait for the 'early-bird' specials and go to bed at nine o'clock. And if you really think I'm too old, then why did you drag me into this mess in the first place!"

Avrum could not help laughing. "Thanks for straightening me out, Hershel! And thanks for demonstrating your confidence in yourself!"

They turned and slowly headed back to the car.

Hershel tried to make light of a serious situation. "Who the hell is confident?"

"Never mind, it just feels good to be able to work together again. A few minutes from here, I intend for you and Nikolai to meet with a former KGB general who was an occasional contact of mine in our days with the Mossad. We know that he also has close contacts with other former high-ranking Communist politicians. Be prepared to hear the same story from some officials time and time again about not being able to feed their wives and children properly. I just hope the damned game is not over for them while we read their info."

His jaw firm, his eyes penetrating even in the darkness, Avrum's voice was low and ominous. "I am not qualified to predict the coming social and economic consequences for present-day Russia, but the entire political situation smells of an ugly crisis for the United States and the rest of the world. There is a lot of resentment against the wealth of the United States. The Russians do not understand why the U.S. has not used more of its wealth to help the transition to democracy here. No matter how much is spent on them, those Ruskies expected a lot more."

Hershel appeared to be in deep thought before he spoke. "It just seems there is a great deal more brewing here than accounting for missing plutonium or keeping track of a stockpile of 30,000 Russian warheads. I know the challenge is especially great because a terrorist group would only need several kilograms of plutonium, an amount no larger than would fit in a soda can, to make a bomb. I just have this uneasy feeling that somehow there is another plot brewing that may have far-reaching consequences."

"Like I said earlier, Hershel, you do have a way with ideas. But without some help, we wouldn't last long in this territory on a quiet Saturday night. That's why I am just damned grateful that Yaakov and Yossi are scheduled to join us for our reunion in a few days. We are going to need all the competent help we can get."

Finished with his quiet plea, Avrum approached the car. "Now we could discuss the question of timing," he suggested.

"Timing? With someone trying to break all the rules it is difficult to plan for accurate timing. Let's think about it down the road," said Hershel.

Chapter Eleven

ALEKSEI TOLSTOY STREET

OCTOBER 17

Delegated by Avrum, Nikolai was in charge of transportation and security. In addition to operating from his apartment, which had now become the "safe house" for the formers, he could also expect to have other obligations as occasions arose.

Sitting in the front seat, his first official duty was to direct the driver to get them all to his apartment building on Aleksei Tolstoy Street.

The driver was not part of the Intourist system, so he didn't have a street map. (And these were almost impossible to obtain in Moscow.) Nikolai's directions to the apartment were given by referencing locations of other buildings.

"Do you know where the museum is? On the street behind the museum there is a yellow building with a black wrought-iron fence," Nikolai explained to the driver. "Turn left at the church and my apartment building is in the middle of the block."

Since the driver was an unknown factor, Avrum and Nikolai had planned to speak loudly enough for him to overhear certain portions of the conversation. It was important to defuse any suspicions the chauffeur may have had, in case he was a paid KGB informant, as were so many Russian chauffeurs driving for business people and dignitaries. Even with the end of the former Soviet Union, the KGB was still actively operating and had a massive network of informants feeding it information.

The driver was therefore fed the misinformation that his passengers were heading to a poetry reading. Poetry readings were not only very popular, they were a way of life, important to everyone in the Russian intellectual community. During the long cold winters, the Russian people needed something aside from alcohol to bolster their spirit, and most of the intelligentsia would turn to poetry. Some did it for entertainment, but others for politics, religious purposes or philosophy—all of which would be expected from the poet of the evening. So in Russia it was not at all unusual for a group like Avrum, Hershel and Nikolai to go to a reading.

Avrum leaned back in the seat and lit a cigarette. To him any bit of intrigue was enjoyable, so he kept up the conversation on the phoney poetry event they were supposedly headed to. Nikolai smiled as he wondered what else the driver knew or thought about them or their destination.

Before arriving at Aleksei Tolstoy Street, Avrum hand-signaled to Nikolai, and immediately Mikoyan requested that the driver stop at a small store they had just passed. He told the driver they wished to buy some bread and wine, but his whole point was to ensure that he didn't know exactly what building they were headed to.

"It's okay. You can wait here and we will walk back," Nikolai said to the driver as he winked at Avrum. He noticed, farther down the street, that two men in civilian clothing continued walking in the opposite direction until they disappeared around a corner.

After the three got out, Hershel, with his keen sense of humor, commented that even if nothing positive was to come from these walks, the exercise was stimulating and good for his heart. Avrum smiled, at the remark and decided to take advantage of their rare opportunity to talk while they were alone and didn't have to worry about listening devices or being spied upon. It was time to get down to facts and disclose what he felt was the reason Yoel Melman was killed.

He spoke as they slowly walked. His voice was low but resonant, so it could not be carried beyond the small group. "It will not hurt if we are a few minutes late. My wife tells me it is more fashionable to be a little late. Anyway, the excuse gives her more time to put on her makeup."

There were some brief chuckles of understanding; then Avrum spoke again. "Okay, my friends, to me the information evidenced in Yoel's letter to Nikolai has become quite clear and pure as the snow that will surely begin to fall before we are done here. In his letter Yoel claimed that he suspected the existence of a secret group of former Soviet military, security and Politbureau die-hards operating undercover. He spoke in his letter of their master plan to return the party old-guard Communist leaders to power and restore the U.S.S.R. to its past glory. We all served and fought together with Yoel. We know how reliable he was, and what he reports is entirely possible. I believe he died for what he learned."

Avrum paused for a moment as the three men looked into a store window. "In his letter he suggested that he was planning to meet with a former KGB general, Ivan Chervok, living here in Moscow, and that's where we are headed. Yoel also said that he was aware the General disagreed with the methods the die-hards proposed to use in overthrowing the C.I.S. But Yoel did not know or did not have time to reveal what, when, or anything—other details—on this dangerous plan."

Avrum again paused, then reached into his pocket to remove Yoel's three-page letter as if it were a grocery list. He studied it for a moment before putting on his reading glasses. "I can remember a time when I didn't need these damn things," he said. "Here it is," he said, pointing to a line.

> Consider that accommodations are made every day
> between people of many stripes, for all sorts of
> different reasons. Together with the cooperation of
> the General and his friends, we can accomplish
> much more than would be possible with the form-
> ers working separately. You must agree that the
> origin of some of the best intelligence information
> sometimes comes from the most unexpected
> sources.

They all stood silent for a moment, considering Yoel's belief, while Avrum carefully folded the pages of the letter, replaced it in his pocket and removed his glasses as they slowly approached the shop.

He continued to speak in a low tone. "Yoel had nerve and no fear, and that was his big secret. He once told me that as a youngster his uncle, whom he was living with on the Lower East Side of New York City, found him bleeding and crying in the hallway of their apartment house. Adding insult to injury, his uncle kicked him in the backside and told him to go out and beat up the bully who had hurt him. 'You should die,' he said to him, 'if that's what it takes, but you don't ever give in.' And that's how Yoel lived his life."

"That's one tough way to grow up," said Nikolai.

Avrum continued: "Yoel knew that he was being tailed here in Russia, but he stated he didn't know by whom. So it is entirely possible that since Yoel was in contact with General Chervok, the General is also being watched. Nikolai, when we get to the General's apartment and after you do the introductions, please go outside and cover us. See if anyone is tailing us. Hershel, as we go in the apartment, study the layout; scan it to see if anyone else is there aside from the General and his house-keeper. Do the usual, but don't be too obvious."

Hershel knew the routine. He was to check for bugs—holes in the mirrors or other places where cameras could be concealed. He also knew that Avrum was the expert on political maneuvering, and that if something was learned at the meeting, they would have a starting place to begin digging for more information.

After entering the small store and looking around, Avrum made his choice. "This bread and wine looks good, let's buy it for the General," he said, handing the items to Nikolai. Avrum waved his hand, as if chasing flies from his face. "Okay, please pay the clerk and let's get rolling. We have a long day ahead of us."

They arrived at General Chervok's high-rise apartment house just a few minutes before the appointed time. Hershel observed that the building showed the telltale marks of power typical of the elite. There were large picture windows, manicured lawns with beautiful landscaping, and clean, modern yellow brick construction. Inside, they proceeded to the General's apartment and knocked on the door.

The door was wrenched open by a tall man with burning eyes and the craggy face of an old-world prophet, someone an artist might have put on canvas.

The General looked them over and stepped back, but Avrum stepped forward at once, shaking his hand and pouring out a torrent of appreciation for the man's taking the time to see them.

Inside, the living room was tastefully furnished in Finnish modern, and the kitchen was equipped with Formica-type counters, a German built refrigerator, a stove and metal built-in cabinets.

The General enjoyed being a host—at least to those present. He poured them all hot tea, then dished out a large amount of blackberry preserves which they could mix into their tea. They sipped the tea in the traditional way, first putting a cube of sugar into their mouths, then letting the tea drain around. It made conversation difficult to understand, but it was the Russian way.

"We apologize for breaking in on your day," Avrum offered.

The General was friendly, speaking to the trio in passable English that was good enough to be clearly understood. But then his words became sharp, almost rude. He showed his annoyance by suddenly accusing Nikolai of requesting a meeting that was supposed to be for some political favor. The General clearly demonstrated that he did not share his information or political favors easily. "You are here in Russia on business or pleasure?" he asked.

"We are here on business, which will provide much pleasure if we can conclude it," Hershel answered as he settled into a chair.

"Success can make an ordinary man a great man, but failure in Russia can also turn greatness into exile," said the General as he smiled thinly, obviously proud of himself for coming up with such a profound thought.

Hershel understood the man's tactics. This must be a tough year for anti-Communists, he thought to himself. Then he waited for some verdict from the General. Hershel wondered: Would Chervok ultimately be cooperative and friendly? Did he intend to carry on this charade for the entire meeting? Would he ever level with them and disclose his precise relationship with Yoel? Hershel asked himself.

"We will talk more," the General stated slowly, hopefully signaling his decision to get serious with them.

To start the meeting in an unfriendly and tense atmosphere would not have been advantageous, so Hershel diplomatically turned the conversation around to the General's former accomplishments. This was intended to gently shift the mood, to lighten up the entire room.

As the General warmed to his subject, he began to speak with nostalgia of the golden age of spying, especially on the CIA, and the good old days for him when it was the KGB versus the free world. Those were the days when both sides clearly knew who the enemy was—although they did not know if their fellow intelligence agents were in fact moles for the CIA or KGB.

"In those days we knew exactly which diplomats in the American Embassy here were spies for the United States. We could pick out those who would have indeed been susceptible for recruitment into the KGB as double agents, or as you say, a control agent or mole.

"I could even walk the 'black cat,'" the General continued, "by telling you about the 'spooks' we had in parts of the White House during the Roosevelt Administration in the Second World War," and he laughed. "Yes, there were Reds under Roosevelt's bed. We even had an NKVD-controlled agent in Roosevelt's office during part of his administration. As a matter of fact, he was Roosevelt's assistant on intelligence affairs—

what you would probably call a penetration agent today. It was indeed a bad time for the anti-Communists in Washington."

He went on to recount, in detail, a number of stories, bridged with ideology, while impulsively throwing his muscular arms around to further make his points.

Suddenly he stood up, gestured for his guests to follow, and—to be sure they could speak confidentially—he showed them into a semi-darkened room of his apartment. It was a large room, perhaps five meters square. Light from the hallway bulb outlined the features of the room until Chervok turned on the small night-table lamp.

As Hershel's eyes adjusted, he could see that the room was dominated by a massive brick fireplace with a marble mantel, three chairs, a desk and a large table.

"We will be able to talk more privately here for a few moments before we must leave to meet another former Politbureau member. I see both of you have that look of suspicion on your face. Do not be concerned. I am the last one who would want to see Communism return to Russia, with the inevitable revolution that would undoubtedly follow. Be assured that you are among friends this evening and that there are no listening devices. I check for what you call 'bugs' every time I come home from being away—even after I take a walk. I know exactly what to look for. Being a member of the Communist Party for almost all of one's adult life brings you experience the hard way.…But I was a member in name only. At the time, it was the only alternative to achieving rank, status and my goals in the U.S.S.R."

The General's face suddenly took on the look of a man who had just received a secret message. He patted his face with a handkerchief, took a deep breath and continued. "It is I, among my close group of friends, who first volunteered to come forward in our mutual best interest, to work on this so-called 'smoking gun' case with you."

The General's luminous eyes seemed too large, too alive, for his age, Hershel thought, as the man continued talking.

"I realize that the most experienced and professional people I could possibly work with would be your group of former Mossad agents. You are among those who have the most to lose or gain by our mutual success or failure. For example, I will provide you with hard proof that former officials of the Kremlin have, and continue to this very day, to be supported by your sworn enemies, the Palestine terrorists. With more than only the moral support of their terrorist friends for the destruction of Israel, they also are able to back their words with arms, money and munitions."

"That's very interesting, General," Avrum interjected, "but we are also well aware of the close relationship between various terrorist organizations and Russia."

"The Western nations of Israel and the United States will always be in constant jeopardy from the Palestinian extremists. Not only because of their killing of Americans and Israelis—but they will also offer the constant threat of sabotaging your oil supply lines and your international trade. Even giving them Gaza and the West Bank will not preclude them from destroying Israel's tourist trade. As a matter of fact, we were informed of their long-range plan for holding the American's by the short hairs. As you are surely aware, the problem of how to deal with these terror groups will create many new dilemmas within Israel and between the Israeli people. You can even look for a threat of insurrection from some left-wing Israelis. Don't laugh, there is always that possibility," the General added.

There were moments when the General sounded impulsive, but as Hershel looked into his eyes he felt that the Russian was sincere and, too, there appeared to be substance in the information that he was privy to. He was coming across as the sincere, disgruntled former Communist he was.

"In the past, our Communist Party Central Committee members even helped finance the Communist Party of the United States, while people here in Russia were literally starving," he continued. "But that is a long story and only the very tip of this 'smoking gun' case. What you may find astonishing is how this renegade group of powerful Communists expect to achieve their ridiculous goals."

Hershel would have liked to make a recording of this meeting with his video camera. Anyone in intelligence who got involved with a breakthrough such as the one he had just heard would love to verify his sources—if the story was to be believed and accepted in the outside world. Hershel realized that almost all of what the General was saying was true and that he was anxious to proceed. Hershel could not imagine, without knowing the full picture, how the formers could counter these immensely powerful renegade elements of the former Soviet military.

While General Chervok was putting on his heavy overcoat, his mood again seemed to change. With the coat on, he suddenly whipped out and held up a full bottle of vodka, offering his guests a drink with a simple gesture as he pointed to the crystal-clear bottle.

Hershel smiled to himself as he silently recalled stories of past Russian military leaders who were famous for telling love escapades at wild parties while chug-a-lugging vodka with whiskey chasers. In the interest of building their friendship with the General, Hershel, Avrum and Nikolai made time for one drink, but not the whiskey chaser or the stories, that always followed naturally.

After the formality of buttoning his coat, the General offered some well-thought-out advice: "You would attract much less attention if you would come with me in my car to meet my close friend and former Politbureau member, Anastas Andropovkin."

Hershel thought the General's warning was a sound one and nodded his acceptance. The four men quickly left the house by the rear stairs.

Once outside, Hershel signaled Nikolai to walk close by his side, as he spoke in a low voice. "Let me give it to you quickly," Hershel instructed. "Have our car follow behind the General's, but at a considerable distance."

"Looks like a fun evening," Nikolai commented.

"Nikolai, this always has the possibility of turning out to be some kind of trap. If so, we are far outnumbered. Stay in the background, don't try anything rash. Just observe. At your first opportunity, after you are clear of the immediate danger, get some word of what we are onto back to one of our friends at headquarters, or even inform one of our former CIA acquaintances as a last resort, if that is more expedient. Until something happens, do nothing, trust no one, and keep a sharp eye on the driver."

Hershel quickly turned away and walked back to the General's car.

Chapter Twelve

THE LENIN HILLS, C.I.S
OCTOBER 17

In the General's car Hershel, Avrum and General Ivan Chervok traveled in silence with lights ablaze, the glow reflecting off puddles of rainwater. They continued on, to the Lenin Hills, overlooking downtown Moscow, to what the General announced was known as the "little dacha" area. There they hoped to find out what they needed to know.

The General made it clear to his guests that the country cottage dacha of the Russian elite was not to be confused with the izbas, the little bungalows of the peasants. Hershel could almost tell the type and size of the beloved Russian dacha from the intonation in the General's voice and the twinkle in his eyes, as he described their various methods of construction. Hershel realized that when General Chervok spoke about a Russian having a dacha, it could mean anything from a small log cabin with no privacy to a reconstructed grand mansion taken over from the Russian aristocracy.

As they drove through the open fence gates and down a long drive, they realized that the special rustic dacha of Anastas Andropovkin was located out of sight, among a forest of birch trees.

Upon entering the house, introductions were made as Andropovkin turned to look out into the darkness before closing the door. He led the General, Avrum and Hershel into a large, double-size, wood-paneled living room with many religious icons. The rooms of the dacha were pleasantly furnished, having comfortable chairs, large beds and throw rugs everywhere.

There was ample lighting, although a bit antiquated, a sauna, huge fireplaces and indoor plumbing, which constantly leaked, as evidenced by the telltale drips in the corners of the rooms.

Andropovkin made his guests comfortable in large overstuffed chairs. Pouring drinks for everyone, he did not waste any time in getting down to the subject of the meeting. But he took a deep breath, like a man preparing to dive off the high board.

"I am glad you are here," he said after the initial introductions. "We have all been worried by the rumors we've been hearing, and if it is acceptable to you I would like to begin immediately, so as not to waste time. This is what I've come up with," he said with an anxious smile. "The truth is that Russian society has given birth to a new class of citizen, all of whom are supposed to be equal.

"Everyone wants a society with permanence and stability," Anastas Andropovkin continued, "but that is not true today in the new C.I.S. Some of the old hard-line Communists who were secure and content with almost immeasurable powers feel that they have now lost everything they had worked for. They feel as if they have become capitalist pawns of Western democracies, and they fully intend to restore themselves to power by whatever means available."

Hershel leaned forward in his chair. He was even more attentive than usual, fully realizing that he would be the authority in charge of planning whatever action would have to be taken, with a maximum of five or six men as backup. Obviously, the main point of their as yet unplanned mission would be to ferret out the true intentions of the diehards.

Everyone heard the footsteps in the hallway as Andropovkin stopped talking and rose from his chair. Walking quietly to the door, he opened it a crack, peered through the small space between the double doors, then walked slowly back to his chair, picked up his drink and made himself comfortable.

Hershel stared at the ornate wood-carved ceiling, obviously relieved that up until now there had been no problems. He knew that everyone in his group was nervous. But his first step in security planning—having Nikolai stay with their driver to see that he did not leave the car to make contact with another party—was on target.

Anastas Andropovkin turned toward Hershel. "Sorry for the interruption. I assure you that my dacha is every bit as secure as your safe house in Moscow."

Hershel's eyebrows raised in unexpected surprise.

"Yes, it is my job to know all about you. But please, let us continue with the object of this gathering. Since it is my assumption that it would behoove you to help us help you, the important question for all of us to ask is…"

Andropovkin strategically paused for a moment to create suspense or to wrestle with his conscience. His rattled features became purplish and his head quivered as he spoke again. "How do our brethren, the die-hard Communist elite, plan to regain their status and power? It has filtered down to me that they have a most violent plan, to which most Russian people in their right minds would never agree. Their political idealism should not be a surprise to anyone, however, and once the world knows they are still in the background—alive and well—it will understand their motives."

Placing his vodka glass on the end table, Andropovkin continued, "You have to realize, gentlemen, that the avalanche pace in which the leadership of the *new* Russia took over is hard for most officials of the old system to comprehend. What I am getting to is that these former high-ranking die-hard officials have their plan in place, which is to shake up and do everything in their power to overthrow the new democratic government before it becomes further entrenched. They are of the opinion that they are being victimized and are unwilling to give democracy a further opportunity to become fully established. It is hard to tell who all the hard-line Communist supporters truly are, since they often ally themselves with our various new nationalist movements to obscure their true goals."

While Andropovkin continued speaking, the General reached for a cigarette and lit it, his hand rock-steady.

"In addition," said Andropovkin, "our former Soviet 'soft-line' military friends, who are presently aligned with our movement, feel that the Communist Party of the Soviet Union always was an undemocratic and illegal organization. But even given this viewpoint, since the breakup of the Soviet Union they are deeply shaken. They feel they can no longer be responsible for the behavior of their line officers and they cannot control their massive arms holdings. Most important, they tell me that they cannot guarantee the military security of the thirty-seven nuclear plants in the former Soviet republics."

Andropovkin's audience sat attentive, their eyes fixed on him. They could clearly see the implications of what he was alluding to.

"I am amazed," said Hershel, as his jaw muscles tensed, "that your former friends think the free world will permit them to get away with a coup or an overthrow of the C.I.S. while they are obviously trying to get their pictures printed on the front of cereal boxes as national heroes. They cannot get away with an overthrow plan in the long term. This sounds outrageous enough to be brought to the attention of the United Nations as an international issue."

"Perhaps you are right, but it simply takes too long for the United Nations to agree and to act on any critical political situation. By the time the world would bring itself to recognize this crisis, the die-hards would have gained control and begun the process of unification of all previous Soviet states—and then some."

"And what's the 'and then some'?" Hershel interrupted.

"That refers to the tens of thousands of innocent people who would die in the attempt," Andropovkin replied. "The die-hards also plan a series of terrorist attacks against the United States, Israel and other countries—to gain respect and a following. And once that is accomplished, they will have even more power.

"As a matter of fact, to prove their point to their superiors and bring any doubters in line, the die-hard Communists just flexed their muscles again. A fire was intentionally set by a group of them at an army ammunition depot in the Armenian town of Abovyan. If you don't know, that is northeast of Yerevan, the Armenian capital. The result was that explosions were set off at the rate of twenty a minute and the fire blazed for two days. This is 'war' to them, after all, and they want to make it clear who will direct the new government."

Andropovkin paused to eye his guests for their reactions.

"But that is not the end of my story, gentlemen. Last week there was more muscle flexing: a blast at the large arsenal in a densely populated district of Vladivostok. The blast triggered thousands of other rapid-fire explosions and thundered on for hours, forcing thousands of civilians to flee the city in panic, fearing for their lives. I was told that the city now looks as though it was in the front line of World War II. Explosions and fires continued burning for several days, and they had to call in the entire military garrison from the area to fight the fires. Windows were knocked out of all the buildings for miles around, and the earth shook from the tremors, almost like an earthquake."

He took a moment to moisten his dry lips before continuing. "More than fifty thousand of the city's residents were evacuated and many of the volunteers and military personnel fighting the fire were wounded by the exploding ammunition. As a matter of fact, I just had the opportunity to speak with Valentin Novikov, the Interior Ministry official in Vladivostok, who expressed extreme concern for the security of the area, even after the blaze was totally extinguished."

"These blokes could be moralists, you know," Avrum said in a troubled tone. They are the players who bomb innocent people on buses to bring attention to their cause. Some of the worst people in history were moralists." Then, as if he had been reminded of something, Avrum went on, "Actually, I wanted to ask you if you know who these people are, where they come from? What the hell are they all about?"

Andropovkin gave an anguished grin. "I don't blame you one bit for asking. What matters now is what they are planning, not who they are." He spoke with lips so close together that Avrum at first didn't realize he was speaking to him.

"The incidents I described just go to prove the character and strength of these Communist renegades you will eventually have to confront— after we identify them, that is. Their actions have certainly rekindled the Communist spirit, which was waning in some of the die-hards. They now have a renewed cause, and a much-needed show of support. You must realize that they are a desperate, power-hungry and dangerous people. I give you my sacred word that they care not who or how many they kill to achieve their self-centered ends. They have lost track of the fact that there are human beings, just like them, in their target sights."

Avrum's eyes narrowed for a moment. Then slowly he nodded. "Sounds like somebody has to put a little reality back into their heads. By the way, how did you come by this information when the rest of the world knows nothing about what is going on here?" he questioned.

"The die-hards are not leak-proof. No organization of this sort is, you know," the General himself brusquely answered the Israeli. "Some of my friends have worked their asses off at great risk to their families to disclose the die-hards' plan to me. And if you cannot agree to work closely with us to put a counter-plan together, all our work and the risks we are taking will have been for nothing."

"I'm a little uncertain right now. I don't know if we are capable of pulling any of this off…without your full cooperation," Avrum added with quiet emphasis. "And incidentally, why didn't you bring this to the attention of the CIA or one of the other Western intell-agencies, instead of us?"

For the first time since they met, Anastas Andropovkin smiled broadly. "Hmmmm," he said, his eyes darkening. "Because there is nothing that can be confirmed officially. Because we have no congressional committee to appear before. Because since the collapse of the Soviet Union the world's governments and intelligence agencies dictate the policies they prefer to us, and your politicians are only interested in the tangible aspects of food and medical aid to Russia that create a positive humanitarian image and publicity to assist them in their reelection campaigns. Because since the fall of Communism and our former system, there is nothing here that can be politically compromised or traded off—except military surplus or nuclear technology. We already lost all of our bargaining chips and we are in the position of having to reluctantly accept almost everything our former adversaries require us to. My friends, the situation is much more grave than you can imagine.

"And not all of God's creatures can survive without help from time to time. Furthermore, you know that American, British, French, German, Italian and other intelligence agencies are considered difficult for both the KGB *and* the politicians to deal with—and in a good many instances, the agencies are widely detested and distrusted. In addition, the integrity of the infrastructure and command in every one of the other intell-agencies is flawed, to those of us in the know. The typical CIA recruit is underpaid, unhappy with his bosses, and after a decade of his being angry and frustrated we can approach him and buy him for a few hundred thousand U.S. dollars! You know it and so does your government.

"That's why we were so successful with the Walker spies, the Ames spy and many others that no one even knows we bought off. And the Brits are even easier because they come cheaper and are more prone to our socialist ways of thinking! So don't expect us to run to the Western intelligence boys for help in cleaning up this problem. We don't dare risk our lives giving them this information. Having been in intelligence, I am sure that the three of you can appreciate that."

As he spoke, Andropovkin's left hand slowly rose above his head until his whole arm was stretched toward the ceiling. "It is not easy to overcome the damage of past errors and scandals, which will make it quite difficult for our group to recruit volunteers for this mission." He lowered his voice in embarrassment. "That is why we need your help."

Andropovkin took a long sip of vodka before continuing. "Don't let it go to your heads, but in my view I always felt that Israel is unique in a number of ways. Probably because it has been in an almost constant state of war and because of its Mossad, which we feel has earned its reputation as being second to none. We know that Israel has been smart enough to recruit large numbers of the best available intelligence agents from throughout the world. Your agents have demonstrated over the years an outstanding ability to collect, organize, screen and evaluate information to your advantage. And most important, there never seem to be the type of scandals that other intelligence agencies suffer—your agents being bought off or turning to the other side.

"I suppose this has something to do with your backgrounds of persecution over the centuries. Your agents know how precarious your country's situation is over there, surrounded by hundreds of millions of angry, bloodthirsty, easy-to-manipulate, fundamentalist-oriented neighbors. Your people know that if they sell out, the consequence could be the end of their country and the majority of the race. These circumstances would tend to keep most people honest. That is one reason we are comfortable seeking help from you Mossad agents."

Hershel enjoyed listening to Andropovkin's comments and analysis. Having been a part of the Mossad, he felt delighted with the praise. "Nice to know someone appreciates us," he said, smiling.

"As for your friends in the Central Intelligence Agency," Andropovkin continued, "in addition to our inability to trust them, their credibility has been lost. For the most part, their gross carelessness, deception and blunders in dealing with the Iraqi problems, the Iran-Contra affair and Saddam Hussein have caused my friends and me to lose all confidence in them. In fact, we feel it is sometimes better to deal with hard-line terrorists by feeding them money, weapons and respect.

"Don't forget, it was the pressure of the Bush Administration that pushed the CIA to support the National Security Directive of October 1989. The directive was and still is secret, and it mandates the U.S.— and I quote," he said, looking directly at Hershel, "'to improve and expand our relationship with Iraq.' What a joke! Then that genius former CIA operative Bush had the State Department give Iraq one billion dollars in new credits to buy food, which Saddam laughingly accepted.

"Saddam was a lot smarter than Bush and the CIA together, and having a Republican or Democratic administration makes little difference to him. He has an uncanny ability to orchestrate events and play off your foolish politicians to his best advantage."

Deep in thought, Andropovkin began working the palm of one of his hands with the fingers of the other. "I am mentioning these recent political events because I know you were deeply involved within the areas I am discussing. You must admit that what Saddam did with the food aid was very clever. Shrewd Saddam off-loaded the food, bought with American loan guaranties, in Eastern Europe, sold it for a nice profit and reloaded the same ships with Iraqi arms, using the food money to pay for the transaction and bartering some of the food for additional weapons. But that is not the best part of the deal. The best part is when Saddam defaulted on the U.S. loan guaranties, never paying for the food and shoving the bill right up his buddy and comrade George Bush's ass!"

With that comment, the entire room broke up in laughter. Andropovkin was effectively breaking the ice and bonding with his new associates. He continued, "Where was the great Central Intelligence Agency that the American politicians speak so highly of?"

"You seem more qualified than we are to answer the question," Avrum said, almost laughing. "For the record, why don't you tell us?"

"Well, the CIA knows now, because your Mossad told them, but they surely didn't know at the time, and they surely never told the sleeping American public." Anastas Andropovkin paused to give his audience time to digest what he had said.

Avrum plucked the cigarette from his mouth and shook his head, spilling ashes over his pants and onto the floor. His other hand brushed away the glowing ashes on his leg.

"Hold on, don't get ready to leave just yet," Andropovkin added, wagging his finger in the air. "I'm not finished—the worst is yet to come! Let me tell you about other projects, the players, their final goals and when they intend to put their whole program into effect.

"I briefly mentioned that the hard-line Communists had a plan to reinstate their beloved government and regain power. This will not be just a political coup, but also a violent plan of destruction," he continued without pausing. "Over the years, Russia has developed a pool of the finest nuclear scientists and biochemists on earth, most of whom are presently unemployed or under-employed. We are speaking of a nation able to build gaseous diffusion plants and plutonium-producing reactors from their inception. I speak of die-hard Communists, ambitious and determined, who are prepared to sacrifice the welfare of their own population in order to regain their lost power."

Again, Andropovkin paused for a moment, then continued. "These are the facts. They will be hard for anyone to dispute. And there is a lot more that we will get into later. Just one more thing, gentlemen: Hold on to your yarmulkahs. Once they get their act together, the hard-liners are planning to launch several of those unaccounted-for ICBMs against a yet-unnamed target or targets. They in turn expect to generate a response in kind—that is, if NATO and the United States are still intact."

The Mossad formers simply looked at one another in stunned silence. It was almost too much to believe. The fatigue and disgust on their faces were unmistakable.

Anastas Andropovkin, a man of realistic sensibility and an obvious master of suspense, took a sip of his almost empty glass of vodka before continuing: "The warheads launched by the die-hards will not be nuclear, because of tight international security controls and technical problems. Instead, these maniacs have decided that they will be filled with a quick-acting deadly bacteria that will be activated upon impact."

Without uttering a word, Hershel and Avrum glanced at each other knowingly. At Mossad headquarters they had worried for years about the possibility of just such a scenario.

"I'm still not quite finished," Andropovkin said, his angry face red and glowing from his three glasses of vodka. "Do you have any idea what will happen then?"

Avrum closed his eyes. Hershel simply shrugged his shoulders.

"After the deadly attack," Andropovkin continued, "I predict that as the world retaliates against Russia, in the aftermath of the inevitable confusion in the former Soviet Union, the hard-line Communists will seize power from the ruling party, placing blame for the incident on them, and call for immediate peace by otherwise threatening more terrorist acts. The new hard-line leaders will be sure to say that the dastardly act was that of a few renegades who will immediately be stripped of their powers and brought to justice—that is, assassinated. So in reality, after the dirty deed is done, there will be no witnesses.

"The plan is relatively simple, but the consequences and aftermath will be disastrous for centuries to come. We cannot allow that to happen—no matter how desperate these hard-liners are and no matter what the costs are to stop them."

The group sat for moments in total silence, thinking of the possible alternatives, before Hershel could bring himself to speak. He mopped his brow with his napkin and said, "Everything you say is probable. With a bit of preparation, I could draw up a plan to pinpoint a mission against these crazy hard-line terrorists. Although this information is great, there is very little we can hope to accomplish without your assistance, gentlemen." He looked in the direction of Ivan Chervok and Anastas Andropovkin.

"Without question," he went on, "the logic of our combining efforts and our motives for cooperation are perfectly clear. Therefore, a powerful counter-plan has to be quickly prepared. If we do agree on a course of action, how do we know it won't be leaked? We don't. So, if we all agree to meet again, total secrecy is mandatory—if we are to have a prayer at being successful. You also have to consider the present danger to yourselves. After all, we don't even know who the enemy is. It could be anyone around you." Hershel gestured toward the Russians. "In addition, in case we fail, an escape route must be planned well in advance."

Hershel paused for a moment to gather his thoughts while the awesome impact of the evil planned by the die-hards sank into everyone's head.

He then continued, "Your communication system in this area is rather primitive compared to other places we have worked, so we will develop our own methods for security purposes, along with a system of codes to ensure the security of the operation."

The small group then agreed to set a time and place within the coming days for their next meeting. They all shook hands, put on their coats, and, with their host, the two Israelis began walking towards the door.

The General made a helpless, shrugging gesture with both hands before he spoke. "I'm sure that you know the old soldier's code: 'Death before dishonor.'"

Hershel was not excited by that idea. He glanced at the ceiling for a second, trying to come up with the appropriate response to this overused comment. But he was rescued by Andropovkin, who diplomatically told the entire group: "We're deeply grateful for your—well, how would I say it—your understanding and friendship."

"*You* deserve the thanks, because you are taking even bigger risks," said Avrum as they exited.

Hershel and Avrum walked slowly down the long path to their car, where Nikolai and the driver awaited.

Avrum mused aloud: "We have no evidence that Andropovkin is not an outright fraud."

"Nope," Hershel said. "No hard evidence. That is a problem."

"You must ask yourself why he and the General are feeding us all this information."

"I suspect someone was not offered a high enough position in the new 'democratic' government and now it's get-even time. Let's just be grateful that we can now try to do something to stop these *mumserim* (bastards). These die-hard terrorists were somewhere at the end of the line when God gave humans a conscience. In any case, we cannot be concerned with the reasoning of terrorists. They are all out for self-gain, or to satisfy their fanaticism. We know that much," Hershel said grimly.

Avrum heard the anger building in his friend's voice. "I am convinced that something serious is brewing here and we are in the middle of it. I also know that our safe house in Moscow is not really safe. If these guys know where we're located, who knows what sort of leaks or integrity their organization has. We should secretly move to our secondary position, tomorrow at the latest. After that we can start dealing with this threat through a clear-cut plan based on fact-finding, intelligence and action."

"Agreed," Avrum said as they reached the car and got in.

On the way back to their lodgings, even though depressed, the formers put on a good act, jovially commenting about the "poetry reading" in a boisterous tone and how much they enjoyed the last reader.

Avrum was very uncomfortable with the driver. He did not have any idea what the driver knew about them at this point and could not take any further chances by letting him learn the location of their new safe house. Their mission was too important to take any sort of chances, least of all, to trust their unknown driver.

As the men laughed, Avrum leaned over and whispered in Nikolai's ear: "When we get to the safe house, ask the driver to take you somewhere else—suggest a red light district. I smell a rat, and I'll wager anything that he is a plant. Something about him rubs me the wrong way and is suspicious.

"Dispose of the son-of-a-bitch and the Chaika. Things are too hot to stay in our original lodging any longer. We'll move to the secondary safe house tonight when you get back. Keep your eyes open. You'll know what to do at the appropriate time."

Everyone in the car fell silent. Only the hum from the engine was audible.

Avrum suddenly felt a little old...and so lost. He wondered how he had got himself into this situation. What was he doing taking these risks at his age?

Chapter Thirteen

THE "DON COSSACK"

OCTOBER 18 & 19

With the single-mindedness of a fugitive escaping from a great Gulag prison wall, Doctor Zavaskayev, director of C.I.S. special operations command, left the grand vestibule of the Politbureau. He strode swiftly, looking neither left nor right, through the side entrance toward his nondescript official limousine.

As he approached the car, his chauffeur sprang to attention, and the doctor gave him a dour look. Before getting in, he took note that the black sedan with two security agents assigned as his protection was behind. Then he got inside.

Once safe in the well-worn cushioned rear seat he made himself comfortable, unbuttoned and removed his overcoat, loosened his tie and looked back at the building he had just left. He observed Colonel Yusol Dubek emerging from the vestibule and knew that he would see him later at a pre-arranged place. It would not be good for the two diehards to be seen traveling together.

Doctor Zavaskayev was bored with the weekly staff meetings at the ministry, where the speakers went on and on, and this bureaucracy inched itself forward, accomplishing almost nothing yet wasting so much of his time. Over the past several months the only worthwhile meetings at the Politbureau were the working luncheons, which came as a perk to those required to attend. At those he flung himself at the food with the enthusiasm of a barbarian attacking a vestal virgin. His fork rose and fell in perpetual motion as he ate steadily, chomping on every morsel. When the ordeal of each meeting ended, Dr. Zavaskayev popped out of the ministry like the cork out of a bottle of vodka.

He peered through the rear window of the limousine to check on his escort car, following close behind.

As uncomfortable as the old car was, he luxuriously melted into the seat, welcoming this interlude of privacy. Lighting a cigarette, he reminded himself that the first order of business for the next meeting he would attend, in eight hours, would be organizational in nature: Who of the die-hards would be put in command of their one, only, and crucial attack against the West?

He did not have the least bit of trepidation or anxiety over what he had planned. A good feeling of confidence and righteousness emitted from every pore of his skin. He recalled that the Russian revisionists had become capitalistic pawns of the Western democracies. His war was against the corrupt politicians and crooks in his country who were running the C.I.S.

So, as Gandhi and Dr. Martin Luther King had died for their cause, he was ready to die for the important cause of the die-hards.

His strategy was to meet with the die-hard leadership on a constant basis, keep them pumped up and enthusiastic. Sending telephone or written messages, despite the worsening conditions their nation was falling into, was less persuasive, so he made it a point of staying in personal contact with each one of his group commanders.

While Zavaskayev possessed many shortcomings, was occasionally brusque and frequently ruthless, he was always a diplomat when dealing with people. His natural talent was to exercise his practiced charm and melt all opposition. Furthermore, it was his style to always speak correctly to ladies, mix drinks for them and make himself agreeable to their conversation, whatever it might be.

When he attended meetings, his opposition became isolated. The doctor walked into meetings fast and erect, like a man possessed. "One of the most powerful men in Russia," someone in the room could often be overheard whispering. The group leader who chaired the meeting became nervous before the real leader—the doctor—even entered. The group leader would look around with great urgency and ask his associate, the second in command, "Is everything in order? Is there enough food, drink? Do we have enough seats? Are the lamps turned up? He's come all this way to meet with our group. Oh, the lamps! I'd better turn up the lamps."

The tension would rise and finally the group leader almost felt ready for the doctor. The leader would gulp at his drink, knowing how important, how very important the meeting he was responsible for would mean to his future, as he swallowed hard. "Yes, I must have thought of everything, nothing is left out!" Then, seeing people collecting at the door, he would leap to his feet, standing ramrod straight, as if called to attention by a drillmaster.

Two security men would enter the room, glance around and keep their distance, melting into the crowd.

Then came Dr. Zavaskayev, cigar in hand, delivering a torrent of friendly greetings as he entered. As he made his way to the speaker's chair, he placed a friendly arm around one or two old comrades, as if to say, "We're going to do big things together." He played the game like a true, big-league politician.

Today, exiting his limousine, he did not hurry his pace, he only chuckled appreciatively as he occasionally puffed at his cigar, getting ready for the coming action. Once inside, however, in the midst of all the activity, the doctor thought about the next day's crucial staff meeting, which was likely to be a tremendous bore. It was scheduled to be held in St. Petersburg and would not be a social event like the function he was presently attending. Tomorrow there would be no fanfare, ceremony or amenities. Secrecy was the word of the day as the great world leaders—those of Great Britain, the United States, France, China and Germany—slept.

They who are now sleeping, Zavaskayev thought, will be burning the midnight oil a month from now, wondering what they could do to save themselves and what had happened to all their power. The doctor confidently snickered to himself.

The earliest recollection the doctor had of his younger years began at age three. It was then that his grandfather hit him with whip and told him, "You are a Don Cossack!" The incident remained with him his entire life. His grandfather had been an officer in the Czar's army, as had his father during the long Stalin regime. As a Cossack, longing for the restoration of the Romanov Dynasty, he thought himself to be liberal, having married an ordinary Russian woman.

The doctor followed all the traditions taught him in his youth. To be sure, he was anti-Semitic, often violently so; and just as everyone around him, he hated everything about the Jews. Of course, the doctor would often declare openly that he had nothing personally against Jews. "I even employed a Jew once," he was overheard saying at a recent die-hard meeting. But the fact was, he had had hatred of the Jews drilled into him at an early age and he proudly continued this tradition among his peers and associates.

At the last meeting of the die-hard group leaders, Zavaskayev had spoken to the small gathering, offering his violent opinion: "If the Jews force me to leave my job, I will return well armed, with a following, and will be sure to kill all of them—mark my words. Those who are presently in power will never live in peace to play with their grandchildren. I will kill the grandchildren too! This is our land, our government, and it will always be!"

The doctor then flashed the other side of his personality: a saber-slashing, whip-cracking vigilante, similar to his fellow Cossacks, who had recently reclaimed their special status by attacking people from the Transcaucuses countries, including a Hari Krishna group in Rostov. He proudly identified himself as a Cossack and knew that he would die a Cossack.

The following day, moments after descending from the military helicopter near St. Petersburg, the doctor was on his way to the command center to further supervise and coordinate the planned attack. This would be his first visit since his plan for the center had been approved, and he enjoyed a feeling of exhilaration. He took a pack of cigarettes and a lighter from his pocket.

The driver, an enlisted naval career man, suddenly came to life as they traveled northeast, out of a densely wooded area surrounding the small airfield. "I'm sorry to bother you sir," he said. We shall have to drive through St. Petersburg before we get to the harbor. Is there anything you will need before we get there?"

"*Nyet, Nyet,* Not necessary," the doctor answered curtly. He casually lit his cigarette, sat back and enjoyed the winding tree-lined streets, catching an occasional glimpse of squat houses, now and then partly obscured by fieldstone walls.

They had been forty-five minutes on the road, and as they came to the busy port of St. Petersburg, filled with ships and cargo from around the world, the driver slowed the car down. The huge iron gate at the end of the long pier was slowly opened by two naval men in uniform who recognized the driver. Another armed patrol officer with a clipboard under one arm flagged them down, approaching the driver's window.

The guard consulted a sheet on the board and nodded his approval, indicating a parking spot next to a two-story gray warehouse.

Leaving the car moments later, Doctor Zavaskayev stretched his chest and shoulders, then hurriedly caught up with the driver, who had already begun walking down the long pier. As he continued along the dock he saw a full range of Russian naval ships, from a few post-World War II museum pieces to others undergoing decommissioning, to the newest-class ships.

Walking quickly, it did not take the two long to arrive at a waiting harbor launch. The officer in charge saluted the doctor as he boarded.

Doctor Zavaskayev loved submarines and he fully understood how they served the special basic purposes for which they were created. The very word *submarine* implied stealth and deadliness to the doctor. He realized that their most common use in wartime was to submerge and secretly attack enemy ships, and that with the introduction of the ballistic missile, submarines were developed that could fire intercontinental missiles in excess of one thousand miles.

The meeting the doctor was anxious to attend today was scheduled aboard a recently decommissioned Russian submarine, anchored near the busy outer harbor. It was a rare moment for the doctor, the first time he'd ever had a meeting on a sub before.

The imposing bulk of the submarine soon became visible through the fog on the surface of the water. At first glance, it appeared no more threatening than a huge sea turtle. Yet despite that, the doctor knew its awesome full range of capabilities. Others understood the submarine in terms of myth or the modern equivalent, a science fiction movie. However, it was a powerful symbol to the doctor and he respected it. Here was a creature that appeared when the commander wished, destroyed what he wanted destroyed, and disappeared in the depths of the ocean in an instant—to strike again when the commander next decreed.

The boat that the doctor was being transported on continued heading toward the huge submarine that was anchored and lashed together in an array of five others that were smaller. Even though decommissioned, this once most lethal of ships was still potentially dangerous to the West. Its communications equipment and weaponry were the most advanced the C.I.S. had, and the die-hards fully intended to take complete advantage of this.

On active duty, this SSBN Typhoon-class sub was among the largest produced by the Soviet Union. It gave Western naval strategists nightmares.

Zavaskayev entered by climbing down the conning tower. As he slowly made his way down some three stories into the hull, he was finally in the portside passageway, just forward of the bridge position of the control room. Once in the control room, he was immediately struck by the fact that the air was clean and fresh and the room brightly lit. The area was filled to capacity with people, mostly in uniform, milling about. In the center of the room was a raised platform with the ship's periscope in the middle. Ahead of him were various status boards, and a place where one could access the periscopes.

Looking behind the bridge position, the doctor saw the masts containing the various sensors for the boat, including the attack and communication masts. Some of them actually penetrated the hull and provided the die-hard missile command staff with communication to the rest of the world and the electronic eyes and ears to observe and track their launch sites.

As Zavaskayev ducked back around the corner, he was surprised to see that at the base of the conning tower a command chair had been placed for him to sit on. From this position he could view the missile launch control consoles in the track alley and the plotting area from which some of the die-hard missiles would be fired.

The systems aboard the submarine had been updated with new equipment to man six positions so that launch control technicians could track and engage several targets simultaneously. The screens were round with red or amber-colored plasma displays and with pen lights to designate die-hard targets and move between various operating modes.

The doctor removed the cigar from his mouth and stared at the small group while collecting his thoughts. He laid the cigar carefully in an ashtray, not looking at anyone in particular. Slowly he settled back into his command chair and closed his eyes, his fingertips meeting his mustache, as he inhaled the still, clean air of the confined area.

After almost a minute of contemplation, he opened his eyes, dropped his hands to the arms of his chair and leaned forward. "Comrades," he said to this secret group, "we have begun the countdown. Together we shall soon achieve the impossible. Within the next month most C.I.S. public officials presently in office will cease to exist. The NATO nations will take care of this for us, once we launch our biochemical missile attack against the West. The theory that we will promote is that the attack was perpetrated by renegade political and military leaders in the C.I.S. This is quite plausible and will certainly be believed."

The doctor took a moment to collect his thoughts before continuing. He maintained his enthusiasm. "We are not engaging in reckless speculation here. For our plan to be effective, the West will be obliged to retaliate.

"Aleksandr Stepashin, each one of your groups will be responsible for their districts and will have to gain the support of the people in their area. Be ready and train your people to be fully prepared to blame and then overthrow the politicians in office by whatever means necessary. Comrades, be ready to seize political power and total control within your areas. You can depend on my having control of the central government in Moscow immediately after the attack. And you can depend on my support if you run into any difficulty," he said as he took an indignant breath.

"Sergei, you are the head of our security and you know the importance of continual vigilance," he commented softly as an inscrutable smile crept across his face. "Keep your people quiet, keep them calm and at all times maintain contact with this command center," he added with an air of authority as he leaned back in his chair, his hands clasped to its arms. "Thank you all, comrades," he roared. "Victory will be ours once again! Long live Mother Russia!"

Chapter Fourteen

SECONDARY SAFE HOUSE, MOSCOW

OCTOBER 20

Nikolai Mikoyan was in an obvious mood of accomplishment, with an ear-to-ear smile as he came striding into the room and up to Avrum. Flinging off his overcoat, he inadvertently got Avrum wet, and small puddles began collecting unnoticed on the floor.

Nikolai's cheerfulness was unexpected, and in a voice that sounded as if he were very pleased with himself, he declared. "Mission accomplished!"

"Does that mean you did what had to be done?" Avrum asked him.

Normally, Avrum thought that Nikolai was about as much fun as a dead fish, but for the moment he had the look of a cat that had swallowed the canary.

"Uh-huh," Nikolai answered, as he brushed away the drops of water still on his coat. He glanced over to Hershel, but Hershel was too deeply absorbed in the notes and sketches he was making on a large pad. "What gives with Hershel?" Nikolai asked, a smile on his face.

"Shush," Avrum answered, holding his first finger in front of his lips to emphasize that Nikolai should keep quiet. "Analyzing sensitive intelligence information is an art, and as you can see, the good doctor Hershel is operating. If the scenario he is planning turns out to be correct, we may be able to have a shot at ending this madness, after all."

"All right," Nikolai responded.

Born in Tripoli, Libya, to European Holocaust survivors, Nikolai's family made *aliyah* in Israel when he was an infant. He had earlier lived through the trauma of his father's unexpected and extremely brutal experiences during the Holocaust.

Nikolai had a recurrent dream: The Nazis were coming to take him and his family. He asked them to have pity on his family. He was outnumbered and tried not to fight with them. Always awaking in a sweat, he recalled that in his dream he was torn and unable to decide whether to run away or to fight and protect his family.

Eventually he explored his feelings, navigating his parents' unresolved burdens of the past despite his guilt of having such a comparatively easy life. He managed to move his mind back and forth between the past and future, between remembering and forgetting, between life and the horror of death at the hands of his family's oppressors.

Nikolai had often heard colorful stories, repeated by his grandparents, that their ancestors had been known as New Christians, or *Marranos,* when they temporarily lived in Spain—where they had been forcibly coerced into converting from Judaism during the bloody periods of persecution at the close of the fifteenth century. Some of his ancestors had been among the earliest explorers to the New World.

Nikolai had, in fact, recently received letters from the descendants of early seekers, eager to retrace their family lineage's, knowing that they came from New Christian stock. These people stated that they wanted to reclaim their Jewish ancestry; this was described in Spanish as *"La Sangre Hama"* (the blood is calling). They claimed to be scorned by Old Christian society and, for the most part, overlooked by Jewish history.

As Nikolai smiled at remembrance of the letters, Hershel raised his eyes from his pad and looked in Nikolai's direction, but did not acknowledge the man's his presence; instead, he went back to his writing. Hershel was totally absorbed in his own thoughts.

"So, this is the way men of vision get when they're thinking?" Nikolai joked, looking toward Hershel.

Avrum gave a disapproving frown. He did not answer; his angry look said it all.

Momentarily, Hershel looked up. Never at a loss for words, he possessed the interrogator's advantage of having all the time in the world to respond. "So, you want to play the comedian?"

Hershel ambled across the room, hands in pockets, reasoning out his thinking. "What we have is a major political power shift about to happen here. It is something that has to be immediately addressed, and here we are, as amateurs, trying to handle it. The die-hards will do their own thing in their own good time, which they feel it is their duty to do. Meantime, this situation is very complicated, it is sophisticated and geo-political, and in part it has become our responsibility to try to prevent. We are not equipped or qualified to play in this league, so let me take this situation down to the basics and get back to reality," he said.

"And, by the way, did I ever tell you what the negative side of this job is?" Hershel asked those in the room while angrily throwing down his papers. "You never get credit for your good work. You only get blamed for the screw-ups."

His outburst seemed to say they were damned no matter how their mission turned out. "Sorry for the outburst. I haven't gotten used to this exalted coordinator status yet," Hershel added sarcastically.

"Please don't overreact," said Nikolai. "Try to stick to what you want us to do to get this job done."

Hershel thought this was odd advice from a man who, along with the rest of the group, would shortly enter the lion's den with little chance of leaving alive.

Standing, Avrum suddenly waved his hand and gestured for Nikolai to follow him into the next room while Hershel, through the corner of his eye, was vaguely aware of them leaving. Hershel was relieved that Avrum had effectively ended the conversation by taking Nikolai out of the room. He got back to his planning pad and continued his work.

They all knew the serious risks they were running, even with the General's help. Even with this help, they could be playing right into the hands of the die-hards. Any degree of success would depend on their being as cautious as possible in their planning—covering all bases and being more brilliant in their coordinating and execution than they had ever been before.

"I know you just came in, Nikolai. It's late and you must be tired," Avrum said to the former Mossad external security officer and one-time member of his squad. "Let's go out for a little walk. It will help me digest my dinner and I can debrief you at the same time."

The two strolled along the almost deserted street. Neither spoke as their thoughts ranged through possible mistakes and errors in this operation. Each, in his own way, confronted the dangers and the possibilities.

While walking, Nikolai said, "I know how impossible the odds will be on us succeeding in this operation. But the way I'm dealing with it is to think to myself that this is not the time for any of us to be timid. It's time for us to be hard-nosed and hardheaded, we've got to approach this operation like the many wars we've fought for our country against vastly greater numbers of Arab attackers. Just as the odds were against us then, and we succeeded, the odds are against us now and we will again succeed!"

Avrum looked directly at Nikolai and thanked him for his words of courage. But by now his curiosity was aroused about something else. When he was sure they were not being followed and were out of earshot of any listening devices, he turned to Nikolai and asked for details on how he had carried out last night's assignment. The speed with which Avrum extracted all the detailed and relevant information of Nikolai's whereabouts and actions showed his many years of professional leadership.

"Did you get the driver to talk?"

"Naturally." Then Nikolai reflected, after a moment. "Your intuition was right on track when you felt there was something strange about him. The way he was somehow discreetly straining to listen to our conversations was one tip-off. Especially when he appeared not to know any English or Hebrew."

"Who was he working for, and what kind of logistical support system do they have?" Avrum questioned.

Clearing his throat, Nikolai referred to the driver as a red-diaper baby, an underling in the die-hard organization doing the dirty work of his superior. "I learned he was a relatively new member of an underground group. They are not like the KGB. They don't obey the tight rules of compartmentalization. His predecessors, the former KGB spymasters, were much more careful. Instead, they are organized in rather large groups, who are supported with unlimited quantities of jets and tanks from their Soviet, Chinese and even North Korean supporters," he added.

"I must tell you," Nikolai said in a more serious voice, "the big mistake the die-hards are making is that they get to know one another too well. Not only that, but they have to rely on still other civilians for support. That leaves them with too many people to depend on for a well-planned secret conspiracy. I suspect they may also not have been able to recruit many of the top, high-ranking members from the former KGB. Most of the smart KGB people figured out a way to cash in on their contacts and are now making big money in the corrupt economic system that has developed here. It's who you know and what kind of muscle you control that counts in this new system of Russian economics. It's a cross between the Wild West and Beirut.

"Another probability is that their codes and communications systems are a bit antiquated because they have not had time to develop new ones, so it may not be too difficult to intercept their messages. But the actions of the driver has me convinced that the hard-line Communists are prepared to sacrifice themselves in order to achieve their goals. We have to consider the fact that the Russians have had some hard lessons during World War II. After having lost twenty million Russians, the die-hards are probably a lot more dedicated and fanatical than we may think they are."

Nikolai paused for a moment, then went on. "The important thing I learned from the driver—before he unfortunately passed away—was the name and location of his contact."

Avrum simply nodded. He did not ask for the details, because he was certain Nikolai would offer them anyway.

"Well," Nikolai said, "I asked the driver to drive to a remote side street in the red-light district. He seemed grateful that he would not have to be driving for too long. He headed the car down one of those dimly lit streets. There, on the left, along the closed stores that run along the street, he told me, was the prime spot for the Russian hooker scene.

"He pulled up behind a black Volga and shut off the noisy engine. And there they were, all dressed up with elaborate earrings accenting their faces and wearing tight mini-skirts. What bodies!" Nikolai's momentary longing came from knowing that he would probably never enjoy their company.

Now he smiled, pondering with satisfaction over how the driver asked whether he could light a cigarette while he waited for him.

"I agreed that it was perfectly O.K.," Nikolai continued, "and when he blew a plume of cigarette smoke toward the ceiling of the car I leaned forward and in a split second had a thin wire around his neck. He looked up in astonishment through the rearview mirror, as he tried to reach the door handle. I could see his face flush and he cried out, 'Don't, don't!' That is when he dropped the cigarette on the seat.

"I told him that if anyone was following us I would kill him on the spot, and then kill whoever was in the other car. I didn't give a shit. I had nothing to lose. I told him I'd kill anybody. 'So cooperate and follow my instructions,' I ordered.

"At first I left some wiggle room in the wire, and then the driver tried unsuccessfully to get his fingers under it."

Aware that Avrum was waiting for him to continue with the gory details, he said, "I just kept pounding him with questions that he felt obliged at that moment to answer. 'This hard-line Communist movement is a crusade with you and your friends, isn't it?' I asked.

"'That's right,' the driver said, 'and you and your capitalist friends can all go to hell.'

"'I will soon enough,' I responded to his suggestion, 'but not with your help.' Then I told him, 'So let's stop playing games here and tell me all you know about your hard-line friends and the name of your superior. Who can I get to sponsor me into your group? I know in the position I have placed you it is hard to believe, but I too want to become a hard-liner! I don't have much time, so speak up if you have any desire to continue living.'

"'Things like this just don't happen,' the driver said.

"'You're the best witness that they really do,' I told him.

"'Pray,' I suggested.

"'I'll pray,' he agreed.

"But he did not really put his trust in providence, Avrum.

"'Okay, okay,' he said, and he continued to get his fingers under the wire. He smacked his lips, took two gulps and began singing like a bird for almost fifteen minutes, in the hope he could work out a deal with us and be allowed to live."

Avrum didn't need all the details. He knew how Nikolai operated.

"Is that it?" he asked.

"Hell, yes! I felt that I had gotten all the possible information from him, including the name and address of his group leader, who I think will prove to be an insignificant underling in a long chain of command. I told him that I was sorry, but my buyout offer had been canceled. I had no choice. Anyway, he confirmed what you surmised. I made him recite his entire story twice. The second time around he enlarged upon his importance in the organization.

"He was among those who were planning to revive the old Soviet Union and bring their Russian comrades back into power. He was only a small fry, but still a considerable danger to us. Regardless of my prodding, at his level he had no knowledge about how the group leaders would accomplish their long-planned overthrow and takeover."

Avrum stood in silence for a moment, looking at the ground.

Nikolai gazed at Avrum and then said, "I never gave him a guarantee. And before I left, I placed his head against the top of the headrest, like he was catching a catnap. I pushed the lids of his eyes shut and removed the wire from around his neck."

There was a brief silence, after which Avrum replied, "I've heard enough, for now. We'd better move to a safer location."

As Avrum and Nikolai turned to walk back to the safe house, a group of young Russians with bright kerchiefs around their necks walked past them singing an old Communist Party song in a sad, mocking tone, urging others to be ready for the call of the new Communist Party. "After tomorrow, there will only be the future," they sang out.

"If they truly believe in what they are singing," Nikolai asked, "I wonder why they are not happier?"

Chapter Fifteen

FAMILY ROOM, SAFE HOUSE TWO

OCTOBER 21

The skies were overcast as Yossi Steckel and Yaakov Vigdor were greeted at the railroad station by Nikolai with big bear hugs.

"This town is really a bloody awful place in weather like this." Nikolai's mouth was locked in a frown, as he gave the two a quick rundown on the die-hard problem. "Avrum will give you the details once we reach the safe house," he added.

"Really? Just like a long time ago, eh?"

Nikolai's thin eyebrows pinched in the center. "The same, but a lot more technical," he said as he made himself comfortable in the car's driver's seat. Nikolai had been Yossi and Yaakov's case worker when they served under him in the Mossad, but always treated them more like their uncle.

Nikolai let out the clutch too fast and the car leaped forward as he began driving, by a circuitous route, to the new safe house, a squat, ugly building that would hopefully be more secure then their last residence.

"Typical Israeli driver," Yossi laughed, as Nikolai pulled into a darkened alleyway before the car crunched to a sudden stop against the curb.

From the dark street they could see the shadows of figures behind drawn shades moving about inside. The compact disc player featured a Rachmaninoff concerto with the volume cranked up—to cover the sounds of conversation in the room.

"Avrum, I could use a drink after that lousy trip," Yossi said after they exchanged greetings.

"How about some orange juice, coffee, hot croissants, with butter and jelly?

"Do you know something I don't? How did you find that stuff here, or is that a state secret?"

"You have to be resourceful, politically connected and know the right people," Avrum confessed.

"I'll decline all the delicacies, I'd better just have that drink. You owe me one anyway."

"A damned sinner, right to the end, aren't you?" Avrum said jokingly. He mixed Yossi a vodka on the rocks and Yaakov a club soda, in some used jelly jars. "Unusual serving pieces, but there is a shortage of glasses....At ease, gentlemen, this is completely informal." He pointed toward the chairs. "Please sit down, take a load off."

Yaakov pulled out a pack of cigarettes. "Smoke, Avrum?"

"Thank you, maybe later."

Avrum sat back to ponder the evening's revelations and to meditate on their present circumstances. The world he had previously thought had a chance of becoming orderly had suddenly begun to disintegrate around them. Perhaps there was still some chance to repair it before it completely tumbled down into a hopeless heap of rubble.

They drank slowly and waited for Avrum to begin while he fiddled with some papers in a folder, as if uncertain where to start.

"Hershel, I wonder if you would begin briefing Yossi and Yaakov?"

Hershel stared at him for a moment, then took a deep breath. "While we have been trained to work in secrecy, our big problem today is that we still have to continue working in secret. We have reached the very limit of our secrecy potential, my friends, and beyond that limit I only see vulnerability and weakness." He then thought out loud: "Look what happened to Yoel. He died in secret with our secrets. If we could just stand up and announce to the world what we realize is about to happen, we'd all probably be safer. As far as I can see, secrecy is killing us—one at a time."

Hershel's gaze was steady as a marksman's. "But I guess we can only do what is possible, given the terrible circumstances. So let's push on."

The two newcomers watched it all going through his head: the mixed emotions, and the struggle to understand the consequences of many problems.

"I always lend credence to the saying that wherever there's smoke there must be a fire," he began. "What I see here is a five-alarm fire. We can't be sure that the data we are receiving is all that accurate, but even if only part is true, what other choice do we have?" He sighed.

"I am not predicting that a devastating event will happen, with certainty. I'm saying, however, that it is only a matter of time before a crippling event will take place that may threaten the safety of most nations."

The two, as well as Avrum and Nikolai, listened intently for an hour. Hershel spoke without interruption, reading from the notes he had pieced together from scraps of information accumulated over the past several days. After this meeting all of the written notes, memos, pictures and sketches would be burned in a kitchen pot and the ashes washed down the sink.

Hershel stood and paced the floor in silence for a moment, then stopped. Again he turned to face the small group before continuing. "First of all, you are well aware that the nuclear and missile threat remains serious enough for the Russians and Americans to continue pushing for more joint disarmament meetings. They want to discuss a joint ballistic missile defense system. The idea may be great theory, but in practice it will never work."

"Things couldn't be all that bad," Yossi interjected.

"Bad enough," Hershel shot back. "It simply makes sense to me that the die-hards have control of Russian missiles and missile components, and are discreetly hiding the fact until it's time to reassemble and launch them. Or as an alternate possibility, they may already have fully assembled long-range missiles secretly deployed in hidden locations."

"I hope you have at least some *good* news for us to take the edge off this bad stuff." Yossi said, trying to lighten the tension that was building.

"I've got lousy news for you," Hershel replied. "The task of tracking down the missiles will be almost impossible for us, given our lack of time and resources. But there are other things to consider. For one, it is general knowledge that Russia has in excess of three hundred SS-18 intercontinental ballistic missiles, with A-10 warheads, and that they are engineered for a range of 6800 miles. They are considered particularly dangerous because of their accuracy and explosive power. I recently heard that the ethnic Armenian enclave of Nagorno-Karabakh, which is inside Azerbaijan, is a possible hiding place for such weapons."

Hershel continued to make his point by describing how the corpses that would result from an attack would be quickly burnt by the nuclear explosions, while terrified and hysterical crowds kneeled in any underground shelters they could find.

"A war of this kind would have an extremely high mortality rate, in addition to the terror and chaos it would cause. If that's not bad enough, there is considerable talk among the die-hards about their biochemical manufacturing factories with their own complete support facilities. They are presently involved in advanced chemical weaponry that Western scientists are not yet trained to handle. To me, it is evident that General Chervok and his followers need all the help they can get."

By now it was not needed, but Hershel continued to explain the significance of their joint plan of attack, because if they did not act soon there was a very high likelihood of mass carnage and chaos. The formers had to take immediate action if there was going to be any hope of stopping the Russian terrorists.

"We'll understand if you have any comments or questions on this rather unbelievable information, gentlemen," Avrum interrupted.

"We get the picture, Hershel," Yaakov said. "Loud and clear. Please go on."

"Fair enough," Hershel replied as he leaned forward in his chair to explain the plan to the others in his soft voice.

"We are at war and no one knows it! And quite frankly, who else can we turn to, if not our friends? Is there anyone out there who would even believe something like this could happen? Or who could we turn to and rely upon in full trust, confident that they would keep our plans from leaking out? Today it seems to me that just about anyone would spill his guts to either his colleagues for political gain, or to the news media for a quick profit. The way the U.S. and British tabloids operate, this sort of a story would be worth big bucks to anyone who had the info to leak. That would preempt an attack, wouldn't it?" he added sarcastically.

Hershel's voice became strained and muffled. He reached for a glass of water and took a sip.

"Tell me, Yossi and Yaakov, are there any former Mossad friends that you're aware of operating out of a station somewhere close by, who might help us?"

Not expecting immediate answers, Hershel continued after a short pause: "If we develop a good plan to counter the terrorists and take action quickly enough for it to be a surprise, we should score a momentary victory for our side before we go forward to knock them out completely. But there are no guarantees. We may be damned to failure when we move against the die-hards, or we may be left helpless and accountable for the ugly consequences if we don't."

"Is there anything we can do right now, Hershel?" Yaakov inquired. "What do you want us to help you with?"

"Nothing for the moment," Hershel told him. "We have to play it smart and gather more hard information—until we get the complete picture together."

"Understood. I don't think your assessments of the dangers ahead can get any worse."

"It's a long story," Hershel interjected. A complete plan to counteract the Communist plot was not easy to develop or summarize to the formers. "And in order to be successful we must fully understand their motivations."

"You have the information, we'll make the time for you to educate us," Avrum assured him.

"As I see it," Hershel went on, "the political essence of the Russian problem appears to be an ongoing difference of opinion between some of the Russian military and the civilian population. The problem is an old one—it stems from way back."

"Yes, I agree," Avrum said. "We know that Russia probably possesses the best history of revolutionary experience in the world. And we all know that revolutionary training, like ordinary military training, is nothing more then the institutional memory of past lessons. For instance," he said, pointing at Yaakov, "your formal training came from those who were more experienced, enabling you to learn from the mistakes of others."

Yaakov, trying to be funny, said, "I guess that must be the reason I rarely make a mistake."

Hershel sighed, not only because of Yaakov's joke, but because of the numerous problems facing him. "The first thing we have to examine are the issues behind the situation here, which are far from settled in my mind. The real economic problems in Russia will take many years—possibly decades—to rectify. Consequently, the different and varied plots that may be going on undercover will also take some time to extinguish."

Again Hershel paused to look down at his notes on the yellow lined pad. "We know that already," Nikolai said with an impatient gesture of the hand.

Hershel raised his eyes and looked at the ceiling in deep thought. "In view of the economic and political realities now facing the C.I.S., I suggest that we are witnessing ongoing not-so-subtle changes that even the Russian military does not fully understand. If I am not mistaken and if my memory is not failing, it was Commonwealth Commander-in-Chief

Yevgeny Shaposhnikov who announced in June that the last nuclear weapons from the Black Sea fleet had been moved away earlier this month. But in reality, there is no true accounting to anyone that each and every one of these weapons has actually been moved. And for those that were moved—under whose control are they presently?

"Today, with all the deep political division we are seeing in Russia, who would even be aware if a few loose strategic long-range missiles disappeared? And if they do get sold to the forces out there looking for this doomsday weaponry, the buyers will be in a position to create unimaginable terror in a world that is unprepared for it."

"What do these disgruntled Communists really expect to accomplish with these weapons?" Yaakov interrupted.

"Well, it still appears to me that the old Communist guard is simply trying to regain its former status and control. The guard's young Communist commissars are ambitious and anxious to cooperate with their former leaders. At a moment's notice, the Generals of their movement could unpredictably put their finger on the nuclear launch button."

Hershel would never have permitted his imagination or his tongue to wander into such dangerous territory without understanding that there had been a confirmed "black operation" in progress, probably from the first day of the new Russian democracy.

He continued: "We also know from what General Chervok told us that there are only long-range plans to take the twelve-story SS-18 and -19 missiles out of service. Some of them are being cannibalized, or used in part for firing non-nuclear payloads into space. However, to me it is only logical that it is impossible for the C.I.S. to pay the tens of billions of dollars it will take for a complete dismantling of the intercontinental ballistic missile system."

Avrum put a fingertip to his pursed lips and pondered a moment, frowning. "We could never be lucky enough to catch the die-hards with their pants down," he said, breaking into his first smile of the evening. "Or to learn where the rogue warheads and missiles may be hidden...without some inside help."

"Agreed," Nikolai interjected, "and the only one who might possibly help us in locating these missiles is our new 'friend,' General Chervok."

Hershel nodded, understanding Nikolai's "friend" implication. "He must know that it will probably pose great personal danger for him and his family if he assists us in locating them. But he agreed to help, so why should we worry?"

He felt the cool glance of the group on him. "Well, I mean, if you want us to play smart, then I've got to have smart backup. And I need the people to supply it. What I mean is, there is no purpose in buying the latest television and shoving the plug under the rug if you haven't got a real electrical outlet to plug it into, is there?"

"I agree, Hershel," Avrum said. "Nevertheless, we will have to use our best charm and stealth, even if we have to do a lot of arm twisting. And we'll have to watch to see that there isn't a double cross at the end. I just can't bring myself to trust the man, for some reason."

For a moment Hershel's expression did not change. His voice remained deliberate, calm, and had a soothing quality—even though deep down he felt he was becoming a bit unnerved by the pressure to come up with a successful plan.

"In my research," he said, "I came across a number of incidents I simply cannot explain. And I never did enjoy engaging in reckless speculation."

Avrum smiled. "For you, that's not unusual. Can you please be specific."

Hershel looked up, startled to find Avrum standing directly over him, studying him, his face looking at him with concern.

"You know full well that I have no hard proof," Hershel replied, "just a lot of circumstantial evidence. There is nothing in writing to prove a massive conspiracy designed to manipulate Russian scientists and other anti-Communist biochemical warfare specialists," he said, closing the cover of his notes.

"However, very strange coincidences have bothered me for some time. At first I thought it was just my imagination, but you will see why it is impossible to avoid the awful truth. For instance, someone or some group have been killing the leading C.I.S. scholars and biochemical experts—those who were most likely to be possible enemies of the diehard movement."

Avrum pushed his chair back as if he meant to collapse into it. "For God's sake!"

"Sorry I have to confront you with what I had learned in my research before we had met, but facts are facts. As I dug deeper, a pattern started to emerge. Initially, I attributed the premature and accidental deaths of so many bioengineering experts to carelessness, bad luck or coincidence. After all, there was nothing to suggest foul play in the copies of the death certificates that our good friend the General obtained at my request."

Hershel leaned forward and handed the certificates to Avrum. "Look here, these are all those who have died at a very young age, of cardiac arrest. Here are eight more, working in the same laboratory, who have died of stroke—again much too young. And look at these, all mutual friends, working in the same laboratory, who lost their lives from pneumonia and so on."

"I can see this is not simply curiosity on your part, Hershel. Is it an obsession? Why all the investigative interest? Aren't you getting just a little off track?" Avrum half whispered.

"No! Not at all! I believe all of these scientists were murdered by the die-hards, or a similar group, for reasons that must have been well worth their while. What those reasons are is still questionable. But the General did cooperate by getting the names and addresses of the next of kin of the deceased for me to interview. He also had some bodies secretly exhumed and autopsied. Here are the results of one autopsy report," he said,, holding out some papers in his hand.

"They indicate that there is an extremely high probability that this person was killed by means of a nerve agent, a DMSO mixture. DMSO, is known to be given to arthritis suffers. However, when mixed with VX, the properties of the VX-DMSO mixture are absorbed into the skin and it only takes a short time for the victim to die. After interviewing the family and learning the work habits of the victim, I assume the DMSO compound was probably smeared on a surface as simple as the knob of his lab door as he left work. The police report states that as he walked down the cast-iron stairs to leave the building he blacked out, struck his head and died in the fall. The report gives no further reasoning or medical cause for his blacking out."

Avrum leaned forward as a signal that he wanted to learn more of what Hershel knew. Hershel went on: "I personally spoke with the widow of another scientist who was in her apartment when the doorbell rang. As her husband answered the door, from the kitchen she caught a glimpse of a person in the doorway holding a child's water pistol. The person suddenly began squirting a liquid into her husband's face. He collapsed to the floor and was dead in a matter of moments. The medical examiner attributed his death to respiratory failure. The police never found a clue of the perpetrator.

"And this death report of a Dr. Zvansky shows that he died of a coronary while in his laboratory. The General had his body exhumed for me, and had an autopsy performed by a leading pathologist which showed that prussic acid, a blood gas toxin, was found in the doctor's tissues. It caused rapid paralysis of the brain's respiratory center, and death followed within minutes. After we checked with his wife, we learned that she picked up his personal effects from the office, put them into a box and kept them at home. I asked the General to have these personal items checked out, and the chemist he hired found the telltale sign of the toxin in the shaving cream soap that the doctor used."

Hershel paused, but only to sip some water from a glass that he had poured from a plastic bottle.

"In another autopsy, a tiny flechette was found in the back of an anti-Communist biochemist which contained saxitoxin, a shellfish toxin. This was a known KGB favorite among toxins that had been used for many years."

"So who do we go after at KGB headquarters—and when?" Nikolai asked.

"The day of reckoning will come soon enough," Hershel answered. "You know if a child doesn't cry, how is the mother to know when he is hungry?" He made this comment in reference to the possibility of using the General's contacts to somehow publicize these murders, and linking them to the existence of the die-hards. "A man like Zavaskayev has to have more than one plan up his sleeve. Keep an eye on him. Let's see what he is up to! We can always get rid of him later. Stalin taught us that," he added with a grin.

"Hershel," said Avrum, "you are saying that the die-hards are systematically killing those scientists who refuse to cooperate with the die-hards' cause?"

"Absolutely. In doing so they eliminate those who understand too well the policies and true intent of the die-hard cause—which includes their plans to take over control of Russia. In addition, by killing these selected scientists, almost no one will be around to countermand what will happen during the retaliation period. And who will be around to develop and disperse anti-toxins or other preventive measures? The people involved in this plot know all about viruses. They are sophisticated spies and killers."

Avrum laid down the medical reports and confronted Hershel directly. "This is the type of plot that spy novels are made of! I would like to believe that this could not happen in the real world today, when everyone thinks peace and *Glasnost* is here to stay," he said. "But the die-hards know they can buy or can simply take anything they need at will—

because of the high level of their contacts and special connections in the still-corrupt Russian government." But Avrum knew full well that Hershel was not imagining what he said. Too many pieces of this puzzle were falling into place.

"We can't lose track of the fact that we are in a country that does not favor our kind," said Hershel, "especially if they ever caught on that we were aware of this plot. Our personal security is constantly at risk." And Hershel recognized the importance of something else: "I suggest that we must go ahead with the next meeting, as planned, with the General," he said. "If we intend to cooperate and have any influence on the General's thinking, we should disclose some of our analysis and conclusions so that he recognizes how helpful we can be. This is the only way to ensure that we remain in the loop on additional information he may have."

"I'm in agreement with you on that," Avrum said, picking up the loose autopsy reports from the living room coffee table and handing them back to Hershel. "I'm sorry that the General is going to have the added risk of further meetings and information exchanges with us, but most likely he knows this. We won't have to convince him to continue helping us and himself," Avrum added. "The alarm has sounded to wake us all up!"

He placed his hands on the arms of his chair as if he was about to stand up.

"Hold on a minute," Hershel said, and Avrum allowed himself to drop back into the chair. "Talk about waking up! I feel that it is time I sent this long-overdue memo that I prepared to headquarters. I have been hesitating for a while, but I think the information is now very timely."

Hershel extended the paper for Avrum to take from his outstretched hand. Avrum raised his head, and his eyes darted from Hershel to the paper and back again without his saying a word.

Hershel continued: "From experience, we know that the enemy is always going to experiment in developing new tactics and methods in every field of combat. Such information in regard to infrastructures rarely comes to light. The only entity that I believe we should release the information to is the Mossad."

Avrum opened the paper and read:

To: Head of Mossad, London Station / Confidential /
for eyes only, OPS Tel Aviv.
Classification: Urgent.

Subject: Information Assurance and Operations.

Suggestion in Basic for Official Use Tel Aviv H.Q.

1.   Because of recent discovery, it is suggested that you take under immediate advisement potential serious threat of electronic incursion to your existing electronic infrastructure.
2.   Transmits of your military electronic communications traffic could potentially be disrupted and degraded, including your routings for communications carriers.
3.   Suggest you implement immediate measures to assure your integrity, authentication, confidentiality and non-repudiation, including protection, detection and reaction capabilities.

Best regards, Former Section 04.

Avrum took another moment to read the communiqué a second time. "It does look sufficiently serious for me to have it sent right off," he said. "Do you mind if I ask more details about these potential intrusions?"

"Sure, go ahead and ask," Hershel said with a smile.

Avrum's eyes widened. "Don't shit me," he laughed.

"First of all, for security purposes I feel that it's important that this not be directly routed to Tel Aviv or be traceable back to us in this country," Hershel added. "As you know, I have for years studied the parameters for national information assurance and operations. I just never got around to writing up a comprehensive report on this subject before retiring. With all of this additional information furnished by the General, it is now the time to tell the right people in Israel that their stability—their economic, political and military interests—are dependant on 'secure' reliable information infrastructures. This, in my opinion, must be defended at all costs against what the die-hards are now capable of doing to us."

Hershel turned and directly faced Avrum. "Think about it," he said. "I call the threat a study in Nanosecond Sorties, in which I anticipate that potential war in the information age will be brutally quick. Destruction of command, control and information systems will be successfully accomplished by potential attacks taking 'nanoseconds,' followed within seconds by secondary information fallout—which could severely damage an enemy's critical information infrastructures. Israel's timelines to react will be measured in fractions of a second for information transfer, compared with the minutes a nation has to react to a ballistic missile launch."

"The information on this critical area definitely needs the Institute's attention. Consider it done as you suggested," Avrum acknowledged.

One by one, the men slowly rose to their feet. "How about a fresh cup of my good coffee, Hershel," said Avrum, as he draped his arm around his old friend and walked him toward the kitchen.

"You, you want to do me a *mitzvot* (favor) and make the coffee? I might as well say my *shema* (prayer to God) now! No thanks, Mother. I'd rather make the coffee myself!"

Hershel walked on, into the kitchen.

Calmly, Avrum began to speak in a voice filled with remorse. "'And there were voices, and thunders and lightenings, and there was a great earthquake—so mighty an earthquake, and so great. And the cities of the nations fell. Come Armageddon.'"

Avrum eloquently expressed the mood of all who were in the safe house.

Chapter Sixteen

THE KUZNETSKY CAFE

OCTOBER 22 & 23

Just after six, the first light began to seep through the shades. Rain was striking the window pane, slowly at first, then quickly developing into a solid, drenching downpour. Hershel dreaded the thought of going out in the rain as he crouched under the heavy quilts, arms folded, hands tucked under his armpits to conserve his body heat from the early-morning cold. By God, he thought, Russia is a bloody awful place in weather like this.

Realizing it was late, however, he raced into the bathroom. After a quick shower and shave he hurriedly went to his bureau drawers and whipped out a freshly laundered shirt, underwear and socks. Unfolding the shirt, he carefully slipped it on over his shoulders and buttoned it. Next came the underwear and socks. He ran back to the closet, yanked out a pair of woolen trousers, pulled them up in a hurry and returned to the bureau for his wallet, change, money clip and wristwatch.

Taking some fifteen steps, he was at the old stove, where he proceeded to heat up the remnants of last night's coffee. Then, from the refrigerator, he removed two sandwiches wrapped in waxed paper. Even though he knew that he would not look like an ad in *GQ Magazine,* he took the time to look in the mirror above the kitchen sink and slightly nod his head, approving of his profile and close shave.

It was not long before Avrum, his face impassive, joined Hershel from an adjoining bedroom for his customary morning glass of piping-hot tea.

After a few sips, Avrum rose, went to the dining-room highboy and opened a drawer that revealed two .09 caliber Beretta automatics with the safety catches in the "on" position and a number of spare clips. "Here is one that looks like it fits you, Hershel," he said, placing the gun and three clips on the kitchen table.

"I hope I don't have to resort to using it," Hershel said as he snapped one clip into the gun and put the other two in his jacket pocket. Then he pushed his half-empty cup of stale coffee to one side of the kitchen table to give himself more room to attack and sort the papers he was compiling for his report.

Mumbling his thoughts aloud, Hershel said, "How in the world can I concentrate on a statistical report in a country where you don't know whom you can trust and where you can't get a decent cup of American coffee? I think we all know that the Russian bear is not simply in hibernation; rather, it is waiting, waiting for a good poke from some fire-breathing nationalist like Vladimir Zhirinovsky to come roaring back with some new expansionist campaign."

Squinting at Hershel, Avrum lowered his glass of tea and said in husky whisper, "We already know all of that, but we also know for a fact that you are better with this intelligence game than the great Houdini was with his magic. The only question I ask is: Will we have a fair shot at developing a strategy for defusing the die-hards before they get an unfair shot at us?"

Hershel winced. "Listen now, Avrum. Even the Great Houdini had his faults, and that's what did him in."

As he flipped an invisible coin with his thumb, Avrum replied, "Mistakes are always a real danger. But I think what we are attempting is a gamble worth taking, and we of course know it could go either way. It's not like we have much of a choice, anyway."

Avrum observed Hershel for a few moments. They were still at the straw-grasping stage. Hershel's eyes were fixed on his notes. His face scowled as he blurted out, "I now know what Jonah must have felt like in the belly of the whale." Hershel never enjoyed the stress of deadlines—they were something that he constantly struggled with. And he hated life or death missions even more then deadlines. "I hope I have the opportunity and the time to question General Chervok about all those Cold War years while he is vertical and sober. If possible, I would prefer to take him on *alone*, with just Nikolai running a 'wire.' I'm willing to bet anything that the General knows a lot more than he has told us. Once he's more comfortable with us, I bet he'll tell us more."

"Russian spying is returning to Cold War levels," Avrum replied. "Moscow's foreign intelligence is returning in strength to its classic methods of spying and intelligence gathering, such as cultivating contacts. And Russian agents are still carrying out a disproportionate amount of activities in Europe. In particular they're involved in those nations belonging to NATO. The Russians are even being assisted by Poland's die-hard Communists, who, although much weaker, have the same goals of recapturing their lost power and glory.

"At this time we have to be alert for those two million or so still employed in the KGB's network. With all of Russia's financial problems, it's interesting how they manage to come up with the salaries for their KGB employees and informants—ahead of everyone else even the military is complaining that they have not been paid for months. Most of the Russian intelligence community feel they have to justify their existence now more than ever."

Moments later, Avrum left the room to set up the appointment for Hershel's proposed new meeting with the General.

The next day was overcast, with light snow flurries, as Hershel left the safe house with Nikolai and they headed for their car.

As they walked, Hershel pulled the collar of his overcoat up around his neck, then wound his muffler around the outside of his collar. He lowered the flaps of his astrakhan hat over his ears, then flailed his arms against his sides to help him settle comfortably into the heavy clothing. Waiting for him to bundle up, Nikolai said, "It is so cold out here that if you spit it'll freeze before it hits the ground."

Where the car was parked, Hershel exhaled a lungful of air and watched the heavy vapor billow in front of his face.

"We will have to stop for a few liters of gas," Nikolai said. "I can't keep too much in the tank at any one time since it is constantly being siphoned out to be sold on the black market. Every morning I have to buy the same gas back that was probably siphoned from my tank during the previous night."

Hershel yanked the passenger-side door open as Nikolai slid behind the wheel. The engine of the ice-covered car sputtered to life after the third try. Gunning the motor, Nikolai turned on the heater and defroster before shifting the grinding gears. Then he cautiously steered the tired old car out of its tight parking place.

Hershel stole a glance at Nikolai's frozen cheek muscles, straining as he struggled to keep the car's steering under control. Almost shouting so that Nikolai could hear him over the roar of the car's overused heater, operating at full blast, Hershel said, "I must admit that I'm really sorry about getting you out on a day like this."

Nikolai, surprised, simply nodded; he hadn't expected Hershel to make such a comment. Hershel casually nodded in return. "I will make a good cup of coffee for us when we get back home."

"It's a deal," Nikolai said eagerly as he moved the steering wheel abruptly to avoid a large pothole, dug up the previous day by workmen and left unfinished without any warning signs. A few more blocks and Nikolai was finally able to find a parking place on Dubrovski Street, near the small cafe where their meeting was to take place. A blast of cold arctic air hit them upon leaving the car.

As Nikolai and Hershel entered the café, a haze of unpleasant, stale smoke drifted toward them. Numerous paintings were hung high on the wall—too high, so that one could hardly notice them, as was the custom in Russia. Some tables had half pitchers of pale beer, glass mugs of a hot red wine and plates of thin liverwurst sandwiches cut into small pieces. Some patrons had their fingers wrapped around glasses of red wine to keep them warm.

Hershel and Nikolai unbuttoned their coats and looked around the room for some sign of the General. Hershel watched a small man walk slowly toward them while reaching into the pocket of his jacket. Out of the corner of his eye he could see Nikolai immediately react by reaching inside his jacket, wrapping his hand around his automatic weapon and even preparing to draw on the approaching stranger to blow him away. Hershel knew instinctively that as soon as Nikolai saw a gun, he would fire.

Instead, the stranger pulled out some tobacco and paper, and began to roll a thin cigarette. Hershel was relieved that his expected scenario never happened, and chuckled at the fascinating speed and dexterity with which the man was able to deftly roll the cigarette while looking elsewhere. The man licked the paper closed and struck a match, holding it to the tip of the cigarette as he had probably done a thousand times before. Hershel could see this from the telltale sign of tobacco stains on his fingers.

When he got close enough, the Russian spoke in a flat voice. "Follow me."

A general cry of laughter went up from the far end of the bar, and Hershel shifted his sights to four Russian men and their girls, the latter perched on high stools. They're too drunk for their own good, he decided. Several empty vodka bottles lined the bar.

Pushing through the main room of the restaurant, the trio carefully walked past the boisterous drunks, entered a small private dining room through a pair of doors and scanned the room for the General. The lighting was subdued, and it took a few moments before Hershel and Nikolai could spot Chervok sitting alone at a table in the far corner of the empty room. The General, a widower, was past the age when he actively craved female company.

Two scurrying waiters in white shirts and black trousers carried trays heaped with steaming blintzes, potatoes, bowls of sour cream and two bottles of vodka to the table. The waiters completed four place settings, added two more chairs and closed the double doors as they left the room.

Hershel took a quick look at the General, who immediately waved his hand at the empty chairs, indicating for them to sit. He did not rise to shake their hands or offer any other manner of welcome. His beady eyes blazed with interest as he turned toward Nikolai. He smiled and shook his head, as if he were trying to remember some damned Russian tune. He couldn't shake his thought out, before saying, "I detected, the last time we met, that you spoke Russian with a peculiar kind of accent."

Nikolai replied tersely, "I am not Russian, I am an Israeli who came here to help those Russians who wish to emigrate to the 'promised land' of Israel."

"If you ask me," the General said after he sucked his Marlboro back to life, "America, not Israel should be considered as the promised land"; and with that bit of wisdom he loosened up and began laughing.

"The world is a jungle," the General went on. "Not all creatures can survive without food, and you're looking at one of them. How would a proper Western lunch suit you?"

Hershel smiled. "Fine with me. But…all of this food on the table?" he asked.

"These are just appetizers. Have a few and then we'll head off to my dacha!" The three men all nibbled on the blintzes, washed them down with vodka and a half hour later rose and ambled out of the café.

Nikolai and Hershel followed in their car as the General and his driver led the way. After about twenty minutes, they arrived at the dacha's driveway, a twisting gravel path that led them slowly through a grove of tall trees. The property was protected by a fieldstone wall with wrought-iron fencing above the stone.

Hershel was instantly energized. He felt that something big was about to happen.

Chapter Seventeen

THE PROMISED LAND

OCTOBER 23

General Ivan Chervok, as Hershel had discovered, was the reputable Russian official Yoel Melman had been in contact with before he was killed. With any luck Hershel's second face-to-face meeting would lead him to other prime sources of information. Co-managing an international mission such as this one would have contributed a major notch in his record if Hershel had still been with the Mossad.

As the General, with the two Israelis, sat comfortably, the living room's double doors burst open suddenly, however, and a stranger in a heavy overcoat entered the room. Hershel's natural reaction was to feel for the gun in his pocket, which Avrum had thoughtfully provided.

As he looked toward the always alert Nikolai for his lead, he noticed that his friend was already backed against the wall, his hand under his jacket, ready to draw and go into a half-crouch, if he had to pull the gun from its holster. His reaction attested to the complexities encountered when an ex-patriot intervenes in an unstable area, even for the most well-intentioned reasons.

"Gentlemen! Gentlemen! Relax, please!" the General exclaimed, jumping to his feet. "This man is also my guest—and trusted friend."

But for Nikolai, the entrance of the stranger was sudden—too sudden for comfort. He continued to watch both the General's and the stranger's faces for any sudden, aggressive moves. He looked into their eyes, noted the muscles of their jaws. This is what he had been trained for by the Mossad. He was determined not to make the mistake of trusting someone who would put his life in jeopardy, especially given what happened to Yoel.

Without an introduction or a word said, the stranger began struggling to remove his overcoat while holding his hat under one arm and his briefcase in the other hand. It was almost like watching a comedy act on television in which the comedian struggles heroically with a coat that refuses to be removed from his body.

The stranger, who seemed like the proverbial absent-minded professor, finally figured out that the only solution to his dilemma was to empty his hands before removing the coat. When it was obvious that this was not an act and that the stranger appeared essentially harmless, Nikolai began to relax somewhat.

But not Hershel. He was like an alley cat. In fact, he had been told many times that he could have made a good second-story man. His cat-like intuition told him that perhaps this day would prove to be one of the luckier ones for the formers. Why else would Chervok have agreed to meet them here if it were not to supply them with additional information? For Hershel, this mission was turning into one of those search-and-seize operations he had studied and participated in on some earlier missions. He continued to watch the newcomer anxiously.

"Before we get started, how about some good Guatemalan coffee?" the General offered, as he reached for a pitcher.

Hershel could see that Chervok wanted to put them at ease. It seemed that he was finally about to cement a permanent alliance by giving them some hard information, and while Hershel wanted that coffee badly, he did not want to delay the info for fear the can of worms would not be opened.

The stranger gulped a loud sip of black coffee, collapsed into a chair and took an unusually long, deep breath before relaxing.

The General wasted no time in making an impression. "There are many ways to die, and we of the military have had centuries to ponder them all," he said like an impresario. His eyes were moving to the others in the room collecting their reactions.

Hershel thought the General must have been well schooled in theatrics before joining the military.

"Gentlemen," the General continued, "I would like to introduce you to my close friend Pyotr Berganov, a former Soviet Health Minister, who for openers will speak to you about politics, medicine and warfare—a strange combination indeed, I must admit. But that is why you are here today as our associates, about to be entrusted with our thoughts and *hard*...information," he said in a gruff voice.

"Our confidence in you," he continued, "is largely due to the considerable data we have collected on your backgrounds. Before you ask, I was able to check on you and your activities while in the Mossad through our few remaining contacts in the KGB. Because you are in the right place at the right time, along with our feeling of your sincerity in helping us overcome a potential nightmare in Russia, we have unanimously agreed to work with you.

Get to the point. Get to the point already! Hershel thought to himself.

As an introduction to Berganov to speak, the General held his hand out in the man's direction with his palm up. Slowly, Berganov began.

"Gentlemen, the nightmare scenario which General Chervok refers to is not the discharge of the world's most lethal weapons, such as fissioning uranium or conventional bombs. The intelligence gathered here," Berganov hesitated, pointing to his briefcase, "is as conclusive as any evidence can be. There are reports contained in here of a potential chemical and germ warfare attack. Our small group of supporters and friends have concluded that the die-hards are in possession, have the capacity and intend to load microbe-filled multiple warheads onto extended-range missiles."

"But we are told that your government has control of all the Russian missiles," Hershel interjected.

"Well, not exactly. We no longer have an accurate account of our stockpile."

"I can't believe what I'm hearing," Hershel exclaimed.

Wriggling in his seat, Pyotr Berganov overlooked Hershel's outburst and went on: "Then let me give you the facts. If you think our missile record keeping is bad, taking into consideration that the C.I.S. is still in turmoil, how about your great friends, the good old U.S.A.? Their defense department inventory records are in such poor shape that when the General Accounting Office tried to count hand-held missiles, the tallies differed by thousands. When the GAO visited all seventy-eight land-based storage sites for the Stinger Redeye and Dragon missiles, they found that 40 percent of the sites did not have accurate inventory records. Our intelligence reports tell us that one depot showed that 7,370 missiles were on hand, but the General Accounting Office counted 12,426. We have information that at another site, records indicated 22,558 missiles were stored, but the GAO only counted 20,373.

"While they found more Stinger and Redeye missiles than the military's count, the GAO found 9,744 fewer Dragons than the armed forces listed in stockpiles. So what do you say to these discrepancies? Incredible, eh?"

Hershel began to appreciate that Pyotr Berganov was a potpourri of talent, experience and information.

"These are tragic examples," Berganov added, "of problems that everyone is going to have to look at very carefully in the near future. Yet disaster is inevitable if nothing is done about them. Nevertheless, biological warfare is what we are concerned with here. That is what is facing us at this very moment. Where and when such an attack will come by the die-hards we do not know—although we have our suspicions. And if you think those few treaties signed by the U.S. and Russia have any immediate consequence, you are gravely mistaken."

Like faraway thunder, this extraordinary danger grew louder in Hershel's mind. Only the discipline of their training kept their emotions out of all their faces, but it was absolutely clear that every man in the room understood the consequences of what Berganov had just disclosed.

Knowing that he had the full attention of his small audience, Berganov slowly continued. "We stumbled on this information for a biological-chemical missile attack quite accidentally, in an espionage drop. Someone on our team copied the papers and replaced the originals before it could be discovered they were missing. I can tell you more about this later. Right now, our focus should be on anthrax, because other viruses and bacteria make poor weapons. Plague and typhus are too unstable to be stored in a warhead. For instance, cholera can only be spread through food and water. The die-hards also do not have the laboratory capability at a missile site to put botulin toxin in the aerosol form necessary to rain it onto large populations. So, that leaves us with anthrax.

"There is no question in my mind that the hardy spores of the rod-shaped soil bacterium, *Bacillus anthracis*, can be turned into an aerosol to become the agent of mass death. To prove my point, the British, in a past experiment, dropped the spores on an uninhabited island off the coast of Scotland during World War II and the anthrax easily spread to the sheep of the island. From there it is just a step to humans....Yes, I believe anthrax is what the die-hards will use. It is cheap and easy to make and available from any number of sources.

"To make you more comfortable about my knowledge and background in chemical warfare, I was working at a secret Soviet bio-warfare lab in April of 1979, when sixty-four innocent people died suffering gruesome but quick deaths—all due to an accidental release of anthrax spores." Berganov spread his hands to further emphasize his statements.

"You should already know, but if you do not, anthrax is a disease primarily of cattle and sheep, but it can also be spread to humans who unknowingly handle their skin, hides or carcasses. When spores penetrate the skin of a human they produce fever, headaches, nausea and highly visible pustules. However, this form of the disease can be treated with antibiotics if available, and therefore is seldom fatal. On the other hand, if the spores are inhaled, the fatality rate to an untreated victim increases to ninety percent. In those cases the spores travel to the lymph glands, germinate into the bacillus form and then travel throughout the body, releasing a toxin that causes nausea, shock, coma and eventual death from massive blood poisoning. It is not a pleasant thought, I know," Berganov added, "but usually, within three days a victim can order his coffin."

It seemed strange to Hershel that such an innocent and fatherly-looking man as Berganov could have been involved in any way with information regarding such a deadly weapon.

The Russian took a sip of his now cold coffee; then he grew serious. "I don't want to miss a single important point or we'll all have egg on our faces. If the die-hards know we are on to them, they will perceive us as a threat and escalate their plans."

He continued, "Can you just imagine the terrified population and total panic where such a warhead lands? There would be total disorder," he emphasized. "But now let's talk about the defenses against anthrax spores. There are protective suits and masks, like those worn in Israel during the Iraqi Scud missile attacks in 1991. The trouble is that the spores can remain infectious indefinitely—which is obviously longer than a populous can wear clumsy protective gear. Additionally, it is difficult to have a large quantity of gear available on an immediate basis; therefore, there will be additional deaths due to panic.

"As far as an anthrax bacillus vaccine to protect against the microbes in advance of an attack, no country has nearly sufficient supplies for its troops, let alone the General population. Also, at this time it takes at least three doses of anthrax vaccine—spread evenly over twenty-nine days—to confer immunity. After that, we are still not sure how long afterward the body builds up full immunity. It could perhaps take months.

"Politicians have known about this problem for years and have kept it under their hats. Anthrax vaccine production is almost nonexistent around the world and that goes for the United States and its great military Pentagon. An anthrax bacillus production facility would require the most extreme safeguards to contain the spores, and could not be produced on a crash program, even in the United States. With these facts at their disposal and the likelihood of success, it should be no wonder that the die-hards have persuaded some very important Russian military leaders to support this surprise attack.

"Once a few major cities are rendered helpless, the die-hards will become the heroes and leaders of a new Communist regime. As I've outlined, the probability of success is close to 100 percent. The only thing that can get in their way is us! And we have to succeed—or the consequences will be more catastrophic than anything imaginable in the history of our world. Restoring Communism and regaining control is the Holy Grail to the people behind this plot, particularly to the former powerful leaders, who will settle for nothing less."

Hershel was silent as Berganov paused. It was his job to look at the fine threads and see where they took him, regardless of how bizarre Pyotr Berganov's statements appeared on the surface. He also knew that people like Berganov would back the formers so long as they didn't get their own feet trampled on. Finally Hershel spoke. "I am not saying that you are wrong, but is it possible your information is incorrect? What we must know is precisely how sure you are that…"

Before Hershel could finish his sentence, Berganov interrupted, smoothing down his mustache with his fingers. "Our confidence level is ninety-nine and nine-tenths percent. We've watched the die-hards for a while now, and I am sure we've got the information right!"

"What would you suggest, Pyotr? How should we attack them?"

"Its a touchy situation at best," said Berganov. "I do know that the die-hards are not going to stay on the sidelines much longer. We need a fresh outlook. What do you feel are our options?"

"In short," answered Hershel, "we all have to work closely together if we are to succeed."

Nikolai nodded vigorously. He was fascinated, and hung on every word. He felt just as he did when he successfully returned from the Entebbe Raid, in the 1970s.

Hershel shook his head from side to side. "Well, I guess we've reached the bottom line. I would like you to review your data as soon as possible and give me fresh profiles of their top leaders."

"I know the die-hards," the General answered. "They may have already come to the conclusion that the best way to bring about a consensus among the former Communist leaders would be to drop a few biochemical warheads on strategic locations of Russia's former enemies, provoking the enemies into retaliating against Russia.

"Even though I believe that no man can walk alone all the time, by now you are probably wondering why I have not proposed to follow this matter up by contacting the U.S. State Department, the CIA or the Mossad directly. Well, if I did, the CIA would probably not believe us and they would not have strong interest since they did not make the discovery through their own direct sources. This is the usual 'interagency politics,' and all the intelligence agencies typically drown in their own arrogance. And if the CIA *did* believe me, they would want to run the show their way and would just blunder it in the end. Furthermore, they move too slowly to be of help in this particular scenario. You also know that it would be difficult to use conventional military forces when the adversary doesn't have a fixed address."

The General cleared his throat before continuing.

"There is simply no governmental agency, that I am aware of, which is quick or forceful enough to handle the sort of grave danger we are confronted with, and to do something about it in time to stop it. Not only that, if the antagonists learned of our activities to stop them through leaks from other intelligence agency sources, the die-hards would just go deep underground and surface at a later date, even better prepared and with more dangerous weaponry. Therefore, we believe the approach we are taking with your team has the best chance for success."

Hershel leaned forward to make himself heard, as he spoke in a subdued tone. "We guessed as much. We must move quickly because we do not know what their timetable is!"

His expectations raised, the General said with a half-smile, "As we say in the military—we must bide our time for the appropriate moment. For now, we prepare the terrain and consolidate the strengths of both our groups. Our time will come, shortly, and with your group's help the die-hards will find that the pendulum could swing in both directions. However, we are faced with a stringent requirement to minimize the number of troops, simply because I don't have that many people upon whom I can depend."

He took a final drag on his cigarette. "Well now, enough of this. Let's go forward. I am inviting you both, along with Avrum, to meet me on

Monday for a short train trip. Everything will be arranged by my staff—the tickets, a private compartment, the food. There are important things that must be seen firsthand, in order to properly understand all of the complexities involved in making our plans."

The General used his old Marlboro to light a fresh one, and for a moment his troubled eyes were earnestly awaiting a reply.

Hershel looked first to Nikolai, then answered with a half smile. "Agreed."

"We have our share of problems in Russia and I must say that I appreciate your working with us."

"On the contrary, General, it is we who should be grateful to you and your friends for entrusting us with the responsibilities of this mission," Hershel smiled back, wishing to encourage him.

The General hesitated for a moment before continuing. He glanced for a moment at Berganov. Then he explained:

"Unfortunately, three of you, with myself, will be doing some traveling. Our destination is not close by. It will be our premier nuclear research center, the Kurchatov Institute, that I want you to see. Nevertheless, I suggest that you do not pack too much, just enough for a few days. The place we are going to visit is Arzamas 16. It is an isolated former monastery in central Russia. The military research and development facility is where the supersecret Soviet nuclear research center was founded after World War II and where the first Russian A-bomb was built. Some say it was built from plans obtained from former Nazi scientists after World War II, combined with information from agents spying in American. However, we were well on our way to making our own bomb here in Russia when the Americans detonated A-bombs over Hiroshima and Nagasaki. The A-bomb that we detonated in 1951 was of our own design—twice as powerful and much lighter than the American bomb."

The General picked up a spoon and began tapping it on the table. "You realize that there is no longer a breach of security in what I am going to tell you," he said.

Nikolai, his hands clasped behind his head, watched the handle of the General's spoon drumming on the table. Chervok noticed him looking, and stopped.

Nikolai relaxed as the General continued: "As you well know, the first real H-bomb was exploded by us former Soviets on October 12, 1952. It was the first genuine H-bomb ever to be detonated. The work of physicist Andrei Sakharov."

"Is this the same Sakharov who became the leading critic of the Soviet State?" Hershel asked.

"Yes," the General replied, "and today, five years after his death, he is held in great reverence by all Russians. You see how time cures old wounds?

"As for the Russian plutonium bomb, only superior intelligence-gathering by our KGB can be credited for its rapid development. The technical materials supplied by the young German physicist Klaus Fuchs, who worked on the American Manhattan Project from 1943 to 1946, was more than impressive." The General did not realize that he was smiling. "If you do not recall, then please let me remind you that Fuchs was a devout Communist who moved to England in the 1930s and began to cooperate with us in 1941. He was angry that the Western powers were not sharing their weapons research with their Soviet Allies during the war. The truth remains that Fuchs' help did enable us to more quickly develop and detonate our version of the A-bomb."

Hershel was enjoying the conversation and the history lesson.

"Most people do not realize," General Chervok continued, smiling across the room at Pyotr Berganov, "that the A-bomb era was a dramatic time for us. In a country where millions of lives had recently been lost and great devastation brought upon us, it was necessary for us to act from strength. It was a matter of life or death for our tired nation. We accepted help from any available source, like the initial calculations for the H-bomb, made by Edward Teller, who was instrumental in developing the American equivalent—although these calculations of his unfortunately proved to be erroneous."

Nikolai shrugged. "We guessed as much."

General Chervok kneaded his lower lip with his teeth, obviously choosing his words carefully. "With a little luck, I will be able to acquaint you with the former superspy of scientists, who to this day will only permit us to introduce him by his code name, Perseus. He is a retired scientist who formerly worked inside the Los Alamos, New Mexico, research station."

"You are the first Russian I ever met who openly admitted that your government cheated a little here and there," said Nikolai with a smirk on his face.

The General nodded in agreement. "One cannot conceal the truth forever. We have hidden behind our deceitful secret cloak of Communism long enough."

"So be it," Hershel added. "But I have always wondered about Julius and Ethel Rosenberg. They were executed by the United States in 1953. Were they ever really plugged into your intelligence network?"

"Not that I am aware of," the General said slowly. "If the couple did get any information to us, it was strictly secondhand. The most important information was obtained independently, from Mr. Fuchs. As far as the United States government's executing them, well, we had little or nothing to do with them, so we never understood what all the fuss was about. We did think that their prosecution and trial ended up helping us, because all of the focus and attention they received took scrutiny and resources away from our other agents who were actively operating at the time in the U.S. Therefore, we could not help them in their defense. Who would have believed us at that period of the Cold War anyway."

Momentarily perplexed, Hershel tried to absorb and digest the information about the Rosenbergs. He emitted a kind of grunting cough that indicated his doubt, irritation and a touch of indignation.

The General pushed his chair back and said, "You will have to excuse me! It's time for the food, gentlemen. We can't keep our stomachs waiting. We shall continue our discussions over dinner."

Hershel, due to his special skills as an information gatherer, was aware of a myriad of threatened security plots against the bipolar world. Threats that do not lend themselves to the application of force in the traditional sense. Hershel was concerned that an attack on a die-hard installation could be seen as an attack against Russia. He feared the consequences and casualties of rash action. He became worried about his ability to explain why this planned action of his group was necessary and justified.

Concerns not withstanding, the reality was that Hershel would be engaged in a military support operation. And, like it or not, once this step was taken, there was a high likelihood that he would engage in additional military support operations in the future.

It was already clear to Hershel that military support operations are not a lesser case of general or limited war. He would have to develop new tactics and training for these new situations. The last thing Hershel wanted to see would be people killed needlessly.

Chapter Eighteen

MILITARY R.&D. FACILITY, CLASSIFIED LOCATION IN CENTRAL RUSSIA

OCTOBER 24

As the train rounded a bend it slowed, and Hershel could see from the window the outline of buildings in the distance.

"We're not too far away now," the General said as he suddenly seemed to come alive. "This laboratory was the first to develop poisons used to assassinate enemies of Moscow at home and abroad. For many years it was called Lab X and was in existence as far back as 1937.

"I am sure you surmise that there are a lot of unusual things that still take place here. Because it is the only way possible, I am going to get you all in through the back door of the operations facilities for the Russian Special Technologies Group. There are some amazing people here working on a variety of cutting-edge projects. When you speak to them, you will feel they come right out of a science fiction book. Within this same complex we have developed both lethal and nonlethal technologies and weaponry that have increased the military options available to Russia.

"What now worries me is that the die-hards could also open these doors themselves. They could use what they find here in a preemptive strike against"—the General paused in mid-thought—"who knows who at this point. It is within this same facility that an arsenal of high-tech so-called tricks have been developed over the years. These have greatly increased our nation's options with an assortment of never-before-used military weaponry that could be employed against any number of adversaries. You will be astounded, I assure you, as you observe Russia's ability to incapacitate rather than destroy an enemy," he concluded proudly.

As an after-thought he said, "You'll be surprised to learn that about an hour west of here, deep in the forest, the government is still running a special Middle Eastern training camp for our favorite terrorists."

That statement turned all three formers' heads.

The locomotive whistled, shuddered and ground reluctantly to a halt while a ghostly tremor from the brakes ran through the passenger car. The small group picked up their duffel bags, then stepped through the open door and onto a well-worn platform.

Barking dogs could be heard in the distance as they walked across the rough, wooden floor planks of the railway station.

The lab they were soon going to view was in some ways a throwback to a U.S. factory town. The facility proved to be a mini-city in itself, with its own government-run apartments, clinics, doctors, food markets, power plant and schools. It still operated under the old Soviet defense industry system consisting of three tiers. At the top was the elite laboratory and research institute. The next tier were the design bureaus, and the third and largest tier were the manufacturing enterprises.

Arriving first at the hidden research and development facility, the group was greeted by an army captain, Boris Felshin, in uniform. He first stood at attention, giving the General a senior salute before laughing gruffly and embracing his old friend in a Russian bear hug.

The laugh immediately transformed into a hacking cough, which the captain smothered with a giant handkerchief. When he regained control and was able to speak he said, "Salute! God bless the long Russian winters."

They walked over to where Captain Felshin's car was waiting and dropped their carry-on bags in the open trunk.

The day was clear and sunny, but Hershel promised himself that if he ever came back to Russia in the winter, he'd remember to bring long-johns. The car took a direct route toward the complex and stopped at a small traffic circle, where the occupants were asked for their security passes. The General reached into his briefcase and removed passes for Avrum, Nikolai and Hershel, with their pictures already laminated under clear plastic.

"How in the world did you get our pictures?" Avrum inquired, his eyes focusing on the identification card.

The General hesitated, then reluctantly said, "As you have your sources, we have ours."

Traces of chemical odors permeated the air as the captain's car approached the main security gate, which slid open as he held up his pass to the saluting guard. Having cleared security, the captain drove to the next checkpoint. As the guard peered into the car, each man displayed his pass. Nodding his approval, the guard waved the car through the next gate.

The car's windshield wipers were working to clear away the early-morning dampness as they slowly drove past a number of large laboratory and research buildings within the complex.

"How many people work here?" Hershel inquired.

"Several thousand, at least," was the captain's reply.

Turning a corner, the captain pulled into an assigned parking place.

Hershel thought this must be the Russian Kurchatov doomsday research facility he had heard so much about in the Mossad. Hershel hoped the General knew hundreds of people like the captain, who were willing to take the risks to stop the die-hards from trying to execute their plan. But which ones could the formers trust?

"As we leave the car, walk directly toward that door," said General Chervok. He pointed in a direction to his right. "Remember, there is a security camera at the top of each building that could be following our every move. Be relaxed, smile and walk in a casual manner while discussing the cross-country skiing we expect to be doing on Saturday. If we are successful, I shall present each of you with a Russian Academy Award. What you are about to see will justify the risks."

To Avrum the General sounded like a skater performing on thin and brittle ice.

"The captain will go first," Chervok continued, "insert his security card into the card-reading computer, and when he gains access we will closely follow and repeat his actions one by one. Now GO!" The General cast a reproachful glance in the formers' direction, expecting that they would do exactly what he wanted, exactly when he wanted.

"What is the time?" Nikolai asked, once they entered the building.

"We are on time. It's exactly nine-fifty, the captain said, as they started down a series of long white hospital-like corridors.

The visit to the lab was like a short trip in a time machine. Equipment, decor, attitudes, and the technologies appeared to have been suspended in time at about 1950. Except for some equipment bought during the early 1980s, most apparatus appeared to have been purchased before the 1970s. Avrum considered it similar to American technology of more than 40 years earlier.

There were large glass windows in each laboratory on both sides of the corridor. Bulletin boards, charts, blackboards and typewritten papers adorned the walls of the lab, while different configurations of long workbenches and high laboratory stools occupied the rooms. Technicians in white smocks seemed to fill every available work space.

The captain stuck his head into one office and said, "Viktor, where is Dr. Sergei Lobov?"

"At the moment, I don't have a clue," Viktor answered.

"Please page the good doctor for me. When he replies, tell him to meet me in room 205."

A hoarse monotone voice was shortly heard over the loudspeaker. "Dr. Lobov, room 205!" The page was repeated twice.

"Gentlemen, these stairs please," the captain said, pointing to a wide pair of doors that opened into a fireproof stairway. On the second floor the small group only had to walk a short distance before entering room 205, which was a small lecture hall. The lights went on and Dr. Lobov raised his hand to greet them.

The General had warned the formers that the room was a quiet place. When people talked there, even if they were discussing the weather, they did so almost in whispers because their voices would carry.

"General, we have missed your visits since you retired. Welcome back!"

After the usual introductions and courtesies, Dr. Lobov immediately got down to the business of the day. The lights dimmed as two large projection screens became white in the front of the room. Turning around to face his audience, he looked like a nervous, fidgety man who was not comfortable and did not want to be speaking before a roomful of people. It took all the courage he could muster for him to start the presentation.

He began by saying, "We are involved in a new vision, a new threat to international security that presages an era of global competition where all sides struggle for supremacy of knowledge and strive for perfection of information technology. This competition will end up penalizing nations that depend upon telecommunications and computer systems for their security, but are unable to effectively defend those systems against attack."

Avrum appreciated the fact that this meeting was not a situation of "you show me yours and we'll show you ours." Instead, this would be a meeting where the host intended to indicate that he knew something we didn't; and he thought we knew and had a thing or two that he didn't. If we put all of our knowledge together, maybe we would have something that would be mutually beneficial.

The doctor's face was perspiring but as if set in stone. The fingers of his hands tightened as his words continued to flow.

"What you are about to see is an abbreviated version of our high-tech arsenal of chemicals and other weaponry. The slide screen to the left will show the weapon or method of delivery. The screen on the right will show the effects of a particular weapon or chemical."

The first picture flashed on the screen.

"What you are now looking at are different versions of special laser weaponry, some of which resemble conventional rifles. In fact, they are low-energy laser rifles with self-contained power packs, which, incidentally, have the ability to flash-blind people. If you now direct your attention to the screen on the right, you will observe the effects of a test made on animals."

Pointing to the right-hand screen, the doctor said, "See that? The animals on the far right are now totally disoriented by a low-energy burst, the ones on the left are unaffected. Now, simply envision the ability soldiers will have to direct fire into a charging enemy! The enemy will be totally disabled, unable to defend itself, before being killed by conventional weaponry from our old arsenal. In addition to non-lethal weaponry, lasers and tasers have a number of secondary purposes: target acquisition, tracking of a target, night vision and even range finding."

"If I may add," General Chervok interrupted, "some of this weaponry is extremely desirable but extremely difficult to maintain, operate and control. Of course, most of these applications also violate international treaties governing war practices. Naturally, I can assure you that the die-hards are not at all concerned with these treaties. I predict, however, that the new weapons tactics observed here could escalate into the most lethal available to mankind for years to come—especially lethal if they got into the hands of our unfriendly 'neighborhood' terrorists....But my apology for the interruption, doctor. Please proceed."

Dr. Lobov went on, "Our powerful laser optics, while initially designed to destroy enemy tanks, could also be deployed to detonate enemy ammunition within a truck, tank, or even an enemy's entire ammunition dump. Aimed at a soldier, laser optics could also explode his eyeballs.

"Portable microwave weapons, shown here in a test"—he pointed his finger to the screen—"can quietly cut enemy communications, and also cook internal organs. Not all that humane, my friends." He looked for the negative reactions on their faces. "But then, what bullet or weapon is humane in war?"

No one responded.

"The next selection of weaponry is this deceivingly simple-looking generator. Shown in this series of slides, it will be easily transformed into a very low frequency sound machine. This could be fine-tuned to incapacitate humans—causing disorientation, bowel spasms, nausea or vomiting. Of course, our acoustic generators do not affect the operator, who is shielded. Therefore, it has the capability to be fine-tuned to achieve anything from mildly irritating the enemy to organ-bursting. While in a few of the applications the effect ceases as the generators are turned off, the intended physical damage will have been achieved, since we would then have the option of destroying the enemy while they are paralyzed. Sorry, no humans are portrayed in these slides. We only have movies of animals feeling the effects at one-third the weapon's capacity.

"Incidentally, United States military research is simultaneously working on similar programs in this same direction." The doctor's tone hinted that it was more than a mere coincidence.

Hershel recalled that he'd seen most of this same technology previously in the United States, but he didn't want to slow things down by bringing this up.

"Gentlemen, I will now brief you on 'combustion alteration.'"

Dr. Lobov noticed that everyone began leaning forward, listening attentively to a new terminology.

"The use of internal combustion engines can be disrupted through special chemical compounds, as shown in these movies of tracked vehicles coming to a halt during maneuvers. These chemical compounds would temporarily contaminate fuel or change its viscosity to degrade engine function. Entire divisions of enemy personnel carriers and tanks could be made to stall as they hit clouds of our combustion inhibitors. This is because inhibitors short-cut the vehicles' metal fibers in their ignition systems. It would take an arsenal of 'smart' bombs and dozens of planes to achieve the same results as our combustion inhibitors.

"During adverse weather conditions, when planes cannot fly, the contaminating compounds can also be dispersed by ground-level half-track mounted generators."

The slides again changed and Sergei Lobov continued: "This laboratory has also developed high technology in computer viruses. Our technology focuses on computer systems, data transmission, fire control systems, and avionics. It involves the covert intrusion of a computer virus logic bomb, or 'sleeper'—also called a worm, by many. This may remain hidden within the system until such time as the system is used or meets specific parameters, causing it then to self-destruct."

"I can see you left nothing out, short of Einstein's general theory of relativity," Avrum observed.

"Sir, I did what I did for many years because I thought at the time it was important for my country, and because I was good at it. But that phase is long passed.

The doctor smiled and continued his presentation. "And how about this one? We call it the Roach Motel. You must admit that it is rather funny to see an easily manufactured polymer adhesive, delivered by air-drop or selectively by ground forces, which 'glues' military or civilian equipment in place and prevents it from operating. There is no reason why several drums of adhesive could not be dropped on airport runways, stopping enemy fighter planes from taking off or landing. Roads leading into an embargoed nation such as Iraq could be temporarily closed by spraying them with super-sticky Roach Motel-like polymers. The enemy equipment could then be permanently trapped by a newly developed, quick-setting 'hard' foam."

"This weapon pleases the politicians," General Chervok added, "since these products are quick to manufacture, can be produced cheaply, and are relatively easy to deliver. It does not require an entire squadron of valuable planes to spray an area. You must appreciate that killing in a full-scale war is generally necessary, to make your point and decisively win the battle. But it always seems so stupid in small police-action wars."

"That's a lovely thought for a general," Avrum said with a smile.

"The Russian police administration," the doctor said softly, "says that this lab thinks too big, that we are only accustomed to thinking up ways to blow up countries. They've said we don't have any idea of practical street-wise technology, something required for them to catch the new Russian gangster—especially a technique to halt a fleeing car without a long, high-speed chase and one of the costliest and most deadly law enforcement operations. But yes, we can now stop a speeding car!" the doctor happily exclaimed.

"Marvelous," Hershel said, laughing, "and how does one accomplish that ?"

"By a burst of microwave energy from this rather small machine," the doctor answered, and he showed the group an enlarged color photograph of the machine in operation.

Nikolai said calmly, "Nice idea, doctor, but what are the drawbacks?"

With a moan the doctor admitted, "The problem comes when we are restrained by the requirements for civilians' safety. We are on track, but the device," he warned, "also manages to stop all other cars within a wide perimeter, as well as every pacemaker in the vicinity."

"Fascinating!" Nikolai remarked.

"Of course. But we do have a way to go before it's perfected.," the doctor confessed.

Everyone turned as the doors to the lecture room suddenly opened and an aide entered, pushing a cart of coffee and tea, kept hot in shiny but dented thermoses. The doctor nodded to the aide in acknowledgment.

"Please help yourselves, gentlemen, while I continue my presentation," the doctor said.

"Here we have another important adjunct to your common instruments of war....I now will focus on our recent anti-traction technology, again delivered through an airborne method as noted in this image." He pointed to the large movie screen, which showed a plane spraying a clear liquid. "Or it can be delivered by human agents, operating on land behind the lines."

He paused for a moment before continuing. "We would provide the operatives with the ability to spread, paint or spray a Teflon-type lubricant, environmentally neutral, on railroad tracks, metal bridge decks, grades, ramps, stairs, and all types of other equipment, seriously disrupting the enemy and denying his use of the local infrastructure for a substantially critical period."

"Why do you say a 'substantial period'?" Hershel asked.

"Because such lubricants are extremely time-consuming to remove—not to mention costly. Look at the screen. Again, it is almost humorous to watch the locomotive pulling the train in this picture going nowhere fast, the drive wheels just spinning from the Teflon-like compound that was sprayed on the tracks."

On the movie screen a train could be seen pulling into a deserted station. Then the camera zoomed in and focused on the spinning drive wheels, skidding along the top of the tracks.

"It would be almost impossible to get traction to start or stop a military transport train before the engineer would lose control and crash," the doctor added.

"Next, you should know that the C.I.S. has specially trained forces that could coat enemy aircraft wings with embrittling chemicals, or spray them with metal-eating microbes—which brings us to the next topic: supercaustics." He took a deep breath.

"Notwithstanding additional worries for the environment and our production problems in making and storing large quantities of this material, the supercaustics that we have developed can be millions of times more caustic and dangerous than hydofluoric acid. Look at these unusual pictures of superacids rapidly eating away at this thick metal bar."

The slide projector clicked on a picture as the doctor continued, "A round of jellied superacids delivered in an artillery shell could destroy the optics of heavily armored vehicles, penetrate bullet-resistant vision panels of glass or silently destroy key weapons systems and their components."

"What about the military personnel in those vehicles?" Hershel quickly inquired.

The doctor became uncomfortable after this question.

"How perceptive! We don't have all the answers yet concerning its killing capacity. I don't mean to avoid the question, but, if the stuff eats through reinforced steel, you can only imagine its effect on cloths and skin.

"Moving along, the next image is a picture of chemicals that crystallize and totally destroy tires. And how about this other concept of a new electromagnetic pulse generator that can be regulated to interrupt radar, telephones, computers or any other type of communication or targeting equipment? Great isn't it?"

"Well, your new weapons are impressive. You have me convinced," Avrum said as he gave the doctor a long glance. His mood became sober as he stood to refill his cup with coffee.

"The weaponry is all real," the Doctor Lobov added convincingly, "including our sleep-inducing chemicals, which could incapacitate combatants by temporarily putting the enemy to sleep. We have even thought of confusing enemy combatants at night with holographic projections reflected off clouds, perhaps leading them to a false road or showing them images of their government surrendering and their leaders instructing them to go home."

The doctor paused for a moment and glanced at Avrum. "I know that all of you are trained and quite capable of blowing a man's brains out along with the best of us. But my favorite concept involving guns— that we've studied so far—is a 'magnetophosphene" gun that induces a visual effect akin to what happens when a person receives a blow to the head and sees stars."

After this last comment, Captain Felshin stood up and addressed the room: "Gentlemen, General Chervok briefed me several days ago. He told me why you are here and that is why I have agreed to join and work with you. I do not want us to further jeopardize the doctor by overstaying our welcome....So I would like to conclude this part of our tour by summarizing.

"What you have been shown here is simply the very tip of a Pandora's box of major biological, chemical, nuclear and technical weaponry, which, if it ever falls into the hands of the hard-line Communists, not even the entire U.S. Army led by the great General Schwarzkopf could help. This information is being closely held, remember that! And while you are in Russia, never hint about what you have learned here. I must warn you: It is a known fact that there are many people working here who have sympathy for the die-hards, as well as for other revolutionary factions around the world."

"Agreed," said Hershel. "And we can't afford to make a long drawn-out career of chasing die-hards. We have to disable them with all dispatch. And doctor, we can only suggest that you play it very carefully until you receive further instructions from General Chervok."

"I am conveniently scheduled to go on holiday to a Black Sea resort," the doctor nodded in agreement.

"Good idea. Thank you for your hospitality and for the 'classified' tour," said Avrum. "Mankind is going through a most disagreeable chapter of history. Tell me, doctor, before we leave, did you ever hear of *novichok?*"

The doctor busied himself with his pack of cigarettes, slowly removing one, but seemingly reluctant to place it in his mouth.

"The meaning is 'newcomer' in Russian," he answered with a look of guilt on his face.

"No, I mean the code word *novichok*, " Avrum insisted.

"Oh, that *novichok!*" The doctor seemed surprised that Avrum was even aware of the existence of this highly classified code word. "Yes, it was the code word by which a new class of poisons was developed by our former Soviet leaders, some of which was transferred to Iraq for use against American forces in the Gulf War. At present other exotic weaponry is also under development—which is more frightening than anything we have seen so far."

"What does Yeltsin have to say about all of these goings-on?" Avrum questioned.

"Yeltsin"—the doctor chuckled sarcastically—"Yeltsin, rather than being a friend of the West, has in great part been a captive of the Russian military and a puppet of the former KGB. The difference between Yeltsin and Zhirinovsky, who has strong military and KGB backing, could very well lie in who is willing to use the Russian 'secret weapon' on a mass scale against one or more Western nations. He who does will be the one most likely to retain control of Russia."

Relentlessly, Avrum dug deeper. "Is *novichok* what Zhirinovsky had in mind when he kept warning that Russia has a secret weapon capable of destroying the West?"

Looking around suspiciously, the doctor quietly commented, "Be careful when you mention the name Zhirinovsky. The Party dominates the Russian parliament and he still has strong ties to the old Soviet KGB. His threat was a boast, not a bluff," the doctor said almost in a whisper. "The truth is that *novichok* exists. And a whole new class of deadly binary chemical weapons have been created in that laboratory.

"A friend of mine, Vladimir Petrenko, is a perfect example and victim of the chemical weapons development program. In 1982, he was a volunteer testing a new chemical warfare suit and was exposed to one of these new poisons being secretly developed. Unfortunately, the suit did not work properly. When I saw him last week he admitted to me that his health was seriously deteriorating. At age thirty-five, he looks twenty years older. He has serious illnesses that require constant treatment. He is half his former weight, haggard and gaunt. I hardly recognize him."

The doctor allowed himself a look toward the three Israelis before continuing. "The *novichok* chemicals have the same effects as my friend is suffering. They can be toxic like a chemical agent or cause diseases like a biological agent. They can be lethal or debilitating. The poisons affect human genes, causing birth defects and infant illnesses among offspring. My friend Petrenko's symptoms exactly resemble those of the worst cases of the ailing American veterans of the Gulf War."

Then, noticing that Avrum, Hershel and Nikolai were listening intently, the doctor rose from his chair and stood facing them.

"During the '80s we came under a lot of heat from the United States and its allies, when the Soviet military began using mytcotoxins, known as 'yellow rain', on anti-Communist freedom fighters in Southeast Asia.

"We are sorry to have to share our problems with you. God knows, we now have enough of them! I'm aware that people in your position may find it difficult to understand how a country as large as ours could still need the help of former agents from a country as small as Israel. But let me assure you that by helping us, you are helping yourselves as well."

"Exactly what are you implying?" said a puzzled Hershel.

"No insult intended," the doctor answered in a calm and professional demeanor. "You are certainly entitled to know a few other facts concerning Russia's history and involvement in various Mideast Wars. During the latter part of 1967, in the wake of the Six Day War, Moscow made the decision to provide Iraq with both chemical and biological agents in their raw, pre-weaponized form, from this facility. Ever since they learned that Israel went nuclear, some Arab nations had kept pressing the Soviet leadership for chemical and biological warfare capabilities.

"If anything, relations between Iraq and the Soviets grew closer over the years. Eventually, Iraq and the Soviet Union signed the Treaty of Friendship and Cooperation, Russia sending about four thousand military advisors to Iraq. I do think that a new form of undetectable chemical warfare agent, such as novichok, was used against the Americans during the Gulf War. And I say again that the reported effects on some U.S. troops are not unlike those I saw in Petrenko. The Americans call it the Gulf War syndrome. The Iraqi chemical warfare agent may not be very toxic, but it could have lingering after-effects, causing many debilitating medical problems for years to come.

This is a nasty, scary issue. You have seen an array of new weapons, most of which would be sufficient to destroy or seriously disrupt the democratic world." The doctor had finished his long lecture.

"What's life without a little excitement?" Hershel asked, trying to lighten the mood while making a bad joke.

Need-to-know had again raised its ugly head in Hershel's mind. He didn't need to know what the Russian warheads or delivery system looked like or how many there were. One would have been enough to do unbelievable damage. Hershel stood up, stretching his legs, as did Nikolai.

The whole thing's a hunt in the dark, Hershel thought. Hopeless situations like this only wear me out, pull me down, trip me up, but he knew he had to press on. He was in the position of having had a glimpse of an insane situation and he felt that he was bloody lucky to get a shot at solving an almost impossible predicament.

Avrum hesitated, wondering for a moment how he should say what he wanted to say before leaving. He had first come to Russia as one would come to a marketplace, to barter and bargain for items he had interest in. In his case, those items were Jews. He was mainly interested in Jewish people who wanted to leave and emigrate to Israel. He locked his hands together tensely and took a step forward.

"I'll tell you what I told General Chervok, 'No man can walk alone all the time.' We fully intend to walk this problem through together."

Then he and the other two formers shook hands with the doctor. Avrum didn't fool himself. Today they were an honored guests. Let the General down, and they could easily become deceased honored guests.

Chapter Nineteen

THE RESTAURANT

OCTOBER 25

The morning routine was exactly the same today for Uri Glebova, despite the fact that he'd been away from home for a month. He awoke at 5:30, an hour that seemed increasingly early as he approached forty-two, and followed the same routine, as closely as possible, as when he was home in Israel. He loved breakfast foods with lots of sugar, fat and preservatives, but in recent years opted for the "guaranteed" health foods. The flesh he carried on his frame was as tight as ever. He looked like the field agent he had once been.

Rising early would give him ample time to shower, dress, check his 9mm Beretta 92-F pistol, put it in his shoulder holster and leisurely read the morning paper—that is, if the publisher had received his shipment of ink to print it. Reading the newspaper usually started Uri's day off on the right foot. He approached the paper almost like an intelligence briefing at the Institute. He had always had his doubts about journalists, especially here in Russia, where their analysis was often faulty. But their performance was often as good as many of the trained employees in intelligence-agency research gathering and dissemination departments

He placed his food on the kitchen table, sat down and opened the paper. What's this, he wondered, as he looked at the headlines for the lead article: "Hundreds of Russian tanks rolled across the border of a rebellious Muslim region in southern Russia yesterday, setting off the worst political crisis in Russia since President Boris N. Yeltsin had troops fire on the Moscow Parliament last year."

Wow, the air is filled with gunfire and smoke again! he mused. All that enormous Russian firepower against its own citizens! Uri thought. There is a real threat here of a full-scale war in Chechnya—just amazing. And it sounds like it was done in the old Russian style—the good old "mass force" Soviet military textbook way! Looks like it will turn out to be another Russian disaster which will last for years.

"The democrats and the intelligentsia will never support this move by Yeltsin. The action will have to be short," Uri mumbled to himself. "I just wonder if he remembers his history—the Czars conquering Chechnya in 1878 and the long and nasty guerrilla war. He should! Nearly every other Russian knows the Lermontov poem about the 'evil Chechen' who crawls along the riverbank, 'sharpening his long knife.'"

Well, thought Uri, it's always easy to get in and hard to get out! Uri knowingly chuckled to himself. Yeltsin should know that too. What he may not have been advised of is that Chechen patriotism is more likely to grow stronger, and that should they choose, the Chechens have the capacity to bring the war home to Moscow by focusing their fanaticism on creating terrorist incidents anywhere.

Putting down the paper, Uri realized that predicting the future was no easier for KGB intelligence analysts than for a Russian sportswriter to determine who'd be the next Wimbledon champion.

All of this is too bad, he told himself, and a worse disaster waiting to happen! Uri was thinking abstractly, but it didn't take him long to come back to earth. He felt that he would rather have accompanied Hershel, Avrum, Nikolai and the General on their trip. Instead, his unusual assignment this day had been to keep a close eye on the activities of another former, Yossi Steckel.

At the age of 38, Steckel looked too young to be retired from the Mossad and appeared too immature to grasp the worldwide wheeling and dealing that was part of the new international business world. But his ambitions knew no barriers that could not be circumvented. He was a graduate of the new school of Israeli operatives and had become the golden boy who married a senior politician, a deputy to Prime Minister Shimon Peres.

Other Mossad agents never cared too much for Steckel—because of his all-knowing, arrogant attitude and the fact that he used his friends and political connections to gain favors and "plum" assignments, skipping over veteran intelligence agents.

While Steckel may have considered himself a supreme patriot of Israel, the line that separated his own interests from those of the state was often clouded. His free-wheeling and dealing frequently brought him into contact with questionable merchants and politicians, and toward the end of his Mossad career the Internal Security Division began to keep him under observation. But Steckel was either innocent or clever enough to cover his tracks, because charges were never brought against him.

Avrum had decided to invite Steckel to join their small group of formers, only because they needed every available hand they could enlist. There remained some doubt in his mind about Steckel from the old days. And Avrum became additionally suspicious when Steckel refused to stay with the formers at the safe house and did not bother to account to Avrum for two days when he disappeared. It was for these reasons that Avrum assigned Uri Glebova, one of the best former tailmen in the Mossad, to keep discreet tabs on Steckel.

Uri considered himself little different from the other formers, although while with the Mossad he had excelled in his training at breaking and entering into places where needed information was located, usually during the night or while the premises were not occupied.

The adrenaline rush that accompanied each of his escapades was totally unique. He imagined it was somewhat similar to how a soccer player felt as he nonchalantly raised both arms as a sign of victory, after the bruised leather ball bounced to the back of the net—the crowd on its feet, a hundred thousand pairs of eyes on this one triumphant human being!

Unfortunately, years had been carved out of Uri's life serving his country. Important years. And in reality there was no cheering crowd, no large bonus, no big pension, and no happy retirement—just the satisfaction of knowing he had patriotically served Israel and had done more to help his people than 99 percent of his peers, who had no idea of the risks he had taken on their behalf. But he could do nothing to change that now. All he could do was, yet again, risk his life to accomplish his mission—although this time he was not even getting paid to do his job, and it was probably the most important assignment of his life.

Uri began his surveillance of Yossi that evening. Years of service had refined his skills to where he was able to take a single long sweep of an area with his experienced eyes, seeing everything that was relevant to see. There was the occasional pedestrian, otherwise he was alone. He did not take his eyes off his target—the rundown apartment building where Steckel was living.

Uri's leathery face was calm. Brown eyes hovered above a brick jaw, and his graying black hair was covered with a ski hat. Having seen Steckel leave the apartment building, Uri's tennis shoes made no sound as, finally, he walked down the dimly lit hallway to Steckel's apartment, checking every door along the way.

Darkness was the lifeblood of the burglary and intelligence trade. He opened his packet of lockpicking tools, guiding one instrument into the lock cylinder. In seconds the door swung open. In this old building there were no pressure-sensitive floor plates, tamper-proof door magnets, infrared detectors or silent alarm systems to concern him. Faster than a thief could steal valuables, Uri set listening devices in each room. Each weighed less than an ounce and was smaller than his thumbnail. Uri quickly looked around. It was not his practice to leave any evidence behind.

As the seconds ticked away, he patiently listened at the door before re-entering the hallway. One minute elapsed and he was out of the apartment and on the sidewalk, walking away from the building.

From down the street, breaking the darkness of the night, a slash of white light from the headlights of a car stared at him. Then the burst of light, coming ever closer, hit him right in the eyes and he almost gasped as he was temporarily blinded, his pupils going from almost full dilation to pinpoints in seconds. His hands—instinctively freed for action—rose from his sides. But there was no shouting, no faces, no gunshots, as the car, missing him, quickly passed.

He was outside Yossi's building the next day crouched down in his car, positioned to survey the apartment house from across the street. He spotted Steckel, a thin smile on his face, walking confidently from an arched doorway of his apartment building onto Mozava Street.

Even from a distance it was obvious that Yossi was considering some pleasant event he had planned. From the smile on the man's face, Uri was convinced that Steckel was up to something strange.

Steckel walked south until he got to the corner of a nearby apartment house and entered it. Ten minutes later the front door opened and a young woman in a long black fur overcoat exited, arm in arm with him. It appeared as if she had known him all her life. She acted as if she was in heaven. A glow of warmth lit Steckel's features. Conversing intently, his head almost touching the woman's, arm-in-arm they continued walking south.

Uri's mind reeled. Who the hell was this broad? It was surely not Steckel's wife—she was in Israel with the kids. There was now no doubt in Uri's mind that Steckel had a girlfriend—and since he was so far from home, he was not a bit worried about their being seen together. But this was improper procedure for anyone involved in a serious, dangerous intelligence mission.

Uri followed in close pursuit for some two blocks, through streets now crowded with streams of pedestrians, until the lovebirds entered a small restaurant. A waiter in white shirt sleeves did not bother to look up as Yossi pointed to an empty table.

Moments later, Uri was not surprised when he soon spotted an obvious KGB tail immediately behind the couple.

Even though the KGB tail was not too smooth, Steckel could not have noticed, for he had been talking intently and was totally absorbed with the woman from the very moment he had come out of her apartment building. He'd even appeared to be trying to convince her of something, and Uri thought he knew what that was.

Even now, as the couple sat in the restaurant, Uri asked himself: Why is Steckel risking himself on what is most likely a stupid frolic?

Uri was confident that Steckel would not recognize him. He was wearing an old raincoat down to his laced-up boots. He was decked out in a Russian fur hat worn at an angle, low on his forehead, almost over his eyes, and his face sported a four-day growth of black and gray stubble. More than anything, he resembled a refugee who had just made a successful escape from the Gulag in Siberia.

Uri watched the woman casually drape her coat across the chair. Why didn't Steckel realize he was being taken? It was a classic setup and Uri was pissed off that their mission was being compromised by a marginal agent who shouldn't have been invited to join them in the first place.

The woman now reached up to flirtatiously fluff her hair, suggestively thrusting her large breasts closer to Steckel. Steckel was staring at her, a few inches away.

Unseen by the two, Uri found himself lucky enough to get a seat at an empty table in the corner of the restaurant behind Steckel, which gave him a clear view of the girl. Uri sat tight-lipped, seemingly ignoring the ridiculous spectacle, but in reality he listened closely to every detail of the pair's conversation and plans.

When the waitress came, Uri ordered a glass of tea, a slice of bread and then feigned sleep before it arrived, his chin resting on his chest so convincingly that from all outward appearances he seemed to have almost stopped breathing.

"But, Galina, I don't intend to get into one of your political discussions. First of all, you must win every argument or you're unhappy for the rest of the day, and last but not least, this is not the time and place," Steckel insisted, as Uri observed his friend's eyes gazing intently at her cleavage.

Uri then heard the woman's voice rise. "I understand, Yossi, but that type of conversation is stimulating for me," she insisted.

"I have a different kind of stimulation in mind." Steckel smirked in nervous excitement. He looked admiringly into her eyes while reaching for her hand.

It was becoming painful for Uri to watch. Steckel was so taken that he was not interested in anything but romancing the woman. He'd lost track of the danger she could possibly represent to him. He only felt confident of his ability to share her bed.

Galina seemed to ignore his statement. "Darling, I do appreciate the attention you are offering me, and hearing you explain things in your intelligent way inspires and thrills me, especially when I can argue with you point by point. For instance, you told me you feel that the end of the Cold War could mean an end to East-West espionage. Do you really believe that?"

"Well..." Steckle muttered.

"I've always loved books about espionage," she interjected. "I really respect your opinion on this subject, so please tell me your thoughts!"

She kept prodding. "I would like to know what you think—as an outsider," she smiled. "I still believe that there has simply been a minor change in loyalties and objectives here. It's just logical to me that there must be a hell of a lot of former CIA, KGB and other intelligence types roaming around Russia, now that things have opened up here. And no one can be sure where their allegiances lie or what those agents could be doing here."

Staring unhappily at the ceiling, abstractly examining the peeling paint, Steckel shook his head, becoming impatient and not really focusing in on Galina's comments.

"I don't understand why you are so caught up with the intelligence balance of the successor states," Steckel said, smiling, "when my love for you is nuclear. I will be exceptionally frustrated if I cannot have you now. I'm in the mood to take you back to my apartment and show you the political miracle of early-morning love-making."

Galina giggled her practiced, charming laugh and replied, "That's not such a bad idea, but doesn't everyone make love in the morning?" Her flirtatious voice was clearly saying "yes," as she twisted the ring on her right pinkie finger. "Let's do something different. You turn me on when you talk to me. You'll soon learn that there is more to me than just jumping in bed every time I see you," she coyly persisted.

Uri noticed how she was holding Yossi's hand, erotically massaging his fingers. She smiled into his eyes. "We must supplement our love with *intellect*—that is the only way love can grow, she said teasingly. "You must tell me the way you think! I have to know your opinions. . .and I will continue to tell you mine."

Steckel's elation turned to disappointment. He had come here to charm Galina, to woo her, to use her—and eventually go his own way. The night before, his sexual fantasies had been fulfilled. So why was she being so exasperating today?

"What do you want me to say? All I can think about is last night," Steckel declared in a thin voice. "Maybe you want to talk about the weather? I thought I saw it starting to snow."

"You are quite right," she said, trying to show that she was understanding. "Last night was terrific. But I need more intellectual stimulation. So what would you like to discuss today, my dear lover?"

"Dear lover"? Bullshit! Damn it, Uri thought. What about your pregnant wife and two daughters back in Tel Aviv? You silly bastard! This KGB bitch is making a fool out of you and you're risking our lives for this whore!

Uri moved his body so that it only seemed he was making himself more comfortable, then turned his head quickly to glance over his shoulder, and saw Steckel caressing the woman's knee and looking deeply into her eyes. She returned his admiring glance with a warm, deep smile.

"It has been a long time since I felt this way," Steckel said. "I feel like the first time I was with a girl and I knew she was going to kiss me."

Steckel took a deep breath and leaned back in his chair to collect his thoughts. Uri wondered where all this could be leading? He laughed to himself at what a fool Steckel was, or was he? Was he aware of what was happening and just leading her on? Could he be so blinded by her...not realizing that Galina might be and most likely was a KGB agent? Where was all Steckel's Mossad training? Where the hell was all that loyalty to his family that Steckel had always bragged about to the other agents? And where was his concern for his fellow agents and the mission?

If Avrum considered Steckel an essential asset to this operation, then someone would have to speak to him—and soon, Uri realized.

Chapter Twenty

BEHOLD IN RUSSIA: DEMOCRACY!

OCTOBER 25

Steckel's and Galina's voices could be heard clearly in the Israeli's apartment by Uri, from the front seat of his car. The bugs he'd placed at strategic locations within the rooms were working perfectly.

Oblivious to anything but her beauty, yet conscious of the weakness he felt when she was close, Yossi began to talk, trying to think of something to say that would satisfy both his nervousness and her need for conversation. "Darling, it's just unfortunate for us both of us," he said, as Galina carefully ran a comb through her hair, smiling at him sitting across from her at the kitchen table, "that this is not the time to ask me all kinds of deep questions. Perhaps... later—first love then talk!"

"And what's so wrong about asking for your thoughts and opinions?" She gave Yossi her puzzled, hurt look. "Why are you suddenly acting like this? What is it all about?" Her mouth curled up in displeasure.

She walked around the table and deliberately kissed him on the lips. Giggling softly, she put her arm around his neck and slowly ran her tongue up and down the edge of his ear. He enjoyed every second of her sudden attention.

"I want to know more about you. Tell me, darling, tell me all about yourself and your friends, tell me everything you do when we are apart," she said as she slipped her hand down onto his leg. "The sound of your voice sends shivers down my spine." She was maneuvering him the best way she knew—with sexual references learned in her training sessions on KGB strategy. But until the right moment came—and it would come, she kept telling herself—she would try to be patient with him.

Steckel, finding it difficult to concentrate, finally answered, "I don't do anything interesting or exciting. Nothing that is important, except for making a living. I only work with my small export business, making contacts through some of my Israeli friends."

"Oh, export, that's very exciting! Do you export guns? Munitions? I want to know more about it. I just knew you were an important person. I'll bet you know a lot and no one appreciates you. But I know how really intelligent you are."

Standing over him, she partly opened her blouse. She was thinking that this nonsense was taking much too long; it was throwing her schedule off.

Steckel answered, "Galina, you are amazing. So sweet and yet so wise! I do occasionally work with some people who happen to be former intelligence agents, none of us are spies any longer or could be considered agents of influence."

Steckel gently pushed her away, suddenly stood up and walked to the sink. There he lit a cigarette. He was standing not far from one of Uri's bugs, as he paced back and forth.

"The truth—for the final time—is that I am self-employed as an export broker. What I once was in my former life has little to do with what I am now. As far as my Israeli friends are concerned, I am not privileged to know where they are now or everything they are involved in, but I'm sure it is not anything spectacular or the least bit interesting, or they would have surely told me."

"Really! Maybe you aren't the man I thought you were," Galina said, sounding angry. "Maybe you just want to impress me and you are really nothing! You and your friends sound like old men living in the past."

Steckel took a moment to collect his thoughts before continuing. Then, beginning to get excited, he spoke much more quickly. "That is not so, Galina. We are involved with the problems of the world. You want to talk about philosophy, feelings, and my opinions all the time, so I'm now going to give you what you've asked for. To us freedom and security are indivisible. I firmly believe that any society which chooses one loses both."

Unfortunately, Galina's inquisitive behavior had still not triggered any suspicions in Steckel. He did not seem to pick up on what was happening to him.

He paused and then softly asked. "How about going into the bedroom?"

"Yes, yes, I want to go to bed with you, but finish what you were saying first."

Steckel sat down, a weary look coming into his eyes. "You know, Galina, rather than you and I constantly having nebulous discussions, what about suggesting to your 'great' Russian reform politicians that they open a dialogue with the Western leaders! As a matter of fact, their cooperation by starting a realistic dialogue would gain a hell of a lot of support from the West."

He took a moment to stare at her and collect his thoughts. Then he continued, "A change in Russian policies will help relations with the West and more Western aid would certainly help Russia at this time of great need. Unfortunately, from what I hear, the aid your country needs so desperately may never get here in time to be of benefit, if your government does not act soon."

She turned and touched Yossi's cheek for a moment, in what seemed to Steckel an act of genuine affection. "You know something, you're really a great guy. Or should I say a sexy fella? Keep up this intellectual conversation. I told you it turns me on, and I am not fooling." She began tinkering with the earring in her left earlobe.

"Turns you on? Ha!" Steckel exclaimed. "I don't think I seem to be doing too good in that department."

He reached for her breast and fondled the nipple. She leaned back and turned her face to his. But then, as he kissed her lips, she gently but firmly pushed him away.

"What do you want from me!" Yossi's voice told of his frustration as he searched for something more to keep her interest.

Wow, he has sure become talkative, Uri thought as he listened through his miniature earpiece. He's just in too much of a rush to get her back into bed and he's bound to make a mistake on the way there!

Uri was concerned about the information Steckel had revealed to the woman about the fact that he worked with former intelligence agents from Israel. But whoever put her up to this game certainly knew that already, and the fact that he told her the truth might make them believe there really was nothing more than exports going on. Maybe she didn't pick up on Yossi's slip when he said we're involved in the problems of the world.

Steckel, now desperate, said, "You say you want to stimulate your mind, Galina? Well, try this on for size. I have one overriding question today: What are the intentions of this Civic Union military group that makes up a good deal of your Russian Security Council? Do those hard-liners have peaceful intentions or are they going to signal a resumption of the Cold War and the beginning of international confrontation?"

"Oh my God!" Uri said to himself, slumping down in his car seat. She did it, she *is* one very clever bitch! She pushed him over the edge. Yossi's taken one step too far by bringing up any knowledge of the diehards. How the hell will he get his ass out of this one? How will we get *our* asses out? When will he stop shooting his mouth off? "Maybe he has all of that political talk in him because he didn't get enough sex for one day!" Uri mumbled to himself, as he pounded his fist on the car's dashboard. Kiss her ear, kiss her ass, do anything—but stop preaching and spilling your guts on what you know to this spy bitch!

Taking Steckel's hand in hers Galina asked, "Oh, darling, tell me what else you think is going on with 'my' Russia. Keep up this conversation, my love, and you won't be sorry! I feel myself getting hot as you speak." She was biting his ear and whispering, "More...more...tell me more...feel how wet I am!" She led his hand between her legs.

For a second, Yossi found himself without words as his newfound love excited him with suggestive caresses. He was beside himself with passion. With a bit of effort he gathered himself together one more time.

"Well, with Russia's economy in a shambles," his words came out in short gasps, "and with military production virtually stopped except for illegal exports to Third World countries, the serious potential for massive unemployment! Civil unrest is overwhelming."

"Oh, God!" he murmured as she unbuttoned his pants. He stopped talking and she lifted her head to whisper, "Don't stop talking or I won't be able to go on." He took a deep breath, closed his eyes and continued.

"Democracy and a market economy don't exist in Russia, for a number of reasons. First of all, there's a severe lack of trained people who can compete in a market-oriented economy." Now he felt her tongue caressing his manhood. He blurted out, "There are former Communists who have succeeded in retaining most of their old political power. There are inefficient state monopolies still controlling most of the economy."

Offering him an inquisitive look, at first Galina appeared rather surprised at Steckel's sudden knowledge of Russian politics, but her training quickly put her at ease. Collecting herself, she responded, "You are clever, my love! Wherever do you get your ideas? To tell the truth, I did once know someone not unlike you, who had only good experiences with the Civic Union people. From what I hear, they are intelligent, sincere, quality individuals, who are dead serious about improving this country."

She paused to kiss him on the nose. "It is my understanding," she added, "that they have district councils that have the power to set the political agenda for the country, give policy instructions to institutions and government bodies, and make sure that they are carried out. It is true that the Civic Union also represents other groups—the military and military industrialists. That is my response to your concerns about our current economy. By the way, tell me about these die-hards and hard-liners you keep referring to?"

Steckel's heavy eyebrows raised as he realized what had popped out of his loose lips. She was sharp. She had picked up on his indiscretion. He would have to cross-check and double-check every word he said from this point on. Perhaps if he changed the subject, Galina would forget his mention of the die-hards, if he spoke casually and replied quickly. He felt that he should try to minimize the damage. Kissing her throat and sliding his lips toward her breasts, he said, "Haven't we talked enough? Now is the time for action..." But the look in her eyes turned cold.

He changed his approach and continued, speaking softly. "I do see good things happening with Russia's young reformers," he said. "Everyone knows that they are confronted by strong opposition in the parliament, but they are actually beginning to triumph on the economic front." But it wasn't working. His ardor temporarily cooled, as he concentrated to complete his thought. "What is making their victory even sweeter is that their struggle is providing reassuring evidence that a rough-and-tumble parliamentary democracy is now beginning to take place. However, the victory that they are working toward would be impossible without the promise of Western aid, and compromising to ensure they get this aid is a small investment to protect Russia's hopeful future."

Galina tried to swallow a yawn, but did not succeed. "Your thoughts are great, but they cannot buy a diamond in Amsterdam," she commented. "Steckel, I respect you for your views, but now I am getting a little tired of our discussion. For now, I am all for your suggestion. Do you still want to go into the bedroom?"

Outside, Uri noticed that after the small talk, and getting all she needed from him, Galina had become bored with the game.

As she spoke, Steckel spotted something in her eyes that he could not explain—an almost feverish shrewdness, a fiery independence. She reached out to hold his hands. Her touch blurred his senses and her closeness again put him at ease, chasing away his doubts.

"Bedroom? Sounds good to me!" He smiled putting his fears to rest. He wanted to believe she loved him.

Yossi took a last puff from his cigarette before crushing it in an ashtray. Galina smiled shyly and coyly, then laughed. Her eyes sparkled as she leaned suggestively against him. She stared into his eyes, as if silently begging him to take her.

He led her by the hand to the bedroom, and her thick blond hair fell in huge waves across her shoulders as they walked over to the bed. His arm around her waist, he steered her onto the bed.

All this firsthand knowledge of Steckel's extracurricular activities had shaken Uri. It was difficult for him to control his urge to jump up, run in and grab Steckel and bring him to his senses. He thought of creating a diversion, but without backup nothing would work. There could be more than one person following Galina, which would complicate things further.

Suddenly Uri saw the "tail" he was aware of slipping out a side door of the apartment building.

At this moment Uri's main priority was to make sure he himself was not spotted. Unfortunately, he would have to remain seated in his car for another minute or two, until he was sure the KGB tail cleared the area.

But why, Uri asked himself, why was the agent leaving before Galina, and why was he walking in a direction where there was no car waiting to pick him up? His only conclusion was that the KGB man knew exactly what was happening in the apartment and felt he was no longer needed. He had obviously gotten all the info he felt he would get.

Uri yawned, stretched, pulled up his coat collar and slumped down in the car seat. He was concerned that when Avrum heard of what had been going on, he would be extremely upset with the misguided Steckel. He wondered, Why do some people have to behave like royal idiots? He knew this would have never happened if Steckel had still been with the Mossad. Discipline would have prevailed and he would not have dared to conduct himself in such a shameless, idiotic, amateurish manner.

Uri's thoughts were interrupted as he stared out of the car window and saw what appeared to be Galina, accompanied by a second man in a heavy overcoat, leaving Steckel's building. Where the hell did *that* man come from? Uri wondered.

Uri listened in his ear piece for any sounds as he checked his watch. It had been three or four minutes since Galina had left with the man and he saw that there was absolutely nothing moving on the deserted street. In the apartment all sounds had ceased after Steckel's last statement. Only the tick of a clock could be heard through his earpiece.

Something had to be wrong! Getting out of the car and walking up to the narrow entrance, Uri looked through the glass of the front door and could see that the hall was empty. He pushed through the door into the semi-darkness and slowly proceeded to walk up the stairs. Cautiously, quietly, as he fingered the Gluck in his coat pocket, he made his way to Steckel's apartment.

Uri leaned forward, his ear against the apartment door. Nothing.

As he touched the door with his finger, it moved. With a slight push, it swung open. Afraid of what he might be in for, he peered around the corner of the door into the semi-dark room. It was empty. Uri cautiously approached the bedroom door, looked through the doorway and received a shock.

Steckel lay in the middle of the bedroom, on the floor, facedown in a pool of blood. Uri bent over his body and felt for a pulse. There was none. He noticed there was a small hole visible behind Yossi's right ear. They had used a silencer. That's why he had never heard the shot. A professional job. By God, his friend had been in a damn trap from the beginning. Galina's every move, her appearance, her questions had all been calculated.

"Bitch," Uri said aloud. "Those KGB bastards!"

His own voice startled him. Not disturbing anything, he briefly looked at Steckel's body. From his position on the floor, it appeared as if Steckel had been shot with a small-caliber bullet by a person hiding behind the door, just as he entered the bedroom. His shirt was half off. He never had a chance.

From the cradle to the grave, he thought, no man dare completely trust people he does not know, for all strangers must first and foremost be considered dangerous—especially if you are in this business. What the hell could Yossi have been thinking! Such a lack of judgment was unforgivable.

Reminded of his listening device, Uri immediately searched out the bugs, retrieving them one at a time, until he got to bug number four, which he had concealed earlier behind a curtain rod. His eyes focused on the floor, below the curtain rod. A stool was placed under the part of the rod where the bug had been placed. When the bug was nowhere to be found, he realized that the KGB people had obviously found the it and that this murder would soon be discovered. They would also be alerted to the fact that Yossi's associates probably knew who was responsible for his killing—which meant Uri and all the other formers would be in serious trouble. The consequences might be immediate. The die-hard agents knew that someone was now onto their game. Uri's face was set in a stony frown. He was like an angry man who had lost something essential to his safety.

His impulse told him to stay and look around for further evidence, because he hated to back down from any fight and he desperately wanted to find something that would help him find the perpetrators of this crime against his colleague and friend. But he had to be practical. Now it was time to take more precautions than usual. Security for his team of formers was his immediate and foremost consideration.

With the information Steckel had divulged, the formers were certainly now in great danger. Just as easily as they had snuffed out Yossi, they could do the same to the rest of the group. It was time to regroup, assess the new dangers, and come up with a new plan to deal with this turn of events.

"Put your dick in the wrong place and somebody is going to whack it off," Uri angrily mumbled under his breath. "You poor, stupid bastard."

He quietly closed the apartment door behind him, instinctively wiping the knob with his handkerchief. It had started out as a bad day and gone downhill from there.

Uri, who had known Steckel all his life, remembered his grandmother saying when they were young that Yossi was a boy destined for a wonderful fate. He was a gift from God, she often repeated. And now, because of his bad judgment, he and his grandmother's prophecy were gone.

Chapter Twenty-One

TWO TOILET APARTMENT

OCTOBER 25

Avrum surmised that the old Russian mystical and religious superstitions, which he had often humorously noted in a small memo book, were an open contradiction within the newfound democratic society of the C.I.S. and had survived the Communist era as well. For instance, he was intrigued that many in Russia today actually believed that Friday was a melancholy day, while it was widely regarded that Monday was auspicious for launching a new undertaking.

Many Russians had a fondness for folk remedies, and some of the superstitions he had noted seemed to have originated in the countryside. However, city people as well as peasants often told him that they preferred medicinal herbs and grasses, or even a mustard plaster, over modern drugs for their ailments.

On page two of his notebook Avrum reviewed an entry that indicated that one way to reduce swelling was to apply a copper coin to the afflicted area. There was also a suggestion to wear garlic cloves in a gauze bag around one's neck to fight a cold. And then there was a warning not to put thirteen people around a table. Some of Avrum's scientific friends would have found it hard to believe these widely followed beliefs in today's modern Russian society—yet they were actually taken as the gospel even by some educated people.

Avrum looked amused, as he waited in the safe house for Uri to turn up.

Meanwhile, Uri passed the quiet, unkempt courtyards and darkened entryways of rundown old buildings on his way to the formers' safe house.

He was aware that the interior landscape of Moscow was vastly different from the often photographed "picture postcard" apartment buildings one saw in the propaganda films and promotional magazines. So massive and aching was the shortage of living space in Russia that the housing norm of nine square meters per person—equal to a ten-by-ten-foot room—established by the government back in 1920, had still not been measurably improved. About one-third of the population still lived in primitive communal apartments.

And yet most people were perfectly satisfied with these meager quarters in the cities of the C.I.S., because they remembered the time when their parents and grandparents lived in *izbas* in the countryside: old wooden houses with absolutely no conveniences. When they compared their present situation with that of their past and with that of their parents, they realized that their situation had improved somewhat. And until they could observe modern conveniences elsewhere in the world, they had nothing to really compare their circumstances with.

Better-connected and affluent Russian families had sets of inexpensive matching lacquer furniture, while the average Russian had a kaleidoscopic assortment of mismatched tables and chairs that looked as if they had come from tag sales and grandmothers' attics. Rugs were nonexistent in most apartments. Furthermore, the door to a communal apartment could have as many as five or six doorbells—one for each large room that would house a family. A curtain across the entire room would separate the sleeping quarters of a child from that of its parents. He saw instances where beds would serve as tables or couches during the day, and then as beds again for sleeping at night. There was hardly a greater double standard than that between the living quarters of the ordinary citizen and the comfortable Russian apartments of the elites. The safe house that the formers had rented came from a well-known Central Committee member who was as elite as one gets in Russia. It consisted of two bathrooms and four bedrooms, plus a large kitchen, dining room and family room.

Uri had noticed that some apartments always appeared to be in a state of permanent disorder, perhaps due to the lack of space. However, it was a seemingly comfortable sort of disorder. If he visited unannounced, his hosts would not bother to neaten up for him, nor would they change from their casual clothes for their guest's arrival. Uri appreciated this casual tradition and found this unpretentiousness one of the most attractive and relaxing qualities of Russian life.

It was shortly past 9:00 P.M. Monday when Uri was observed by Hershel, who was watching from behind the window curtains of the safe house. He noticed that Uri was using every known trick he was taught to see if anyone was following. He walked past the entry of their building, then made a U-turn to cross the street and walked into a building opposite them.

Uri gave the appearance of a cat, pacing and unworried, but cautious, with eyes that were wise and alert. Hershel observed him as he cautiously crossed the street one more time. From the various angles on one side of the gutter to the other, Uri had a complete view of the street, windows and rooftops. After a few moments he triumphantly entered the safe house, thankful that he wasn't followed.

As Uri walked down the long and deserted hallway, he was reminded of a similar hallway at another time. It was in 1976, when Uri was serving at the Mossad station in Nairobi. The special interest for Israel was that Nairobi was not far from Cape Horn and was one of the most important capitals on the continent. Nairobi was where diplomats, spies of all nationalities, and meetings of African Unity Organizations took place. Together with Nigeria to the West and Zaire in Central Africa, Kenya was also one of the three most important centers of Israeli intelligence activity.

The hallway then, Uri remembered, was one that belonged to Bruce McDermott, a British businessman and farmer who had settled in Kenya and whom Uri knew very well and considered a good friend. But crossroads like Kenya inevitably attracted terrorists, too.

On January 18, 1976, less than half a year before Uri would be involved with the hijacking drama at Entebbe, Kenyan police with Uri accompanying them arrested three Palestinians on the edge of Nairobi airport with two Soviet-made shoulder-fired SAM-7 rocket launchers.

The Arabs had been planning to shoot down an El-Al airliner with 110 people aboard that was due to land an hour later. Based on Uri's interrogation, Kenya's secret police arrested a West German couple, Thomas Reuter and Brigitte Schultz, as they arrived in Nairobi three days later. Schultz's family tried to discover her whereabouts, but the Kenyan government denied holding any foreign prisoners. Eventually, Israel confirmed that all five terrorists were under arrest. Uri, with McDermott's cooperation, arranged an extra-judicial extradition whereby the Kenyan authorities handed the terrorists over to the Mossad. In Israel, they were tried, convicted and jailed. If tried in Kenya, the terrorists would have been freed within the year.

At the end of June, 1976, with many Israelis among the hijacked passengers in Entebbe, Uri again walked down the long hallway to McDermott's office—with a need for even greater assistance.

McDermott secured President Kenyatta's approval for the use of facilities in Kenya by Israeli intelligence. Within a few hours, dozens of Mossad agents flew to Nairobi to set up a planning center for intelligence and military operatives. Uri and the other Israelis, rowing tiny boats, crossed the border into the Entebbe area—just across Lake Victoria from Kenya—on reconnaissance missions to watch the airport and plan entry and exit routes. He also received permission for the Israeli aircraft that served as their field hospital to land in Nairobi after the successful mission. The clandestine connections forged by Uri paid off with the success of the Israelis' lightning raid on Entebbe.

Two years after the Entebbe assault, Uri received word that his friend McDermott was killed because of his cooperation with Israel. Libyan agents working for Uganda's dictator planted a bomb on McDermott's private jet. It was Ugandan dictator Idi Amin's show of revenge for being made a fool.

Uri thought about McDermott and the long hall to his office as he now approached the heavy wooden door to the safe house.

The second he was ready to knock, the door was abruptly opened by another former Mossad agent, Yaakov Vigdor, a well-built man in his early fifties whose eyes looked out rather cautiously from behind heavy tortoise-shell glasses. He still had the look of a warrior on his face that was both good-natured and deadly serious. At the moment it was the former.

Without saying a word Uri walked into the family room, where Avrum and Hershel were seated behind a long table. Hershel had turned the table into a desk, with maps and neatly stacked notes on one end. He had been busy working on a large graph that lay half completed in the middle of the table, listing names, countries, locations and sketches of weapons—some old, some new—that were of obvious interest to all present. One was a map of Russia whose legend was in Cyrillic.

"How is it going, Hershel?" Uri asked, not really expecting an answer.

"We could save a lot of time if we had the liberty of listening at the right keyholes," was Hershel's answer.

The new arrival remained silent until Avrum spoke. "It's not that cold in here, so take your coat off and sit down."

"Well? We are waiting anxiously. What gives with Steckel? Have you been able to keep up with him?"

"Like a Siamese twin," Uri replied. "But not close enough."

"Then he must have given you the famous Steckel slip."

"That could have been a problem, but he was not that elusive and that's not the full story. I must unfortunately say that..."

Uri hesitated, not finding the right words. "Avrum, we have a situation."

"How bad?" Avrum said, looking directly into Uri's eyes. He'd noticed an edge to Uri's voice.

There was what seemed like a long silence. Uri squeezed his fists together tightly.

"All right, Uri." Avrum's voice became authoritative. "Enough's enough! Where the hell is he?"

"With Satan. But as far as I know, sir, his corpse is still in his apartment, facedown in the middle of the bedroom floor with a bullet in the head."

Avrum stopped and squinted at Uri. "That's not funny. What's going on? What's happened?"

Uri rocked back and forth uncertainly, gazing back at Avrum.

"I agree," he finally answered. He shrugged his shoulders upward and let them drop, signifying that he didn't know what else Avrum wanted of him. "It wasn't pleasant finding him that way."

From the dejected look on Uri's face Avrum could see that he was not joking.

"For God's sake, what the hell happened?" Avrum asked.

Everyone's attention was abruptly riveted on Uri Glebova.

"The only explanation I can offer is that it happened very fast. And he was definitely set up."

Astonishment gave away to bewilderment as Uri told the gruesome story of finding Steckel's body. Then he answered an avalanche of questions, as if he were before a jury.

Avrum finally spoke. "I just find it strange that anyone bothered to kill Steckel. There has to be more to it than we know." He scratched his head as he thought. "I cannot believe that he gave away information about us. Nor could they ever get him to talk by torturing him. And I feel he would never give away our identities or whereabouts, under any circumstances. Most likely, killing him was a definite signal sent to anyone who might be part of what Steckel was up to here."

Everyone in the room remained silent—listening.

"They couldn't have concluded that there were others out there with the same cause, or they would have begun to uncover us before now. The KGB has little patience and takes very few risks. But, what I don't understand is, why they didn't arrest and torture Yossi to get more information. Unless," he reasoned, "they were not acting in an official government capacity."

He sucked on his lip for a moment, his deep-set eyes ringed with circles, deeply in thought, as Uri spoke out, "I have to feel sorry for Steckel meeting that woman. She could turn heads in any city of the world. She was a classic KGB temptress, too beautiful for any but the most disciplined man!"

Slowly, pensively, one by one, the four former Mossad agents nodded in agreement. Avrum parted the window curtains and stared outside. There was the feeling of snow in the air. The sky was dark and low.

Hershel spoke. "You know there's a term used to describe the destruction of someone who gets too close to a military project or source. That term is identified as 'collateral damage.' The death of Yoel, and now this incident, is unfortunately our collateral damage. It is one thing when a state kills someone as an act of war. In the cases of Yoel and Steckel, their deaths were simply plain, cold-blooded murder. Those bastards took their sweet time about setting Steckel up. After looking at all of the facts, I'm now certain they must have felt there were others out there, and they enjoyed sending a message to whoever that might have been by killing him."

Avrum's lips kept opening as if he were about to add something more.

"It's agreed then," Avrum suddenly announced. "Contact Nikolai at his aunt's house at once. I want him to discreetly and with great care remove the body for shipment to Israel. Even though we are former agents, the tradition of the Mossad is that we never leave our own behind. We had plans in place, from the beginning, to remove any casualties on this mission. Steckel's body will be shipped out aboard an El-Al plane in a wooden packing box marked 'rejected machinery parts,' and given the sad circumstances of his death, the 'rejected' marking will be appropriate.

"Pass the word," Avrum said slowly. "There will be no gossip, no rumors, nothing negative is ever to be discussed regarding Steckel after this meeting. For the benefit of his family, the cover story of his death now—and in the future—will be that he was struck by a car driven by a drunk driver. I will make all the appropriate arrangements in Israel." He gave a deep sigh. "It's too bad that Steckel's overconfidence, success and stupidity had him careening around like a wild beast. Since he left the Mossad he'd become too brash and took too many chances. Now his wife and children are left with this tragedy.

"But we will not let this setback shake us or hurt our mission, he thought; sometimes the worst turns out for the good in the long run. We must think positive."

Avrum gave the following message as clearly as he could to those present: "Uri, take all the precautions you feel are necessary and the extra security you require to make sure you are not observed. In order to confuse the scent, invent all the pretexts you must without drawing the eye of the enemy. Any record of Steckel's involvement with us must be purged." Avrum was not being melodramatic when he told Uri not to leave any trace of Steckel's existence in Russia after the body was removed. "We've achieved so much in a short time on our mission here. It's tragic that because of one guy with hot pants it could all go down the goddamned drain. His decadence has put us all at risk."

Avrum glanced over to the pile of papers that Hershel had collected at his end of the table. "Now, what do we do to keep our mission on track? First of all, we have to get back to work and concentrate on our objective....I will speak with the General and see what *he* can learn about this mess. This puts us in an awkward position. Never before have I been compromised on a mission because of this kind of outrageous behavior!" Avrum said grimly, with an obvious look of disgust on his face. "Steckel took his chances and lost, and that's too bad. We've just got to make ourselves leak-proof from now on. No one must be able to trace anything back to us. As sad as it is, I know that we are capable of doing this."

Uri was confident in his abilities to do his job, but not exactly sure in his heart that everything would be the same from this point onward. He moved toward Hershel.

His brow narrowed by his fur hat, his broad, barreled chest, his heavy overcoat, and his square jaw made Uri suddenly appear forbidding. His hands were thrust into his coat pockets as he looked into Hershel's face.

"I nearly forgot some news that you may find interesting," he said. "It may or may not have any significance to you, but the day before Steckel was murdered, Dmitri Kholodov was killed in his office when he opened a booby-trapped suitcase. The story is, he had been told its contents would help his investigations of corruption in the Russian Army. Here are several news clippings about it I removed from Steckel's inner jacket pocket."

Uri handed them to Hershel. Hershel studied the writings for several moments before raising his eyebrows.

"News clippings about the hard-liners were published under Dmitri Kholodov's byline in *Moskovsky Komsomolets.* That paper is the center of investigative journalism in Russia. They charge that General Burlakov, who recently returned to Russia after serving as the commander of the Russian troops in Germany, was involved in arms smuggling, black marketeering and other crimes during his tour of duty. They also call for the indictment of the Russian Defense Minister, Pavel Grachev."

Hershel slid from behind the table and added. "Incidentally, I read an article in today's paper about Dmitri Kholodov's murder. The paper said he was a crusading journalist who has become the latest martyr in a campaign for total democracy in Russia. It also said that over a dozen journalists have recently been killed when they got close to any big dirty political stories about the hard-liners or the Russian Mafia."

Avrum puckered his lips thoughtfully. "The truth about all of the corruption here is in the records. It always eventually comes out, it's just a question of how many journalists and investigators get killed first. All of this just shows what the future holds for people who seek the truth here. I rather doubt that we shall ever have the time to find Kholodov's or Steckel's killers."

As Uri readied himself to leave, he realized how his discovery of the news clippings made obvious logic out of the events leading to Yossi Steckel's death. The clippings also put together a few more missing pieces of the hard-liner jigsaw puzzle.

"Oh yes, one more thing before you leave, Uri," said Hershel. "You, like all of us here, keep referring to the KGB as the KGB. It is not officially called the KGB anymore, even though it still exists and is still powerful. It is now rectified and reinstalled into the new Federal Counterintelligence Service—FSK for short. The director is Aleksandr Stepashin, and all but a dozen of the two hundred fifty top officials from the KGB still run the agency. What began in 1917 as the Cheka, on the back of the czarist Okhrana, later became the OGPU, the NKVD, and in 1954 the MBG. The KGB has changed its name no fewer than seven times since the aborted coup in August 1991. It may be called the FSK today, but the KGB is alive and well—a government within a government. Sorry to hold you up, just thought you should be informed. I wanted you to know exactly what we are up against."

Without uttering a word, Uri buttoned up his overcoat, wrapped his muffler around his turned-up collar and disappeared out the door. He looked around him carefully to be sure he was not under surveillance, as he slowly walked from the building out onto the street, disappearing into the darkness.

In the apartment, Avrum's eyes gradually focused on the top sheet of the pile of Hershel's papers. "What...the hell is this?" he said with a slight hesitancy in his voice.

"It's not an immediate problem!" snapped Hershel, "but I predict that it will be one before too long, because it involves some of what we are after—Russia and China and the hard-liners—strange partners indeed. They are not the only partners the die-hards are dealing with. There is Saudi Arabia, Taiwan, Iraq, Iran, India, North Korea and other Third World nations."

Avrum interrupted, "Where in the world did you get this information?"

"As we were leaving the General's car at our last meeting, he sat next to me and quietly slipped this folded manila envelope into my coat pocket." He held up an empty envelope that had held the papers. "So, if he wanted us to have this information, it must be worthwhile and it should give you added insight into the situation we are confronted with."

Leaning over Hershel's shoulder, Avrum added, "I see you are not quite done translating the documents from Russian. Why not just give me a short brief on what you have so far."

"I will, I will, in just a moment," Hershel said, collecting his notes. "The General is pooling his resources with us. He is confirming that the hard-liners will prove to be clever, resourceful and strong. They are promoting violence and chaos and recognize that these are the key ingredients to their success. In the meantime, their wallets are benefiting nicely. The pattern of Russia's arms sales has changed considerably since the Cold War, when they realized billions of dollars of profit every year from nations such as Libya, Syria, Iraq, Cuba and others. Some of those sales were made at bargain-basement prices with long payout terms. That was when they were making their best efforts to expand their military influence. Today it's a different story. They are promoting one thing and one thing only: hard cash for their near-bankrupt arms manufacturing plants. And they don't give a damn about adverse publicity or Western preferences on who they sell to."

"And from the rest of the world there's not a peep, no matter which terrorist groups they sell to," Avrum interjected.

"What they are doing," Hershel continued, "is so obvious and so irresponsible that we all know the world's leading powers are aware of this activity. They are choosing to ignore it because they realize that if the hard cash from these arms sales is not realized, it will mean that even more money will have to be given as subsidies and loans to this bankrupt nation. Furthermore, the Western military leaders are delighted that the formidable arsenals of the former Soviet Union are being sold off and dismantled, presenting them with less of a threat—even if the weapons are headed toward terrorists, dictators, and other unsavory end users. Let's face it, the powers that be have chosen to look the other way. Then again, what we are working on could only be appreciated by a fraction of Western politicians. While the hard-liners are for 'national strength, the Motherland and Communism,' let's be realistic—they also like the hard profits from their wheeling-and-dealing free enterprise activities. And we can be sure that these guys are taking a cue from what is going on in America.

"Take for example America's 'private' army in Bosnia. While U.S. troops in Bosnia have been kept below 20,000, a Dallas-based private contracting firm was hired by the U.S. Government to work in Bosnia doing a host of jobs, from engineering and supervising workers to re-building pipelines, sewage systems and housing. And they've even undertaken the solemn task of readying the bodies of U.S. fatalities for shipment home. It is none other than Dick Cheney, former U.S. Secretary of Defense, who now runs that Dallas-based firm. The support-staff contract, which has already pocketed over $300 million for this company, was originally won when Cheney was still Secretary. Not too bad an example of how to feather one's nest, is it!" he added.

Avrum hung on every word, yet this explanation was still not enough for him. "We need more specifics," he exclaimed in an excited voice. He knew this was an old, complicated story, but he did not want Hershel to waste precious time seeking out items that did not directly relate to their immediate problems.

Hershel took a deep breath and another moment to get his thoughts together. He looked down at the papers in front of him, studying them for a few seconds before speaking. "The Russian hard-liners are focusing on the countries that are willing to pay them cash for the goodies they are selling. To date, their top priority and best cash customer has been Iran. China has now begun increasing its purchases as it buys weapons at bargain-basement prices—below even China's low costs to produce similar items! China is also buying high-tech stuff that it should not really be allowed to purchase, given the fact that Russia knows the Chinese will be stealing the Russian technology as soon as they can take these new weapons apart to copy them!

"From my viewpoint, the Chinese cannot get such high-technology weapons systems from any other suppliers. What they are developing is a dangerous marriage of convenience. The hard-liner officials have even resorted to selling sophisticated, Russian missile-guidance technology to China. Since China's air-to-air missiles are not fine-tuned enough to seek out enemy planes, the added Russian technology can be expected to enable Beijing to greatly improve China's offensive capabilities. China's surface-to-surface missiles would also benefit, since the ones they presently have are inferior to the Russian guidance systems. You can be assured that will soon all change."

Avrum nodded grimly.

"And, as if we didn't have enough to worry about, the General's notes also state that there are negotiations going on for joint production of tactical missiles and other highly technical weapon systems in China. Anything to make a fast ruble! Can you believe this?" Hershel said, looking down at the Chervok's papers. "They are not only selling tanks to Beijing, they are selling them their latest military tank manufacturing technology. Don't panic just yet—there is more to come....Now, I know you haven't had time to give it much thought, but just tell me, what do you think about this outrageous scenario so far?"

"The more complicated it gets, the simpler it gets," Avrum spat out, his mind too boggled to want to think about the stupidity of what the Russians were doing. "Aside from cutting their own throats, they are strengthening a dangerous, unstable, hostile, unpredictable neighbor— with a vastly superior growing economy that was running circles around them."

Hershel added, "The die-hards even filtered some of their surplus funds from these arms sales back into the weak Russian economy in the form of hard business investments. I guess they are trying to shore it up before it collapses. That included some of the money from the 14.8-billion-dollar sale for combat jets to Taiwan and Saudi Arabia that was recently completed. I believe this exceeded the value of American arms sales to all nations of the Third World last year. That's an incredible figure. The General indicates that the hard-liners are also negotiating with Iran and Syria to sell them an unusually large quantity of weapons this year, regardless of world opinion. And they don't even bother to be secretive about the sales. It's high time that the world listened in to the pulse of what is going on in Russia."

"As usual, only a small circle profits by all this and the Russian people don't get any direct financial benefits," Avrum interjected. "Their misery continues, as has always been the case over here."

"Exactly! There's no mistaking that the die-hards control the profits," Hershel affirmed. "They divide them as they please, among themselves. In fact, they claim that weapons exports are only a cushion for the Russian arms industry. They say their country is making the transition to a civilian economy."

Briefly toying with the thought, Avrum added, "Why shouldn't they sell these weapons?" He laughed. "They need only recall the story of Dick Cheney and the example the United States set. The U.S. is also selling arms and technology to some of the same countries. Why, just last year McDonnell Douglas sold seventeen specialized machine tools to China, with the full permission of the U.S. Commerce Department. The machines had been used to make the U.S. Air Force B-1 bomber, C-17 transport and the MD-80 and MD-90 airliners. These machines were to go to a commercial machining and tooling center in Beijing. But they were recently found to be in Nanching, 800 miles from Beijing, at a military plant that makes cruise missiles and fighter planes. The Chinese lied when they were caught red-handed at cheating—saying that it was a mix-up! Which only adds insult to injury. We all know that the machinery should never have been sold to the Chinese in the first place. It was only a matter of time before the machines would be illegally, knowingly and willfully diverted and used for military purposes."

"A perfect Chinese Communist plan," Hershel reasoned, "allowing them to get what they wanted at the expense of the foolish Americans who let this deal be done in the first place, satisfying their own agenda.

Russia now is justifying the recent sale of three diesel submarines to Iran. They've simply stated it was their way of raising cash during a difficult transition period. We already know that Israel regards Iran as the greatest long-term threat to its security. But Washington always considers the Mossad's warnings of Iran's military threat as mostly knee-jerk reactions. When Iran uses these weapons on U.S. targets, perhaps then the Americans will understand our warnings!"

Hershel reached for his throat, indicating that he was getting hoarse from talking. Avrum held up his hand as a sign for Hershel to stop, and walked to the kitchen. After a few minutes he returned with a porcelain pot filled with more Russian coffee in heavy mugs, as well as stale doughnuts on a plastic tray. Hershel tasted the bitterness of the coffee and made a sour face.

Clearing his throat he said, "Thank you Avrum, my good friend and lousy coffee maker. It's strong enough to set off the metal detectors at Moscow airport."

"I love you too. Next time, make it yourself, if you think you can do better."

Hershel put down the cup and turned toward Avrum. "Were you aware that Patriot-like surface-to-air missiles known as S-300s, designed to shoot down planes and missiles, have also just been sold to China? I just found this out in this document! China purchased them along with twenty-four SU-27 fighters, including all the technology necessary to assemble them at home. The hard-liners have put everything up for sale. Russian officials are offering Third World nations the opportunity to purchase most of their military hardware out of existing inventories or off present production lines, and they are even willing to custom-manufacture specially configured weaponry. And all of this is going on under Yeltsin's nose and he can't do a thing about it. Where is the protest from the rest of the world? Is everyone asleep at the wheel?"

As if he were looking to the stars for answers, Hershel gazed up at the bare light bulb hanging from a wire in the ceiling. Then he continued.

"Listen to this: Did you ever wonder what happened to all those Iraqi aircraft Saddam Hussein ordered flown to Iran during the Gulf War? I'm referring to the large group of fighter jets that the Iranians said they would not return? Well, they are now working just like they did when they were new, thanks to the spare parts the hard-liners are cheerfully selling them. Oh, I almost forgot about the latest group of T-24 tanks sold to Syria," Hershel said looking down at his translated notes.

"With all of this sophisticated weaponry being sold to anyone with a checkbook, world peace is not going to be part of the long-run picture.

"The corruption is rampant. I also found out that a private Russian company, Glavkosmos, is selling rocket boosters to India in violation of their treaty agreements with the United States to restrict technology transfers for ballistic missiles. We should find out who is actually running the company." He took a deep breath and began again.

"What is a real worry is the die-hards' sale of advanced dual-use technology. This can be employed to enrich uranium for nuclear power plants. China, in turn, is planning to modernize its nuclear power plants with this technology, making them much more marketable to Third World nations. Both Russia and China have recently sold nuclear power plants and technology to Iran. So what do you think will happen?...My guess is that it will soon help Teheran enhance Iran's expertise in developing the nuclear weapons that they so desperately want."

Avrum interrupted. "There is one more thing I'd like you to be aware of. The hard-liners are systematically manipulating Russian people backwards, back towards their old Communist ways. 'Divide and conquer' is probably what they have in mind. This country is adrift in the schemes of the die-hards. And their economic and military power will soon turn into political power. Through economic and military pressure, they are maneuvering to divide Ukraine, split Kazakhstan and subvert Azerbaijan. It's even possible that once Ukraine is made submissive, they will start their same tricks with their Communist friends who are trying to do the same thing in Poland. Yes, Poland could be next—depending on how successful things are in Russia. We could assume any number of possibilities and argue the points all day."

After a brief silence Avrum got to his feet and started pacing.

"But this is bullshit! We can't stop all the problems of the world. What the sons-of-bitches are doing is developing a new, more sophisticated generation of terrorists. We seem to be living in a calm before the big storm. So what should we do? How in the world can we stop it? We have to concentrate on stopping the immediate problem with the Communist die-hards."

"We may not be able to stop all of it, but maybe we can slow it down a bit...slow it down," Hershel suggested. He sighed, his brow wrinkled. "Perhaps create a longer calm before the big storm. Just look at our own history. Remember the reports about the years 1963 to 1967? Soviet policy back then was involved in the use of chemical weapons in Yemen.

"And what about the Russian nerve agent shells, which were discovered among the munitions captured by our troops in the Sinai during the Six Day War? Don't forget that Russia had previously furnished Iraq with chemical and biological agents in the fall of 1967, when they decided to counterbalance the Israeli nuclear threat. And Iraq just went on to use those same C-B agents in their war with Iran, killing tens of thousands."

"All quite true," Avrum agreed. "Your point?"

"You know that I didn't get involved with the Mossad until the Yom Kippur War in 1973. Keep in mind that as far back as then, Egypt was prepared to deploy Russian-made chemical and biological munitions, associated with Russian-made SCUD deployments, against Israel. When our team analyzed the captured Soviet equipment, we could see that it had been designed for fighting in contaminated environments. I will never forget the massive amount of protection gear we found at the front, including the medical treatment kits. All kinds of chemical and biological equipment were present. After analysis, it was found to be superior to the U.S.-made equipment, which had been neglected and allowed to deteriorate even before we received it. We gradually forgot about the Soviet equipment supplied to the Egyptians and would have kept on ignoring it, had it not been for the massive use of Russian C-B agents in Iran, Iraq, Southeast Asia and Afghanistan."

Hershel drew a deep breath. "What's the point, you ask? Well, we may eventually have to deal with a bunch of Russian crazies who have stockpiled anthrax, available for sale to our enemies or anyone else who can pay for it! And it doesn't matter who starts this problem: the fact is, we're going to be the ones in the middle of it."

"You mean we could be dealing with more than a few dozen lunatics on the loose with canisters of anthrax, who would use them against civilian population centers?" Avrum was painfully conscious of the sweat that kept forming in his palms.

"That's certainly a possibility, isn't it?" said Hershel. "Do you think anthrax fired into a population center via a SCUD missile or via a canister released by a suicidal terrorist is such a farfetched scenario? Did you ever think it was farfetched for suicide bombers to strap explosives to themselves and blow up buses full of civilians? Well the anthrax scenario, I'm sure, would please these suicide assholes even more—getting them to meet Allah and become martyrs even faster! That is the sick mentality we are up against!"

Avrum's reply was not angry, but matter-of-fact. "Nothing has ever been easy for us. I don't expect the hard-liners have any more love for us than do the Arab terrorists."

In spite of the ugly odds facing them, Avrum decided that he had to lighten the tension of the moment. "I'd better look up in my funny little memo book to see what superstitions are in store for us traveling about in this part of Russia."

"I beg your pardon?" Hershel said with a surprised expression, as he pulled a handkerchief from his pocket. "Are you trying to make a funny?"

"Here it is—page 5," Avrum continued. "'All members of the household must sit for a moment of silence before anyone departs on a journey.' Evidently this is a holdover from an old Russian religious practice. When the moment of silence has ended, the senior member of the family is to say, 'Go with God.' Others have to be careful not to mention the precise destination of the trip so as not to attract the attention of the evil eye."

"That'll work. So *Mazel tov*—whatever turns you on," Hershel said with a frozen smile on his face.

Chapter Twenty-Two

THE ORGANIZATSIYA CONSPIRACY

OCTOBER 26

The already crumpled, poor-quality yellowing pages of Pravda lay strewn about the kitchen table. For an hour Hershel had been sitting by himself in the kitchen, reading incidental details of emerging morning stories. It had become a morning ritual for him. Every once in a while he sat back to reflect on what he had read about recent revelations in Russia. He knew that no point was too small or insignificant in the larger scheme.

On this particular day he noticed an article that caught his interest. He had to squint to read the small print. It was written by a Russian journalist who was reporting on a revolt of Muslim separatists in tiny Abkhazia, on Georgia's western Black Sea coast. They had been fighting Georgian government forces for the past twelve weeks in what had reportedly become one of the former Soviet Union's bloodiest ethnic battles.

In an article written by the Itar-Tass news agency, Russian Defense Minister Pavel Grachev had warned that Georgia planned to take control of all Russian military equipment on its soil, a move that would violate agreements between the two countries and could very likely spark an all-out war between the former comrades. Hershel figured that with what he now knew about the way things operated here, the Georgians probably wanted to get in on some of the arms sales action, so they figured they'd make a play to get the Russian equipment and sell it on the black market for a hefty profit.

Avrum was now up and about. He noted that it was 7:00 A.M. He recognized Yaakov's distinct footsteps in the hallway getting louder as he approached the door to the apartment. Yaakov turned the key to the lock and opened the door without knocking.

Without a smile or uttering a word, he thrust a manila envelope into Avrum's hand and sat down in a chair. His face in his hands, Yaakov finally offered the fact that the envelope had been given to him by one of the General's retired KGB clowns as he got out of his car. It was obvious that Yaakov was unhappy.

"All right, what's the problem?" Avrum said. "And don't complain to me that we pigeonholed you into the same boring task, Yaakov—even though we both know this is true. We just need every bit of cooperation we can get."

"That's not it," Yaakov answered. "I feel a lot of anxiety at the moment."

"Anxiety?"

"I happened to overhear some older Russian citizens talking about life here today. Things are so hard for them. Democracy has brought them only poverty, pain and hunger. They are paying for sixty years of economic stupidity that put the concept of the 'good of the state' before the welfare of its citizens. They had no choice at the time, because of their totalitarian system, so how can we blame them now for those past problems? But most of all, they're now paying the price for so many years of wasteful, excessive, corrupt and cruel Russian regimes. You know that I try not to concern myself with politics too much, but it hurts when I hear about the problems of the senior generation. It reminds me too much of my parents and grandparents."

"I know," Avrum said softly, "but we can't solve all the problems. We have to think about immediate ones for the moment. Now, I'll bet that the General would not risk an additional meeting with us if the contents of the envelope were not urgent."

Avrum sat down and tore it open, pulling out papers one by one and holding them under the lamp as he set the empty envelope to one side. What he saw was beyond anything he could have hoped for.

Looking across the room at Hershel, he said, "We have just received a positive message from General Chervok with plans for us to have an immediate meeting with Morat Progalin. He's a former member of a group known as the Organizatsiya," he read. "Trained with the international elite of the Russian Mafia, he has returned from the United States to conduct his business and live again in Russia. From what I see here, as a favor to the General he is willing to offer us some information that may be extremely important to our mission. It seems that the Organizatsiya has been pressuring Progalin. He thinks that by giving us some information it will score him points with the General's people, which will help him to take some of the pressure off him from this Organizatsiya. In any case, the General says Progalin would give us his full cooperation."

"If he is willing to collaborate with us, what the bloody hell does he want from us in return?" Hershel asked.

"That remains to be seen. Anyway, that's not our problem. The General was to play the part of the dark-suited moneyman, if that's what it takes to get what this guy has to offer."

Hershel chuckled. "Wrong question. Right answer."

"In his memo," said Avrum "the General makes the statement that Morat Progalin 'has no face,' which is some sort of a Russian slang saying. I do not know the actual translation of what this implies, so keep it in mind." Avrum skimmed the rest of the report, translating as he was reading. "He also said that this Progalin, who once also had strong KGB ties, is now in hiding in Garaga from the KGB boys who once supported this new breed of home-grown Mafia criminal."

He paused for a moment to find just the right translation. "The General feels that Progalin is not a bad person at heart; but that may be more a function of the fact that he's a friend. We will have to be the judge, when we get to know him better. And the General strongly suggests, in these notes, that I warn anyone we send to interview Morat Progalin about several issues: First, that the area where Progalin was hiding is in Abkhazia, where there has been a rebellion going on. Last Sunday, Georgian warplanes bombed the resort city of Garaga, not far from where Progalin is in hiding—he could feel his building shake and he is concerned. Apparently, the bombing was in retaliation for the previous day's fighting, in which the rebels forced government troops from the city, leaving eight Georgians dead and seventy-six wounded.

"The General says here that there were forty thousand reservists called up to stop the rebellion and that a helicopter carrying Eduard Shevardnadze and other leaders to the region's capital of Sukhumi was unsuccessfully attacked. If you recall, Shevardnadze was the former Soviet Foreign Minister. We formers knew him to be tough, but also fair. Now he heads Georgia's ruling state council. The seizure by the rebels was timed to disrupt parliamentary elections planned a week from Sunday.

"The General also warns in these notes that after the breakdown of the Moscow-brokered peace talks, Shevardnadze intends to take an increasingly militant stance toward the Abkhazians, and to him it appears that additional fighting is now inevitable.

"The second important warning is about Progalin and the danger of the Russian Mafia. He noted that Progalin would be hard to spot in a crowd. Thin and tall, he's a lean one hundred ninety pounds on his average-looking six-foot-one-inch frame. He was recruited out of a Soviet prison labor camp by the KGB, in 1973. After extensive training by a special KGB unit, in December 1975, in the midst of the Cold War, he emigrated to the U.S., masquerading as one of approximately five thousand Jewish refugees at John F. Kennedy Airport in New York."

Not excited about what he'd learned so far on Progalin, Avrum stopped reading for a moment while he thought about the man's background, then he continued, "In a clandestine KGB plot, he was chosen to develop a special Mafia group in Russia that would become an off-the-books profit center for the KGB. Since there already exists a fast-growing and enterprising gangster underworld throughout Mother Russia, he was able to recruit a large-sized organization leaning on the muscle of the KGB to back him up. And his crime family is not to be messed with, given who his Godfather is. After successfully running this organization for a few years, he scammed his way into the United States and settled among some twenty-five thousand other recent Soviet émigrés and several hundred other KGB agents or informants in the Brighton Beach section of Brooklyn.

"As a professional 'spook' educated at Moscow Center, he was planted in the United States to create trouble and disrupt anything he could. He engaged in any crime that paid well—including espionage, counterfeiting, looting, illegal gambling, torture, prostitution, burglary, extortion, terrorizing businesses and contract murder. He kept all the proceeds—tax free.

"The KGB taught him how to be liar a with a sweet tongue. He completely understood that the world of the Russian Mafia often worked through terrorists, criminals and cowards, who hid and assimilated among the innocent, in places like Brooklyn. And he played his part well."

In his report to Avrum, the General also disclosed that not long after his arrival in the States, Progalin varied and widened his enterprises through negotiated alliances with leaders of other new Soviet émigré criminal rings, which in turn diversified and spread themselves in other major cities across the United States.

Called the Godfather by the cohorts of his now-thriving Russian émigré underworld, Progalin mimicked the life-style of a Mafia Don; he was always chauffeured in long black limousines when he was on business making collections from Brighton Beach businessmen or to stop at a local bar to loan-shark money at astronomical interest rates compounded on a weekly basis. The unfortunate borrower would probably never be able to pay it back in full, and would eventually suffer the consequences. He held 'high court' in several of his favorite neighborhood restaurants, just like the real mobsters did, where he met and joined with the local Italian Mafia to merge, and divide territory, and expand his underworld ventures, which included his ownership of a chain of bootleg gasoline dealerships in the New York area.

Reading further, Avrum allowed himself a knowing smile of understanding. "At his peak, the General tells us, Progalin was doing his best to screw up as much as he could in the U.S. while accomplishing his goals. He has been involved with anything illegitimate, from low- to high-tech. But gentlemen, this gets even better. His rap-sheet also suggests he's a major player in the international illegal weapons trade. He has bent all of the known rules on the sale and distribution of weapons. We're talking anything from guidance and navigation systems, fighter planes, munitions, custom-built motor torpedo boats, every type of small arms and ammo, missiles and their launchers, and from military rations to body bags.

"You'd better believe this guy is a villain. He actually believed that he could advance his enterprises without getting more assistance from those who backed him in the beginning—but he realizes that is no longer an option for him. He's now trapped. He knows the only way out is for him to risk working with the General, relying on him to get rid of one of the KGB factions so that things can go back to the way they were for Progalin."

Avrum read another page, then went back to reread it very carefully. He looked up and announced, "Crazy smart! The General's story of the KGB's infiltration of the West in the middle of the Cold War was a bigger operation than we all could possibly imagine!

"These documents state that the Soviet Union wanted to clear their overburdened, harsh Russian prisons and penal camps of career criminals, thereby ridding the nation of their most violent and troublesome offenders. The KGB came up with a brilliant plan. They were getting a lot of annoying media attention on their handling of the Russian Jews, so they came up with a nice solution to several problems: They would release some of the troublesome Soviet Jews every few months, and mix in a few career criminals with each group. They would brief the criminals on the basics of Jewish religion, and give them cover stories and documents to use when they emigrated.

"The KGB was delighted with the results as this operation continued successfully for many years. The criminals did what they did best: they preyed on whatever Western societies permitted them to emigrate. They committed all sorts of crimes, giving the majority of the legitimate, hardworking, impoverished Jewish Russian immigrants a much more difficult time in their new communities in foreign countries.

"Perhaps you've heard that earlier this year, several owners of a club in Hialeah—near Miami—Florida, were indicted in federal court for negotiating to sell a submarine from the former Soviet Union to several Cubans to transport cocaine to the U.S. Well, these same men were also found to be part of a large network of Russians established to ship stolen four-wheel-drive vehicles to Lithuania from South Florida. The indictment claims that the Russians held meetings and telephone conversations that were all conducted in Russian. The phone calls were recorded and the participants were videotaped at fancy places like the Fountainbleu Resort in Miami Beach. Another deal they were reportedly involved in included aircraft missiles. They were also selling tactical nuclear weapons to Arab terrorists in the United States. The charges against the Russian immigrants include conspiring to deal in explosive materials without a license and 'to transfer and disperse without lawful authority nuclear materials, knowing that they will be used to do substantial damage to property in the U.S.'"

"Officials of the United States Customs Service said that this case showed how readily available illegal arms from the former Soviet Union have become since the breakup of that country in 1991.

"The authorities even seized documents in which bills of lading were provided—reportedly signed by the Lithuanian Minister of Defense—asserting that the shoulder-fired anti-aircraft missiles would be delivered to Lithuania, when, in fact, they were destined to be delivered by cargo vessel from Bulgaria to Puerto Rico," Avrum pointed out.

"Federal officials in the U.S. said this case also pointed at the growing presence of mobsters from the former Soviet Union *throughout* the U.S.," Avrum continued. "These papers claim that more than twenty-five Russian criminal organizations are presently operating in the United States. This is particularly troubling because members delve into all types of crime, including financial fraud and extortion. They have proven adept at cooperating with other criminal groups, be it the Mafia or the Cali drug cartel in Colombia."

Avrum picked up another page and quickly scanned it before explaining to the rest of the shocked team that in establishing the Organizatsiya in the United States, the single most important goal of the KGB's braintrust was for the crime organizations to repatriate a share of the quick, untaxed profits from their criminal activities to help finance the worldwide clandestine KGB operations. But apparently Progalin thought like a chess master who was also willing to throw the dice. He'd even paid a fraction of his profit to the KGB, keeping the lion's share for himself!

"This guy has really big balls to pull that kind of crap on his own KGB masters!."

"If you were wondering, Hershel," Avrum said, as he looked down at Morat Progalin's résumé in front of him, "why we have never heard of Progalin or why he is now in hiding in the C.I.S., well, in keeping with an ancient Russian criminal custom, Progalin surrounded himself with an underworld confederation of tight-lipped ultra-loyal criminals that proved hard, if not impossible, to penetrate. Any Russian refugee-immigrants that might have had an inclination to go to the police were threatened with reprisals against family members if they ever spoke out or identified those responsible for some criminal action. And as the group got bigger and stronger, even potential witnesses refused to appear or testify against an Organizatsiya member—no matter what. And there you have it," Avrum said, putting down the papers for a moment.

As usual, Hershel's curiosity continued to be aroused. As he had done countless times, he squinted his eyes in thought, then turned to Avrum beside him.

"If Progalin was so damn powerful and successful, why the hell can't he work out his KGB problems on his own? Can't he just pick one of the two KGB factions and team up with them to get rid of the competing faction? And why is he back in the C.I.S. and in hiding?"

"You're on the right track Hershel. But he is working with two rogue KGB groups that are so high up and so connected he can't play one off against the other." Avrum laughed, scratching the side of his neck, and said, "Well, this couldn't have happened to a nicer scumbag!

"Let me finish the memo from the General," Avrum suggested. "Then you will understand some of the realities which the Organizatsiya may not have come to appreciate yet. The United States Federal Drug Enforcement Administration broke up a major Mafia heroin smuggling gang in New York last December, and Progalin was fingered as the go-between to the Italian organized-crime distributors. The drugs were being smuggled in from Southeast Asia by unsuspecting women couriers, via Warsaw. Polish women were working as household help and frequently went back to visit their families. A perfect cover."

Avrum glanced at a picture of Progalin which the General had attached to the report. "Not a bad-looking guy for a con man, KGB-backed Mafia Don, informant, drug dealer, counterfeiter and turncoat!" he commented, as he handed the picture across the table to Hershel. "Hershel, meet Mr. Progalin."

Studying the picture, Hershel did not wonder or care about Progalin, his parents or where they came from, whether he listened to classical music, had a wife, children or a dog.

Ezra Gur, who had joined Avrum's little team from his office in Paris only hours before, was seated next to Nikolai. Life for him while in the Mossad had not been a popularity contest. Even though he was extremely trustworthy, capable and loyal to the Institute, he'd been unpopular with his immediate superior, who considered him the rich kid on the block—haughty, smart enough, but with no drive, politically shallow, and with too expensive a wardrobe.

For years after Ezra resigned the Mossad to go into business for himself, he boiled with anger at the disregard with which he had been bypassed for promotion. He only agreed to work with Avrum for reasons of his own and to prove to himself that he was still worthy. For one who was once a trusted agent in Israel's most elite intelligence group this trip into the Russian unknown was strange indeed!

"One crooked dude, this Progalin character," stated Ezra. "I've seen guys like him again and again. They do the deals, other people take the fall."

As Ezra ceased speaking, Avrum decided to return to substantive details. "Progalin thought himself untouchable in the U.S. He was protected by his small army of aides, bodyguards and that impenetrable émigré code of silence. He was untouchable until the year 1985. That is when Progalin and his associates raked in about one hundred million dollars in profits, and that's when the Organized Crime Strike Force and the United States Justice Department got on the case and tried to press charges and indict him. Hours before a grand jury indicted him, Progalin escaped to Garaga.

"Of course this frustrated the federal law enforcement agencies monitoring this piece of garbage's whereabouts, and they requested that he be extradited from the Soviet Union. In return, they heard nothing but silence. Progalin is not an easy person to find, even in Russia. He is such an expert at what he does that you almost have to admire the man."

"I think we all see the big picture on this guy," Ezra spoke up cautiously. "So what do you want us to do about him? Do away with him? Plan to spy on him?"

"Well, that is the way the system has been working. Everybody spies on everybody else and they also check out everyone we come in contact with whenever they can," said Hershel.

Avrum had an especially warm smile at the thought of taking time to spy on Progalin. "I'm afraid that we just do not have time enough in this instance, Ezra. Anyway, it wouldn't work out. He has friends all over Russia and he's too insulated and protected for us to spend the limited time and resources we have."

Avrum then added the following thoughts: "What followed in Progalin's absence, when he decided to disappear, was a power vacuum, a leadership struggle which put the Organizatsiya in the U.S. into a state of disarray. Progalin is a wanted man by his own people, who would love to get rid of him, and by U.S. law officials—by everyone! His enemies and the other opportunists moved into the void and took over his organization with their own violent administration. Now Progalin has a fire raging in his belly and wants to talk about it with his old friend the General. It's obvious that he also wants Chervok's help in many areas. He expects one hand to wash the other. He still has dreams of taking over his old position, but these are dependant on the General's backing."

Avrum laughed under his breath. When he spoke again, his voice seemed to echo through the room. "Time. Time's valuable, every minute of it. Ezra, you are to go along and meet with the General and Progalin. You are a skilled interrogator, one of the most capable in developing a rapid and meaningful discussion. You must get inside Progalin's head. I believe you can do it better than any of us, if you put your head to it."

"Fair enough," Ezra agreed.

Avrum painstakingly put his briefing papers back in order and slipped them into a loose-leaf folder. He then slowly made his way back to his chair next to Hershel and sat down. He was thinking about their next inevitable moves.

"We may have the opportunity to use our swords again before rust collects on the blades," Avrum said to Hershel. Both men sighed heavily.

Everything had to be perfectly planned. Nothing left to chance. They had no intention of putting their trust in providence. From the moment when they attacked the die-hards, all had to be precision-coordinated by their strategist, Hershel.

Chapter Twenty-Three

SOLDIERS OF THE BEAR, GARAGA, GEORGIA, C.I.S.

OCTOBER 27

The morning train to Garaga left from the Moscow station at 5:00 A.M., still on the old Communist schedule designed for maximum use of the rolling stock, not for the convenience of the passengers. Russia always had enough people, but not nearly enough trains. As had been decided, Ezra, accompanied by the General, was going to meet Morat Progalin in Garaga.

The station looked like a vast, dim warehouse with groggy bodies moving as slowly as possible, as if slow motion would preserve their energy until their train arrived. Some passengers looked as if they had been waiting days for their train, their tired bodies draped over large wooden benches apparently designed for the express purpose of preventing comfort.

A policeman walked slowly down the aisles, tapping people on their legs with his baton to wake those sleeping. "The station is not a hotel, comrade."

It was finally time for Ezra and the General to board, and they prepared themselves for the freezing walk from the station to the train outside. They hugged themselves against the cold as they finally boarded. Their breath blew away from them on the bitter north wind.

The seats in their compartment were folded down for daytime use as the two entered their car. Ezra sank into his. He was tired enough to fall asleep sitting up. He closed his eyes for a moment, but there was a resounding screech—the noise of the train starting to move at a walking pace through sleeping Moscow. It was the brief hour before daylight. To save power, the city's streetlights had been turned off before dawn, and the Russian capital became a collection of dark square objects hovering over the banks of the river Moskva.

The conductor now opened the compartment door and fumbled with Israelis' tickets, as the car rattled from side to side. In a few moments, he was back again with pillows and blankets. Ezra noticed a sly glance from the conductor as he slid the door closed behind him. Ezra said, "You know, General, if I were paranoid I would think the conductor was spying on us."

"That's a charitable way of putting it in a Communist country where everyone was brought up to spy on everyone else."

The vastness of the Russian countryside appeared endless in the night, as the speeding train rumbled noisily toward the seaside resort of Garaga. Here and there the sporadic moonlight outlined an occasional farm and a remote village, its dim lights burning in a few lonely buildings. The winding railbed, twisting and turning beneath the train, did not feel as if it had been laid with any care.

"Why are there so many turns in an area where the countryside is flat?" Ezra asked, breaking the silence.

"Because there are many offshoot roads to small towns," the General pointed out. And since many of these roadbeds were laid out during the Second World War! You see, a turning roadbed would be more difficult to bomb from the air."

This morning, Ezra saw many railroad stations crowded with young people carrying bedrolls and crude backpacks, headed along to sit by the sea or hike and sleep in the open air of the countryside. Ezra understood that the Russians had an extreme passion for their countryside and that the real point for most people was to take a stroll in the country—to get away from it all. And anywhere there was open space, Ezra saw people playing soccer or volleyball, sometimes simply hitting the ball around a human circle if no net was available.

But the one Russian outdoor hobby that bemused Ezra was "mushroom picking." It had approached a national craze.

Mushroom aficionados hid the location of their favorite hunting grounds for a premier species, as a military man would guard a top-secret document. The General, a connoisseur, insisted that each species required its own proper brand of vodka to accompany it. The milk mush-room was best with brown vodka made with refined sugar, which the General called petrovka.

"In fact, the beautiful little redheads demand crystal-clear and very cold vodka, which will not numb your sense of taste," said the General.

Ezra knew, however, from what he'd been told, that the General would be one of those mushroom gatherers who did it because he simply needed another excuse for drinking a variety of vodka.

At peak season, competition among dedicated mushroom pickers became so keen that they organized into groups and expeditions, rent-ing buses and spending entire nights on a bus so that at daybreak they could be first to get a crack at tender new mushrooms found deep in the countryside. It took a very practiced eye to distinguish poisonous from nonpoisonous mushrooms.

For Ezra, the trip began to seem endless as the train rolled along. The sun played through a strand of birches and majestic pines, casting a spell on him. Feeling a need to move, he changed positions in his seat. For a long time he found the open countryside a disappointment, since it did not offer dramatic scenery. He found a good deal of Russia to be a continent of vast flatland, stretching beyond the horizon in every direc-tion. It reminded him of the time he had visited the open, limitless prai-ries of Kansas, which lacked the picturesque hills of Bavaria or the breath-taking vistas of Switzerland. This part of Russia was even plainer, wilder, more undisciplined and more rambling. This was the Russia of the yel-low light reflecting from the oil lamp in the farmhouse window, of the rustling skirts of peasant women and of the rutted, muddy, unpaved roads.

The train finally slowed to take one of those offshoot roadbeds that headed toward the sea. After another thirty minutes speeding due east, it again slowed to a crawl as it came to the outskirts of Garaga.

The metallic sound of the train wheels resounded in Ezra's ears as they drew near the small station. He saw a number of military trucks looming in the distance as a group of uniformed soldiers, obviously stationed in Garaga to protect the railroad from rebel attack, circled a glowing campfire nearby. The dark silhouettes of several men with rifles and sidearms approached the train as it jerked to a complete stop. He looked at them with interest as they moved at a serious pace and with firm steps.

General Chervok told Ezra they would be passing through a military checkpoint and that he should get ready to deal with the approaching soldiers. Ezra forced himself to stand on his stiff legs and they both moved in the direction of the train's doors.

Departing the train, Ezra walked in front of the General and was immediately confronted by an officer who held his right hand up as would a traffic policeman. "You will permit me, sir?" said the officer, standing directly in front of Ezra.

"Permit you what?"

"You seem to be a foreigner. I am sorry for the circumstances, but it is customary under marshal law to show me your papers, to search your person and possessions. You have papers with you, da?"

"Papers? No papers—just a passport and a visa."

"I see." The officer said politely. He dropped his head as he inspected the dates of the many entry and exit stamps and visas stamped within Ezra's passport. With swiftness and efficiency the soldier then probed the contents of his overnight bag.

"You have no weapons on you, either?"

"Of course not," Ezra answered convincingly.

"Wait here a moment." the soldier said, and he strode back toward the fire with Ezra's passport.

"I'll wait for you to come back with my passport," Ezra shouted after the guard.

Other guards glanced toward Ezra, some with rifles poised under their arms. Several of the soldiers carried two-way radios, and made a show of looking busy by speaking to one another; but from what Ezra overheard, they were not discussing official business. Farther away, small groups of men in work clothes walked slowly toward the center of town, speaking to one another as they met. They did not seem especially interested in the people leaving the train.

After a few moments, the officer returned and handed the passport back to Ezra. He had a stance that arrogant Russians do best—hand on hip, shoulders back, one knee cocked. This was not a face to play cards against and lose. His officer's lapels carried the emblem of the Special Security Forces. "You did say that you are a correspondent?"

Ezra became cautious. "No. I am here on holiday and to see an old friend. He said that he would show me some of the historic sights," Ezra added, as he triumphantly pulled a tourist map from his bag.

"A holiday here? Haven't you heard? This is not a tourist resort right now. With all the shooting going on, you had better take care to leave some instruction with your relatives on what to do if you don't make it out. This is a war zone, not a tourist area!" The soldier's hands stiffened. "You may enter Garaga on your two feet, but we cannot guarantee that you will exit the same way. If you wish to continue, good luck!" The soldier snapped a hasty salute and turned to interrogate the next departing passenger.

Ezra looked toward the General, who had at the same time successfully completed another officer's questioning. The General acknowledged the salute of the soldier with a casual waved response.

"They take their jobs pretty seriously, don't they?" Ezra commented.

"They are a bit of a hassle, but under the circumstances its only appropriate," the General offered. "I could have gotten through this nonsense easily if there were a problem. But in an insignificant instance such as this, it does not pay for me to identify myself, pull rank or think of making a scene. Some of these guards are rank amateurs, totally inexperienced. Their officers are trained to believe in practically the same doctrine as the American FBI: 'Find 'em, bust 'em, incarcerate 'em.'"

He chuckled, pleased with himself at having delivered his joke so smoothly. The General then picked up his bag and started walking. "Let's get on with the journey before some trigger-happy Muslim cowboy in the hills decides to take a potshot at one of the soldiers, or worse yet, at one of us. We are in territory claimed by the Muslims, you know, and are probably standing in the line of fire between the Muslims and those soldiers at this very moment."

Looking back at what he had learned about the hard-liners from Avrum, Ezra was totally convinced that the conspiracy was real enough. Avrum, Hershel and the others were still not sure whether they were right to not disclose this information to the highest intelligence levels in both Israel and the United States.

As a Mossad operative, in the past his superiors had always drilled into him that many of his assigned missions were not really worthwhile because of the risks of damage that might result from international exposure. But the superiors could not neglect an order from the "home office," and would have to exercise the utmost caution in following their instructions to get their missions completed.

Now that they were retired, the formers rarely thought about all the niceties—those rules and regulations they were forced to operate by in the past. But one thing was in the back of all their minds: If a mistake was made and things went awry on this mission—which the formers had assigned to themselves—then the state of Israel would invariably be blamed, because of the past ties of all of the agents involved. No one would ever believe they had been operating on their own.

Some former intelligence veterans like Ezra believed that every export deal they initiated in their new private business life would ultimately benefit their former employers, the state of Israel, which was good for both parties. The country benefited from exports or imports that they were able to stimulate through their activities. However, on rare occasions, there were other intelligence veterans, like the operatives who had trained the security services of Mobutu's Zaire and Idi Amin's Uganda, who took advantage of dealing with unsavory regimes and enhanced their personal bank balances through their contacts. In 1988, to the embarrassment of both Israel and the Bush Administration, agents of Israel's Bar-Am organization assisted in the sale of military hardware to Iran's Ayatollah.

It had always upset Ezra that with all of the Israeli government's good intentions, they would occasionally end up with adverse publicity by inadvertently dealing with regimes that would later turn out to be undemocratic or even totalitarian. He was determined not to permit this to happen through his forthcoming dealings with Morat Progalin of the Organizatsiya.

Ezra believed that the export and import world he now worked in was divided into fiefdoms of favorite old-time formers, especially where Israel had established an official foreign ministry. His recent business experience showed him that much of the real export/import business between a particular country and Israel was done by ex-Israeli operatives, many of whom he had met. "You never truly retire from the intelligence community, you are always at its disposal," Avrum always used to say to him—and as usual he knew that Avrum was right.

Ezra Gur, one of the Mossad agents who had retaliated against Arab terrorists after the 1972 Olympic massacre, was among those former operatives who did not have friends in high places—except for Avrum. Ezra was just not good at kissing asses. He was a compact, outgoing man, with an apologetic smile that he seemed to use for self-protection. He appeared nimble and in his prime of life. The twinkle of his eyes had always caught Avrum by surprise. But Avrum expected more dynamism from Ezra, more intensity. The man's mildness of manner within a large frame was something that troubled Avrum.

The son of an Israeli customs inspector, Ezra was a *"sabra,"* (born in Israel) having been born in Tel Aviv in 1931. He followed a career similar to many military men of his generation—in the Israeli intelligence field. He served in the pre-Israeli Shai, Palmach and the volunteer army; and as soon as the State of Israel was proclaimed, he was invited to join the intelligence community. Serving with distinction as a foreign ministry security officer in the Shin Bet (Israel's equivalent of the FBI) during the 1950s, he directed operations in 1972 and 1973 for the assassination squads hunting Palestinian terrorists—until the unfortunate incident, identified by the Mossad as the Lillehammer blunder: the misidentification and assassination of the wrong man, who was incorrectly identified by a Mossad agent as a Munich terrorist. Only Ezra and three members of the hit team managed to escape Norway. He never forgave himself that the three other members of his team were arrested. He'd always felt he should have done more to insure that all of his group escaped.

Ezra was able to put in the next fifteen years in anonymity at the Mossad home office. In these years, no Israeli public official dared to voice open criticism of the Mossad and no one spoke of the Lillehammer incident. It was a bad accident that everyone obviously regretted.

After that period, Ezra, as a veteran operations man, was sent to the agency's major station in Mexico City. His assignment was to track the activities of Palestinians living in the area and to promote the sale of Israeli armaments. There he became indispensable to Panama's General Noriega, training the general's bodyguards and advising them on the purchase of light arms for the Panama Defense Forces. However, Ezra had always felt uncomfortable in the role of arms salesman. He was, after all, an intelligence officer, and he had no illusions about being anything else.

In 1988, when Ezra learned that General Noriega was about to be indicted by the United States for alleged drug smuggling, he received permission to return to Israel; there would be no further business interaction with anyone close to Noriega. After walking through the "looking glass," he saw that he was caught up to his eyeballs in the hall of intelligence mirrors, and he didn't give a second thought to resigning from the Mossad. He had lost his desire to continue playing the game.

Ezra didn't have a clue about what he could expect to learn from Morat Progalin today. He did not have the luxury of receiving the latest e-mail or fax on the situation. But whatever he learned from Progalin, Ezra's background and hands-on experience had prepared him to handle the present situation, no matter how difficult.

Chapter Twenty-Four

THE CULT OF LENIN

OCTOBER 28

With Ezra close on his heels, General Chervok walked briskly along the well-worn, uneven paving stones that made up the narrow main street of Garaga, C.I.S.

Not a word had been spoken since they left the train. The General did not want to be overheard on the street by another Russian, no matter how unimportant the conversation. There was always the possibility that a simple joke, saying or phrase, overheard by a stranger who might be spying on them, could be misinterpreted. Garaga's townspeople moved past the newcomers slowly and with caution, giving them a wide birth while viewing them suspiciously with half-glances.

Some of the low buildings the two passed were newly painted, while others had canvas or wood slats covering blown-out windows—reminders of the recent street fighting. Many buildings were constructed in the traditional Russian style with ornate carvings; the windows of these structures were completely intact, but they were protected by shutters. Electrical wires sagged from skinny wooden poles everywhere. Dangerous bare wires had been spliced together where some wires had been sabotaged. Then, suddenly, there would come the distinct sweet odor of bread baking over wood-burning fires from one of the buildings.

"Smells like a bakery making goddamn baklava—and I love it!" the General exclaimed, his eyebrows arched as he broke the silence. "See, the smell is coming from over there." He pointed across the street. "The store and ovens are on the main floor and in the basement. The baker probably lives behind the store."

"Maybe we will have time to stop there on the way back," Ezra said encouragingly, noting the General's weakness for sweets.

As they moved on, Chervok's eyes lingered on the street sign painted on the side of a building. Everything was in Cyrillic. "Here it is—Zagorsk Street." They started up a small incline. "Look for number thirty-seven," said the General.

Some townspeople huddled in doorways, obscuring the barely legible numbers painted on their doors. Ezra recalled that the area where Progalin lived was called "the hill." The "hill" overlooked the beach, and the house there—he soon saw—resembled a fortress.

"Just one more detail before we meet," Chervok warned. "Morat Progalin feels that his obligation in life is to be independent, to drink, to entertain his few friends…and to womanize. But if a woman is there we will probably not see her."

"There it is, on your left, General, the house on the hill with the tunnel-like entry—number thirty-seven," said Ezra.

A young man in civilian clothes stood partially hidden beside a hill or a bunker made out of rock, right next to the house. He had an automatic rifle under his arm but made no effort to move as the small party approached.

Several black iron bars were fastened to a heavy wooden door with a small slot for a peephole at eye level.

A knock by the General did not receive a response from within. However, Ezra noticed a heavy-set man coming toward them from his resting place in the courtyard of the house diagonally across the street.

"Da? Who sent you?" the heavy-set man demanded.

Under the man's jacket Ezra could see the outline of a pistol tucked into his belt. Staring the man down, the General did not reply.

"Who sent you?" he again insisted.

He was not a KGB man, only one of Progalin's bodyguards, the General reasoned, but Chervok was the kind of man who was always ready, even somewhat eager, for combat. After all, he had survived the age of Stalin's purges. Ezra's eyes widened as the General nodded his head aggressively, making an angry face as a statement for the man to open the door. It was the type of provocative behavior that let his opponent know that he would find his balls hanging up to dry on a clothesline if he didn't cut the bullshit.

With a last-minute impulse to be rational, the General muttered, "Hell of a way to run a railroad," and then reluctantly said the prearranged password: "*Na levo*."

"On the left," the guard angrily pointed. His stubby fingers reached for the door handle and gestured for them to follow him through the entry and into a large living room, its floor covered with oriental rugs from this region.

Holed up in this comfortable house, which resembled a KGB sanitarium on the Baltic Sea, Progalin had had time to reflect on the indignity of having to return to Russia to hide and to purify his ever-sinking spirit, but ever-bulging pockets, from his illicit operations. That purification came to him through the miraculous healing power of vodka.

"Ahhh-ha! Welcome, my old friend," Progalin said as he rose from a padded recliner. At this early hour he was already somewhat pleasantly adrift in a pumped-up alcoholic haze.

Wrapped in an old terrycloth bathrobe, and sporting a two-day growth of gray stubble on a gray face that obviously hadn't seen the sun in months, Progalin was the perfect example of someone out of sight and in hiding. He greeted Chervok with two cheek kisses and the old Russian bear hug that was reserved for close friends.

Long echoes of the calls of sea gulls, mixed with the smell of the nearby sea, came from an open window. An undercurrent of noise could be heard from children playing soccer in an empty field nearby. One child called out, others yelled, their clamor resounding off the glass window panes.

"Here!" Progalin said, pointing to his collection of a variety of half-empty vodka bottles.

Extending both arms with palms up, the General said, "Da, perhaps we will have just a little."

Like the Organizatsiya's form of corruption, vodka is an indispensable lubricant and often the sole escape mechanism from the difficult Russian life. The mere mention of vodka had started the General salivating and put him in a mellow happier mood.

Ezra did not question the mentality that invested vodka with the symbolism of machismo in Russia, but practically speaking, it also eased the tensions of the difficulties of life and helped people to loosen up so they could better get to know one another. In addition, he was constantly reminded of the saying in Russia that you cannot trust a man until you have drunk seriously together.

Progalin soon spoke of eating local delicacies together, such as khachapuri, shashlik and steaming khinkali served with vodka before a pleasant fireplace—all of which sounded good to the General.

Picking up the tempo of the conversation, Chervok began by introducing Ezra and reminding Progalin that he could feel 100-percent confident in disclosing all the information that Ezra would request of him.

With this opening, Ezra chimed in, "First of all, this information will be held in the strictest of confidence. No one shall ever be told of its origin. You need not be concerned with this, for we will be acting on your information without the need to secure any further approvals beyond those of our existing team in Russia."

"That's what I need to hear," Progalin replied sarcastically. "But you have to know that at this point in my life I cannot pass up an opportunity to embarrass or confuse the hard-liners. For me it is payback time." Obviously, he felt that fate was about to hand him another opportunity.

Why? What is his connection, Ezra continued to wonder to himself. If he is willing to collaborate with us, what the bloody hell does he want in return? Can he be doing all of this just to curry favor with the General, or is there more at stake here? A man like this never does anything without expecting gain.

Progalin's bushy eyebrows twitched nervously. "If it were not for the General, I would be rotting in a U.S. prison instead of rotting here in comfort—but in safety and seclusion!" he exclaimed with resentment in his voice. "My Organizatsiya group in the United States became an encumbrance to our Russian counterpart. While I shared my profits with them, they decided they wanted to squeeze me and take it all. If they were rid of me, they indeed would have it all. My own backers in the KGB were the ones who reported me to the United States Department of Justice and the other government agencies.

"But...I will not put myself into the considerable danger I will soon be in—after I give you the information I possess—without substantial consideration in return. I have to be assured of my safety and have certain other benefits to live comfortably. General Chervok tells me to trust you. Well, I trust him! So on his word, I trust you! In addition, I have a few scores to settle and I have some business interests that I am counting on the General to help me with," he said cautiously, looking intently at Ivan Chervok while speaking.

Ezra was almost tempted to give Progalin his honest opinion of the man, but the General spoke first. "We can't make promises until we see what you have, my friend."

Ezra knew, at this point, that there was even more evil in Progalin than what he'd been told. The man oozed with deceit. Progalin was about to double-cross the double-crossers he had been allied together with! And who knew what he would do against the Mossad formers, if given the chance? The whole plan was going to be like sleeping with the enemy, Ezra thought.

Wrapping both hands around a vodka bottle, Progalin poured another double shot for himself. By the time he took his first sip he had made up his mind as to what he would say next. The guy, Ezra could see, had an incredible ability to hold his liquor.

"The die-hards are making big promises to the people," Progalin resumed. "They promise to employ millions as they gain more and more control. We are looking at a major organized effort that has the capability of doing what they brag about. As ruthless as I will admit I am, my problem is that I could not go along with all of the hard-liner plans, since these guys were talking about mass murder on a scale beyond anything you or I could imagine!

"I am in this game for the money. These assholes are in it for ideology and the money, and believe me when I tell you that killing millions of people is part of their plan to achieve their objectives. I am no humanitarian, as I'm sure you are aware," Progalin chuckled, "but I am also not a Hitler or a Stalin, and I will not work with people who are planning large-scale murder—especially when I can't trust these bastards to pay me what they promised!"

Ezra realized that this last sentence had more truth in it than the rest of his speech. Basically, Progalin couldn't depend on his buddies to pay him and that was why he was suddenly turning soft and had a problem with their plans, Ezra surmised.

Progalin continued, "Furthermore, the die-hards have plans for Russia to be the world's incubator for organized crime. While there will be billions to be made, they wouldn't agree to cut me in, even though it was my idea to begin with. I have been completely excluded from the profits from this area—which is yet another example of how untrustworthy and ungrateful the bastards are to deal with!"

Ezra thought Progalin was actually serious about this last bit of nonsense, and realized that these Russian Mafia types were even crazier than he had believed.

Progalin went on, "They intend to compete with me or they may do away with me. Those people are going to promote and export organized crime and corruption. They will create chaos anywhere it would line their pockets." His face was deadly serious and drawn, his deep-set eyes ringed with dark circles. "Oh yes, I know all of their plans, because I was suppose to play a key role in this whole scheme. But believe me when I tell you they will be sorry when they learn what I have done to them! They will be sorry, big time!" he repeated.

Looking at both of his visitors, Progalin reached into his bathrobe pocket, removed a handkerchief and wiped his nose before continuing.

"The hard-line Communists have already created one of the biggest money-making machines they could ever have hoped for by turning the C.I.S. into the world's biggest money-laundering capital. Yes, my friends, it is a hard fact that the C.I.S. is now offering billions of rubles for sale to South American drug rings—who are using them to disguise illegal profits from their drug sales. They use the rubles, which are now more easily convertible into other currencies, to purchase commodities, oil, metals, diamonds, weapons, gold and cotton from the C.I.S. They then turn them around and sell them on the world market."

Ezra did not show any emotion as he and the General exchanged glances.

"There is a question that I must ask," Ezra cut in. But the General nodded, and whispered, "Be patient. The main purpose of our visit involves information that is yet to come."

Progalin paused—his mind, like his eyes, focused elsewhere.

For several moments no one spoke. Then Progalin said in an almost breathless voice, "Your greatest concern should come from the danger of tactical nuclear and chemical weaponry. The die-hards have made it easy to transport these weapons now. With the technology available to them, they could pack them into an artillery shell that weighs less than one hundred pounds! I've seen these shells with my own eyes! Alarms should be going off all over the world about how vulnerable you all are to the 31,000 nuclear and chemical warheads that the C.I.S. have access to, give or take a few. But do you hear anyone even publicly bring up this subject in any of the leading world powers? No, they actually believe the situation in the former Soviet Union is stable and under control! The stupid politicians are asleep everywhere."

The General's head bobbed in agreement, as if he too were trying to take credit for uncovering this dangerous plot. Okay, thought Ezra, both of you assholes can take the credit! Just give me the info we need to stop these crazy murderers!

Progalin's eyebrows arched in an agony of affirmation. "Do you guys understand where this is going? As a matter of fact," he confessed, "agents of Saddam Hussein have already purchased four consignments of enriched uranium at black-market prices. They paid four million U.S. dollars! Usually the going price for one nuclear weapon here starts at five million, so Iraq got a special deal."

It was not necessary for Progalin to explain to Ezra that if the lead-lined canisters temporarily stored in unsecured military warehouses throughout Russia ever reached Iraq, they would eventually be aimed at Israel.

"An additional three nuclear weapons," Progalin continued, "have been sold by the die-hard Cult of Lenin to Iran. These strategic weapons were shipped from Kazakhstan, which has an additional fifteen hundred of them for the taking—by anyone who can pay the right price. I don't know why the United States or the NATO nations don't buy them, just to get them off the market," he added.

"And if you ask NATO intelligence or the U.S. top brass, I could almost guarantee you that they will deny any knowledge of these sales. But you can rest assured they know about them! Still, all NATO is interested in these days is expanding membership to Poland and other nearby countries.

"Another important point for you to be aware of is that Russia's nuclear power plants and stocks of nuclear materials are vulnerable to terrorist attack and theft. This is a very serious problem, and it can result in unbearable consequences....Ah, I see from the look on your face, you know about some of this," he said to Ezra. "Last week, the Igalina nuclear power plant in Lithuania was temporarily shut after mobsters threatened a terrorist attack against it.

"And I'm sure you heard that just last month, Russian officials tried to minimize the importance of six-tenths of a pound of smuggled plutonium found on a Lufthansa plane coming from Moscow. The officials said it was not from nuclear weapons. If this is true, then you can bet that the material originated in a civilian plant—which is just as bad. Fortunately, it was just luck that the stuff was confiscated in a sting operation by German police. But how much more got through that you didn't hear about?"

Progalin rose and walked across the room to his desk, where he unfolded a world map. Pointing to an area of western Russia, he began speaking to his visitors with some intensity.

"The world had better give the Russian people a taste of Western democracy real soon so that they have a reason to oppose the radicals seeking to take power. If the Lenin Cult dissidents get away with their master plan to regain Communist control of Russia, you can forget about democracy here for the next hundred years. As a matter of fact, I know for certain that some one hundred sixty-five pounds of weapons-grade uranium are stored at the Kharkov Physical-Technical Institute in Ukraine. That is more than five times the amount that they publicly acknowledge, and enough for five nuclear weapons. That surprises you, doesn't it? Well, I've got more surprises for you. In Belarus, the Institute of Power Engineering cannot even locate its records of nuclear weaponry inventory.

"Problems at Sosny involve locating another seventy-five pounds of highly enriched uranium that are missing!...Russia has the world's most sloppy accounting practices, when it comes to keeping accurate track of its nuclear and chemical arsenals! The government has absolutely no idea of the exact quantity of nuclear or chemical material they've got on hand. The situation is as you say in America, 'all fucked up!' "

Progalin pressed his eyes closed. "I think I can say this positively," he declared in his most serious voice: "The critical information you came for is that there is talk that the Cult of Lenin plans to launch a limited ICBM chemical attack against their old enemy—Japan. There are other targets they also plan to hit, but they are still undecided as to what these will be. Unless aggressive action is taken immediately, nuclear terrorism will soon be a reality. You guys don't have all that much time to stop the problem."

Ezra tried to keep his composure and not let his actual feelings show. His head sank back onto the headrest of the couch where he sat. He breathed heavily through his lips. When he regained his self-control, he simply blurted out, "Japan? Why Japan? And why the hell do they feel they should attack anyone?"

The seriousness of his tone demanded a substantive response.

Scratching his forehead, Progalin said, "The plan they've come up with is surprisingly simple. It stands a better-than-good chance of being successful. Please follow exactly what I am saying: While the world is totally shocked by the attack, the U.S. has soldiers stationed in Japan to retaliate against just such an event. You can be assured that retaliation will come through the efforts of the United States and not that pathetic paper tiger, NATO. After the attack, Japan and the entire E.E.C. Bloc will be in total disarray and unable to come to an immediate solution. The site of retaliation will be limited to the area from which the missiles were launched."

"So what are the Cult's short- and long-term benefits from such an attack?" Ezra asked.

"First of all, it will convince many nations not presently purchasing weapons from Russia to buy from the hard-liners. The successful Japanese attack will demonstrate that the merchandise is excellent technical weaponry, even though the Russian arms industries suffered an embarrassment during the Persian Gulf War, something that was the result of the American and Allied aggressive action and not because the Russian equipment was inferior. The equipment the Iraqis purchased from the Soviets was almost totally destroyed.

"There are reports that say some of the equipment sold the Iraqis was defective and couldn't compete against the U.S. military's weapons. So this will also be the Russian military's so-called payback. The former military leaders want to redeem themselves in the eyes of the world. However, you must already be aware of the fact that at that time, of the Gulf War, the Russian Defense Industries Committee did not export its top-of-the-line arms—for security reasons—and that many of those arms sold to Iraq were in fact improperly used, old and volatile."

"But if what you say indeed happens, the Japanese will be sitting ducks," said Ezra.

"Do not blame me, I did not make this judgment. You want information, I give you information. Sure, there will be death, lots of it, and don't forget the long-term consequences from the fallout of a chemical attack—especially in a crowded country like Japan. Die-hards are not only harboring long-term resentment against the Japanese, they are playing a game which I believe the Americans call hardball. Ever since the Japanese beat the Russians and confiscated their offshore islands, the die-hard Russians intended to get them back by whatever means were required. Communist die-hards laugh off the consequences because they feel the Japanese, along with the rest of the West, have it coming."

Progalin took another sip from his glass of vodka and a deep breath before continuing.

"You have to understand, these people are fanatics. But they certainly are not fools. Their second and most important reason for the attack is totally self-serving. Their aim is to overthrow the present Russian regime, which is already in trouble, and regain complete control, restoring Communism in its fullest glory. Keep in mind that the die-hards are not your ordinary 'radish' Communists!"

"What the devil are 'radish' Communists?" Ezra asked.

"I thought everyone knew that," Progalin laughed. "Red on the outside, white on the inside, unlike the die-hard Communists, who are red throughout. The goal of the die-hards is not all that difficult to understand, since a disintegrating country with a struggling economy is always the ripest for political reform and takeover."

Ezra appeared almost startled that Progalin would know such details, not being a member of the radical die-hards. "How did you get all this information?"

"My access to secrets on both sides of the spectrum is almost endless," Progalin practically whispered. Then he added, "Unless your group can make things happen and take speedy, decisive and effective action, the Organizatsiya conspiracy will become permanent, and it will be deadlier and more sophisticated than anything seen before. Afterwards, it will be too late to stop them."

Rubbing the side of his large nose with the ball of his thumb, Progalin measured the General and Ezra with a cold eye. "Well, gentlemen, I have told you the 'what' and 'why.' I have not given you the 'where' and 'when,' because...I do not know, at this time. For sure, you can see that I can be of help to you. I know that we can find some way to continue working together that benefits you, but also has some benefits for me."

Chervok and Ezra both appeared deeply worried even angry

"Perhaps a glass of vodka will calm your nerves, Progalin remarked, as he crossed the room like a man walking the heaving deck of a ship in a storm, to get a new bottle.

The General muttered an obscenity under his breath, and there was no stopping his anger. "I know you have 'clients' coming to you for favors." He then paused, but only to sip some vodka from a glass. "I am sure they flatter, they fawn, over you they come laden with gifts, but they are not sincere—they always have a personal motive. We are not here to exploit you. We are here because we feel it is not right that innocent people will be murdered in large numbers, when you or your contacts are in a position to help us avoid this kind of catastrophe."

Progalin exploded, unable to endure any more of the General's guilt trip. "The world is a jungle," he said. "Not all creatures can and should survive. It is survival of the fittest."

"None of us are citizens of paradise! You should realize that Morat," Chervok countered.

"You're right, General, but since this boils down to a fight for money and, most of all, for control, the die-hards do not intend to obey any law or honor any code but their own."

The General replied, "Basically you understand what we are up against, Progalin. Honor is nothing but adherence to a code, and those who comply with the code define themselves as a nation and try to live by their honor. But it's *not* so with the people we are dealing with. And we in this room all realize: If we want to play it smart, we've got to have very smart backup. *And* the proper people on our team to help us execute our plan. It is no good buying the latest refrigerator, filling it with goodies, and shoving it in your *mud hut*, if you haven't got the electricity to run the thing! Now, is it? Am I right or wrong?"

Ezra plunged his hands into the pockets of his pants and his face offered a lazy smile. Very profound, he thought, as he and the General gazed at each other waiting for Progalin's reaction.

Progalin beamed, holding up his glass. "To us and to the vodka!"

After taking another mouthful, he wiped his face with the back of his sleeve. Then he offered glasses of the vodka to his guests.

"This is good, isn't it?" he said.

"It is good," Ezra answered.

Ezra Gur found that the vodka burned less now, after the shock of the first sip that felt like fire down his throat. Or perhaps his tongue had just died from the strength of the 100 proof, he thought. He knew that his brain cells would begin twinkling like the evening stars if he were to swallow another mouthful.

Chapter Twenty-Five

SELLING RUSSIA—GARAGA, GEORGIA

OCTOBER 28

Morat Progalin not only disguised his appearance, he kept a very modest profile by never going outside in daylight. While standing motionless by the window overlooking the beach, he envied the man running along the water's edge with his dog.

Progalin gave the General a great deal of credit for his being kept in seclusion—and alive. Now all he had to do was survive. I'm tough, he told himself with bravado. I know that I can do this. I've been through tougher things before.

General Chervok interrupted his thoughts with a sarcastic comment. "How many rubles is it going to cost us for your thoughts, Morat?"

"Rubles? Thoughts? I'm all thought-out for the moment."

"Since we now know more precisely what to look for in the diehards' plan," the General said, "now all we have to do is to find out who is running the show and the location of the launch site where the attack will originate."

"Is that all?" Progalin said sarcastically. "Without my help that's not going to be so easy. I know my way around and can get you into places you would never find without me. To tell you the truth, I am very tired of this self-imposed imprisonment. I would like you to convince your friends, the former agents of the Mossad, to include me in their plans. Don't let my past history detract from my value in helping you get this job done," he pleaded.

"I beg your pardon. You say you have great value to the formers?" Ezra questioned, knowing full well that Progalin was nothing better then a carpetbagger looking for a quick buck.

"But of course," Progalin replied exuberantly.

The General looked in Ezra's direction before speaking. "We understand that you have a lot of talent and knowledge, plus some old scores to settle, Morat, and the fact is, we could use some reliable assistance. But my opinion is that you are an asset only as long as your presence does not become politically disastrous or jeopardize our security."

Progalin slowly answered, "Let me obtain the information you need. I have a plan that will work."

Encouraged, his eyes excited and alive, the delighted host then told his guests, "It would be my honor if you would all join me now in a very unboring supper. This way!"

Progalin pointed in the direction of a large dining-room table in the center of an adjoining room. Progalin's table, like so many other tables in Russia, functioned as much more than a place to take meals. It also served as a meeting place.

For hours, on many occasions, Ezra had sat as a guest with Russian families around their kitchen or dining-room tables, laughing and drinking vodka or strong tea. Most preferred their tea dark, piping hot, usually served in a clear glass. Some Russians even put a lump of sugar between their teeth and sipped the tea through the cube. This they called *prakusky*. Others would sit at the table and guzzle vodka while nibbling on hard toast or a piece of cheese. The ritual could take an entire afternoon or evening, with stimulating conversation lasting well into the night and on almost any subject.

In the Russian home, the room where meals were eaten was the center of social life, a place for communion, a bridge between individuals; and the table in that room became the center of the universe. It was here that they found refuge from poverty, shortage of goods and pressure from the government. Among family and friends, they could relax and become candid and open in their discussions.

Russians usually considered their friendships to be immensely important, and visited with each other on an almost daily basis. This was precisely how the General and Morat Progalin became so close, starting with their parents' gatherings from the time when they were children. Russian friendships were very intense, demanding, and often longer-lasting and more rewarding than those of Westerners.

Progalin was living proof that Russians would go to enormous trouble to help a good friend, regardless of the dangers or inconvenience. And now Morat Progalin wanted to return an expression of true friendship by offering to help the General in his cause to expose the die-hards. Of course, he also intended to gain something back that he needed, at the same time.

"You are going to have to trust in *someone*," Progalin said. "Over the centuries, we Russians have developed an animal sense about each other. We can drink with some people, talk to them about family, world events, pretty girls and those sorts of things, without ever developing a serious friendship. I think this would be referred to as being good 'bullshitters' in the West!"

Ezra was flattered that General Chervok and Progalin were talking to him openly—*dusha-dusha,* or heart to heart and soul to soul, as they would say in Russian—since it often takes a Russian a long time to get to know someone and come to trust him. There was an intensity in the General's relationship with Progalin that Ezra found both exhilarating and exhausting.

The veal that Progalin served his guests was especially good. In particular, Ezra enjoyed the white wine that was served with the meat. In fact, everything was so good that the Israeli former could not believe he was in Russia, where food was usually far from tasty. Just getting a decent cut of meat was a major challenge and generally required a special relationship with the local butcher.

The only disappointing note at the meal was the highlights of Italian operas that oozed out of a small speaker in the room. These detracted from the conversation and were an annoyance. But Ezra didn't dare insult his host by asking him to lower the music or turn it off.

As Chervok developed a personal liking for Ezra, he began to open up and tell him more about his life, feeling an obvious sense of intimacy and involvement. In fact, after they had drunk more vodka, the General felt that he had found a soul brother in Ezra. Chervok got so comfortable with him that he began revealing and discussing military strategies—which surprised Ezra.

Meanwhile, Progalin slumped in his chair, snoozing.

"You know," said the General "the more I think about Progalin's information regarding the attack on Japan, the more sense it makes. I followed the U.S. attack on Iraq with intense interest, since I was involved in designing Soviet first-strike strategy against the West as far back as 1956.

"To understand the die-hards' tactics, you first must take a good look at the United States' Gulf War strategy. It was almost a mirror image of the old Soviet strategy for all-out nuclear war, which the Cult of Lenin helped plan under the old Soviet regime. Like the United States in the Gulf War, we in the KGB designated an aggressive offensive strike capability designed to strike, first, the same types of targets in the U.S. as the U.S. had struck in Iraq, and with the same priority. This strategy, which we've somewhat revised, is still in place today. It also recognizes the importance of maintaining a relentless attack until all U.S. offensive forces and important military and industrial targets are totally obliterated."

Chervok glanced at this watch before continuing: "We knew full well that there was only one really effective way to minimize retaliation against Russia, and that was with a massive, surprise first strike that destroyed the U.S. offensive nuclear strike force before it could be used against us."

"What do you think would happen if a nuclear war erupted right now between the United States and Russia?" Ezra asked, leaning forward and intently waiting for the answer he might hear above Progalin's snores. Despite the cool evening breezes now sweeping through the open dining-room window, Ezra was beginning to feel the sweat roll down the back of his neck from the effects of the vodka.

The General took a deep breath, thinking about what he should answer.

"As things stand now," he said "the same type of asymmetrical outcome we just witnessed in the Gulf War is a deceivingly real possibility. Just multiply the Gulf War statistics by a factor of one or two thousand, and envision a war that is even faster and more devastating. A Russian nuclear or chemical war situation vis-à-vis the United States would be disturbingly similar to the Gulf War. It would be disturbing because in a nuclear situation the strategic factors responsible for the United States' victory in that war would, in the case of a Russian-U.S. nuclear war, be totally reversed. Furthermore, the U.S. would have big problems if such a war were to occur today.

"The U.S. strategic leadership has not only allowed us, the Russian military, to achieve an unstoppable advantage in our first-strike capabilities, they have provided and continue to provide essential technical and financial assistance to the Russian bloc. This same U.S. leadership under the Reagan, Bush and Clinton Administrations has enabled the strategic balance to shift to such a degree that the only likely U.S. option in the case of a nuclear or chemical war initiated by us would be to 'elect to receive.'

"You see, our strategists have played out the various war-game scenarios and we believe that if we launch a first strike and then contact the U.S. leadership and the U.S. media, blaming it all on a hard-liner faction in our government, the U.S. military will not risk global nuclear warfare and world destruction because a few of our generals acted on their own. Consequently, the U.S. military, under pressure from the media and the politicians to act with restraint because of this 'unauthorized Russian launch,' would inevitably force the military to consider acting with restraint and to 'elect to receive' rather than to launch.

"Following a lot of apologies, Russia would be in an incredibly powerful military position vis-à-vis the United States. To make matters even worse for the U.S. and its European allies, the geniuses who run the long-term military strategy have disrupted, delayed and effectively blocked any past efforts to build strategic defense program that might have provided the best hope of deterring a chemical or nuclear war—thus preventing their countries from prevailing or possibly even from surviving a war of that type."

Ezra leaned back in his chair, breathing deeply to absorb all of these outrageous statements. "Just like that? The hard-liners are going to risk global nuclear warfare on an educated guess that the U.S. military will be restrained from responding to the Russians' accidental first strike? Do the dissidents really have the capability to commit their chemical and nuclear blackmail against the rest of the world?" he asked.

The General responded, "The West is totally unaware that the danger of the Cult of Lenin is even greater now than it was in the time of Stalin. If civil war here is unavoidable, it will involve chemical and nuclear weapons of mass destruction. Yes, we may all perish, and it is possible the die-hards will take the whole world to their grave. It is a chance they are willing to take. Ezra, you and the formers will surely perish with us. I can assure you that there will be no borders to this coming conflict. The die-hards' conflict will ignore borders, creating a world catastrophe. This is a deadly serious business."

In a gesture of frustration Ezra threw his arms in the air. In an accusatory voice, he snapped, "They're fucking nuts! They are nothing but animals with multiple warheads filled with bio-chemicals. In the long run, and even if they were wildly successful, they would only gain control over a skeletal country."

"Exactly my thoughts, Ezra," Chervok added. "That's why I wanted you here today. We have to do what we do *effectively*, considering the unexpected from them."

By now Chervok was speaking breathlessly, like a runner who had just finished a marathon. "When some people rejoiced at the collapse of the last empire—the U.S.S.R.—they were seriously mistaken. They should have been concerned with preserving the U.S.S.R., and thereby preserving the balance of power, which worked, for around forty-five years since the end of World War II up until the collapse of our system. Now there is no balance of power—just a void that will, one way or another, be filled. That is why those in power in the West should be interested today in preserving the C.I.S. and securing its internal stability."

Suddenly awakening, Progalin interrupted, "Hope you enjoyed the dinner, gentlemen. Now, shall we continue our conversation in the *lykus* (steam room) and in the luxury of my *banya* (bathhouse)?"

"Your hospitality, as usual, Morat, is second to none," the General said as he extended both arms in preparation of giving Progalin a bear hug.

Ezra cleared his throat several times, as if something was stuck deep in his gut or as if his anger over the hard-line dissidents was a bone that could not be coughed up. "Yes, it was excellent indeed," he finally added, realizing that he hadn't fully appreciated the excellent dinner because he was captivated by the conversation.

As Progalin led the way to the bathhouse, Ezra lagged behind a few steps, whispering into Chervok's ear, "How the hell do we know that everything he is telling us is true?"

The General's expression darkened. "We don't have time to wait for a clear day to get a better picture. So don't knock it, this is the best evidence of the die-hards' activities to date. I know that Progalin would not dare lie to me. Doing business with him is the price we will have to pay, and we'll be paying it for a long time. 'Only when the well runs dry do we appreciate the value of water,'" the General added, quoting from a Russian proverb.

"I guess we only have to let him finish connecting the dots to this puzzle," Ezra replied tactfully.

Chapter Twenty-Six

STRANGE NEW PALS IN THE BANYA

OCTOBER 28

It had been difficult for Morat Progalin to return to the old-fashioned, simplistic, Russian way of life after knowing the pleasures of a respected multi-millionaire mobster in the United States. There were the amusement parks of Coney Island close to where he lived in Brooklyn, along with all the culture and excitement of the latest movies, plays and restaurants nearby, in vibrant Manhattan. Once back in Russia he had soon realized that his only means of diversion, television—except for sports and the biased news reports—was dull and the balance of the C.I.S. a land with almost no entertainment when compared to the United States.

In Russia, there were virtually no skating rinks, bowling alleys, amusement parks, decent movie theaters, video or game arcades, as there were within walking distance of his Brooklyn home. Of course there were ballet and opera, but that sort of high-brow, upscale entertainment was not Progalin's cup of tea.

Even though he would not have openly admitted it, he had now reached a point in his life where he wanted people to admire and respect him, as the Dons in the Mafia received respect wherever they went in their neighborhoods. He constantly craved an image that cried out his power, strength, success and greatness. He would be patient until somehow he got out of Russia and back on the fast track he was accustomed to.

Some Russians believed in health cures, even if they had nothing to cure. Sulfur treatments and mud baths at a sanitarium were activities preferred by many Russians. Progalin's *banya* was a cross between a

Finnish sauna and a steamy Turkish bath. It was a welcome release from the men's intense exchange of information.

"This hot sauna bath will cure any disease you have—even those you were only thinking about," he joked to Ezra with a knowing smile as they entered the banya. "I think I've heard that your name for it is the *shvitz*."

A look of reminiscence came over Ezra's face. "You are right, my friend, it is called shvitz where I'm from, and it does work wonders!"

The anticipation of the *banya* proved to be one of the few things that Progalin was able to enjoy while in seclusion in Russia. It was his chicken soup, flu vaccine, mind-melting, and body-healing delight.

Ezra could also tell that it was as much an addiction as was the General's beloved mushroom hunting. It was not merely the act of bathing that counted for Progalin, it was the entire process, from the walk to the rear lower level of the house where the baths were located, to the ritual of weighing-in, soaping one's entire body and then steaming, flogging, toweling, washing—and starting all over again.

"How is the steam for you, or would you prefer it cooler?" inquired Progalin.

"It's just fine," replied the General.

"If it's too hot, speak up," demanded Progalin, eager to accommodate.

"No, it's just right for me. How about you, Ezra? Are you used to it this hot?"

"This is only the second Turkish sauna I have ever been in, and I feel it is tolerable," he said, recognizing that his host was expecting a much more enthusiastic reply. He then wrapped the hot, wet towel around his waist. "But I will reserve final judgment until later—if I am not totally exhausted by the impressively hot steam."

"Seven minutes is all you should take, if you are a tenderfoot," Chervok advised, laughing.

He then pulled a large towel from the wood bench, wiping away the sweat that had formed on his chin. "I simply cannot get along without a good 'sweat' at least once a week. Some think I'm crazy. People don't understand. I feel that when I walk out of the sauna, I'm different than when I walked in. No more trouble! No more pain! It is one of the great joys of my life!"

Ezra tried to envision the presently bare-bottomed general in one of those long military overcoats with red sideboards. When the Russian soldiers marched while wearing them, they looked like uptight, little shit puppets doing their goose-steps, Ezra thought, as the General continued.

"I can remember a meeting of KGB and other top Soviet leaders in Moscow, back in 1982. We reported that we were seriously concerned that the possibility of a chemical and nuclear war had significantly increased and that the source of our fears was a secret group within Russia. The members of that same secret organization now comprise the nucleus for the leadership of the Cult of Lenin. At that time, we implemented special intelligence collection requirements, and sent warning alerts to all KGB agents and our strategic nuclear force commanders. The information was also leaked to the CIA, but we have no idea whether they took the report seriously."

Sitting there, Ezra blinked away the sweat as he watched the General thrash himself, with a branch of oak leaves, into rosy pinkness and soothe himself with occasional mutterings and undertones of swearing and contented-sounding grunts. The Israeli former checked the illuminated dial of his waterproof watch. The sweep hand appeared to him to be moving ever so slowly. He wiped the sweat from his eyes, hoping that when he opened them the watch hand would move more quickly. He knew full well that it wouldn't, as the General went on.

"I have to tell you that as a career military man, I admired the Bush–Schwarzkopf Gulf War strategy. It was a really well thought out plan—only the ending was a flop! But while it was not unlike our Soviet strategy for a nuclear attack against the United States, in my opinion it was incredible good luck for the Americans that they were up against such a nut as Saddam. He gave the U.S. the opportunity to win. And it was only because of Hussein's curious strategic decision to give the United States the chance to strike the opening blow.

"If Hussein had aggressively responded against the U.S. forces right from the start, as they arrived in Saudi Arabia in mid-August, the fortunes of that war might have turned out differently. At that time the U.S. deployment was highly vulnerable. The U.S. depended heavily on high-tech systems for its defense and those were in short supply. Those that were available were still unmanned. In addition, there was no allied coalition in place yet. Just think about it: The only one truly ready to fight, in reality, was Iraq. But for some unknown reason the madman Hussein did absolutely nothing. He foolishly elected to 'receive.' So the

U.S. was permitted to fine-tune its plan, deploy its forces, and call the shots about when and where to massively attack.

"For several decades, we in the U.S.S.R. have recognized the U.S. military strategy as set-piece operations. Unfortunately, this type of plan—which the U.S. seems to be committed to—does not always work, except when there is sufficient time to deploy, plan and execute. This slow response time by the U.S. is another reason our small group must intensify its around-the-clock intelligence gathering. We have to advise Hershel to coordinate all aspects of the information he is picking up, as soon as it is supplied to him. He must, in addition, keep me advised about how much progress he is making, so that we may coordinate our efforts. It is essential that we try to give our allies in the West as much time as possible to draw up their plans of defense."

Ezra was pleased with the General's enthusiasm, and nodded his head in agreement, the sweat now dripping profusely from his face.

"Here, do my back, will you?" Chervok said, handing a branch to Progalin.

In the Russian steam room, there is always discussion about "good steam" and "bad steam." Some complain that it's not hot enough, and constantly open and shut the door to the oven, throwing water on the rocks to make the steam rise. Only the old, real shvitzers can take the appropriate amount of heat. The young are driven out of the steam room when it gets too hot and the old-timers sit on the top-tiered, hottest, bench—like the smug, pompous machos they think they are.

"More on the back of the legs, the legs, the legs," the General insisted. "Now the *platza*" (shoulder blades)." He began to look as red as a beet. Like borscht.

He then pointed to the metal water bucket next to the fire-brick oven. "More water!" he shouted at Ezra, who, trying to look as if he knew exactly what he was doing, found himself duty-bound to dash the water on the hot bricks, making the steamy, heavy air even hotter.

The General was not only a military veteran, he was a veteran of the steam rooms and was not yet sweating to his satisfaction.

It was becoming clear to Ezra that General Chervok had to endure great pain and suffering in order to fully enjoy himself. That was the kind of guy he was. As the steam filled the room, the General gasped, cleared his lungs and continued with his story.

"We will have to do with the hard-liners what the United States did in the Gulf War. The U.S. carefully prioritized its tasks for the destruction of the Hussein military machine, concurrently undertaking to demolish the three key elements: Hussein's command, communications control and intelligence. This decapitation strategy worked just fine, since it cut off Iraq's ability to communicate with its forces and brilliantly prevented them from coordinating an effective counterattack."

The General slammed his open palm down on the wooden bench to emphasize his next point. "If they *survive,* soldiers always learn from battlefield experience! At first, the 'smart' weapons that the United States used against Iraq were immensely effective. Hussein was unable to respond even if he wanted to. He did not know what was happening to his forces unless he watched it on CNN, and the U.S. kept up the attack on his communications throughout the war!

"There were two other tasks that also took high priority, the first being to cut Iraq's air defenses, the second to destroy SCUD missiles and Iraq's strike aircraft. I mention this to you because once our strikes begin, there can be no letup. The Mossad formers will have to plan a strategy similar to that used in the Gulf War in order to defeat of the Cult of Lenin. You would have to kill all the hard-liner defenses and offenses before they can be used, in order to blind their communications and command centers!"

As Ezra continued to listen to the General, he suddenly realized that he had almost forgotten one of the most important rules of his Mossad training: "Never become too intimate with your sources."

Despite all the lavish food, entertainment and time spent over the past day with General Chervok and Morat Progalin, he asked himself if he was not in a position that directly conflicted with those wise, long-standing instructions. He realized that he was getting much too close to Progalin. He could not take any chances that might leave his associates, the formers, exposed and vulnerable to some kind of trap. He wished that he could have created only a loose alliance with Progalin and the General, without risking the safety of one of the formers, one who would have to stay almost constantly at their side as a liaison. He now also felt responsible for whatever might go wrong as a result of working with Progalin's and the General's information. He would have preferred to obtain the information in total secrecy by penetrating the die-hard ranks, thereby not being beholden to anyone outside the small group of formers he knew intimately and trusted with his life.

Ezra was unaware that his gaze had become cold and unflinching, as the General continued: "As Schwarzkopf did to Hussein in the Gulf War, it will be crucial for us to methodically destroy the critical elements of the hard-liners' chemical, biological and nuclear weapons. Once we start our strategic attack, there will be no turning back—or we will lose the element of surprise, and have no opportunity to recapture it. Unlike Schwarzkopf, who was not given the opportunity to complete the assignment he was given, we must make every attempt to destroy the die-hard leadership or they will simply return again in the future to destroy us. We Russians—and that includes KGB staff—believe that, in essence, Iraq 'won' the Gulf War because the U.S. permitted Saddam to remain in power, continuing to run his country and making mischief."

"Morat, what is the chance of your infiltrating the die-hards?" Ezra asked.

Progalin's face lit up with a wicked grin. "It won't be easy, but it will be far more interesting than being stuck in this 'prison' here."

Ezra was aware that it was difficult for him to be convinced of Progalin's sincerity. He became even more unhappy knowing that he was working with a violent, savage, murderous, mob-tied criminal who was a disgrace to humanity. And how the hell did Progalin expect to infiltrate the die-hard ranks?

There were a lot more questions Ezra would need to ask. Nevertheless, since in the Mossad he'd been trained to exercise good healthy skepticism, he would need to give himself time to think, time to wait for the right opportunity to start his probe, asking harsher and harsher questions.

On the other hand, Ezra realized that Progalin's disposition was perfect for a covert operation. Everything he was able to learn so far indicated there was the possibility of a successful penetration of the die-hard organization. Properly connected, as Progalin was, and a convincing enough liar and double-crosser, with the right cover story he had the means for a good chance of infiltration. A rare opportunity such as this would not come again and, besides, there was no one else they had who could remotely get near the die-hards. Of course, Progalin too would be taking a big chance.

Still, right now Ezra was grateful that the General was continuing with his boring lecture. It gave the Israeli the opportunity to put the loose pieces of the past two days together.

"General, I find all of this very interesting," Ezra said with a smile on his face. "What is remarkable to me is how you have related the Gulf War events—which are still being analyzed at the Pentagon—to the situation we have here."

"Indeed, but I am not the final authority on the subject," said Chervok. "You see, if there is anything the die-hards learned from the United States in the Gulf War, it is that a tremendous advantage accrues to the side that strikes first. They are aware that they will have to seize that strategic initiative and advantage if their objective is to be accomplished. The die-hards still need several weeks' advance preparation to complete a viable plan of attack. My sources tell me they've been working for the past two weeks—which leaves us about two weeks to formulate a counterplan.

"I know that my former military comrades who are now die-hards have extensive training in tactical and strategic deception, which will be the major component of their preparation for an attack. In fact, I can vouch for the fact that the former Soviet officers involved in this plot are all masters of deception."

By now, the sweat from the steam room was running down Ezra's chest, even with heavy towels wrapped around his shoulders. He hoped he had received the necessary quotient of suffering to prove to the others that he was indeed a man's man and could keep up with the others.

The heat was at last becoming unbearable, even for the General, the macho aficionado of baths. He announced: "Time for our beer, comrades!"

Many occupy themselves by watching TV, sleeping, eating, drinking, going to a movie, playing cards and talking. In Russia, the steam bath is a place both for getting away and for getting together: a safe haven where the *shvitzers* can brag, reveal secrets and make deals—in their own retreat.

The temperature now measured close to 195 degrees, as Progalin and the General poured buckets of water over their heads and shouted, "ACHHH!"

When the door to the steam room was finally opened, it reminded Ezra of so much of Russian life that he'd observed: Relief came at the moment of escape from self-torture.

The sweating bathers fled the steam room in loosely wrapped sheets, moving into the changing room, where they all jumped into shockingly cold showers. The three then toweled themselves dry, each man feeling supremely energized from the extreme shock he had just put his body through.

The General asked a servant who stood nearby to bring them some vobla, a dried bony fish that is chewed or sucked on to replace lost body salt.

Back in the main house, they found an amazing spread of beer, canned sardines, salami and plenty of bread, enough snacks to last for an entire evening of socializing. But the camaraderie and male bonding was not yet complete until out came a well-worn set of dominos.

The longer Ezra studied Progalin and the General in this environment, the less he remembered their former association with barbarism and ruthlessness. He was aware how his judgment about them was changing as he saw them as regular, fun-loving guys with good senses of humor. But Ezra realized this was exactly the type of impression his hosts had hoped to convey, lulling him into believing and trusting whatever they told him. His guard was up, despite all the deep bullshit he was surrounded by.

The General picked up one of his half-smoked cigars from a nearby ashtray and re-lit it, puffing away.

A half-used cigar, Ezra thought. Does that make sense for a senior Russian general who is connected to the highest levels of power in one of the most corrupt countries in the world?...Sure! he realized, if you are in Russia—where a good stogie is as rare as a lean T-bone steak.

Chapter Twenty-Seven

GORKY STREET:
GARAGA AND MOSCOW

OCTOBER 29

With the sun high above the horizon and throwing long shadows from the trees, Ezra and the General, the two new close friends, left the comfort of Progalin's house. With the fog now lifted Ezra could clearly see the magnificent scenery of low, steep ridges, plateaus and mountains rising in all directions.

As they walked back through the gate to the road they could see that it was made in the old Georgian style, with ornate iron latticework. The fieldstone wall surrounding the compound was topped with broken bottles and sharp shards of glass set into cement. Behind the stone wall, row upon row of fruit trees were loosing their leaves.

Two young men, roughly dressed, made a show of guarding the house. Another man stood just inside the gate, staring at them as they passed. He wore dark baggy cotton trousers and a shirt that almost formed a military uniform.

The Georgian town was coming awake; dark-eyed workmen were watering down the dusty central square. As Ezra and Chervok walked to the railroad station they passed through the old quarter of Garaga, whose back streets were no wider than the distance a man could stretch his arms. The bustling bakery shops, boot makers, tailors and barbers reminded him of Beirut—before the civil war. He observed how the area and its people had their own distinct Latin flavor, closer in appearance to Mediterranean than to Russian. The few street signs denoted the names of poets and not commissars, suggesting to Ezra the new but unmistakable independence of these people.

At the Garaga railway station, Ezra was amazed at how these people lingered in anguish when parting with their friends or families. This was certainly in contrast to the usual Russian gruffness. Tame and out of character, without embarrassment they gave each other continuous bear hugs and numerous kisses on both cheeks, as if there were no other onlookers around.

An old woman held up a bunch of flowers for him to buy. "From my garden," she said softly. "From a man such as you, a young lady would appreciate these flowers."

"Thank you," he said smiling, "but not right now." He handed her a kopek and smiled.

Several young girls walked by in obscenely tight Levi jeans as they polluted the air with the noise of Western rock music from a cheap boom box.

Ezra and the General had an uneventful train ride back to Moscow, both sleeping in their seats, grateful that they could finally relax after the active day they had been through with Progalin. In Moscow, they parted at the train station and the General indicated he would telephone later.

The lights were already on inside the safe house when Ezra arrived. Avrum and Uri must already be here, he thought, as he hurried into the building and up to the large apartment.

Uri, sitting in an overstuffed chair reading a newspaper, glanced up as he heard the resounding click of a key turning in the door lock.

"So what's new?" he said.

Ezra smiled and nodded as he closed the door softly. He shuffled across the room to shake hands with Uri.

"Nothing new, except that it's another nasty day."

"That should be good for the garden."

"Not this time of the year," Avrum interrupted, entering from the kitchen.

Hershel soon arrived and greeted everyone before he made himself comfortable. Over the weeks, Hershel felt himself becoming harried and frustrated, almost groaning aloud under the burden, as he examined reams of information collected by the formers. As much of the data as they could compile was now at their disposal.

Flitting from report to report like a bee from flower to flower, touching each of them only briefly and sporadically, hoping some sort of information would spring from his magic touch, Hershel once again doubted his physical and mental ability to perform the monumental task assigned to him.

He tried Avrum's patience by going over, in detail, every minor bit of information, time and time again, as if it were of tremendous importance. Yet for him to understand or follow up a particular lead, every one of his "how" questions became distinct from the "what," "where" and "when."

"It is surprising how much one hears, if one listens carefully," Hershel said, not expecting a reply.

Once the die-hards' assembly and launch area had been positively identified, Hershel would be responsible for coming up with a plan for their transportation, infiltration and destruction of the enemy facility. He folded his hands behind his head. Smiling slowly to himself, he recalled a passage about guidance in the Bible: "And the Lord went before them by day in a pillar of a cloud, to lead them the way; and by night in a pillar of fire, to give them light; to go by night and day."

Hershel was the grandchild of long kitchen discussions. In his youth he was used to his grandfather describing how his ancestors aimed their sextants at the stars and sun, using celestial navigation to plot their courses by land or sea to find their way. After joining the Mossad, Hershel had some training in charting global positioning of satellites circling the Earth in 10,900-mile-high orbits, constantly broadcasting data containing orbital parameters, time count, clock parameters and other data, which was then interpreted and converted into readily accessible information. Obviously this hi-tech equipment would not be available to Hershel while he was in his present surroundings.

The ring of the telephone was only an echo in the other room as Hershel continued idly to examine the papers before him.

"This is interesting," Avrum said as he re-entered the room. The General just called and said there've been recent developments. He suggested that we have an immediate get-together." Avrum then told his colleagues, "Honestly, I can't imagine why he would have to see us on such short notice. There was an edge to his voice, however. He sounded quite excited."

Putting down his papers, Hershel nodded. He paced across the room, then turned to face Avrum. "I believe this is it! The General has his own style—and balls of brass. I have a feeling he has the info on the location of the launch site and may even know the time of the attack. We just have to make sure there is water in the pool before we all jump off the diving board!"

"Right again, Hershel," said Avrum. "We have to keep in mind that General Chervok and his followers are really desperate to achieve success for their own damned cause. In the long run, they couldn't care less if we live or die."

Once they took in the destruction of the hard-liners' facility, what reason would the General and Progalin have to ensure their safety? That was the question.

Chapter Twenty-Eight

THE AGGRESSION PACT

OCTOBER 30

The people of Moscow struggled with bitter north winds that blew in overnight. The gray day began with intermittent fine snow mixed with drizzle that froze, melted and froze again. Black, gritty slush and salt were everywhere.

His dacha looked dark from the outside; the General stood by the window overlooking the wide street.

He was turning to get himself another cup of coffee, but stopped when a black four-door sedan pulled up in his driveway. He recognized Nikolai behind the wheel, and the other passengers were Avrum and Hershel, who opened the rear door.

Nikolai, who for a short time had served as an ordnance technician in the Israeli Army, was wearing a Russian-style black fur hat and an overcoat that was sufficiently old and worn so that it looked very Russian. His wool scarf clashed with it, protecting his neck and hiding a stained tie. The weather was the great equalizer. Planning to live through the Russian winter, Nikolai had begun dressing and acting as would a Russian during late autumn, even to the point where he looked downward when he walked.

All three continued rapidly up the narrow path to the front door of the dacha as the General pulled the heavy blinds closed. Chervok flicked on a large floor lamp, squinting in the brightness, and saw that Avrum was the first to enter into the living room, clenching a legal-size manila folder under his arm.

Striding through the door, Hershel walked, back erect, almost defiant, like a military officer on an important mission. He knew that, once inside, he was the man. He was the one who would be barraged with questions.

Nikolai walked in, removed his heavy outer garments, and stood motionless for a moment before all took their seats.

The General was now standing before the fireplace at the far end of the room and the air was as oppressive as the look on his face. After a brief hello, the rest of the formalities were quickly concluded. Hershel sensed that this was to be their most important gathering so far, and he noticed that the General did not offer his usual gregarious warm greetings before beginning. He was all business, which was fine with everyone.

The General started by inquiring, "Your progress so far, Hershel? Has analyzing our leads brought you to any definite conclusions?"

By not being able to personally seek out the enemy—their limited time and resources prevented this—Hershel felt that the formers were going to have to risk that the information they were to receive from the General and Progalin was reliable and not a setup.

In replying to Chervok, Hershel was sharp. "My leads are as hot as they can possibly get without additional input from you, General. Why don't you do the honors and bring us all up-to-date?"

The fingers on the General's right hand slowly curled into a fist and then uncurled. Hershel took the gesture as the General's readiness to turn the screws on the die-hard bastards.

Nikolai stood, walked to the window and parted the drapes to peer outside for any sign of unusual activity. For him it was second nature to be on the alert.

"Don't worry," the General said. "The house continues to be watched by my most trusted security people, especially while you are here."

"I may sound paranoid," Nikolai responded, "but even with the trees around the house and the heavy drapes to distort most voice surveillance, the new lasers have improved technology that can overcome that. *The new technology can pick up a whisper.* Let's all keep our voices low to be safe."

"Of course," Avrum agreed.

Hershel fell into a comfortable armchair, impatient to learn what the General would say and what new information he might have gained since their last meeting. The four men present clearly understood the reason they were meeting. Time was growing short, and the formers had to learn a lot more before they could go forward. At the moment, the General was the only one with the necessary information that their small group could turn to.

Hershel started to say something but stopped himself. He really wanted to know the answers to several key questions: Which of the die-hards was the General communicating with? Did he know them personally? Were they reliable? How accurate was the information he had obtained for today's meeting? Was Progalin coming through for him? Most important, there would have to be a definite main plan and backup plan subject to the review of those present. Hershel hoped that the General had acceptable answers to these questions; otherwise, the former Mossad agents had no intention of risking their lives on this distant battlefield.

While the General may have not intended to answer all of these questions, the stakes were too high for anything less than total candor. Hershel knew that once they began the operation, there would be no turning back and all would be in great danger. Any action they took against the die-hards must be decisive and deadly.

Hershel realized that given all of the factors stacked against the success of the mission, it might very well be a one-way suicide job. But given the stakes involved—trying to stop a nuclear war and a biochemical surprise attack that would most likely involve missiles hitting his country and injuring his family and relatives—there was never a question of whether or not to proceed.

The General was standing, looking very official, his head lifted, staring in the direction of those facing him across the room. The fatigue in his face was apparent for all to see. His skin was paler than usual. "Well, I have here what you would call some goodies," he said, prying at a rubber band wrapped around a roll of maps on his coffee table.

He paused for a moment, looking up. "Since I retired I have spent many pleasant days in the library, reading everything in sight. Even Aleksandr Solzhenitsyn, Ankady Shevshenko, Anatoly Scharansky, and other authors once banned here. I finally realized that I have been deceiving myself, and I've probably been in the wrong career because I feel that I can write with as much feeling and as much insight into the flaws of our former Soviet system as they have. One day, I hope to have the opportunity to receive an offer from a big New York publishing house for my memoirs. Some may find my story quite remarkable, especially the part that keeps unfolding now before us. It would certainly make the list of the New York Times, and I have enough information here for other exposés that are for another time and place." He began unrolling the large military map he had placed on the coffee table.

Now, that's some buildup, Hershel thought. He rose and approached the map, noting that it was topographical, with extreme detail. He smiled, recognizing that whatever this was, it was certainly not for public consumption, especially not for a group of former Mossad agents who planned to soon decimate a group of fanatics with the same skills they had used over the years to snuff out thousands of Mideast terrorists.

Hershel realized that the Arab terrorists were probably tougher foes than these power-thirsty Communist outcasts whose main motivation was to regain their lost positions, power and prestige—not to mention trying to cash in on the big bucks everyone else has been making selling off Russian weapons. These Ruskies were not half as motivated as the Arab terrorist who hoped to kill Jews and meet Allah after Israel's Defense Forces would catch them and dispense justice. Hershel decided he'd rather be up against greedy Commies, all things being equal. But then the General started speaking again, quickly and in secretive whispers.

"What I am pleased to contribute is the location of what Progalin feels is the precise likely launch site for the hard-liner's Inter-Continental Ballistic Missiles."

Hershel was wondering how the launch site could be the "precise" location and at the same time the "likely" location, as the General had stated, but he realized that this was the best info they were likely to get.

The General bent over to open a drawer under the table and pulled out a large manila envelope. Tearing open the flap, he scattered a half dozen photographs helter-skelter on top of the maps. "And it doesn't take a rocket scientist to see the launch tubes in the clearing next to those trees," he said, pointing to one of the enlarged photographs.

Hershel's expression froze for a moment as his curiosity was satisfied. He surmised that it *was* Progalin, after all, who came through for the General. Progalin may not only have been the anchor to Chervok's game plan, but he was very likely the best source for quick information. After all, if the General had had this data earlier, he probably would have showed it to them. Now Hershel's immediate concern was to confirm the identity of the target and set out the game plan.

After studying the photographs for a moment, Avrum said, "It certainly looks like a recent construction. In fact, I can see remains of construction debris over there to the right of the second frame."

"Well, I'll be damned!" Hershel added, a slightly cynical smile shaping his lips. "Those die-hards sure went through a lot of trouble. Let's make certain it will have been for nothing!"

"I might even go so far as to say that Morat's work was brilliant," the General noted. "He was able to get the pictures from the reconnaissance camera of one of our military reconnaissance planes. Don't ask me who he bribed or how he paid for them."

Avrum's eyes examined Chervok in a professional way, revealing nothing of what he thought or what he felt inside. "We never implied that Progalin was an amateur," Avrum said, begrudgingly. "In his former occupation he was just a son of a bitch—a criminal, a murderer, a psychopathic aspiring mobster with delusions of grandeur. Aside from these things, he's a great guy who really knows how to party—according to Ezra."

Then Avrum added, with fire in his eyes, "What makes you think he has changed from his Russian and New York Mafia days? Has he told you he reformed and is going straight? Is he any less of a troublemaker than yesterday? How much can we really trust this double-crosser who has sold out everyone he's ever committed crimes together with?"

The General did not immediately respond.

"Don't take this the wrong way General," Hershel interrupted, "but our asses are on the line—yours too—and none of us want to be hung out to dry. Tell us why Progalin is working so hard for so little. What is the real story, or as we say in Israel, what's the tachlass (the actual facts)?"

The General's expression became grave for a moment and everyone could see that he was angry. He did not like to have his judgment questioned. He slowly answered, "Because, without us, he would not be able to enjoy the good things that affluence has to offer, like the martinis served before lunch, the different wines between courses, and the exotic brandies afterwards. We are his one and only last chance. This guy has burned all his bridges, my friends, and you and I are the last game in town."

However, the General's look did not change Avrum's demeanor. "Sorry, but damn it, sir, we just can't overlook his past history and the fact that he always was a two-timer who deceived his business associates—even the KGB, the Russian Mob, the American Mafia, the CIA, everyone. This guy fucks with them all—and doesn't seem to give a shit. Why wouldn't he jerk our chains as well? And how do we know these pictures were taken from the area he says they were?"

"Don't knock him too hard!" the General exclaimed, excited. "This is the best evidence of die-hard activity we have received to date. He had to put his life on the line to get us the information, and yes, his greed had everything to do with his newfound courage. He will have to be well rewarded for what he has done, and for what he's still willing to do for us."

Hershel considered the answer for a moment, then said, "Sounds like a catch-22. We're dammed if we trust him and he's wrong, and dammed if we don't and he's right. I saw this coming all along. What did you have to promise this scum of the earth for his help—half of Russia?"

"You're...not far from the truth," the General said, emitting a short bark of a laugh. "For Progalin, his reward is something as good as owning half of Russia, and it's tax free. But let's be realistic: At this moment Progalin is not our problem. We are facing a situation involving some dangerous, terrible business here. We're dealing with weapons that are beyond belief in what they can destroy, weapons that have never been launched in the history of warfare."

"Before you go on, General, I would like to get back to Progalin. What exactly are you implying about him?" Hershel asked, a serious look momentarily frozen on his face.

"Well, gentlemen, we are all fully aware that Morat Progalin is nothing more than an ass-kissing gangster with delusions of power, even though he had become famous for spawning one of the world's most aggressive and successful Russian Mafia gangs. After the die-hards are defeated, Progalin will be out of danger from his most serious and life-threatening enemies. In his mind, this will be a very valuable accomplishment. We will be giving him his life back—which will enable him to go back to his lucrative mob activists in Moscow. Now you ask, What's in it for him as the big payday for all his help? I'll explain it simply. Aside from the fact that he'll be running his crime empire again—which should yield him millions in profits—he will also be rewarded with something very very sweet!

"Since private security companies in Russia have now started to develop in large numbers and are supplementing the inefficient police, we have guaranteed Progalin the exclusive rights to manage all the anti-crime private security organizations in the Moscow area. He will be in the enviable position of controlling both sides of the fence. He will be the equivalent of Al Capone running Chicago's private security forces. He will be like the fox watching the chickens. He already knows every trick in the book.

"We in Russia know that the Mafia will be with us for a long time, just like the Americans had their serious mob problems and Mob wars for decades. If America couldn't slow down the Mafia for more than thirty or forty years, how can we in Russia with all of our economic and social problems, our infrastructure nightmares, our inability to collect taxes and our limited resources, hope to succeed in getting rid of organized crime? We simply can't hope to succeed—just like America did not succeed.

"By the way, America, with all the bullshit, still has an active Mafia in every major city—they just operate in a more sophisticated way than they used to and are involved in fewer murders and more white-collar crimes, according to my information. We'll have a Mafia that we in power will work with and, to some extent, control. And we'll give Progalin incentives to cooperate with us in his capacity as the director of Moscow's private security organization."

"What an incredible business opportunity!" Avrum stated. "Your boy Progalin should be ecstatic."

"Normal people can't live quietly anymore," the General said, pacing before the fireplace. "Do understand what I am saying. I don't kiss asses and I hate to buy favors. But you don't have to worry about Morat Progalin's honesty in this instance." He looked anguished. "He is not concealing anything. If we don't succeed, neither does he. At least we don't have to question each other's motives. We know what Progalin wants, and only we can deliver it. He knows what we need, and if he turns on us, he loses out on a golden opportunity."

The General's face was now heavily lined and sagging under the strain of the moment. But then he continued: "We all know that it's damned impossible to completely protect the world from people like the die-hards. Our choices are to react after the worst happens or try to do something now to prevent the worst from happening. We cannot go by the book. There has never been a book written about this type of scenario. We have to know where the where will be, when the when will come, and as many other details as Progalin is able to give us."

Hershel responded. "It's almost impossible to prevent a chemical-biological attack, with the world currently in such an extremely poor state of preparedness. Actually, what is amazing is that we haven't already had one or two disasters....I remember the story in the U.S. of a truck accidentally spilling a container of talcum powder while crossing the Oakland–Bay Bridge. It took eight hours for the authorities to get their best experts to expeditiously identify that the specific agent was talcum powder. All that while the bridge was closed to traffic! Can you imagine what would have happened if this had been a real terrorist threat?"

Avrum sighed, indicating his acknowledgment. "All you say is very true. A solution is not going to be easy, and no one said it would be, Hershel. But let me hear from the General. What do you think they have in mind for the immediate future?"

The General began speaking in whispers, his lips so close together that Avrum at first didn't realize he was talking at all. But his eyes stayed on Avrum. "I believe they will use missiles to launch chemical and biological weapons. The die-hards are a clever, ruthless bunch. They know that chemical-biological weapons pose a far lower risk than attempting to set up and discharge a nuclear device. They are also much cheaper and easier to manufacture and deliver. Furthermore, chemical-biological devices could even be delivered in person in suitcases, or be disguised as regular cargo freight or as one of the existing Russian missile systems available on the black market—all with a high degree of reliability."

Sucking in his stomach, as his wife often reminded him to do, Hershel sat up straight in his chair. He surveyed the solemn gathering as everyone recognized the severity of the situation. "As you probably know," he began matter-of-factly, "the die-hards are not the only ones to worry about. Any resourceful terrorist group can build a formidable chemical-biological, or C-B, weapon with the help of a few scientists. All you would need is an engineer, a microbiologist knowledgeable in disease processes, a microbiology laboratory, a vegetable bacterial pathogen—to mix all this stuff—and a good plan of attack. Everything that cannot be easily purchased can be easily improvised by any of the professionals, and then it's chemical-biological warfare time for your unfriendly neighborhood terrorist."

The General folded and unfolded his hands. He began speaking in a hushed voice and his words almost tiptoed through the room as he delivered his words with a good deal of emotion. "What everyone thinks about, but hopes and prays will never happen, is about to happen." He was in deep thought for a moment. "Gentlemen, we are at war, and war is just a continuation of politics by other means. I'm pleased and honored that now we're on the same side."

He stood erect. "Gentlemen, in spite of the down side, which Hershel has made quite clear, we are fortunate that Progalin has agreed to work with us. Let us quickly finalize a plan of attack and implement it so we can stop these madmen."

With this closing comment, the General sat down and everyone was ready to adjourn this meeting to get on to the planning stages of the actual mission.

Hershel was piling his new notes and maps into his briefcase, while Avrum hurried through the door of the room, Nikolai following close behind. One half-sigh of tiredness, frustration and impatience emerged from Hershel's lungs, reminding him of his childhood. It echoed in every part of his body.

He felt his heartbeat increase. Mist gathered across his eyes, and he became vulnerable and weightless. In his memory he saw his long-deceased brother Moishe as a youth, his face bright and smiling. He and Moishe had left their house in Palestine to play in the street. He heard the shuffling of feet, followed by the unexpected reluctant struggle of his brother against a surprise Arab attacker, who slashed out with a knife against Moishe's neck. He recalled his brother's one long, cathartic scream, to summon help—in vain. He rationalized that perhaps the permanent memory of that terrible incident of terrorism was reason enough for his being here today.

Chapter Twenty-Nine

SUBMERGED DISPLACEMENT

OCTOBER 31 & NOVEMBER 1

While Avrum, Hershel, Nikolai, Uri and Ezra were sleeping fitfully, cold, rough water splashed against the side of a rubber dinghy in which Yaakov Vigdor and five Russian frogmen crouched expressionless. Yaakov looked at his watch—it was minutes before midnight.

They drifted slowly and deliberately toward the die-hards' command submarine. Camouflage makeup, dark green in color, was across their foreheads, cheekbones and jaws, with light green in the hollows of their cheeks and under their eyes.

Yaakov had been trained by the Mossad at Atlit, the top-secret Israeli naval commando base. For him, tonight's mission was no different than the many night training sessions he had taken at Kfar Sirkin on how to sabotage ships. Not to mention the many missions he was involved in where they blew up the safe houses of Arab terrorists.

The huge docking area of St. Petersburg covered the entire waterfront. There were acres and acres of containerized cargo with thousands of tons of food, cigarettes, pallets of used clothing, automobiles, and warehouses filled with sacks of sugar, cement and every other conceivable consumer and industrial product. There was even military equipment awaiting export.

Dozens of ships were off-loading still more cargo, while others were lying offshore, anchored with their running lights on, waiting to berth in the already overcrowded port. Yaakov could make out the Russian writing that marked the names of some ships.

Not fifty yards from where the six were, a small fishing trawler shot forward like an attack boat from her mooring in the inner harbor. The oversized motors growled deeply as she advanced on her fishing assignment toward the open sea.

Just after 3:00 A.M. it started raining again, slowly at first, then developing into a torrent from which there was no escape.

It was now pitch-black as Yaakov crouched in the front of the dinghy, arms folded, hands tucked under his armpits in order to conserve as much body heat as possible. Even with the full body wetsuit on, his face was gaunt from the cold, his skin stretched tightly over his cheekbones. He kept track of his exact location in the harbor by keeping an eye on the running lights of the merchant ships and the lights from the pier.

As a senior intelligence officer Yaakov had once refused a Mossad home-office desk job because he felt there were so many wonderful things to know and see in the world. Tonight, the sea had been a welcome improvement over the boredom of the past few days. Now, more than for the nourishment, he needed some food to divert his thoughts and nervousness. Slowly and quietly he withdrew a food bar from his packet and tore open the aluminum wrapper with his teeth. He chewed the bar slowly, as his mind dealt with the stress and fatigue.

"Still with us?" The commanding naval officer asked cheerfully in a hushed tone, a silencer-equipped AK-47 assault rifle resting in his lap.

Yaakov nodded. He said nothing. He simply sat, anxious to get the mission over with. He was more concerned with how tomorrow's...er, it's midnight by now, he realized looking at his watch...today's mission at the missile base would turn out for Avrum, Hershel and the General, and whether the timing and coordination of their attacks would work out as Hershel had planned.

There had been no opportunity for the General to arrange the equipment necessary for a direct communications hookup between the demolition team at the missile launch site of Nagorno-Karabakh and the team at the submarine site at the port of St. Petersburg, in time for these coordinated operations. In any case, communications by voice or satellite would have been exceptionally risky. Russian intelligence agents were constantly monitoring the airwaves, keeping tabs on all forms of communication.

The dinghy and the trawler drifted closer, and for the moment Yaakov's only concern was destroying the die-hards' submarine command headquarters, which lay straight ahead.

The hard-liners' communications center had to be cut off from activating other possible cells or alerting other die-hard teams pre-positioned in Europe, who may have had access to hit the rear lines with incapacitating or lethal chemical agents. The die-hards, or any other terrorist group, could achieve their point with biological sabotage, without even bothering to take the risks of destroying the political or industrial infrastructure of a country.

The rubber raft eased cautiously toward the black outline of the trawler. The commandos slowed about 500 yards from the boat and drifted to a stop when the commander held his left hand in the air—the universally understood silent hand signal for the team of frogmen to immediately stop making noise, cease all movement, and remain silent.

Fortunately for their attack team, the General had learned that the submarine's command center no longer had its original high-capacity radar equipment, which ordinarily could detect a swimmer in the water and practically tell his shoe size and blood type. Apparently the device had long since been stolen off this deactivated sub and sold on the black market to the highest bidder.

Even in the darkness, Yaakov could make out the outline of two lookouts, lowly seaman about twenty yards apart, slowly pacing the de-activated submarine's's narrow deck.

It was time for Yaakov to use his AK-47 with the night vision scope and silencer. Pffft went the nearly-silent bullet as it left the rifle. The seaman jerked slightly, as if he'd stubbed his toe in the dark. Then his body tumbled forward, breaking the water's surface with the faint sound of a fish jumping out of, then falling back into, the water. The other guard ignored this familiar sound.

"Say 'when,'" Yaakov whispered to the Russian commander, who was just now lowering his rifle after taking out the other guard.

"When. It's time for us to use our skills," he answered in a hushed tone, while he hand-signaled the other frogmen silently into the water. All had their air tanks and masks fastened snugly to their bodies. A knapsack holding explosives was pulled underwater by two frogmen.

"Don't forget, keep low and try to stay right here for twenty minutes," the commander said to Yaakov and the others, whose job it was to swim to the trawler, plant the explosives and blow it off the face of the earth. "In fifteen minutes hold the direction beacon under the water in the direction of the trawler. If we are not at the designated rendezvous location in a half hour, get yourself the hell out of here."

Few things can be as unnerving or as disorienting as swimming underwater at night.

Good bunch of guys! Yaakov observed while swimming from the dinghy, watching the team make their way toward their objective on course two-six-five. Whatever might go wrong tonight, it wouldn't be for their lack of effort, training or skills.

Yaakov forced himself to take deep breaths of ice-cold oxygen and continue his mission in the numbing water. At his age, Yaakov worried about the extreme cold water on his body and muscles. Even in a black neoprene wetsuit, the added burden of the weight belts and the cold Russian waters could sap the energy from his tired, out-of-condition body in minutes. Of course, there was no turning back now. But for those on intelligence missions, there never is.

Yaakov calculated that it was almost time for them to have arrived at their main target. The rain continued to fall steadily. Good! he thought, the guards on the decks of other ships will be huddling to stay dry. The dreary, cold, uncomfortable night will bore them more than normal, and bored guards are less alert.

The tension was building. Yaakov's eyes were sweeping everywhere, searching for danger, for something unusual—finding nothing. His visibility was limited because the water was as black as hell.

When Yaakov finally reached his destination, he noted that the Russian sub was an older model with a modified hull, which made her somewhat faster underwater. When she was on active duty her twin screws and larger rudder made for far greater maneuverability. But none of these improvements would be of any use after this evening.

As the commando team approached the large black shape, it appeared darker than the water that glistened with the light of their undersea flashlights. From a distance, the sub looked as if it were a silent dolphin.

Yaakov often looked at dolphins with affection and wonder, considering the knowing gleam in their eyes and their playful disposition. Swimming toward the sub, he admired the easy gracefulness with which the creatures could speed through the water. He recalled a dark time, not so long ago, when the Russian Navy maintained a special force of trained killer dolphins at a Black Sea port. These dolphins were taught to seek out specific items and to kill swimmers. The programs were discontinued when Communism fell, but if they were deployed in this port today no one would be safe in these waters.

Magnetic mines were slowly lifted from their watertight carrying containers pulled by the frogmen and carefully secured to the sub's hull. Air bubbles randomly making their way to the water's surface, the empty containers, slightly longer than they were tall, were allowed to sink to the bottom of the bay. They took on the appearance of mini-submarines.

A moment later, after checking their depth gauges and air supply, they hand-signaled one another to head back on a pre-set compass course to a remote dock.

Twenty-five minutes later, Yaakov raised his head above the water only enough to expose his eyes. He reached up with his hands to pull the rubber hood back on his head, allowing his ears better access to the sounds of the area. He heard the unmistakably clumsy noise of his fellow frogmen following behind him, flapping up the dock ladder from the water below. But there were all sorts of noises and loudest of all the pelting rain.

Crouching in the dark between pallets of fifty-kilo bags of the chemical Urea, one of the frogmen whispered to Yaakov in a hushed voice, "Where's our transport?"

Before answering, Yaakov unsheathed the diving knife strapped to his leg and slashed their rubber raft, sending it to the bottom.

Pushing his night vision goggles back into their case, he acclimated his eyes in the darkness to the surrounding shapes. "Just head for the black hearse at the end of this pier," Yaakov chuckled, as he patted the shoulder of the frogman.

The hearse was only fifty yards away, and at the moment it was totally vacant except for the beefy chauffeur.

"Dreadful night," the man said as the last of them climbed aboard.

"Bloody awful weather," Yaakov replied. The words were their pre-arranged code of recognition. He stripped off the wetsuit, stuffing it into a duffel bag.

The hearse driver wound his way through the city to lose any possible tails, as the first flashes of the distant explosions seeped through the drawn drapes of the hearse, followed by the concussions.

Rain again began striking the windshield, slowly at first, shortly developing into a heavy downpour. The commander of the frogmen passed around a flask of vodka. "Take a sip—for medical purposes," he advised his associates.

After Yaakov took a swig, he felt the warmth in his belly as the vodka spread throughout his system. It allowed his mind and body to relax. In that relaxed state he felt rejuvenated. "Let's cheer this bloody place up," he informed the others.

From his window, Avrum could see a tug pushing a coal barge up the Moscow River. As the rain stopped, across the river the intermittent rays of the moonlight glittered off the windows of an apartment tower. The rays danced over the streets, the branches of the trees and the ripples of the water created from the wake of a tug, slowly trudging upstream.

In an adjoining room Hershel could not fall asleep, not even though a preliminary phone report from the mission's other support personnel indicated that the performance by Yaakov and his group went off without a hitch. It was too early for the morning paper, nor would the early paper necessarily even contain news of today's incident. Beyond the excitement he always felt while planning commando attacks, Hershel was impatient to learn if all his hard work, planning, wisdom and technical activity would now pay off.

That was when Avrum burst into the room. The silence of the morning was broken with Avrum saying sourly, "We are no longer safe here! I was just speaking on the phone with my office in Tel Aviv. They were shouting to me that they were under some sort of attack. And then we were disconnected. I tried calling back several times without success. Then I got an Israeli operator on the line in another city, and she said that her telephone circuits would not go through to Tel Aviv, either."

"But...but...but," Hershel tried to respond. His veins ran cold. He could say nothing; his lips moved and chattered but no sound came out. His mind danced and panicked. He felt it could be the end of everything.

"For all we know, at this very moment, the die-hards may be onto us and they may have launched whatever they've got left at their designated target," Avrum offered.

He walked to the bathroom and inadvertently glanced at himself in the mirror. His hair was matted to his scalp with sweat, from the strain and pressures of this evening. And now the General's and their cover seemed to have been blown and they had no idea how badly their operation had been compromised.

Chapter Thirty

EN ROUTE TO NEGRO-KARABAKH, AZERBAIJAN

NOVEMBER 1

It was a moonless night and close to 1:00 A.M. when Hershel awoke from his catnap to look out the window. The sun would not appear for many hours—if at all.

A few moments later, Hershel could hear everyone in the safe house beginning to scurry around.

"Good morning, hope you slept well," Avrum said.

"Uh-huh." Hershel was struggling to focus his eyes before putting on his glasses.

"We don't have much time," Avrum announced as he headed for the kitchen to try his hand again at coffee-making. "Better get moving. Get a bite to eat—I don't know when we will have another chance."

"I'm up, I'm up!" Hershel said flatly, as he walked toward the dresser. Feeling slightly balmy from exhaustion, he did not exactly move at the speed of light. "Well, I guess we're finally going to find out if our plans will work."

"That's for sure," Avrum shouted back from the kitchen.

Hershel reached into the dresser to remove the package with the heavy brown wrapping paper with his initials on it. He tore off the wrapping and found a pressed Russian army uniform, military combat boots, a visored officer's hat, and a belted holster with an unloaded pistol. He threw them all onto a chair, then picked up the pants and browsed through the pockets.

"By God, the General thought of everything," he laughed. "Even a new ID. Avrum, look at your uniform and see if I outrank you."

"That'll be the day!" Avrum laughed. "I was just field-commissioned what would be the equivalent of a full colonel in the Israeli Army."

"You would cut a splendid figure in a colonel's dress uniform with the lovely plumes," Hershel jested. "But, if you're a colonel, I can be chief aide-de-camp to the General. On second thought," he smiled, "I could never be a self-serving apple polisher with delusions of promotions."

"Damned impertinent civilian!" Avrum shot back, laughing.

"Details, details," Hershel mumbled under his breath, buckling the belt of his trousers and reaching for the lightweight bullet-proof vest. He stood motionless, holding the gun before inserting the entire clip packed with ominous brass-capped 9mm shells.

Hershel did not have cause to consider the possibility of chemical nerve agents being unleashed against him today, as he silently recalled his discovery in 1986 of chemicals at a site in Iraq known as "Tall al Lahn." At a later date he again reminded the Institute that specialized vehicles had been seen at the site and that the area was renamed "Kamis Iyyah." At the outbreak of the Gulf War the Mossad shared Hershel's information with the CIA. Warned by the Mossad to avoid the site, the CIA failed to share this information with the U.S. military, who in March of 1991 blew up the bunkers, directly exposing some 100,000 U.S. troops to nerve gas and other unknown chemicals. CIA analysts incorrectly concluded that since Iraq had previously been unknown to store chemical weapons in an unusually designed "S" shaped bunker, they had incorrectly concluded that the information Hershel furnished about chemicals being stored in "in-line" bunkers could not have been used for chemical weapons storage, and therefore was not accurate.

Seven years later, in 1993, Senate investigator James Tuite obtained, under the Freedom of Information Act, a Livermore National Laboratory report, dated and sent to the Pentagon three months before the bombing of Iraq began. The previously classified Livermore report clearly predicted a broad dispersion of chemical warfare agents in northwest-to-southeast directions that could expose allied combat positions to nerve chemicals. Neither General Norman Schwarzkopf, who led the 1991 Persian Gulf War liberation of Kuwait, nor General Colin Powell, chairman of the Joint Chiefs of Staff during that war, received the study on chemical fallout prior to the allied attack. The idea that there were intelligence reports done that did not always reach down the ladder to soldiers in the field was not new to Hershel. Over the years he had seen other examples of that.

Today, there would be no heavy bombing to release chemical nerve agents possibly stored at the die-hard's missile launch site. However, the security around the site was expected to be heavy. The General had made plans for the formers and a trusted group of his military officers, along with their commando units, to gain access to the site. The plan was to have them enter the complex within minutes of one another, dressed as garbage men, food vendors, delivery people and truck drivers. The formers would be dressed in their new uniforms as Russian military officers.

"You look terrific," Avrum said, walking into the room.

Hershel grumbled something that Avrum couldn't quite make out.

Avrum replied, "Yesterday we were businessmen, today we are soldiers. Soldiers can better accept the risks of combat in uniform. As a matter of fact, I never thought I would be caught dead in a Russian uniform!"

"What do you mean caught dead?"

"Sorry, but I didn't mean it the way you took it."

With a troubled expression on his face, Hershel spoke in a reasoned voice, across the room to Avrum: "You know, this whole thing is amazing. I came to Russia to make some money in the import and export business and got hit with the equivalent of an asteroid. At this very moment, this part of the world is supposed to be at peace. If you take any time to give it some thought, this entire operation seems incredible. We hear the drums of war beating, and no one except the dissidents and our group knows anything about what is about to happen. A few weeks back, I would never have dreamed any of this could be possible."

"Calm down and loosen up! This will all be over soon," said Avrum.

Hershel shot back, "Give me a break. Assuming we stop them today, what new wrinkles on the theme are some son-of-a-bitch crazy terrorists going to come up with tomorrow? And why can't we get Tel Aviv on the phone?"

The tone of the former agents' conversation was still entirely calm: they were just a couple of professionals sorting out their thoughts before a tense operation.

"Come on, Hershel. Let's tackle one problem at a time. Anyway, it's time to go and see how close your predictions come to reality."

The other formers were milling around the living-room, cheerfully comparing their Russian campaign ribbons pinned to their dress uniforms.

Their plan was to enter the base as visiting Russian officers on a surprise inspection tour.

"Everyone, please calm down," Avrum instructed the group. "I think we have to go over a few more points before we move out of here. We should now match the dress of the personnel at the base, but don't forget, when we board the plane and are told the details of the green security color patch of the day, make sure to pin it on your left lapel."

After a moment of silence, Avrum inquired, "Does anyone have any questions of Hershel? If not, then Hershel, please bring us up-to-date once more with anything new that we should be aware of before we leave." From past experience Avrum knew that Hershel would not hesitate to direct questions back to him if he was unsure of any aspect of the mission.

Before speaking, Hershel collected his thoughts for a moment, looking down at the coffee table in front of him. On the table was a pastry tray and a pot filled with a liquid that Avrum kept insisting was coffee.

"Before I start," said Hershel, "I just have to affirm that we Israelis—regardless of our differences—feel that we are all dependant on one another. Our country is quite vulnerable, as you well know. We have limited supplies of air, soil, and water. And we have extremely dangerous borders with vicious, fanatical and dangerous enemies all around us. We avoid annihilation only by the care, the commitment, and I will say the love we give one another and our fragile country. I appreciate what you are attempting to accomplish today."

After a few more seconds he again spoke. "Well, there's not much more I can add to what you already know. The weather is cooperating. It's still a 'go.' Despite whatever problems are going on at Avrum's office, it seems we have not yet been compromised and our schedule is right on time."

Hershel didn't need a computer for this day's' operation. All he had to do was study the information, maps and images given him, piece-by-piece. He was programmed as good as a computer to pinpoint items of importance and overlook those that appeared to be unimportant.

He continued, "I remind you to be alert. The die-hards you can expect to run into will not only be tough, they will be experienced. Many have long histories of combat experience, so don't underestimate them. There is no other short and enlightening explanation other than to remind you that they cannot be trusted for an instant. Never take your eyes off them and never turn your back on them."

Everyone understood these orders and no one in the room questioned his statements.

He added, "From what we learned yesterday, there may be several dozen guards stationed at the main and rear entrances, and another forty to fifty from different military police and security groups scattered around the inside of the complex. Some will be off duty or on break, but they will all still be armed.

"The perimeter of the complex will be surrounded by a few more uniformed and plain-clothes agents, on foot and in vehicles. And they have been known to be accompanied by guard dogs from time to time. You know what to do in that instance."

"Yes sir," Uri volunteered.

"And what is that?" Avrum sharply shot back.

"Since this is a high-risk situation—shoot first and ask questions later!"

"Exactly," Avrum confirmed.

Hershel's gaze had gone from the group back to Uri. "One more thing. I'm not ashamed to say that it looks like Progalin has given us the right stuff and I was wrong. While we know that he is desperate and dangerous, he proved to me that he is a reliable ally in this battle against the die-hards. And that's what matters!"

Hershel stared around the room, thinking that he has spoken enough. Then he added, "We are going in with our eyes wide open. You know what I mean—no head in the sand, no illusions. We may not all return. And incidentally, Progalin was not sure if the machine-gun emplacements were manned around the clock. Keep low, stay close to the buildings, and watch out for possible automatic weapons crossfire from rooftops."

Despite what he had just said to pump up his commando team, something inside Hershel's gut couldn't bring him to trust Morat Progalin completely. But the men putting their lives on the line didn't need more to worry about, so Hershel decided to keep this to himself.

Avrum's smile was chilling and his voice was calm. "That's all we have time for. We must leave now."

"Do we know how many are in the complex, Hershel?" Ezra asked, as he pushed himself out of his chair.

Hershel shrugged his shoulders. "Progalin did not have that information, so your guess is as good as mine. An accurate count was just not available without several days surveillance, and we don't have that luxury. However, you can figure a minimum of two men in each tower and bunker, probably fifty off duty in the barracks, and who knows how many on patrol."

Hershel had relied on stand-alone secondary information—possibly incomplete—to come up with his assumptions. He would have rather had the opportunity to build a simulation of a homogenized model plan through an Internet-like computer for his scenarios and final analysis. In that way he could have conducted thorough computer simulations to predict or determine alternative courses to take before the conflict, and therefore test his tactical doctrine. If only he had a computer and a simulation software kit to give him a point-and-click environment, it would have been simple to change a particular simulation with a keystroke and immediately see the changes on the screen. But "what if" no longer mattered. Instead of his computer, he used what information was available—and, even though somewhat slower than a computer, his brain power.

Hershel started pacing. "We will have hand-held rocket launchers and enough automatic firepower to hose the towers and bunkers. The trick's going to be for us to get the initial strike teams in fast and close. The assault element has to get in past the towers and then blow the bunkers, with the main assault team hitting the reinforced missile launch building."

He carefully picked up the photographs and notes, folding the maps before placing them in a carry-on bag. Nothing of a personal nature would be left in the apartment. They would not be returning. Everything was wiped clean.

"Time to take the gloves off and eradicate these madmen," Hershel added as his voice dropped.

"Eight more minutes, you guerrillas, and we're outa here," Avrum said, rising to his feet. "Get your gear together. We have instructions to board the plane two-by-two."

The briefing ended with an orgy of handshakes and pats on the back as they acknowledged their good feeling for one another.

"Bloody good," Avrum said, and in silence they all left the safe house, piling into the cars waiting to take them to the transport plane.

The area near the airport was flat and they could see for blocks. There was no traffic until they neared the gates, and now for the first time Avrum saw what he feared they might be up against: six tanks and a dozen armored personnel carriers lining one side of the avenue under the trees.

An officer stood in the turret hatch of the lead tank, a military radio headset casually resting on his shoulders. Not far from the trucks, a group of demonstrators were pacing back and forth, talking to one another, ignoring the soldiers as they carried placards of protest.

"Democracy is rotting and it stinks," one of the protesters shouted.

"Looks like the die-hards have organized a propaganda event with their supporters, a warm-up for things to come," Avrum sighed.

Their cars passed by the tanks and personnel carriers without incident, continuing to the airfield. The airfield complex was dimly lit when they arrived and the waiting plane looked like a black stencil against the moon. Avrum tried not to concern himself, but he knew that the pilot would probably fly at least part of the way to the missile enclave by an auto-pilot-radar-computer system that was obsolete by Western standards.

The airframe of the great Russian TU-95 "Bear" was probably twenty-five years old, but that was not unusual for a Russian plane. This wasn't so bad if the plane had been well maintained. But Avrum realized that this was doubtful.

"Hershel, do you think the pilot is any good?" one of the clever former Mossad agents inquired.

"I practically taught him myself," Hershel answered, making light of the question.

However, he knew full well that flying low over rough terrain was dangerous, especially during a pitch-black night. A pilot could easily become disoriented if he did not pay attention to the instruments, and at night even experienced pilots had guided their airplanes accidentally into the side of hills. But Hershel felt there was no point in discussing these fears.

"I've got no problem checking the pilot out," he offered, loud enough for everyone to hear. He then mumbled to himself, "Just don't ask me to check the maintenance log—that is, if there ever was one."

The formers boarded the plane and stored their gear in an orderly fashion, checking to make sure that everyone had everything he was issued. The commandos took their seats along the sides of the bare cabin without breaking stride. Hershel looked out the window of the aircraft. There was nothing unusual about the pre-departure. No special security guards were visible, only the ground crew lazily going about their preflight duties, prepping the plane before departure. It appeared that they would be taking off as planned, without incident.

The large plane door was closed while the flight crew went through the usual start-up procedures. In a few moments the Bear slowly began moving. Several minutes later they were taxiing down the runway, and within seconds they were in the air, banking away from the city, heading northwest. As Hershel sat on the bench-type seat inside the wide cabin, he found himself contemplating the down side of what he and the team of formers were doing.

On the books, the formers did not officially exist, and if anything with the mission went wrong they would take heat from all sides. They'd be disavowed by their former bosses in Israel, they'd be blamed for espionage by the Russians, and worst of all, they'd probably be shot on the spot by the die-hards—who would know they were responsible for taking out their submarine launch headquarters.

Not aware that he was cracking his knuckles, Hershel closed his eyes and leaned back as he thought: Dear God, please don't let us screw up!

While he was a team player, he fully realized that he was half a world away from any real help. Despite his trepidation about the dangers of this mission and his desire to be involved in every crucial step of the operation, Hershel hated the reality that he would not be able to participate on the front line of this attack. It would just not be prudent for him to take the risk of injury while everything was riding on his planning. Unfortunately, the mission would be totally beyond his direct control.

Despite the earplugs issued to the men on boarding, there was a constant high-frequency whine from the engines and turbulence from the rough air through which they were flying. The Russian military didn't spend money, as commercial airlines did, on sound insulation. Every person flying aboard the plane, except for the crew, was wearing earplugs. This made any attempt at conversation most difficult, and after a time didn't really block the drone of the noise anyway.

"At least we won't have to worry about unfriendly radar coverage on this trip," Hershel shouted to Avrum over the roar of the engines. A few minutes after take-off, he had seen the reflection of the moon above the cloud cover shimmer from the wings.

The plane settled into its course, and from a mixture of tension and not enough sleep, some of the commandos drifted off to dreamland for the balance of the ride, despite the loud whine of the engines.

The worst part of military air travel was the boredom, made even more unbearable by the sound-induced isolation.

Hershel awoke, slightly confused as to where he was until he overheard the pilot speaking in Russian into his headset.

"Tower, this is B-245 heavy. Requesting permission to land—over."

A few moments of silence went by and the pilot began speaking again.

"Roger, B-245 turning runway two-seven direct. B-245 heavy—out."

The pilot turned, first to the left, then the right, visually checking for other air or ground traffic, but there was none. Close to the missile enclave, the red runway lights, blue perimeter lights and finally the black tarmac runway of the military air base at Negro-Karabakh, all came into view. The silver pods of the Bear's engines roared through the morning fog, whirring down as the pilot eased back the throttles, maneuvering the plane into an isolated position on the far side of the airport.

A ground crewman walked backwards in front of the plane with lighted wands, waving for the plane to follow him. As he brought them to an "X" configuration, the pilot stopped the plane and cut the engines.

The massive doors opened with a whirring sound and the attack group headed by the General and following Hershel's plans, quickly departed. The Chervok's "special regiment," all volunteers, was the elite combat unit of Russian commandos. They were all highly trained killers, by instinct and practice. Each would sacrifice his life for the success of a mission.

Chapter Thirty-One

MISSILE ENCLAVE, NEGRO-KARABAKH, AZERBAIJAN

NOVEMBER 1

Avrum and Hershel were the last to leave the noisy transport plane. They shook their heads to clear off the dizziness induced by the loud flight and from wearing earplugs.

As they walked down the ramp, it started to rain again and the General looked to the sky, concerned about the inclement weather.

"Weather's a weapon too. It should add to our element of surprise," he said with an air of confidence.

"The weather predictions were right on target," Avrum declared. "The low-pressure front is passing through here now."

Then, almost casually, it began happening. No commotion, no shouting of orders, no running about—scarcely a sound beyond the rumbling of engines. If anything was remarkable at all, it was not the noise but the quiet.

Large military trucks immediately pulled up to the staging area next to the plane so the commandos could quickly load. As Hershel spoke, above the noise of the idling engines, a downpour suddenly drenched him and the others.

He stated, "General, I need a truck with a half dozen men and a scout who knows the area."

"Hell, we have no time!" the General shouted, almost losing control in a sudden outburst. Then, in an afterthought, he calmed down and spun around to face Hershel. "What the devil for?"

Hershel said, "I never argue with generals, and I apologize for not being perfect. But I did not think of it until we were almost here—that's my fault—please hear me out. Then you can make your decision....My idea is certainly not going to compromise the attack. If I am right, it should greatly help."

The tension was building. Hershel felt his heart rate increase.

"Talk, damn it! The clock is ticking!" The General snapped.

Hershel took a huge breath, like somebody about to spend a length of time underwater, and stated "At the first sign of our intrusion there is absolutely nothing to stop the officer in charge from launching several missiles. I reviewed the plans of the site again on the flight, and noticed from the grid symbols that electricity for the site was supplied by Mosenergo, the power-generating facility on the other side of town. All I have to do is cut the high-tension power lines and the site would be blacked out. Even if the die-hards were in their underground bunker with the command codes already entered into the launch mode, and even if they had their fingers on the button, their launch would be delayed until they switched to their back-up power. This delay would give you the additional time that we will need to get into the command bunker and destroy it.

"I'll need some plastique explosives, several accurate timers to coordinate the precise moment of your attack, a few of your demolition experts, some commandos...and your approval."

General Chervok stopped in his tracks and exclaimed, "That's one hell of a plan!" There was a look of admiration on his face. "I'm sorry that I initially sounded critical. Implement your plan. It makes good sense."

Hershel rubbed his forehead with his fingers. He was as nervous as the General. "You probably didn't think of this because, for most people, the ordinary light switch is often taken for granted. When we turn the light switch on we never take the time to consider the source of the power."

"Good luck," the General obligingly commented.

"I don't need luck, General, I need your Colonel Viktor! But thanks for the good-luck wish," he said. "I do appreciate it."

The General immediately signaled for the Colonel and his adjutant to join Hershel.

As the newly assembled group started off in the direction of the power plant, Hershel's driver pounded on the gearshift to get the truck into gear.

The General got vicarious exhilaration watching Hershel and his newly formed group prepare to depart on this spontaneous side-mission.

Speaking softly to his troops, the General's voice was low but resonant. Not a sound but the General's words could be heard. As Chervok spoke he stood straighter than usual and began to walk back and forth in front of the men, water running down his slicker. He was in his element. He felt as if he were a young man again.

"I know that you were always the best—the elite—and there is no doubt in my mind that you know exactly what to do. It is most important that you understand the underlying situation and the reasons for your being here.

"The purpose of this operation is to defend and protect the process of democratization. The first duty of a democracy is to defend itself, and that's what we are about to do! We are defending Russia against a group of renegade rogues, die-hard military men who have decided to take the law into their own hands and are now planning unauthorized missile attacks against our allies. These traitors must be stopped to ensure the integrity of the Russian government and to prevent a catastrophic loss of life which will be forever blamed on our country. This is your first test. God's speed!"

He stared into the group of soldiers, as if trying to memorize faces. His troops treated him with respect, almost awe. He was always charismatic and stimulating to them. Someone called out, "Okay men, form up." It was an officer whose lapels carried the colors of the Special Forces.

General Chervok watched them file off, wondering what to expect next...and if this would be his last command. He still had the look of a deadly serious warrior on his face—a look you didn't want to get in the way of.

The problem of the sudden downpour was solved by the General's ordering the commandos to enter the rear of the canvas-covered trucks. The troops settled themselves on the benches, awaiting their order to proceed, as the General followed the illuminated hands of his watch turn to the operation's agreed-on starting time.

The perimeter zone was demarcated by a double ten-foot-high chain-link fence, barbed wire running along the top. Small, thin trees surrounding the complex were reduced to thickets, nearly fifty yards across, growing between rocky terrain. The narrow perimeter roadway running between the fences was just wide enough for one vehicle to pass. Soldiers armed with high powered rifles and German shepherd dogs occasionally patrolled the inner and outer perimeter.

The fences were surrounded by walls of electronically generated waves that threw off static, disrupting anyone trying to listen in with external devices to conversations within the complex. Sensitive motion detectors placed in the ground kept track of potential infiltrators attempting to tunnel under the fence.

As Chervok and his convoy of soldiers slowly approached the missile base, a group of commandos was immediately stationed around the perimeter fence and the access roads were blocked.

The lead command car carrying the General came to a stop at the main gate. Two military policemen dressed in rain slickers came out of the guardhouse and approached the car. Avrum noticed that one limped and the other seemed to have something wrong with his arm.

"Hmmmm, they must be veterans," he observed.

This was both good and bad news. People with military combat experience were very different. When the time would come for action, they would most likely react well. Their instincts would kick in, and they would probably fight back effectively, even without leadership.

As the two military police snapped a hasty salute, the driver lowered the window and held up some papers. The guard came closer, leaned forward, and the driver discreetly raised his other hand, revealing a small gun.

The impact of the tiny air dart was no greater than that of a mosquito bite.

"What the...?" The guard raised his free hand to swat what seemed to be a bothersome insect. A lethal drop of poison rapidly entered his bloodstream and he fell to the road. The second guard standing directly next to him did not have an instant to react before a second dart struck him. He turned and looked toward the shooter, clutching at the dart that had struck his throat as his eyes tried to focus. All his speech and thoughts were cut off as he, too, fell down in a heap.

"Incapacitate soldiers without warning, and all their experience and training becomes a moot point," the General pointed out. "It certainly makes our situation a hell of a lot safer."

No sooner had the second guard hit the ground than three commandos jumped from the tailgate of one of the trucks. One shimmied up a pole to throw a covering cloth over the security camera, while others opened the gates for the convoy to pass. Two removed the two bodies to the nearby bushes and took up the positions of the fallen guards, creating the impression that nothing was wrong.

The situation that the base commander faced in defending the facility was a problem of size: hundreds of acres of open space and miles of perimeter fences, exposure to a heavily wooded area, dozens of buildings, sensitive equipment and munitions that were all at risk. And the only backup to the sentries were dozens of passive closed-circuit television cameras (CCTV), monitored by several guards watching a bank of mind-numbing monitors. Detecting intruders or following an unauthorized vehicle as it moved in and out of camera range, from camera to camera, was problematical.

The dilemma that the CCTV security men faced was not their fault. Their antiquated, frail warning system was designed to be a passive watchdog. Real-time monitoring of dozens of cameras was simply beyond human capacity.

Avrum recognized that if the Russians had installed a new generation of active digitized CCTV system, he would have had to contend with an increased level of Russian security. Rather than rely on a security officer to catch an intruder in the act, the new system would alert security to the event's location and continue to track the interloper, or multiple images, by automatically zooming or panning the cameras. The new system's intelligence would also project the direction and speed of the intruder and automatically switch camera views to the next camera in the field of view. The guards would have been given ample time to study the intruder and could act upon multiple situations at one time. Avrum was thankful that this was not the case today.

He took his 7x50 binoculars from their case and began observing the camp. Guards were stationed in all the towers. Avrum rubbed the sweat from his eyes and checked the focus on both eyepieces before he continued his survey.

"Hershel and the Colonel were successful," the General stated authoritatively, noticing that the lights had suddenly gone out and the entire base was blacked out. "Let's move quickly—before the auxiliary generators automatically kick in," he said.

Six of the trucks swung out of the convoy, racing in the darkness to different pre-assigned positions. The lead vehicle, with a truck full of commandos following, pulled up to the main bunker entrance and screeched to a stop.

A single guard snapped to attention as General Chervok approached. "Your identification card goes here sir," he said, pointing to a slot in the security console, "and your hand print goes here, on the flat surface."

"I have dirty hands and I don't have time for stupid cards," the General said angrily in a voice that told the guard to go to hell.

His aide lowered the pellet pistol in the direction of the man and fired a deadly shot to his neck.

Two of the soldiers in the nearest guard tower were casually chatting with each other. One could see that they were bored. This would be that sort of duty. A comfortable and grossly normal routine, conducted by men who'd been doing the same thing for months. Stay bored, guys, he told himself. Their weapons are not chambered—a safety precaution that will count against them today!

The muted flash of a shoulder-fired missile launch could be seen, and barely a second later, the blinding white flash of a fragmentation shell hitting against one of the towers and disintegrating it on impact.

The echo was still resounding as the other towers were similarly destroyed.

Gunfire abruptly erupted from the direction of the barracks. Seconds later, the General's commandos returned fire, pumping white-phosphorus exploding rounds into the windows. Any semblance of life within the barracks was lost in an instant.

Following the General and his aide, Avrum climbed a bank and crossed a gravel path, disappearing around the corner of a building. They walked slowly and deliberately in a tense crouch, careful that they did not expose themselves unnecessarily.

The sound of objects hitting metal and shattering glass could be heard as the result of explosives going off from the different positions taken up by the commandos around the missile site. A nearby truck looked like a gutted pineapple, blasted door panels peeled back by the force of a grenade exploding and only scraps of the seats still burning inside.

The die-hard guards on the rooftops and bunkers had noticed nothing unusual, before they were devastatingly attacked. Now their video surveillance cameras placed at strategic locations were put out of commission. But that did not matter because most of the security officers watching their consoles were off eating in the mess.

Then, the emergency generators finally kicked in and a few dim lights were restored to parts of the base.

In a moment, one of the commandos was able to activate the controls to open the double security doors. There was nothing to use as cover and for all they knew there could be an armed battalion waiting to blow them all away as soon as the doors opened.

The commanding officer whispered to his men, "We go in two-by-two. No one is to go in alone. When they surrender, disarm them and leave a few of your men to guard them. Open fire if you have to, but give them every opportunity to surrender first."

As the doors swung open, the commandos plunged in through the opening. It was like stepping into the control room of NASA. There were men behind green illuminated console screens and large tables with miniature replicas of missiles and their targets. A few of the die-hards were at the screens, entering data at the keyboards, while most were aimlessly standing around, still wondering why there had been a power failure.

Avrum wiped the rain from his face and noticed a tall dissident whose eyes were moving as rapidly as his own.

The man's eyes and body turned in the direction of the console. Avrum pointed at him and shouted to the team of commandos, "Stop him!" A gun with a silencer went off.

The soldier fell to the floor and the room of approximately 30 people was quickly secured as the die-hards were each handcuffed and led to a nearby stockade.

"What is your name and what are you doing here?" demanded one of the die-hard officers who had surrendered.

"My name is not important for you to know, nor are my orders for you or these other criminals to review. You'll get all your answers at your trial," the General answered. "You must realize by now that you and your friends are finished. You are all under arrest for treason."

"That remains to be seen," the die-hard officer said surprisingly, as he was shoved out the door by a commando guard.

"Arrogant bastard!" Avrum interjected.

Turning toward a just-arrived Hershel, as he left the crowded bunker, the General said with a smile, "My congratulations. Your idea helped ensure our success!"

Outside in the well-lit compound, Chervok shook Hershel's hand, his eyes staring intently and never blinking. If there was anything unusual about Chervok that would startle anyone meeting him for the first time, it was his eyes, for they were the intense eyes of a man who loved confrontation.

"I need a casualty report," the General shouted to his aide. "All commanders are to report in. Find out if the perimeter is totally secure."

Avrum anxiously asked, "What plans do you have for Doctor Zavaskayev? Do we go after him at KGB headquarters?"

"A man like Zavaskayev has to have more than one plan at a time up his sleeve," said the General. "Keep an eye on him, let's see what he is up to. We can always take care of him…later." Then he added with a smirk, "Stalin taught me that."

Reports of group leaders directing the mopping-up operation shattered the momentary silence. The battle was short but hard fought, and had taken only slightly longer than anticipated.

With the missile base secured, the General signaled to the commandos, "Mission accomplished!"

"What we've accomplished is not exactly a framework for world peace, but it should certainly make a good start," Avrum said to the General as Colonel Viktor handed Chervok a report.

"But not good enough or thorough enough," the General replied after quickly reading the brief report. Chervok gave the quintessential Russian gesture that the Russians call *fig karmane*, the sign of the fig—the thumb thrust irreverently between the second and third fingers in a clenched fist— meaning, roughly, "nuts, we are screwed!" While making this defiant gesture, he said, "we have been screwed by the die-hard Communists."

Disbelief crept into Hershel's face at the frightening prospect of a die-hard victory. "What's happened?"

"Colonel Viktor just handed me this report. I had no way of knowing," the General said, gathering his wits with a visible effort. "The situation appears to be desperate. While the world was dragging its heels, the die-hards launched worldwide attacks from multiple sites, including bases overseas."

Hershel turned away from the General, his eyes sweeping the horizon. He realized that the General had been tricked by his life-long friend. Chervok was caught in Progalin's trap and as much as the formers tried to help, their efforts were for naught.

The General's lips were compressed into a thin line. He knew that Hershel always disliked Morat; and now, so do I, he concluded. He looked back on his decisions in anger

"Morat did what I never could imagine he would do....He double-crossed us! He gave us one location and not the others. Damn! Double-dealing is nothing new for people like him. It must have been the same under the Czars. Everyone double-dealing everyone else. Morat is that same type person. He's now in the lion's den and it will be difficult to get to him—and his cohorts.

Although the formers had inside information from the General—in part from that gangster Morat Progalin—it was not sufficiently specific for them to issue an alert regarding the die-hard's plans. Even the best intelligence in the world can fail to prevent every single terrorist attack. Their target, they believed, was the only missile base in the C.I.S. controlled by the die-hards, according to Progalin.

There would be no overnight, magical solution to this international crisis. Hershel's analysis, although impressive, was based upon disinformation Progalin furnished to the General. The present world maladies might have been cured, having been given more time, greater accountability, improved coordination and more reliable sources. Now, however, it will take many years to repair the serious damage done to the entire world in just one night by the die-hards.

"Whatever happens, I wish us luck," the General said.

"I wish everyone luck," said Hershel. "The whole world, if there's enough luck to go around. We'll all need it!"

Chapter Thirty-Two

NEW YORK STATE, U.S.A.

NOVEMBER 1

The sun had just began setting in the western sky as two men in a four-wheel-drive pickup truck came to an abrupt stop on the gravel berm of the seldom used reservoir ring road in Croton, New York. A steady breeze blew through the trees surrounding the large lake. There are few places in the eastern United States as rural, sleepy or beautiful as Croton in November.

It was community with a crime rate so low as to be nearly off the charts, except for the occasional note of misbehavior or improper parking on the police blotter. The only real problem was the way the people drove, and for that they had the Croton police, who gave an occasional warning to an erratic motorist.

Middle-income one-family homes on the opposite side of the narrow ring road abutted the heavily wooded area surrounding the lake.

At the rear of her house a woman wearing an apron had just finished removing clothes from a line where they hung to dry in the fresh, clean air. The two men in the pickup truck watched her quickly fold the clothes, put them into a laundry basket, then walk back into her house.

The driver of the truck had a large round head perched atop a thick neck. A pair of awkward, black-framed glasses dominated his face. When he spoke to his partner, it was in Arabic, and his heavy eyebrows seemed to float up and down on his forehead as if out of control. "It's dark enough, let's go!"

Abdullah acknowledged Saleh Makdiah's statement with a grunt. Some years ago Saleh, 11 or 12 years old at the time, was a Palestinian refugee living in Lebanon when his family fled in fear of advancing Israeli forces from his home—a tin-roofed, cement-block two-room house—where he had lived with his parents and nine other siblings. They ran, while some of their Arab neighbors stayed and prospered under Israeli and Christian martial law. He was fond of the fig trees growing near there and often worked as a day laborer picking the fruit. Fleeing this home, he was transplanted deep within Lebanon to a refugee camp, with perhaps a million other Palestinian and Syrian workers who had also been transplanted into Lebanon. None of them where permitted to work freely by Syrian controlling factions. Private charities that helped the camp were, at that time, dealing with more immediate crises in Rwanda and the Congo, so the camp had difficulties dealing with the most recent influx of refugees.

A wiry man with a bushy, black beard, Abdullah was Saleh's partner in frequent clashes against Christian malitia soldiers in Lebanon in the 1970s and '80s. With nothing better to occupy himself, Abdullah soon joined one of the Black September Twelve Battalions—named for the "black day" when the late Israeli Prime Minister Yitzhak Rabin and Yasir Arafat shook hands on the White House lawn. Paid about $35 a month by one of Arafat's support groups, he was sent to Russia where he received advance training as a guerrilla under the tutelage of die hard communists. He proudly sent his parents a picture of himself from there, posed with an AK-47 assault rifle. After many letters back and forth, he convinced Saleh to join him in Russia.

Having been promised a life of leisure and wealth by the die-hards, both Abdullah and Saleh came to the realization that it would be impossible for them to return to Lebanon. They were soon recruited by their Russian trainers to work as paid terrorists for a Communist die-hard group, which is why they were in Croton today.

The two exited the truck, walked to the rear and pulled the tarp off the truck bed, revealing a large cardboard box and two big aluminum cylinders. The cylinders were painted black so as not to be obvious or reflective in the dark. Making hardly any noise, the two men only took moments to cut through the wire fence, and make three trips to the water's edge with their cargo.

Afterwards, in a cluster of trees, as they had practiced countless times before, they expertly donned their cumbersome protective suits and oxygen respirator hoods. Then, carefully placing the containers just under the surface of the water, Abdullah unscrewed the caps with a wrench while Saleh held each container steady, releasing deadly type A botulinus toxin into the reservoir.

Patrolman John White was casually driving along his regular patrol route. Every so often, something "real" would happen while on patrol, and he figured it was his job to know everything going on in his assigned area. He was about to conclude his tour of duty when he spotted the parked pickup truck on the side of the road.

That's unusual, he thought. No one should be parked there. And directly in front of the "No Parking At Anytime" sign. What nerve!

At first, the lone officer in the big Chevrolet police cruiser did not know what to make of the parked truck. He slowed the cruiser and pulled over on the gravel, stopping some twenty-five feet behind it.

The hood's not up. Doesn't look like it broke down, he told himself. Must be a couple of kids neckin' again, he quietly assumed. When he put his patrol car's spotlight on the truck he could see that the tarp was pulled back in disarray and that the truck bed was empty.

White put his uniform hat on, adjusted his pistol belt and lit up his car's red and yellow rotating roof lights.

Following the police manual to the letter, he cautiously got out of the patrol car and walked up behind the driver's door of the truck, flashlight raised above his head in one hand, the other hand routinely on the butt of his gun—as he'd been taught. He'd approached the driver's door from the rear and leaned in closer after he saw that the truck was empty and the doors locked.

Directing his flashlight toward the trees, he saw nothing. Without backup present he would not follow the path into the woods.

Walking back to the car, he stabbed the mike on his radio. "Four-two-four to H.Q."

"H.Q back," came the reply. "Go ahead, four-twenty-four."

"Looks like we got us some more lovers or fisherman on the northwest bank of the reservoir. I need a 10-28 on New Jersey tag Charlie-Kilo four eight zero Fox-trot, a 1994 silver Datsun pick-up." It's a long way from New Jersey to go fishing, White thought.

"That's a roger," a voice from police control crackled over the static. ".Stand by."

After a minute the same static-filled voice came back on the police band. "Four-twenty-four, this is H.Q."

"Go ahead, H.Q. This is four-two-four."

"Charlie-Kilo four eight zero Fox-trot, registered to a 1989 Ford red Bronco; owner Herman Brant, number twenty-three Filor Lane, Montvale, New Jersey. There are no outstanding warrants or a 'stolen' on the plates. The plates are definitely not registered to the Datsun. We are running a further make on the owner. Do you want backup for a ten-thirty-seven, four-twenty-four?"

"That's a roger, ten-seventy-four. H.Q., four-two-four will be ten-seven at northwest bank of reservoir."

"Roger."

The officer put on his flashing headlights, got out of the car and slowly readjusted his gun belt and hat. Holding his flashlight to the side, he cautiously began walking toward the path leading to the woods, when he was met by a barrage of automatic gunfire. The force spun him around before he fell in a heap at the side of the road. He barely had time to gasp as the Teflon-coated bullets easily penetrated his bullet-proof vest.

The gunmen quickly peeled off their respirator hoods and protective suits at the side of the pickup truck as a dark blue sedan driven by a female accomplice pulled up behind the police cruiser. The terrorists planned to abandon the fingerprint-free truck where it stood.

Before the three sped off in the sedan, they could hear the voice over the police car's loudspeaker. The communications sergeant on desk duty at police headquarters was calling, "Four-twenty-four, signal 1, four-twenty-four, signal 1!"

"The New York countryside is very peaceful this time of the year," Saleh said to the woman driving the getaway car.

"Yes, but it's not as nice as Palestine," she countered.

Almost at the same moment, a panel truck, lights off, coasted to a quick stop in the parking lot of the Croton reservoir dam and pump-house.

It only took a few seconds for two ski-masked intruders to disengage the alarm system, tear the lock cylinder out with a special lock-pulling tool, and kick open the employee entrance with a resounding crash.

One of the technicians at the control console spun around in his swivel chair, knocking his half-filled coffee container to the floor.

"Everyone on the floor," barked one of the intruders. "Move, move! Hands behind your back!" he demanded.

He fired a round from his automatic weapon into the ceiling while his accomplice handcuffed the technicians. Once they were all handcuffed, the first intruder switched his gun from automatic to manual. Just a few short years ago this gunman was a shepherd playing his flute while tending a small flock of bony sheep on a Jordan hillside. He could neither read nor write.

As he walked behind each hostage he systematically put two quick rounds into the skull of each captive without showing the slightest bit of emotion.

Moments later another masked intruder entered the pumphouse, wheeling in several five-gallon buckets on a hand truck.

As soon as the two finished checking to see that all of the captives were dead, they shut down the water purification valves, put on protective rubber clothing and respirator hoods that were connected to oxygen packs, and began pouring the highly poisonous contents of their buckets into the intake system.

Their work was completed at this first-of-several locations they planned to attack. They turned the valves back on, and in a matter of minutes the die-hard terrorists calmly slipped out of the building and drove away in their van, leaving behind empty buckets and the bodies of the three water supply technicians.

It would be hours before the bodies would be discovered, dead from their wounds. Even more time would pass before the water system's security force would learn who had done this and what poison had been used.

Neither of the terrorists spoke for more than a minute; then the driver turned to the others. "The doctor was right when he told us that the facilities are poorly protected."

The second man agreed. "For sure. The Americans only react after the worst happens. It's hard to believe that we put together a knockout punch right here under their noses, without them ever suspecting."

"Well, it's only a matter of time now and our friends will be in complete control of the C.I.S.—or should I say the new Soviet Union?" he added, laughing, as this death squad traveled to its next assignment.

A similar scenario would occur later that night at the main water pumping station in the middle of New York City, as a gauzy mist hung in the trees and dew covered the broad lawns of Central Park.

Without warning, several long-range missiles launched from a remote missile site in eastern Russia exploded over Tokyo, raining down AC and CK lethal blood agents upon early risers who were on their way to work.

Blood agents immediately attack the chemistry of the blood of those exposed by destroying its oxygen-carrying ability, clotting characteristics and other life-supporting attributes—causing severe internal organ damage and death to whomever comes in contact with the agents. In this case, they descended upon tens of thousands of innocent people.

Panic raged as crowds of commuters were doused with the deadly agents. It was impossible, at first, for any of the crowd to know what was happening to them. Fear of the unknown and memory of past biochemical attacks in the city's subway system sent the commuters into a frenzy. People parted, running everywhere, then surged together, seeking cover as a barely visible cloud mass moved over them. People clung to one another, or tried to hide—even under flimsy awnings, in shallow doorways or deep in a pile of already trampled bodies. But as if by the force of a moving tide, everyone was exposed—unwillingly pushed along by rolling waves of the masses.

There were shouts, cries of pain and of anger. Some of the people got a whiff of it, and knew its reek. "Gas!" they shouted. "Run! Hide! Get away!" They did not even know the people they were shouting to. Panic pushed them against a stream of bodies trying to push in the opposite direction. They struggled to get to open space—fresh air—but then the gas cloud rolled over them, again. Nausea overcame them; then they sagged and fell to the pavement as they retched uncontrollably.

But Tokyo was not alone. Streets in international cities throughout the world were suddenly a mass of dead bodies. None who breathed the poison would survive. Through all these cities, bodies were scattered helter-skelter. People on all fours were puking violently; here and there individuals holding handkerchiefs to their faces wandered aimlessly, until they too received a whiff and were overcome.

Until this moment it had been man's natural instinct to think the best of his fellow man, not the worst. At the end of Friday's workday, millions frequented their favorite restaurants to enjoy a drink, a meal, or just a snack with their friends. They did not have a clue that just hours before their revelry, die-hard sympathizers had visited those same eating places, deliberately spreading botulinus bacterium in the salad, intent on causing a worldwide outbreak of deadly food poisoning. They took their lead from what had happened in Dalles, Oregon, in 1984 when followers of Bhagwan Shree Rajneesh had deliberately contaminated salad bars there. This was the beginning of maliciously planned food poisoning around the world.

In New York City the telephone rang, jarring Kathy out of a fitful sleep. She was a demure little creature, about twenty-two, had blond, shoulder-length hair and dark eyes. Her face was that of a classic model with a finely shaped nose and full lips.

Disoriented at first, her eyes centered on the rising sun reflecting around the edges of the dark window shade. The phone rang a second, then a third time. Whoever it was seemed determined.

Blinking, she looked toward the source of the commotion, and after hesitating picked up the receiver. Glancing at her dresser clock, she saw that it was just eight-fifteen, and it was, after all, Saturday morning—her morning to sleep late.

"Yes, hello," she said. "How are you, Mom? No headaches...or anything ghastly?...I'm glad you're going out early....Yes, I did have a good time last night....Yes, I did think about what you said....I'm not going to move out of New York City....No, I don't agree. Hold on a minute while I get something to drink."

Holding the portable phone to her ear, she walked to the kitchen and turned on the water. Letting it run for a moment before filling her glass, she started back to the bedroom, sipping its coolness as she went.

"It's no more dangerous here in New York City than where you are. I'm sorry...I didn't think that I was yelling at you....I just woke up," she said as she lifted the glass to her mouth.

Pressing the phone to her ear, she tried to ignore her mother's next question. She struggled with the answer as she put on a sour face.

"Don't try to be clairvoyant, Mom. There is no chance of Bob and I getting together again. Now, Mom....*Honestly,* what do *you* think? You know we weren't getting along too well....For all I know, I may have told Bob I'm allergic to him!"

"When are you going to see me? I guess the next holiday is Thanksgiving. How about then?"

Suddenly Kathy shouted into the phone, "What's happening? What's hap-pen-ing to meee?..."

A wave of nausea passed over her and she began sweating as if she were in a sauna. She reached for the wall to steady herself. Her legs turned to rubber.

What's happening? she kept thinking, as the light coming from the window went gray and then black. Gasping for breath, she grabbed her throat, collapsing into a heap on the floor, arms twitching wildly as her face hit the rug. Her now motionless eyes stared blankly at the brick wall of the building next door.

"Hello, Kathy? Hello?? Hello?...What's wrong?!"

If Kathy could have looked into other apartments she would have observed the same scene repeated in hundreds of homes with men, women and children sprawled on their floors. Before it struck, a few people had time enough to leave their buildings. Their bodies littered the street. Unaffected passers-by stopped to help, or, in typical New York fashion, pretended not to notice and walked by these unfortunates.

Everything about them looked normal, there were no wounds, no blood, no destroyed buildings. Something unbelievable had happened.

From around the corner an ambulance hurtled into Kathy's street. Three EMS technicians jumped out as it stopped. They fanned out among the sprawling bodies and began conducting a hasty triage. One EMS technician turned over a man lying on the pavement and started mouth-to-mouth resuscitation after clearing away the man's vomit. After a moment he felt for a pulse in the man's throat, but he was dead, just like all the others.

The ambulance stood empty as the technicians walked back, stepping over bodies. They had been alerted to the break-ins at the pumping stations and sent out to help survivors. "Murderers!" one of them shouted. "Who said this could never happen here? Damn murderers! Whoever would have done this?"

It was decisive. It was the end of life as Kathy and others had known it.

A week later Saleh and Abdullah sat in the shade of a fig tree on a hillside in Lebanon. The rough dung-colored landscape stretched for miles around them, devoid of another living being.

Abdullah broke the silence. "What we did could be bad for our reputation." He had no remorse.

"Why is that? You feel we have made a mistake and wish to repent?"

"No," Abdullah replied. "Our reputation is for killing with a gun, a knife, or a bomb. Not with chemical weapons."

"Maybe it is bad for your reputation, but it is good for the soul," Saleh replied. "How many do you think we killed?"

"Countless millions," replied a bored Abdullah. Then he asked Saleh if they should think of remaining in Lebanon.

"No," answered Saleh, "I think my family will like living in Russia with the new generation of Communists. The die-hard fight to re-establish the Party is so much like our own goals to take back all of Palestine from Israel that it makes me feel as if I belong.

"And don't forget that the die-hards are helping our cause by establishing terrorist cells in the United States—and throughout the world! Why shouldn't we be comfortable living among them? After all, we may have a lot to offer by teaching them a few new wrinkles about terrorism."

EPILOGUE

Among the lowlands of the Ramapo Mountains the sun was rising for yet another hot, humid September day in 1997. With trepidation, I had just finished listening to a newscast originating from New York. The commentator sadly disclosed that some one-hundred "suitcase size" atomic bombs had just been discovered missing from the vast Russian arsenal. What will eventually happen to them, I wonder?

Intelligence sources had known this fact a year prior to this public announcement. Most intelligence communities are extremely proficient in obtaining and objectively evaluating information from potentially aggressive areas, offering advice, analysis and wisdom to their political masters. There is no guarantee that advanced intelligence dispatches are disseminated or acted on correctly. Intelligence is basically an extension of a nation's policy. If a nation's decision making or handling of the information by the political administration is faulty, even the most excellent intelligence can not be effective in preventing potential disaster.

While *Secret Agenda* is a speculative exercise, the scenario remains, however, entirely feasible. It is a regrettable fact that some terrorists are willing to embark on a journey beyond that known to any living being on earth. They are willing in their cause to join Allah for the eternal life.

Former intelligence operatives, who now only occasionally visit me, suggest that, in fact, humanity is a singular entity, bound together by dignity, honor and the desire to survive in peace. It is up to the individual to persuade their political administrators to set up their own *secret agenda* of international mechanisms to ward off increasing world terrorism.

We share in a mutual role of responsibility to humanity in protecting one another and preventing Armageddon.

Today is your day. There may not be another like it.

SELECTED REFERENCES

Biotechnology in the U.S.S.R. (1979–1989).

Carnegie Endowment for International Peace, Nuclear Nonproliferation Project, 1993.

Chemical Warfare in Southeast Asia and Afghanistan. Special Report No. 98, U.S. Department of State, 1989.

Chemical Weapons Threat. Defense Intelligence Agency, Washington, D.C., 1990.

Chemical Weapons: Arms Control and Deterrence. Current Policy No. 409, U.S. Department of State, 1991.

Combat Fleets of the World. Naval Institute Press, 1993.

Conference Report, "Terrorism and Other 'Low Intensity' Operations, International Linkages." Institute for Foreign Policy Analysis, 1994.

Continuing Development of Chemical Warfare Capabilities CIS. Department of Defense, Washington, D.C., 1992.

Desert Shield Order of Battle Handbook. U.S. Army, Sept. 1991.

International Analysis: "Commercial Biotechnology," An. U.S. Congress, Office of Technology Assessment, OTA-BA-218.

International Defense Review (1989 & 1992–1995).

Jane's Armor & Artillery (1986–1994).

Jane's Defense Weekly (1989–1995).

Jane's Soviet Intelligence Review (1988 through 1995).

Jane's Weapon Systems (1986–1995).

Land Warfare in the 21st Century. U.S. Army, 1993, 1995.

Monterey Institute of International Studies. Nonproliferation studies reports, 1994.

National Defense. American Defense Preparedness Association. Arlington, VA, (1985–1995).

Naval Institute Guide to World Naval Weapon Systems, The. Naval Institute Press, 1989.

Red Thrust Star, January 1992.

Report of the Chemical Warfare Commission. Washington D.C., 1985.

Soviet Air–Land Battle Tactics. William Baker, Presido Press, 1986.

Soviet Bloc and World Terrorism, The. Jaffee Center for Strategic Studies, Tel Aviv University, 1988.

Soviet Military Concepts. Directorate of Soviet Affairs, No. 4-90, U.S. Air Force, 1986.

Submarine Review, The (1996–1994).

Submarines of the Russian & Soviet Navies. Naval Institute Press, (1918–1990).

Terrorism: The Role of Moscow and its Subcontractors. Hearings before the Subcommittee on Security and Terrorism, Senate Committee on the Judiciary, 1991.

Testimony on Biological and Toxin Weapons before the Subcommittee on Oversight and Evaluation of the House Permanent Select Committee on Intelligence. Department of Defense, (1993–1994).

Weapons & Tactics of the Soviet Army. Jane's Publishing Co., Ltd., 1981.

World Airpower Journal (1991–1995).

AUTHOR'S BIOGRAPHY:

Howard H. Schack was born and raised in New York City. Trained in design and engineering, he has spent most of his life working for the family construction business, which he later developed into an international enterprise.

Schack has had business dealings with foreign governments around the world. He has specialized in military projects, especially in the rapidly developing Middle East region, particularly during the region's greatest expansion period.

Concerned with the possibility of another Holocaust for the Jewish people after Israel was attacked by the combined Arab forces during the Yom Kippur War in October of 1973, Mr. Schack volunteered his services to Israel's equivalent of the CIA, known as the Mossad or as the Institute for Intelligence and Special Operations. Using his cover as an international contractor, he served in the capacity of intelligence operative for fifteen years.

However, as a family man and father of four sons, he agonized over his extended periods away from home and the need to hide from them his secret life of intelligence activities.

Among Howard Schack's activities was the discovery of Saddam Hussein's plans to turn Iraq into a military power. He reacted by personally gathering photographic evidence of Iraq's Osrack nuclear facility, which he turned over to Israeli intelligence. This information led to the Israeli Air Force's attack and destruction of that facility, in 1981. Ten years later, his information helped pinpoint targets for Operation Desert Storm.

Schack had also furnished details and bombing coordinates of the in-line bunkers storing chemical weaponry at Tall al Lahn, (also known as Kamis Iyyah) Iraq. This knowledge was passed on to the CIA, which failed to share it with the U.S. military before they bombed this facility during the Gulf War. Approximately 100,000 U.S. servicemen were subjected to nerve gas and chemical exposure as a result of this ignored information.

Mr. Schack's first book was the best-seller *A Spy In Canaan*. It was chosen as Book-of-the-Year by the Jewish Book Council in the category of Autobiography/Memoir, and was selected and republished as "Today's Best Nonfiction" by *Reader's Digest* magazine.

Howard Schack presently consults with an international task force on terrorism and unconventional warfare. Nationwide, he also makes appearances and lectures on this subject.

OTHER EXCITING BOOKS FROM S.P.I.

Illusion or Victory: How the U.S. Navy SEALS Win America's Failing War on Drugs *by Richard L. Knopf*

Reveals the recently declassified details of the U.S. Government's secret war against the international Drug Cartels and Narcoterrorists. You will learn the true story of the U.S. Military's involvement in fighting the organized drug trade through the author's many revelations of secret military operations around the world. Included are details on operations involving U.S. Navy SEAL Teams and other U.S. forces engaged in combat with armies of drug barons and mercenaries equipped with state-of-the-art weaponry.

RICHARD L. KNOPF is the pen name of a former U.S. Navy SEAL who for security reasons wishes to keep details of his private life secret. He lives in the western United States.

ISBN 1-56171-959-4 • PRICE: $21.99

U.F.O.s Are Real: Extraterrestrial Encounters Documented by the U.S. Government *by Sergeant Clifford E. Stone, U.S. Army (ret.)*, Director of Research, Rosewell Enigma Museum. *Introduction by Stanton T. Friedman, Ph.D.* author of *Crash at Corona* and *Top Secret Majic*

The U.S. Government's official position is that there are no flying saucers, landings by or encounters with extraterrestrial beings. Government sources like the U.S. Air Force, on the other hand, do have extensive records of unexplained sightings of what we all call Unidentified Flying Objects (UFOs). For too many years none of these classified records were available for release to the public.

Now, however, U.S. Army Sergeant Clifford Stone (ret.) has finally obtained declassified documents going back to the 1940s that will shake up any UFO skeptics. Using the Freedom of Information Act to patiently outduel bureaucrats at Air Force and Navy Intelligence, the CIA and the State Department, Stone obtained documents with minimally excised portions but with significant testimony still intact. One UFO documented sighting was especially sensitive since it flew over an air corridor dividing NATO and Soviet air space at the height of the Cold War.

SERGEANT CLIFFORD E. STONE, U.S. Army (ret.) served for more than 20 years as a Nuclear/Biological/Chemical Retrieval Specialist. He has been studying the Roswell, NM incident and the government's mysterious relationship to UFOs for decades and presently serves as Director of Research at the Roswell U.F.O. Enigma Museum.

ISBN: 1-56171-972-2 • PRICE: $18.95

The Covert Operations of the CIA and Israel's Mossad: The Shocking Truth About America's Hidden Agenda in the Middle East *by Joel Bainerman*

Throughout the 1980s, the CIA and Israel's equivalent, the Mossad, worked hand-in-hand on some of the most sophisticated and delicate intelligence operations ever conceived. Now, readers are taken deep undercover behind the scenes of some of this era's most astonishing cloak-and-dagger actions. Many of these revelations are exclusive scoops that will be followed up by the news media.

JOEL BAINERMAN is the publisher of *Inside Israel*, a monthly political intelligence report on Israeli affairs. His editorials and analyses have appeared in *The Wall Street Journal, The Christian Science Monitor, The Financial Times, National Review, New York Newsday, The San Francisco Chronicle, The Baltimore Sun*, and *The Toronto Globe and Mail.* He currently resides in New York City and Israel.

ISBN: 1-56171-350-3 • PRICE: $5.99 (Canada $6.99)

Crimes of a President: New Revelations on the Conspiracy & Cover-Up in the Bush-Reagan Administrations *by Joel Bainerman*

The first book that exposes the constitutional crimes and miscarriages of justice of the Bush-Reagan years. This riveting publication documents the secret agendas, covert crimes, and massive media cover-ups of those two Republican administrations. Readers will learn the whole truth about: Oliver North and why George Bush needed him as a willing scapegoat; the details of the new Iraq-gate scandal; Bush's plans to arm Saddam Hussein and orchestrate the Gulf War and his plans for a "New World Order"; the Justice Department's attempt to conceal the BCCI scandal; the little-known details of the secret mission of 248 U.S. soldiers that ended in a mysterious plane crash in Canada; CIA involvement in the bombing of PAN AM 103; and more.

JOEL BAINERMAN is the publisher of *Inside Israel*, a monthly political intelligence report on Israeli affairs. His editorials and analyses have appeared in *The Wall Street Journal, The Christian Science Monitor, The Financial Times, National Review, New York Newsday, The San Francisco Chronicle, The Baltimore Sun*, and *The Toronto Globe and Mail.* He currently resides in New York City and Israel.

ISBN: 1-56171-188-8 • PRICE: $5.99 (Canada $6.99)

Crisis in: Israel: A Peace Plan to Resist *by Yechiel M. Leiter*

Is the future of Middle East peace in terrorists' hands? The peace initiatives between Israel and the PLO have given the world cause to rejoice. But has Israel's government entered into an accord with a reliable bargaining partner, or is Arafat's PLO seizing upon the global community's increasingly hardline stance—demanding territorial concessions from Israel that will ultimately jeopardize regional security?

YECHIEL M. LEITER was born in Scranton, PA, and is a veteran of the Israeli Defense Forces. He served for three years as mayor of the Jewish community of Hebron, Israel. A frequent contributor to *The Jerusalem Post,* Leiter is also well known on the North American lecture circuit.

ISBN: 1-56171-338-4 • PRICE: $4.99

Condemned Without Judgment: The Three Lives of a Holocaust Survivor *by Bert Linder*

An unforgettable and harrowing true story of one man's will to survive Hitler's death camps. *Condemned Without Judgment* is, in the author's words, "the story of a victor rather than a victim." It is the inspiring adventure of a man who, despite bearing witness to evil and carnage beyond comprehension, remains steadfast in his belief in the ultimate good side of humanity.

"Bert Linder's deeply moving autobiography will remain an important contribution to the literature of testimony. It is a story of infinite pain and great courage."—Elie Wiesel

BERT LINDER was born in Austria in 1911, and lived there until that nation was annexed by the German Reich in 1938. From 1938 to 1945, he was either in hiding or interned in concentration camps. Mr. Linder has been a resident of the United States since 1951.

ISBN: 1-56171-340-6 • PRICE: $19.95

Evil Money: The Inside Story of Money Laundering and Corruption in Government, Banks and Business *by Dr. Rachel Ehrenfeld*

"Must reading for anyone interested in the frightening intricacies among drug traders, terrorists, bankers, and government officials."—Alan Friedman, *The Financial Times* (author of *Spider's Web*). A chilling and fascinating exposé of how one trillion dollars in annual drug revenues is laundered through banks in the U.S. and abroad. *Evil Money* exposes readers to the existence of a sophisticated worldwide underground economy that links drug cartels, terrorists, and even legitimate governments and businesseses in illegal enterprises. The results are the growing numbers of multi-billionaire drug lords, crooked lawyers and bankers, and corrupt political regimes—with no solutions in sight if present trends continue.

DR. RACHEL EHRENFELD is an investigator, scholar, and political commentator and one of the leading authorities on the topic of banking and drug money laundering. Her writing has appeared in *The Wall Street Journal, The New York Times, The Los Angeles Times, The New Republic,* and *National Review.* She has also offered expert commentary for ABC-TV's *Nightline*, CNN, and PBS's *Frontline.*

ISBN. 1-56171-333-3 • PRICE: $5.99

Inside the Cocaine Cartel: The Riveting Eyewitness Account of Life Inside the Colombian Cartel *by Max Mermelstein, with Robin Moore* (The French Connection) *and Richard Smitten* (Bank of Death)

The firsthand account of how Max Mermelstein built up, then tore down the world's largest cocaine cartel. In this amazing story behind the headlines, a young man from Brooklyn marries a Colombian woman and is propelled into the inner circle of the Medellin cartel. The Colombians didn't have a man who could organize and open the lucrative American market—and that's where Max came in. The fantasy lifestyle suddenly crumbled when Max was ordered, on the threat of death, to kill CIA operative Barry Seal. Max turned on the cartel, and became an even more damaging witness to it than Sammy "The Bull" Gravano was to the Mob.

MAX MERMELSTEIN is currently in the U.S. government's Witness Protection Plan; authors Moore and Smitten are based in Massachusetts and South Florida.

ISBN: 1-56171-254-X • PRICE: $5.99 (Canada $6.99)

A Soldier's Story: The Life and Times of an Israeli War Hero *by General Raful Eitan*, Chief of Staff (fmr.), Member of Cabinet

A dramatic insider's story of Israel's military history! For all readers of war, adventure, and Mideast history—an autobiography of one of Israel's most daring and controversial military and political leaders. *A Soldier's Story* views the development of the nation's military strategies, including vivid descriptions of many of Israel's most dramatic and historic battles. Leading key battles in 1956, 1967, 1973, and 1982, General Eitan became a greater-than-life legend by his bravery and success in the field. Beloved for his dedication to his fighting men and for his no-nonsense approach to politics, he tells an exciting soldier's story that exemplifies the best of Israel's past and future.

RAFUL EITAN served as the Chief of Staff of Israel's armed forces and is now a cabinet member in the key post of Minister of Agriculture. He is one of Israel's most outspoken military and political leaders.

ISBN: 1-56171-094-6 • PRICE: $5.99

Thrill Kill *by William R. Vanderberg*—An electrifying new crime thriller from a former cop on the beat.

A stunning literary debut! Like other cops-turned-writers, including William Caunitz and Joseph Waumbaugh, author William Vanderberg puts down his nightstick and picks up a pen—and the results are truly arresting! Washington, D.C., is being terrorized by a brutal psychopath known as the Capitol Hill Carver. He stalks his victims armed with a gun, a buck knife, and an unquenchable thirst for human blood. With the skill of a seasoned hunter, he leaves no tracks...only the gutted corpses of his victims. On his trail is Ronnie Bell, veteran cop and the mother of a twelve-year-old son. One false move in her desperate hunt to stop this killer, and she—or her son—could be his next trophy.

WILLIAM R. VANDERBERG is a decorated veteran of the Washington, D.C., Police Department. While with the force, Vanderberg was a street cop working one of the most violent and deadly areas of our nation's capital, the northeast sector of the city. He is currently Sales Director for a leading life insurance firm and resides with his family in Burbank, California.

ISBN: 1-56171-353-X • PRICE: $5.99

- -

Buy them at your local bookstore or Xerox this convenient coupon for ordering.

S.P.I. BOOKS, 136 West 22nd Street, New York, NY 10011
Telephone: 212-633-2023 • FAX 212-633-2123

Please send me the books I have checked above. I am enclosing $_____ (please add $2.50 to this order to cover postage and handling for the first book, and $.75 for each additional book). Send check or money order—no cash or C.O.Ds. Make checks payable to S.P.I. Books. New York State residents please add appropriate sales tax.

Name _____

Address _____

City _____ State _____ Zip Code _____
Allow 2 to 3 weeks for delivery.